VISION QUEST

VISION QUEST

a journey to happiness

JANE RAMSEY

Clovercroft Publishing

Vision Quest

Published by Clovercroft Publishing, Franklin, Tennessee

Edit by Adept Content Solutions

Cover Design by Nelly Sanchez

Interior Design by Adept Content Solutions

Printed in the United States of America

978-1-948484-71-8

"Who looks without, dreams.
Who looks within, awakes."
—Carl Jung

To Rich Ramsey, the man of my dreams and love of my life. Thanks for coming back for me.

Acknowledgments

I am deeply grateful to my family, friends, teachers, students, and the many advisors who assisted and held space for me as this book came to life. I firmly believe that the people who dance in and out of our lives are not random.

I have immeasurable gratitude for my husband, Rich, for the deep love we share and the journey we are traversing together. I am grateful to my siblings, whose unique gifts and talents surface again and again throughout life; I appreciate all we have experienced together and the life lessons we are still unraveling. I am also grateful to my dad, who taught me that it is possible to live a deeply spiritual life and still be "in the world."

Reverence and gratitude to my beloved teachers: Dr. Deepak Chopra, Roger Gabriel, Dr. David Frawley, and all the teachers at the Chopra Center; Dr. Jean Houston, Peggy Rubin, Robin Rice, Nicki Scully, Linda Star Wolf, Wendy Weatherwax, Jenn Poniatowski, Laurie Rivera, Dr. Larry Senn, Dr. Jon Kabat-Zin, Dr. Daniel Siegel, Dr. Emiliana Simon-Thomas, Dr. Dacher Keltner, Dr. Amit Goswami, Alan Seale, and Dr. Bruce Lipton.

To my dear friends who have witnessed my journey, thank you for allowing me to evolve and still be in my life; deep gratitude to Annette

Smith, Beverly Richardson, Jenny Donaldson, Robin Rice, Ann Plunkett, Tim Plunkett, Phil Funkenbusch, Judy Matthews, Doug Williams, Sandy West, Curt Mudd, Jenn Falor, and Charlie Carey.

To Tammy Kling, Tiarra Tomkins, and team at On-Fire Books who educated a first-time author and led me to Nelly Paez, who designed the cover. To Larry Carpenter at Clovercroft Publishing who patiently led me through the needed steps and introduced me to Lori Martinsek with her talented copyediting staff. Special thanks to Cindy Birne, my publicist, whose energy and drive make me describe her as a force of nature.

Thank you to my students who asked me to share my journal, and to readers for choosing to take a look at one person's journey to seek answers to life's most interesting questions and find happiness along the way.

Prologue

In a dreamlike fog, I surface. Bella is standing by my side of the bed, gently insistent, with her nose rutting against my outstretched hand. I pat her head to buy a few more seconds. The air conditioning is on, but I can dimly hear a bird chirping outside the window. I glance at the clock—4:44 a.m. Normally, I would be starting my workout, but not today; starting today, things officially change.

Rich and I are nested like spoons. Not wanting to move, I pat the bed lightly, and Bella hops up. Rich feels solid next to me as he cocoons my bottom, and Bella lies next to my legs. Heaven. Gratitude washes over me.

It's not light yet. I relish my new reality. I don't have to get up. Rich is snoozing. Bella is content. I am free to just lie here. I start to meditate, using the loving-kindness practice I learned from listening to Sharon Salzburg.

"May Rich be happy, healthy, safe, strong, and live easily. May Bella be happy, healthy, safe, strong, and live easily. May I be." I send metta to my entire family, Rich's entire family, my closest friends, people I know who are sick or suffering, neighbors, and work colleagues—former colleagues. Can it really count as meditation if you are burrowed beneath the covers with your husband?

Rich is sleeping hard. I ease out of bed and pull a long-sleeved denim shirt over my nightgown. Bella and I go downstairs, and I unlock the side door to go outside. The dew on the grass is cold on bare feet, so I stand on the brick sidewalk. I watch Bella run to the backyard in the grayish-pink predawn light. The air smells fresh, like cut grass, and I gaze across to the misty pond in the morning stillness as I listen to the frogs' deep morning sound. As I open my senses to see, hear, and smell this good morning, I wonder how Rich and I will change.

I can feel the muscles in my legs as I stand and stretch. It feels so good to just move. I take a few paces on the sidewalk, so I can see the half moon. I make sure no one is around to see me in my nightgown and attempt a couple of yoga postures. After a clumsy down dog, chaturanga, and cobra, I lift my arms above my head, stretching my whole body from heels to fingertips as if to embrace the morning. Learning yoga is another thing on my list. I want to learn the whole sequence of a sun salutation, the names of all the poses, and proper form and technique.

I keep thinking, "This day is finally here." My mind is racing with all I want to do, learn, and think about. The idea that we only use a small part of our brain keeps popping into my mind. Humans don't use all their potential—not even close. I want to learn how to use more of my potential. Such a paradox when now, presumably, I could be doing much less than before. I got a "congratulations on your retirement" card yesterday that teasingly referred to napping every day. The idea of not being productive or useful scares the hell out of me. In fact, I still feel a tremendous drive for achievement.

I know I have some kind of calling or mission. My whole life, I have been somewhat aware of subtle energies and the invisible domain beyond the five senses—something just beyond my grasp. I feel a call to learn and obtain wisdom, to go deeper inside, unlocking creativity. There is something stirring me: ideas of paintings that almost have a life of their own, as though they want to use me as an instrument to move from subconscious to canvas. I also feel a strong desire to learn how to be healthier and how to maximize potential in mind, body, and spirit—a kind of coming-of-age vision quest. I think ruefully that maybe it's a "coming-of-old-age" vision quest.

And now, there is time to understand what has been calling me. The idea of unstructured time with no set goals, no deadlines, and no drop-dead dates is more daunting than freeing. As I have started my journal over these last few weeks, I have given myself one year. I want a deadline for my own comfort. In my mind, I call it a sabbatical. I will study my own life transition and see what I can learn. I will faithfully record what happens: the good and the bad. If I have not figured out a way to make some kind of vocation out of my quest of being wiser, healthier, and more creative, I will go back to work.

The thought of going back to corporate life, while very familiar, makes me suddenly feel ill. That strong reaction is surprising because work has been such a huge part of my identity.

From somewhere in my subconscious, I remember a commercial. It would be insulting today. "She brings home the bacon, fries it up in the pan. And never lets me forget I'm a man." It was a fragrance commercial. I will not be bringing home the bacon anymore.

That thought sends a chill of fear through me. Rich has told me that we are going to be just fine financially, if we don't do something crazy. I picture the wife in Lost in America who loses all their savings in Las Vegas and see Rich admonishing me instead of Albert Brooks: "Perhaps I have not properly taught you the concept of the nest egg."

My role in the family had been clear for thirty-six years. I contributed as bread-winner. Now I have to come up with a whole new identity. My heart thuds, and I feel a little breathless. Who am I now?

I'm going from a corporate executive role where I knew how to handle everything at work to being at home full time. I don't know how to do anything here. I do not even know how to turn on the TV because the remote control seems overly complicated. I haven't paid the bills, run the vacuum cleaner, or taken clothes to the dry cleaner in years. I've never taken Bella to the vet. If I had to call the plumber, I would not have a clue who to call. But Rich is almost giddy with the thought that I will pick up "the house stuff," and I'm game to learn.

We have had helpers in the house for years: housecleaners, a student who runs errands, and a personal chef who cooks several meals a week. Rich has suggested that they all stay for now, so "the house stuff" is really just managing schedules and tasks, planning meals, handling contractors, taking care of Bella, and planning travel.

I ponder how my career has been all-consuming up to now. I didn't have kids because my career was so important. Rich and I once lost our marriage because of my focus on my career, and thanks mostly to Rich, we now have it back. We married, divorced, and remarried. I am grateful that we are back together now; we have over thirty-seven years of shared history. I gave up weekends to get an MBA for my career. We moved to new cities six times for my career. Now it's over. After all the sacrifices I made for my career, the ending was abrupt, embarrassing, painful—and maybe just the call to action I need.

I remember my first year of business school when I learned through case studies that publicly traded companies are expected to do better, to have top- and bottom-line growth, and earn more for shareholders every single year. I remember coming home to discuss this with Rich, who was a banker at that time. "Honey, did you know that corporations are expected to improve results every single year?"

Rich replied, "Uh, yes. How did you not know that?"

I said, "Wow, think of the stress and pressure that puts on an organization."

My dad was a small-town business owner; he had a construction company. There were good years and bad years. I was embarrassed that I had not ever known this concept of continuous improvement. I started to read the *Wall Street Journal* and watch business shows with Rich. I learned my business school lessons through first-hand experience. If my company didn't grow on the top line, we cut resources to make our numbers. I was always on board with whatever needed to be done and, as a result, got moved or promoted nearly every year and thrived in corporate life for over thirty-five years.

Retail is a tough business: fueling growth and investing in newness while closely watching costs. Many times, it felt like my foot was on the accelerator and the brake. I hired people only after careful thought because the new associates were often cut in the next downsizing. But pressure always existed to fund growth areas with the right talent. This past year, for the first time, I felt out of step with corporate life. When I was in my twenties, thirties, and forties, and early fifties, no task or request was too daunting. I was focused, tough, and unyielding in leading whatever needed to be done for the business. In my thirty-six years of corporate life, I participated in or led over a hundred resource shifts, mergers, business closings, restructurings, sell-offs, and downsizings.

To my surprise and somewhat to my shame, I have not gotten emotionally tougher with wisdom and age; instead, I seem to have gotten more thoughtful and quieter, and I feel things with more intensity.

Treating people with dignity has always been the priority for me and the teams I led through the years. But the impact on people during change has deeply unsettled me in recent years, invading my dreams and making me feel stressed.

People would ask Rich, "When is Jane retiring?"

He would jokingly answer, "Tell me when the next downsizing is, and I'll let you know; I'm not sure she can take another one."

Bella runs to the edge of the lawn. Her electronic fence keeps her from going into the street. A runner comes by, under the streetlights. Dawn is about to break. This has always been my time of day. A month ago, I would have been that person running in the dark. Now I will get to do my workout in the light like a civilized human, but I wonder, *Will I miss the quiet of an early run in the dark?*

For another moment, I watch Bella. Our ten-year-old Labrador/golden retriever mix is absorbed, completely focused on what she is sniffing. The single-minded in-the-moment intensity is something I envy. Mindfulness training via canine. The sky is brightening. I walk out on the cold wet of the grass soaked with dew and look to the east.

As I softly call Bella to go in, I wonder—how will *we* change? Rich does a huge amount—everything financial and all the house logistics. But he has always done some things just for me. He is not demonstrative or outwardly adoring as a husband, but he does little things that tell me he loves and appreciates me. I chide myself for being ridiculous and needy but wonder, *Will he still bring me coffee in the mornings and offer a glass of wine at night? Will he cut my little square of dessert chocolate four ways so I can savor each tiny piece? Or does my new status as not breadwinner mean those little things between us will change, too?*

I dry my feet, and we go back upstairs. Bella sprints up the steps. I slip into bed next to Rich's tall, solid frame and snuggle in for a few more minutes, matching my breathing to his, relishing the feeling of his skin next to mine. He slides his hand to my bottom, gives it a pat, and says, "Good morning."

I say, "Good morning, my bear. How did you sleep?"

"Great. How about you?"

"So good. I feel—just great."

He stretches and says, "Come on, Bella. We have to get Mom some coffee."

Chapter One

July

In July I begin my year-long commitment of keeping a daily journal to chronicle my journey and honestly record how my transition unfolds.

July 1

Rich and I are in the air on the way to Tucson to go to our beloved Canyon Ranch. I look out the window at cobalt sky and whipped-cream clouds. The lead pilot is a woman, and both pilots are black. It makes me feel happy to see these tangible signs of progress. Rich did his goofy *Beverly Hillbillies* tradition when we took off. When the plane was taxiing, he grabbed my hand and said "Darling, if this driver doesn't slow this bus down, it's going to leave the ground." I laughed and thought, *It's lovely to be married to someone your own age so you can share stupid TV references.*

I feel exhausted and imagine I look haggard—pinched, tired—but I appreciate that Rich looks at me with love. To him, I am beautiful, even now, and he is beautiful to me. I am apprehensive to see family. This trip is a gift from Rich and me to them, but they are critical of me. I imagine how I must seem to them—too driven, too politically correct, too serious, and now becoming a new-age kook.

I have made a commitment to write in my journal and catalogue what happens and what I think about for an entire year.

Today I began writing about the range of reactions I have gotten from friends and colleagues who know about my retirement, from pity because my career is now over to others who wish they were in this situation. I remind myself not to worry about anyone else right now. For once, I get to focus on what I want. I keep writing.

Rich and I have a couple of private days at Canyon Ranch before family descends. I need to get my head together. My wishes for retirement:

- I want to be healthier in mind, body, and spirit.
- I want to use more of my potential.
- I want this to be my most fulfilling time of life.
- I want to be an artist.

Mind

- Explore how learned people think about the big existential questions and mysteries
- Consciously notice and appreciate moments throughout the day
- Learn a language
- Be more proficient at technology
- Think in new ways and use more of my brain
- Practice gratitude

Body

- Get great sleep
- Avoid stress
- Daily cardio workout

- Lift weights three times per week
- Learn Pilates and yoga
- Eat vibrant fruits and vegetables daily

Spirit

- Connect to family and friends
- Build more intimacy and passion in our marriage
- Get a daily belly laugh
- Meditate
- Be in nature and enjoy fresh air every day
- Interact with animals
- Travel
- Keep a journal and truthfully record what happens and how I feel

When I turned fifty, Rich gave me a pen and a new five-subject notebook with a red plastic cover and said, "Here is a project for you. Start thinking and planning what your retirement could be like."

So, on and off for eight years, I have used the notebook to record thoughts and ideas. I am grateful for the advance preparation; maybe this transition will not be that tough. Most of the notebook is still blank. Over the past few years, I've scribbled wishes and fantasies, pasted post-it notes of random ideas, and doodled: sketches of images for paintings that have come to me at odd times, meditation symbols, interesting shapes and patterns, and color combinations. I have imagined how post-retirement days could be structured and how I could fill my time, and now I can look back with fresh eyes.

As I opened the cover of the red notebook today, I momentarily flushed with dread, thinking that as I read what I have written, it would probably seem sophomoric and naive.

Rich—the voice of experience because he already left corporate life—warned me. "The transition to retirement is really tough; you have to bring the energy to every interaction. If you don't make a call, you don't get a call. If you don't send an email, you don't get an email."

Privately, I thought that sounded a little like heaven, but I nodded gravely.

I have never not worked. I have never even taken a break between jobs. I worked in grade school, high school, and college. Rich and I got married the day we graduated from college, and we both started jobs a week later. Every time I switched companies or got promoted, I started the new job immediately. Even vacation was never a real break because of conference calls, emails, and random emergencies that had to be handled.

Emotions flood through me as I leaf through the notebook. I highlight some things that still seem relevant and wince at a few things that were ill-considered, and now new ideas are skating through my mind. I read notes about the portfolio of hobbies and interests I have attended to sporadically over the years and feel a nugget of excitement. With no kids, I have been able to devote occasional time to abstract painting and take evening and weekend art classes in New York. I have sold a few paintings and now wonder, *Could my new job title be artist?*

For me, art is about expressing something spiritual. Most people don't resonate with what I make. I smile as I recall one colleague who remarked, "That looks like my five-year old painted it." But when people like my paintings, they really like them. I imagine that my art might speak soul to soul with some. It's almost as though the art I make is generated by some inner need to create. Images, forms, spirals, colors, and geometric patterns come into my mind and don't let me rest until I get them down on paper or canvas.

I have always pondered big, philosophical, mysterious questions in odd spare moments, such as waking up in the middle of the night, on long plane rides, on a run, or in long meetings at work. I write the questions I want to delve into:

- *What is the meaning of existence, the purpose of life?*
- *Do we really have souls? If yes, what is the nature of a soul?*

- *What is my reason for being here? Do I have a "soul mission?" Does everyone? How should I live the rest of my life?*
- *What happens when we die? What is the nature of reality?*
- *Does God or spirit or oneness really exist?*
- *If yes, what is God's true nature? What role does she, he, or it play in our life? What do all the different wisdom traditions believe? What do atheists believe?*
- *Which traditions believe in reincarnation and karma? Have any of these ideas ever been scientifically proven?*
- *Do souls reincarnate? Do people reincarnate together? Which wisdom traditions believe in reincarnation? Which believe in the laws of the universe?*
- *Do we have free will, or is there a predetermined plan that the universe has for each of us?*

I have a deep yearning to study, learn, experience, and understand. And yet, I also have an embarrassed sense that others know the answers to these questions, and somehow, I have been left out of the loop.

As I worked closely with leaders over the years, I often found myself pondering what they believed and what they think it's all about. Many times, I felt that I was only bringing part of myself to work. When people told me I seemed authentic, integrated, and genuine, it made me feel like a fraud because I left the philosophical side of myself out of the picture. I stop and enjoy a little fantasy about being in an important business meeting with a cranky group of senior executives deciding on budget cuts and piping up, "Sure, profit matters, but let's just pause to ask ourselves: Why are we really here on earth right now, together? Why are you here? What is the purpose of this life?"

I think about years of drama at work: every incident of jealousy, greed, stupidity, and spite; leaders inciting unhelpful competition or subtly or overtly trying to influence a situation to get more resources in their part of the business; executives making terrible decisions and getting fired as a result. Leaders would jockey and maneuver for a bigger bonus or push for the promotion of "me and mine." I saw the foibles and eccentricities of senior leaders, yet I also remember times when they would do something extraordinarily kind, helpful, or philanthropic and make a thoughtful sacrifice for the greater good. They were complicated humans with good and shadow traits who were making their way through life the best way they knew how. I will miss many of them, the problem-solving, and the mediation role I often played. I will not miss the daily drama and stress.

I wonder how much of the drama was about karmic lessons being played out. Karma is one of my big questions. When I had conflict or someone did something aggravating or spiteful to me or one of my teammates, I felt compelled to ask, What is the bigger meaning behind this? Is there something that needs to be worked out between me and this person? I try to set ego aside and see if I can see their point of view, let it not be personal, and forgive.

For years, I have been criticized for being too forgiving. Rich would often say, "Stand up for yourself," "Stop eating shit," or "You are making excuses for their bad behavior." In those instances, I vacillated. I wondered if I truly was weak, or unable to stand up for myself, or could too easily understand where they were coming from. I could see that what they were doing made sense to them somehow. Maybe my lesson in the interaction was to learn to detach from caring too much about the outcome. I have felt for most of my life that I could see myself from a distance—dispassionately, like I was watching my life as though it was a movie, and I was just playing a role of one of the characters.

For a while, I have had a feeling that I am being called to go on an adventure—almost a vision quest. I ask myself, *Why am I drawn— more like pulled almost against my will—to dive more deeply into thinking about existential things?* I wonder. I feel thrilled that I now have time to do it. *But how to start?*

It seems like every wisdom tradition says that the answers are within us. In meditation, we are asked to go deep to try to answer the question, "Who am I?"

I think about the first questions on my list: What is the meaning of existence—the purpose of life? What am I here to do? I wonder if the purpose of an individual life is to maximize your potential. Is it a "be all you can be" type of notion? I read somewhere that it is to manifest the possible. Yet, what if those wisdom traditions have it all wrong? What if we get to the end and realize it really *was* about maximizing profit? Or having the most laughter? Or having the most stuff? Or having the most fun? Is it different for each person?

I wonder if I am ready to retreat into a life focused on going within myself, home, and family. If my future success exists on a very small stage, am I OK with that?

Paging through the notebook, I find an entry in my journal that notes the three things some spiritual practitioners say we are here to do in life:

1. To know ourselves from a soul perspective
2. To discover why we are here
3. To learn our life lessons as we discover who we are

I find sketches and notes for paintings that want to be born. One idea is the notion that the universe is a single living substance: mind and matter are one. The sketch I made looks like a shimmery, wispy blob of transparent color shot with light. Another note and sketch shows paired opposites: male/female, light/dark, vertical/horizontal, positive/negative. Others have yin/yang symbols, lines, geometric shapes, and colors. There is a whole page of spirals, Fibonacci numbers, and nautilus shells.

My emotion turns to gratitude as I write in the red notebook.

This will be our thirtieth trip to Canyon Ranch. Through their spiritual and metaphysical resources, I now know a few things about myself. Though I am not sure I believe all I have heard, I know that I have an openness not to reject new ideas out of hand. And there is some consistency in what I have heard from different practitioners, which somehow makes it all seem more believable—like the ideas are triangulating. Once you hear the same thing from a few different sources, it seems more credible.

As I sift through those old pieces of feedback, I remember something that I have not thought of in years. We are landing, so I will journal about this tomorrow.

July 2

I'm so glad to be here in this perfect place on the heels of deciding to retire. Canyon Ranch is a respite: a place for renewal, reflection, and making leaps.

I wish I could bring all my close friends here. I am incredibly grateful to have the means to bring my family. Rich reminds me that it's not for everyone. There is only healthy food, no alcohol, and no carbonated beverages, and the agenda in the evening consists of dinner, lectures, and occasionally bingo.

I had a short, steep hike before breakfast. I now have time to journal until class. The memory that came to me yesterday has been haunting me all night. It will be good to get it down on paper.

In 1995, I received a letter at work from a high school boyfriend, Sean. I had not heard from him in eighteen years. He had gone to medical school, gotten married, had a couple of children, and lived in Texas. The letter said he had been on a spiritual journey and discovered some things he felt compelled to tell me. He said we had shared past lives and that I should read a couple of books.

I remember opening the letter, reading the first paragraph, and folding it up again before I finished it; I was beyond startled. Baffled, I asked myself, *Why is this coming to me?*

One of books he talked about was *Autobiography of a Yogi* by Paramahansa Yogananda. And, included in the letter was the phone number of a clairvoyant. He had prepaid for a consultation. I didn't know what to do with this unexpected information. Feeling bewildered and a little annoyed, I tried to just forget it, but it kept coming back into my awareness. Sean had always been intentional, so taking the time to track me down must mean he took this very seriously, and thus, I couldn't completely blow it off. Plus, he meant a lot to me a long time ago.

But, busy at work, I put the letter in a drawer. Rich and I talked about it, and I finally read the whole letter and wrote Sean, basically saying, "Hey, thanks for thinking of me; hope you are well. I am still processing this." I didn't do anything for months, but the notion that there was something more out there kept sneaking into my thoughts. I finally decided, out of curiosity, to call the clairvoyant and talk to her.

The medium told me that I had indeed had past lives. She began to describe some; the one that sticks in my memory was a life in ancient Ireland where I was the husband, Sean was the wife, our thatched-roof house burned down, and our three children died in the fire. I was horrified, mystified, and somewhat intrigued but unable to really comprehend what the clairvoyant was saying.

At some point, my senses were overloaded, and I could not take in any more. The medium gently stopped the conversation and said, "Jane, you are not ready to hear this now, but at some time in the future, you will be. You are an old soul, and you will be on a big trajectory of discovery some time later in your life. When you are ready, you will be supported in your journey."

Too overwhelmed to say something coherent, but intrigued enough by what I had heard, I felt compelled to ask her, "Can you tell me anything about my mom?" Mom died over thirty years ago after a sudden, two-month illness. I was in my early twenties. Rich and I had been married a few years.

The clairvoyant explained. "Your mom is happy and safe."

I asked, "Where is she? Is she … in something like heaven?"

"If you imagine something like a school, she is graduating from middle school and ready to go on to high school. She is learning."

I told her that my siblings said they sometimes feel Mom's presence, but I never had. The medium said, "She is with you."

I asked, "Why don't I feel anything?"

She answered, "Imagine your face is damp and you are out in a mist; it is so subtle it's hard to discern."

Though I filed this away as some weird thing that happened, the idea that the soul goes on gave me some measure of peace. Around that time, I read *Many Lives, Many Masters* by Brian Weiss. I loved it and gave a copy to each close friend who had lost someone. And then I read *Autobiography of a Yogi* for the first time of many.

I remember how I felt when I realized that reincarnation could be a universal idea. I thought if it existed, it was reserved for the Dalai Lama and Indian mystics. I never imagined it could be for normal, everyday people. I felt a whole world open. This push might have been the trigger for me to somewhat skeptically begin to take advantage of metaphysical services during Canyon Ranch visits.

I pause to write down fragments of metaphysical feedback I have gotten:

"You are a very old soul."

I wonder if they teach them to say this at metaphysical school? If reincarnation exists, aren't all souls old? Or are some souls newer in the cycle of death and rebirth?

"You will be a spiritual late bloomer."

"You will be coming into a transformative spiritual awakening that is very tailored to you."

"Later in life, you will go on a vision quest."

"You come reluctantly into this, but your guides are advising you to open your mind."

"Your soul is like someone with a PhD. Right now, you are in kindergarten, but you are going to get a fast and deep education."

Interesting: another school reference. Is this how they teach it in metaphysical college? Is there metaphysical college?

"You chose the life you have. All your memories from past lives have been erased. Your job is to rediscover them."

"You have one leg in the spiritual realm and one firmly planted on earth. You will build a bridge between the two worlds."

"You have a specific role to play in this life. But you must develop to take advantage of that opportunity. You may develop slowly, because you have a lot to learn and accomplish. So, the significant part of your journey may take place later in life."

These ideas both unsettle and secretly delight me. I feel intrigued and want to be open, but I also want to be sufficiently skeptical and analytical. I don't want to be naive or taken in by charlatans. I like the idea of a vision quest.

I imagine becoming a new-age kook dressed in a flowing tunic with long silver hair, wearing crystals, and driving a cerulean blue pickup with dogs leaning out of the back and bumper stickers that say NAMASTE and VISUALIZE WHIRLED PEAS.

But right now, I am off to indoor cycling.

July 3

Nourishing sleep last night—more than eight hours. I feel excited and content.

Rich is so supportive; I am filled with gratitude for him. I'm glad he is here, though my family is coming, and he may not be able to take it. My three sisters, Teresa, Bethany, and Gussie; my brother, Joe; my sister-in-law, Emma; and our niece, Sasha, are on their way. I am especially glad Sasha is coming; she brings out the best in Rich.

We had the sweetest morning. Rich and I woke up at the same time, lay in bed with legs on legs, held hands, and talked about puppies (he wants a black one, which are harder to get rescued; I want one that loves carrots like Beau). Lounging in bed was an unexpected, sweet luxury, and I felt almost overwhelmed from the pleasure. I didn't want it to end.

We had an outstanding before-breakfast hike; the air felt very fresh, like there might have been a rare Tucson overnight rain. From time to time as we hiked, we touched hands for a moment. Amazing how after thirty-seven years, his touch still gives me a tingle down deep inside, and as I look at his tall frame, beautiful brown eyes, and now white hair, I still feel so attracted to him.

Something smelled great; wild sage? Kind of spicy sweet, a little like someone smoking pot. It's so nice to just pay attention and notice and not be weighed down by a conference call or urgent email or some bitter drama going on at work. I feel like I am even breathing deeper.

We walked to the top of our favorite hill and shared a kiss, looking out at the mountains and the morning sky. We took a selfie. Then I went to meditation. I want to savor the memory of this impeccably perfect morning. At meditation, the facilitator gave us a mantra, "So hum," but said, "If you have your own personal mantra, feel free to use it."

After class, I went up to him and asked, "How do you get your own personal mantra?" He told me that until very recently, you had to go to India and study with a guru to get your mantra, but now there are teachers in the United States who are trained in the ancient Vedic practice and know how to assign your mantra. He said to check out the Chopra Center. I am definitely doing this! There is something about having a mantra that is tailored specifically to me that feels very right.

I attended a lecture in the Spirituality Center called "Divine Qualities of the Heart" about the essential preconditions to achieve a strong spiritual life. It was perfect timing. The story of "The Alchemist" by Paolo Coelho is the idea that every element in the universe supports the boy's dream.

Wouldn't it be the coolest thing if it were true that you can get clear about your dreams and then you will get help from the universe to make them real? Do I believe that the universe is in league with us to make our dreams come true? Maybe I should say, "Hey, Universe, I want to be an artist."

Being at Canyon Ranch makes me feel more alive. Memories and ideas are being sparked. My senses are more alert. My mind is buzzing—radiating out—noticing and appreciating what I see, hear, smell, and taste. My journal calls me. Ideas are spilling out of me and the journal is the receptacle. The idea of exploration: a compulsion toward learning and understanding stays in my thoughts.

Today is arrival day for my family. Sasha and Teresa arrive first.

Complicated thoughts and feelings arise in the wake of knowing they will all come. What is it about siblings especially, but other family, too, that brings up so many emotions? It must be the years of shared history: the wounds and victories, joys, and hurts delivered to each other and witnessed by all. I do not want to take them, or this time of fresh thinking and open eyes, for granted. I am describing them in my journal to see them with expanded awareness, greater insight, and hopefully, gratitude.

I am hoping for a good, drama-free visit. Here is my attempt at writing about everyone. Teresa is my oldest sister. We call her T. She is six years older than I am, and she has always nurtured and supported me. She more that anyone realizes my yearning to go deeper in trying to learn universal truths; she encourages me to go deeper and spurs me on.

Teresa lives in Santa Fe, has long red hair, and plays in an all-woman marimba band. She is a jewelry designer and a spinning instructor. Her "real" job is a leadership role in IT, working for the state of New Mexico. We tease her because she could be on the cover of Santa Fe magazine. She embodies that earth mother, aging hippie, artist, new-age cowgirl hat and turquoise necklace-wearing Santa Fe vibe. She is enthusiastic and sees life as full of possibilities. She loves babies. Her life is filled with synchronicity, and she makes connections that others can miss. She is artistically highly creative and makes beautiful jewelry, art, quilts, and much more.

She loves being the center of attention, and she loves affirmation from others. She gives other people, even strangers, confidence, appreciation, and support. She often blurts out what she thinks, so she can sometimes hurt feelings and offend people, but we are used to it. She and my brother, Joe, can both speak backwards. She has synesthesia, so she sees music and experiences in colors. She once walked past a painting in an art gallery and loudly told her friends "that's what my orgasms look like." She says she is the universe whisperer and that she can make things happen. We believe her. She is my big sister, and I love her.

My niece Sasha is Teresa's daughter, nineteen years younger than me. She is tall, slender, brunette, confident, successful, charming, gorgeous, and funny. She is married to Drew, and they have two young daughters, Avery and Sloane. They live outside of Baltimore.

I have loved her fiercely all her life and watched with wonder as she has evolved. With Sasha, I almost can't wait to see what happens next. I would defend her from anything (not that she needs any help). Sometimes when I wonder if I experience less emotion than other people, I think about how much I love this girl, and my heart feels expanded. Sasha and I text a lot, and we are on the same wavelength. She is the one I worry most about alienating if I go deeper down a path of spiritual discovery. She can barely keep from rolling her eyes if I mention the laws of the universe or something existential.

Sasha and Rich have similar personalities. They are both warm, empathetic, and responsive and always dialed into the emotions, motivations, and potential of people. Sasha and Rich can walk into a crowd, pick out a couple of people to watch, and construct entire stories about their lives in detail. This is one of their most advanced talents, and they like nothing better than to do this together.

Sasha also has a goofy sense of humor around other members of our family. She brags about things like being able to eat as much as two men at a meal even though she is tiny.

After an exuberant welcome, Sasha, Teresa, and I hustled to get to women's stretch class on time. Women's stretch is my favorite daily ritual at Canyon Ranch, and Rich loves men's stretch just as much.

Class was so good today! Lots of hip openers. The instructor said, "We all keep a lot of emotion in our hips; it's so important to stretch every day."

Teresa shared a private moment of hope and dread with me, confiding, "I hope Gus will be OK this year."

"Me, too. I'm worried."

"Did you talk to her before she got on her flight?"

"Yes. She sounded like she was out of it."

"Shit."

"I know."

My brother Joe and his wife Emma arrived stressed out; they need this vacation badly.

Joe is a CEO of a not-for-profit that helps low-income families get housing and healthcare. He gives everything to work, community, and being a dad. He has two incredible sons, Brad and Richard. He often ignores his health. I want him to be healthier, and he wants to try. I'm proud of him for being open.

Joe is eight years younger than I am. He was sixteen when Mom died. They were so close; in many ways, he has never gotten over it. He has always carried some extra weight but has lost over forty pounds since he has been coming to Canyon Ranch. He can now actually jog on the treadmill, and he is a demon at racquetball.

He has a booming radio personality voice, blond hair, and blue eyes. Joe is opinionated and decisive, a natural leader. He is also the life of every party. He notices anything that is illogical. He constantly brags about things he has done to make life more efficient, like drive-time to work, and setting up the kitchen for cooking. He can shower and shave in less than two minutes.

He is a planner and, like me, is always on time. He is full of life. He is my baby brother, and I am so glad to see him. But he can really be a pain in the ass.

He is extremely high maintenance, and I can barely stand to be at a restaurant with him when he orders because he tells the waiter things like "I can only drink coffee in mugs that have a thick wall structure; my lower lip is very sensitive to heat."

He is also a neat freak; there is nothing touching his garage floor other than car tires. His office is paperless with nothing on it except his computer, photos, and a plant. He can do the daily jumble in less than thirty seconds.

Joe was uncharacteristically late coming to meet me. "Hi, baby brother; welcome to Canyon Ranch! Where have you been?"

He said, "Oh my God, did you know they have a pillow menu here? They have like twelve pillows you can try to see which one you like best. So, I called, and they brought each one, and I tried them out."

Emma is a great mom and caregiver. Her elderly parents both rely on her. She takes care of everyone else and puts herself last. I love her like a sister and am so glad she is in our family. I know Canyon Ranch is rejuvenating for her. I hope she can relax and breathe here and do some things just for herself.

Emma is petite, blond, and curvy. My brother adores her and can't keep his hands off her. She is bright, sturdy, tough, and occasionally, irreverent. She claims she has a superpower to make her house look clean when it really isn't. She can be a little *too* saintly; she is always saying "it doesn't matter to me; I'm fine with whatever." But once in a while, she can be very commanding and bossy, too. I love when she gets like that.

I have been most nervous about seeing Bethany; she texted that she was on her way. She has never been to Canyon Ranch before. Sasha, T., and I were waiting out front to meet her. We saw a car pulling up, and T. said, "There's Bethany." I think Bethany was startled to see us all there, a greeting committee. It has been so long since I have seen her—too many years. We just stood there under the Canyon Ranch entrance and hugged. I thanked her for coming. They wept, and even I had tears in my eyes. We took a photo under the Canyon Ranch sign.

I am sure I would have recognized her, but I had not seen her in seven years. She is taller than I am, and she has let her hair be natural; short and gray with a perky, spiky cut. Her eyes are bright blue, and she wears no makeup and no bra. She has a very pretty smile when she decides to actually grace us with one, and her laugh is contagious. She carries a little extra weight like our whole family tends to do, but her legs are long and shapely.

I am conscious that the first visit to Canyon Ranch can be a lot to take in. So, I wanted Bethany to go on the tour that program advising does, to find her way around the place and get settled in her room. Gus will be her roommate. We agreed to meet for a late lunch.

Bethany is four years older than I am. She lives in Utah, and she is founder and president of a manufacturing company. She is very creative. I have always been a little scared of her because she is very bright, brave, critical, and quite outspoken. She does whatever she wants and has strong opinions, quick wit, and a hilarious gift of being able to tell a joke. She is an animal rights activist and a strict vegan. She has five dogs and got funding for a new animal shelter in her town. She has always been a big believer in giving back and donates her time to causes she believes in.

For years, I had a grudge against Bethany, and I didn't invite her to Canyon Ranch for the family trip. A few months ago, in some work to try to go deeper in my meditation practice, I realized it is stupid to hang onto old baggage. I always thought if she wasn't my sister, I would find her very interesting. I am committed to finally letting go of all this history. When I asked her to please forgive me for being an ass, she did instantly. And now she is here. But I barely know her.

I spent the afternoon with Bethany. Everyone else was off unpacking, doing spa treatments and classes. We went to breathing class together and learned that when you are having trouble sleeping to focus on breathing in and out of your left nostril. Who knew?

We talked things out. I told Bethany how I felt when she moved West. For the first time, I learned the whole story of what happened. In 1973, Bethany decided she wanted to leave the Midwest. She went down to the train station and told the ticket agent she wanted to go west—but she only had $100. She could get to Spokane, Washington for $97.50. She bought the ticket and went to the library and found a college to apply to in Cheney, Washington.

She came home for Christmas and said she was moving. She withdrew all of her savings—about $1,000—and got on a train with three suitcases, a black-and-white portable TV, an ounce of marijuana, and 100 hits of an upper. She met a fellow traveler, a lady she later realized was a hooker. Bethany and the lady were getting high in the bathroom, and somehow, the other lady got kicked off the train. Bethany was lucky she didn't, too. She probably still had an innocent, Midwestern look about her.

Bethany said she stayed awake the whole forty-four-hour trip thanks to uppers. She described being in the top deck of the observation car going through Glacier National Park on New Year's Eve with a breathtaking full moon. She says she still has images of that night burned into her memory.

What stayed in my memory was the worry and fear because I did not know what had happened for days. And there was the resentment of my childhood and teenage years when our parents focused their mental and emotional energy toward Bethany even though she had hurt them.

It felt good to let go of forty years of history in one afternoon. Bethany talked about her kids, but mostly focused on her grands. Later, I told Rich that I felt like a little girl whose big sister finally played with her.

Then Bethany seemed to get excited about the Canyon Ranch routine, taking a private session with an exercise physiologist so she would know exactly what to do to get healthier. I thought, *If she can even get one healthy habit from here and take it back, it will be good for her and for her grands.*

Augusta (Gussie) arrived. I am glad she got here safely. I hope and pray she is OK. Canyon Ranch is good for her: a healthy vacation with no alcohol available. Fourteen years younger than I am, she was only eleven when Mom died. She has had many challenges of alcohol and other addictions, depression, anxiety, and a difficult marriage. She might have bipolar disorder.

She has long brown hair and is tall and graceful. She was a talented music teacher for twenty years but lost that job. She is creative, outgoing, and great with kids. She can sink deeply into sadness, yet at other times be an exuberant lover of life, people, and material comforts. She can be very formal and likes to use big words and be seen as highly educated. She is also very funny, has a great sense of comedic timing, and has some amazing talents, like being able to whistle like the birds in Cinderella and pretend to be fluent in any foreign language with proper accent and intonation but made-up words. She's a mom with two talented college kids, Mark and Mia.

One of her favorite things to do at Canyon Ranch is the Desert Drumming class. She flings the drumsticks around and shakes her booty, making seriously embarrassing noises at the top of her lungs and getting everyone fired up.

Over mocktails, Sasha, T., Joe, Emma, Bethany, and Gus wanted to know the "real scoop" on why I decided to retire. I told them that a feeling of being out of step with corporate life had been building in me. The 24/7 schedule was exhausting. Being an introvert, I craved solitude to recover from interaction and time to process big decisions. The weekend suddenly did not seem like enough recovery. And, there were times when weekends didn't exist.

My weekday routine for years was to get up at 4:00 or 4:30 to get a decent workout in before going to the office by 7:30. Days with back-to-back meeting schedules were typical.

Rich's father, Raleigh, lived with us for several months while being treated at the cancer research hospital. He had thirty-five radiation and six chemo treatments on the last visit. I only managed to get to one appointment with him; all the rest fell on Rich.

Two months ago, our oldest dog, Beau, died of cancer. He was a sweet-tempered, low-key black Labrador retriever whose biggest character flaw was to bark at the garbage truck. Every day when I got home from work, Beau and Bella would greet me, and it was the best part of my day; my heart lifted, and I laughed to see his tail wag so hard it looked like it could fly off.

The vet said, "You will know when it's time." At work, I was busy, traveling on weekends and working late nights. I knew I was missing Beau's last days. I managed to take a Thursday off to be with him, watch him get excited when the garbage truck came, and take him on a slow sniff walk around the pond. Soon after, when he could not go outside without being carried, we let him go.

Rich and I were devastated. My heart felt like it was buried beneath a ton of sand. I felt almost sick with sadness that I did not get to be with him much in his last days. For the first time in my life, I began to resent work, especially the weekends away, an emotion I had never felt before.

Feeling sick, sad, and exhausted, I had been getting ready for the next change at work. I was leading the next big downsizing: moving resources from the central organization to the brands. I didn't agree with part of the reorganization direction—decentralizing departments that were saving the enterprise money by capitalizing on efficiencies and shared resources—but my arguments were not accepted. This was the first time I felt misaligned with the direction we were taking. It took a surprisingly hard toll on me.

I don't get sick; I had not had a sick day since 1981. But stressed and not sleeping, dreading the exits of many close colleagues, I developed an itchy rash that now covered my whole body, even my scalp and inside my ears. My vision became so blurry that I had been afraid to drive. Rich had been driving me to work every day. He saw the pain I was in and urged me to leave.

It had crossed my mind that perhaps *my own* role could be eliminated. I had been given a huge, multi-million-dollar budget challenge to cut in my own department. After many late nights going over and over the numbers, I could not find a way to get there. If I eliminated my own role as department chief, that could get us to the number.

Many of the former brands in the enterprise had been sold. In the remaining brands, the team leaders who report to me are strong and capable. Corporate direction is less needed in the new model. In recent days, I honestly wonder what value I add.

And then, two weeks ago, my boss, the chairman of the company, announced that since the downsizing was focused on the corporate resources, the downsizing would be led by the brands. One of my direct reports was assigned to lead the project, and it was taken from me. I tried to not let my ego get the better of me and to even to see this as a gift instead of a humiliating wake-up call.

Then my boss called me, said he needed to talk to me about something, and then left me on hold for forty minutes. My intuition kicked in and during the time on hold, I prepared myself for what seemed inevitable. I expected I could be fired but wanted to stay open to hear what was on his mind.

I called his administrative assistant on the other line and said "Susan, I've been on hold for a half hour. Should I stay on hold?" Susan apologized and said yes.

My boss finally got back on the phone and said that he had made some decisions, and he wanted to change my reporting relationship from reporting directly to him to report to the COO.

And I heard the words coming out of my mouth without really knowing I was saying them. Heart pounding in my ears I calmly said, "If you could see your way clear to eliminating my role and making me part of the team that is exiting so I can get a separation package, I would like to leave."

Silence. He seemed surprised and asked me, "Are you sure this is what you want to do?" I said I would want to make a smooth transition and give maximum notice, but yes. He graciously said he would support me if this is what I wanted and that he would be fair.

I put down the phone thinking, *What did I just do?*

A few minutes later, the COO came to my office and said, "Are you sure this is what you want?" and I said yes. His only request was to call the exit a retirement. I agreed. So—just like that, a thirty-six-year career ended. We agreed on a month's notice, but effective early August, I will be done with corporate life.

They all cheered me with a mocktail.

July 4

Holidays at Canyon Ranch are like any other day. Great hike with Sasha and Rich this morning—four miles in before breakfast.

We all called Dad today. He seemed so happy we were all together. He was optimistic and upbeat but is not feeling great in his body. I need to visit him soon.

Rich and Sasha played tennis in the Tucson 100-plus degree summer heat, and they both nearly expired. I saw Sasha with a tomato-red face laying on a couch in the spa lobby fanning herself. "Are you OK? and Sasha squawked, "We played death tennis." After I made sure Sasha was going to be OK, I sprinted back to the room and found Rich similarly sprawled out. Now death tennis will be a Ranch legend.

We all went to much needed stretch class and then indoor cycling.

At lunch Rich and Sasha documented the lives of everyone in the dining room in confidential whispers and significant eye gestures. T. pronounced the Mexican food on the menu with a Santa Fe accent. I'll have the QUESadilla. Sasha begs her, "Mom, say it again." They crack up. Teresa is in heaven with the attention. Everyone tried to keep from lecturing Gussie, but I could not keep from suggesting that she go to the AA meeting at five o'clock.

Teresa, Gussie, Bethany, and I made necklaces after lunch with Kevin, a very handsome Native American art teacher. This is the kind of guy T. especially loves, and so there were many good-natured comments about him being hot, cool, and "holy"—a perfect trifecta.

I did Pilates with Sasha in a full class of thirty people. Darcy taught. Rich calls her "Evil Darcy" because she is so kick-ass tough. We were doing backward/forward rolls, and from the big dude over to the right, we hear pfpfpfpfpttt, brrrrr—rrr.

Farting in class happens sometimes at Canyon Ranch. Darcy, the consummate professional, just kept teaching like nothing happened. I was afraid to look at Sasha but knew we were both barely breathing and staring straight ahead, so we would not erupt into hysterics. Some girl laughed so hard she started to kind of hiccup from stifling it, and she had to leave class—so everyone thought she was the culprit. It's all the fiber from the veggies, whole grains, and fruit.

Sasha and I can't stop giggling after class. We realize how juvenile it is to laugh at passing gas. Are we five years old? And yet, somehow emotions are close to the surface here, and everything gets magnified and embellished.

Everyone falls into a nice routine, taking classes, getting spa services, and going to lectures and appointments that were booked in advance. It's fun to run into each other during the day and hear what each person is doing and learning.

Each time Joe or Gussie goes by the big outdoor sculpture of the bell, they ring it. As it slowly swings from side to side, it gongs, and the sound reverberates throughout the property. The group comes together at breakfast and dinner.

This morning they played a joke on me. Sasha put everyone up to it. They agreed to only say positive things at breakfast: no bitching, complaining, or negativity whatsoever. Rich and I walked in, and they were already seated. The conversation went:

Me: "Hi, everybody! Good morning; how did you guys sleep last night?"

Joe: "Awesome, maybe the best night of sleep I have ever had in my whole life."

T.: "Incredible."

Emma: "So good."

Gus: "In my whole life, this is the best bed I've ever slept in."

Bethany: "My pillow is so soft!"

Sasha: "I think I had one of the happiest dreams ever; talk about sweet dreams—wow!"

And breakfast goes on like this. At the breakfast bar, they go into ecstasies over the quality of the fruit: "Wow, this pineapple is out of this world!"

Emma's eyes well up a little. "I am just *so* grateful that someone cut up this delicious fruit for us. The variety is every color of the rainbow."

Joe says, "This omelet is perfectly prepared. I *love* the tofu bacon."

I am beaming and overwhelmed with love for my family. What a pleasure they are!

Then I asked, "What did you guys do this morning?" Gus answers, saying, "Emma and I went on the morning hike and we saw a snake! They look at each other. "But we *loved* it. It was a growth experience—a *beautiful* snake!"

I said to Rich after breakfast, walking back to our room, "OK, I love my family."

Later they told me about the positivity stooge and said, "How did you like the trick we played on you?"

I said, "I love it. Do it forever."

The trip is going well, but there is always the undercurrent of worry and frustration about Gus: Can she get well? Does she want to get well? What is her path forward? Do you think she smells like alcohol? Do you think she is telling the truth? Do you think she is drinking? But she seems upbeat and funny most of the time, and only gets surly if someone mentions rehab or AA.

We laughed so hard at dinner that our stomachs hurt again. Rich just mostly rolls his eyes at us, but when he does belly laugh, it is a gift because his laugh makes everyone else laugh harder. Daily belly laughs are the best ab workout ever. I am not kidding. Studies show hard laughter is the best ab workout. And it is great for your nervous system. We *have* to do it every day.

I went to meditation with Rich, Bethany, and T. There is something so great about meditating with people you love.

After meditation, I had some time alone to catalogue this day, get dreamy about retirement, and make some more notes.

I know meditation is a pathway for me. After ten years of meditating sporadically—mostly on vacation and the weekends—I started a more regular daily practice when I turned fifty. Some days, it was only focusing on deep breathing for five minutes a day as I got ready for bed at night. The idea of having more time go deeper in meditation is very appealing.

In addition to going deeper in spirituality, I want to take classes and study new subjects like quantum physics. I fantasize about exploring nutrition and becoming incredibly healthy in mind, body, and spirit.

Travel for *fun* has always been appealing. With Beau gone, and Bella sad being alone, the possibility of getting a puppy is daunting but kind of thrilling. Being able to paint every day will be remarkable. But I worry that pursuing these ideas might not be enough to sustain me. Will I get bored? Will I be able to cope with a less structured life?

I have watched others have a tough time retiring. Stories abound where people get sick and die soon after leaving corporate life. I have friends who retired and went back to corporate life within a few months. Many go through a period of grief and mourning in which they struggle to carve out meaning and purpose. How it will be in the same house together all day with Rich? Will we get on each other's nerves? Will our relationship change?

Performing a ceremony—conducting a ritual—can help you let go of the past and move on. Part of me says, "This is silly," and part of me wants to be open to try it.

I did a "Rites of Passage" ritual in the Spirituality Center with Julie. Julie explained that this is a time to examine life more deeply to find the right place to start. Everything we need for success and joy lies within. This is a time to let go of life's debris, identify what matters the most, and let go of past hurts, wounds, and blocks. This is a time to reconnect with power, raw instincts, and intuition. When we examine ourselves to these depths, we are able to find what we wish to bring to the surface and what we wish to let go.

I made some resolutions:

I will let go of confinement, feeling stifled, and conflict. I will fully explore creativity with a focus on painting. I will embrace and bring in spiritual growth and opportunities to learn while moving at my own pace and schedule and be a better wife, sister, aunt, daughter, and friend. I commit to daily joy and laughter.

The last day, everyone teased me about a childhood story. In kindergarten, my classmate Lisa called to see if she could come over and play. I hesitated. I liked her, but her natural exuberance exhausted me. So, I made an excuse off the top of my head. "Lisa, I am sorry you can't come over now. Our house is so dirty, a monkey can't see in." As a tidy housekeeper, Mom was mortified. It became a family legend.

Now, "a monkey can't see in" is our family's superlative for "a really humongous amount" whenever words fail us. Examples are: "It is so freaking hot outside a monkey can't see in. I am so hungry a monkey can't see in." Last night everyone thanked Rich and me for the trip: "You guys are so generous a monkey can't see in." Very nice.

I almost made it through the trip without a fight with Gus—but not quite. She kept it together most of the time, but yesterday in the hot tub, she started crying and talked about how hard her life is. First, she claimed that she quit drinking. I asked her to please just tell the truth. Later, she said she is trying to quit drinking and quit smoking. Then she went on at great length about how terrible it is to never get to taste a great Pinot Noir or Sancerre again. She feels like a loser since she lost her teaching job. She hates her current job, and she hates how she looks. She complains about her body.

She is devastated about her marriage, and she has lost confidence. She says she has no money. She says her kids hate her, and she doesn't blame them. She says she has no friends. She says she wants a divorce, but then, in the next sentence, she thinks of ways to try to make Mason fall in love with her again. She knows she is ruining her health, and she is afraid she is going to get sicker and die. I listened and held her hand while she cried. I asked her if she wanted me to listen or if she wanted advice. She said she just wanted me to listen, and so I did, for a long time, making gentle noises and finally helping her out of the hot tub, wrapping her up in a towel, and rubbing her back.

I feel sad for her life but so frustrated, too, because she has made terrible choices, and she keeps falling back into the same patterns. I bit back the words until she got mean. Sobbing, she said, pointing at me and raising her voice, "How would you understand any of this? Your life is perfect. You have the perfect job, the perfect marriage, the perfect body, and the perfect life! You can't understand! You are four-teen years older than I am, and everyone thinks you are the younger sister." Then she dissolved into tears, bending over with her head in her hands.

I said quietly, "Gussie, you have the power to change all of this. Stop being a fucking victim. You can get your life back under control. Why don't you go to rehab again or start going to AA? You keep saying you want to quit drinking. It's hard to do it alone. Why won't you get professional help?"

And she said, "Just because you paid for this trip doesn't mean you run my life. Stay out of it."

And I said, "Listen, let's not have this fight again. Let's enjoy the last night here. We always get to the same place every time we have this argument. I love you, and I'm sorry you are unhappy. I hope you decide to get some help. If you do, and you need money, just ask. OK? Truce?"

We all said goodbye after breakfast. Despite the ongoing heartache with Gus, it was a good trip. I hope I can afford to bring everyone next year. I am going to count on the law of abundance and trust that Rich is such a great money manager that we can think of a way.

July 8

We are home. I am sitting at our kitchen table, drinking a cup of tea and reviewing my red notebook. A page is filled with color, shapes, and notations, such as, "Is imagination real? How to experience higher states of consciousness? What is the point of an individual life?"

Other pages contain notes, ideas and exercises from sessions I have had with spiritual teachers over the years. Exercises from Alan Seale's book, *Soul Mission Life Vision*, where for the first time, I pushed to identify my real self. What did you do for fun as a child? What talents emerged as a child? Which ones multiplied, and which ones got buried? Which talents do you most cherish?

What did you want to be as a grown-up? *A nun and a mother.* Note to my childhood self: those might be mutually exclusive. Well— Mother Superior might be all-encompassing.

What most excites you about the world?

When people transcend situations and do more than they ever thought possible. To dare mighty things. To do something tangible to right a wrong. Surprising acts of humanity. Making and appreciating art, music, food, wine. Great books, bold ideas, positive humor, aesthetic excellence, finesse, beauty in nature, athletic capability. These uplift us and help us live life joyfully and fully.

When individuals and groups change the culture and gain personal growth and greater perspective. Understanding that people do things that make sense to them at the time. The notion of presuming innocence and positive intent. These can be bridges to resolve misunderstandings.

When people make a commitment to live in a healthier way and then follow through on that in mind, body, and spirit. Getting better as you get older.

What angers me?

Man's inhumanity to man or beast. Not valuing and appreciating others. Not having perspective to be able to see the other person's view.

People who go through life cranky, unhappy, taking no risks, being disappointed, being a victim, taking no responsibility, looking for the bad instead of the good, and wasting life.

Selfishness, entitlement, laziness, narrow points of view, people who don't care about others, people who don't take care of or invest in themselves. People who don't make a commitment to learning, achievement, health, and happiness.

I flip through more exercises.

Write a story about where you want your life to be:

I will strive to exude health, positivity, grace, confidence, vitality, gratitude, and appreciation—to be my best self every day. I will make home a refuge of peace. Rich and I will have a fun, passionate, intimate relationship. I will recover through meditation, reading, painting, learning, and gratitude. I will consciously enjoy more daily moments. I will stop and appreciate interactions and conversations and realize that each time I connect with someone, it is another soul. I will enjoy vibrant fruits and vegetables every day. Each day I will strive to say—and mean—I am working to be my best self.

I am in limbo at work during my notice period. I slept later today with no need to rush into the office. We took Bella for a walk, and I relished being in our neighborhood when it is light.

On the walk, Rich said, "Bella, do you see all these people driving to work? Is Mom one of them? No, she is not! Won't we be happy to see Mom during the day? How many of them do you see smiling? Here's a dude in a big fancy Mercedes. Is he smiling? Let's see. No! Not smiling. Here, this lady has a vanity plate MOMX4. Is she smiling? No! She is not. Look at this guy in the Porsche. Not smiling! Texting! Not good. Bella, we are the only ones smiling."

I went to the eye doctor and found out that I have cataracts in both eyes. No wonder I can't see. I look at it from a gratitude perspective: I'm glad I'm not going blind. I'm glad I can afford glasses. I'm glad to be aging instead of the alternative.

I found a page in the notebook I wrote at fifty; it is how I dreamed I could be as I aged:

- Look and feel great
- Passionate about work that is fulfilling
- Painting: selling work and donating paintings to charity
- Feeling fulfilled in my creativity
- Taking classes—constantly learning
- Meditation daily—growing spiritually
- Strong marriage built on great love, passion, and companionship
- Living in a beautiful home with views
- Incredible garden with heirloom vegetables
- World travel
- Strong friendships
- Olive trees, hummingbirds, dogs

- Appreciating every moment
- Writing
- Lots of laughter
- Cooking incredible, healthy meals together in our state-of-the-art kitchen
- Running, biking, and swimming
- Financially secure
- Functional in three languages
- Giving back to community in ways I am passionate about

Looking back, I am not sure how I expected to do all that in a corporate executive role. Olive trees don't actually thrive in Ohio. Some of the "wishes" were ambitious, and some were right on the money. The desire list still seems pretty valid. One definite theme that carries over from then to now is being healthy in mind, body, and spirit. Again, I ponder what my new, fulfilling work could be. Secretly I dream I can be an artist.

I look back at more writing exercises inspired by Alan Seale's *Soul Mission* book. I have read his book so many times that it is dog-eared. I took a word, drew a circle around it, and filled a whole page with free word associations inspired by the middle word. The words in the middle were Freedom, Success, Power, Love, Difference, Positivity, People, Nurturing, Fulfillment, Journey, Light, Health, and so forth.

I remember meditating on the center words to discover circumstances where my soul could flourish. What themes show up consistently for me?

- Natural positivity and optimism, having perspective
- Being inspiring, motivating, and nurturing
- Seeing good, bringing light, peace, respect
- Being genuine, authentic, kind, caring
- Creating, painting, exploring
- Fulfillment, being on a journey, using gifts and talents

- Spirituality, light, choice
- Gratitude

One theme I see is understanding other people's perspectives. I wonder if this comes from reading. Every time I read a story, I can imagine being that person and what it would be like to be: for example, dying of AIDS, in a Nazi prison camp, a monk who loves his daily devotional practice and the routine of the monastery, a slave, or a wife whose husband is fighting in a war. What would it be like to be a soldier fighting, a Jewish leader expelled from Spain in 1492, or a scared child who is being abused? The idea of seeing through the eyes of another person feels natural for me. Could this understanding be from past lives? If someone is truly an old soul, how many lifetimes could there have been? Ten? A hundred? Thousands? Are fragments of memories or life lessons retained somehow?

At work, I was a peacemaker. I would calmly and patiently explain to someone (the self-ascribed "victim") why someone else might have done what they did "to" him or her.

I would tell them that the other person did what made sense to them at the time.

In mediating disputes, I can easily see both sides. When someone did something very wrong or broke policy and had to be dismissed, I always tried to do the exit with compassion, often saying, "You are human. You made a mistake. You need to leave the business, but don't let this ruin your life. Go, reflect (get help if needed), learn this lesson, and then be a better person because of it."

As I am leafing through the notebook, another old story comes to mind. I add it.

I was working at Lord & Taylor in New York. It was a cool, clear spring night, probably in 1989. I left the office after a long day. It was dark. I walked down 39th street to 6th Avenue. Cabs were zooming by. I put my hand up. A driver pulled to the curb. A woman came up and said, "Want to share this cab?"

I said, "Sure, if you are heading to the Upper West Side." Yes. She was going to give a lecture on astrology, the world's oldest belief system. She asked me my birthday. I said "May 20."

She looked at me for a long moment and said, "Me, too." Wow, that's amazing. She asked, "What year?" I told her. She shook her head and laughed. "That's a big synchronicity. Me, too." We compared driver's licenses. As she got out of the cab, she ducked her head back in and said, "Get your chart done. This has to mean something."

At the time, it was just a good cocktail party story, but as I think about it now, it was one of several calls to adventure, like the letter from Sean. It is as though hidden forces or subtle energies were saying, "Wake up! There is a lot more here than you imagine."

I have always been a person who looks forward more than back. But something about journal writing is taking me back to moments of synchronicity and signals about a search for deeper meaning. Now that I am dredging up old stories, I remember another and write it in the notebook.

I was nine years old when a tent revival came to Carrollton. It was August in Missouri, humid and muggy. I was Catholic but somehow got invited to the Protestant revival and went. I got completely caught up in it. I had never witnessed such a display of intense and passionate feeling. Everyone had a paper fan and sat in the sweltering tent, sweating and fanning themselves.

The preacher would say something, and the congregation would call back, "Amen!" A large lady near me in a white cotton dress was fanning and moaning. The intensity, zeal, and vehemence of the minister was spellbinding. Something deep stirred in me—emotions I had never felt before. For a long time, I held back while gospel songs I had never heard before went on and on around me, and I felt a rapturous feeling of being lifted up.

Deepak Chopra says that in India, they call it being "mad for God." I was. After the preaching, they kept singing "Sweet Hour of Prayer" over and over again as people walked down the aisle to be saved. I was embarrassed to go because I was an outsider as a Catholic, but I *wanted* to go. I was not an outwardly emotional kid, but I remember tears coursing down my face. And I still remember the words to that song.

After two or three nights of this, they announced they would have a movie at our town theater the next night. I begged Dad to take me. Somehow, I thought if he would have the courage to walk down the aisle and be saved, I would, too. Looking back on it, he was in his late thirties, a devout Catholic, and here was one of his kid begging him to do something that would get her closer to God. I am sure he struggled to decide what to do. This evangelical demonstration was nothing a Catholic would ever do in their matter of fact, "Say your rosary and get it over with" way. But he took me. He didn't want to be there, and I was embarrassed he was embarrassed. We arrived after the movie started and sat in the back of the theater. I'm sure he was glad it was dark. He might have been a little curious, but mostly I think he was just trying to be a good dad. I am sure the movie was contrived and obvious, but to a nine-year old, it was emotional, stirring, compelling, tear-inducing, and near the end, I *wanted* to walk down the aisle and get saved. I whispered, begging, "Dad, please, let's go down there." He hesitated for a moment and grabbed my hand, and we rose to our feet. I couldn't believe it; we were going to do it! My heart leaped into my throat.

Then quietly, he led me to the exit, whispering, "No, we're leaving. We're already saved."

But I wasn't quite done. The minister had said, "If you *feeeel* the Holy Spirit, you will go ask the retail stores on the town square to close at noon tomorrow so that everyone in town can come to the last day of this revival and be saved." I look back now and can see that all the store owners knew this was coming and had aligned on a response. In my fantasy, I imagined there would be hundreds of us banding together, asking the store owners to close—fueled by the Holy Spirit.

I rode my bike to the town square, screwed up my determination and then, stammering and red-faced, walked in and asked the jewelry store owner if he would close the store for the finale of the revival. My cousin was working, and she said nothing but gave me a little head shake as I started to speak to the owner. He said gently, "Honey, I can't do that. You get on home now." I walked out of the jewelry store to the sidewalk, dejected and humiliated, took a few steps, and stood outside the hardware store next door and tried to catch my breath and build up my courage to go in and talk to the store owner. I debated, and then I just chickened out. I didn't go into the hardware store. I rode home on my bike, feeling sure I wasn't worthy of the Holy Spirit.

My heart started pounding, and my face got red just now, remembering this story dredged up from who knows where. In our small town, all the store owners knew me and my family. It took about ten seconds for my bike trip uptown to get back to Mom and Dad. Looking back on this memory, it is amazing because I was so introverted. I would not even order an ice cream cone for myself at the Dari Maid. I felt an urge or a calling that made me act completely outside of my personality.

Later that afternoon, I went to the piano room to practice. My parents' bedroom was behind a louvered door; I heard them talking. Mom said, "Should we be worried?"

Dad said, "I can't get over it. Who would have thought this of Janie? I think we should just act like nothing happened. It's a phase, and it will pass. These damn zealots with their revivals—ridiculous."

I wonder what the purpose is of my remembering that story. Maybe going deeper in spirituality can cause those I love to think that I am going off the deep end? Or it can cause pain, embarrassment, and separation? That this quest to go deeper has been with me all my life?

There is a central idea I have triangulated in most wisdom traditions: a desire for connection to the Source or the Supreme Being—a type of unity consciousness. Even before I heard of the laws of the universe, I had started to hear some of the concepts from quantum physics and the idea that there is oneness among all creatures. Everything connects to everything else.

I once had a spiritual teacher at Canyon Ranch who talked about unity consciousness and seeing God in everyone. This involves suspending judgments: all in God and God in all. He gave me a lesson: every time someone does something incomprehensible, just tell yourself, "They are enlightened."

That afternoon, someone left wet towels all over the steam room. I said to myself, "They are enlightened."

I can get there pretty easily. "They must not see that towel receptacle five feet away and all the other guests who put their wet towels there," or "They just got some terrible news and have forgotten all their manners."

Today I did an old meditation I remembered. I lay on the floor and followed my breath until I got to a point of stillness. I thought about times I do and don't resist the flow of love that is available to me. I asked, "What am I here to do? Do I believe I deserve love? Do I believe I deserve abundance?"

The incredible, unexpected gift of a separation package to leave working life feels like an unmistakable sign of grace and abundance. I have to work to not feel guilty about it. Do I deserve it? Is deserve even the right word? Someone once told me that we need just enough money to go on our spiritual path. I like thinking of the severance package this way—as something to fund my vision quest.

I wonder about the best way to listen to what my true self has to say to me. The true self is what many of spiritual teachers talk about; it seems to basically mean the same thing as soul. I remember from psychology classes that Carl Jung wrote about individuation, which is the process of finding your true, authentic self. This is when you recognize your persona (the way you project yourself to the outside world) and integrate it with what is below the surface in your unconscious mind, including your shadow side (the hidden part of you that exists in the background).

By connecting to your inner voice—your authentic self—you become conscious and aware of your true vocation. This is the journey toward the person you are meant to be; this is your journey to wholeness.

How do we find that inner voice and begin to travel on the journey to wholeness, to be the person we are meant to be? Is it about following your passion or your bliss? I think painting, meditation, and journaling are what I will try for now.

As July dragged by, I continued going in to the office, dreading walking through the doors each day. It was painful, boring, and embarrassing. I was the lamest of ducks. Someone told me I was now a "PIP": a previously important person. I tried to laugh it off, but I did feel as though I was moving to obscurity. An acquaintance saw me out walking and told me how sorry she was that I had gotten fired. I started to explain, "Oh, I wasn't fired; I'm retiring," and then stopped myself. What did it matter what people thought?

My email inbox was remarkably light, other than meeting cancellations pinging through. I tried to keep a sense of humor about it, joking with Cherri, my administrative assistant. A month ago, I was so busy in back-to-back meetings that I could barely find time to go to the ladies' room. Now there are huge blocks of time on the calendar with nothing at all. I never realized how long the workday is: as long as a night with insomnia.

I struggle to take ego completely out of it. It's not personal. It will be over soon. I am moving past caring what people think.

July 15

I find the section in my notebook where I had written the laws of the universe. Along with a page of tiny handwritten notes, I found a post-it-note to myself saying, "You are at the beginning of a long spiritual journey." Ha. Pretty prophetic.

I remember that even the notion that there *were* such things as principles of the universe blew my mind.

These seven universal laws or principles are ancient mystical and secret teachings dating back over 5,000 years. From ancient Egypt to ancient Greece to the Vedic tradition of ancient India, common threads lead back to these principles.

They are:

1. The Principle of Mentalism
2. The Principle of Correspondence
3. The Principle of Vibration
4. The Principle of Polarity
5. The Principle of Rhythm
6. The Principle of Cause and Effect
7. The Principle of Gender

Mentalism	• Everything begins with thought
	• We are all connected—all one
	• Habits are formed by thought
	• You can't destroy habit—must transform it
	• Seek the divine in yourself
	• You can change the world with positive thought
	• The law of abundance is linked to this concept
Correspondence	• The person you wish to be exists within yourself
	• As above, so below—as within, so without
	• What is seen and unseen
	• Different perspective produces a different vision
Vibration	• Energy is vibrating and in motion
	• Positive thought attracts positivity
	• Learners remain engaged throughout life
	• Your body's vibe creates your aura
	• Change is constant
	• Birds of a feather flock together
	• The law of attraction is linked to this and other laws

Polarity	• Everything is a shade of gray on a wide spectrum
	• There are infinite possibilities
	• All possibilities and wisdom we need for life already exist within us
	• We are here to learn even from poor choices
Rhythm	• Every person has their own rhythm
	• You are either growing or dying
	• Synchronicity
	• Living a full spectrum life that's wide and free
	• Feel and experience life fully
Cause and Effect	• Karma
	• Being consciously aware of choices
Gender	• Everything in its own time
	• Faith
	• Yin and yang in everything
	• Every creative process needs balance
	• Let go of urgency and let it happen

These seven principles have been handed down over centuries and are known as hermetic laws. They are originally attributed to Hermes Trismegistus (thrice greatest Intelligencer). He is thought of as one of the first to communicate celestial and divine knowledge to mankind by writing.

Wisdom traditions have interpreted these laws according to their various belief systems.

Just having the space to think about these concepts is an amazing gift. I have always wanted time to identify what concepts I know and believe and what I still need to learn, without being interrupted by an urgent conference call.

The Principle of Mentalism

The first principle states that the universe is mental, and thoughts become tangible. Our world is created from our perceptions: our thoughts, feelings, ideas, beliefs, biases, and points of view. Billions of humans with different perspectives share the planet. The Sufi story about the blind men and the elephant explains that one blind man feels the elephant's ear and describes the creature as flat and thin. Another, touching a leg says, "No, the creature is thick like a cylinder." Another, grasping the tail, says that the elephant is like a rope. Each one, within the limited context of their finite senses, describes an incomplete piece of the whole.

The inscription on the ancient Greek temple of Apollo at Delphi says, "Know thyself and thou shalt know all the mysteries of the gods and the universe." The ancient teaching is that we are all one, and we are all connected, not only to each other, but to all of nature and to everything in the universe. What we do to others, we do to ourselves. To create the ideal reality, thoughts must be mastered. It is possible to experience happiness, true love, excellent health, creative expression, abundance, wealth, and anything else by bringing oneself into vibrational harmony through the creative power of thoughts.

The concept of abundance is linked to the law of mentalism. The thinking is that what we believe we can receive, we *do* receive. If we believe in scarcity or lack, that's what we experience. If we believe in abundance, we experience abundance. There is a popular book called *The Secret* that explains this.

I am now beginning to understand the concept; if we truly believe in overflowing good, we will receive and create it in our lives. This is the idea I have heard in the past with both skepticism and hope, that we are in partnership with the universe in the joyous creation of our lives. What if more people believed that there is *enough*—enough food, love, compassion, wellness, and resources for all of us?

It's easy to ask whether it's right to feel joy and gratitude in the midst of suffering throughout the world. But maybe elevating our own thoughts is a gift we can give the world, and through that, others' thinking can also rise to be more grateful, conscious, respectful, and joyful.

The Principle of Correspondence

The law of correspondence resonates with me because it contains the idea of having perspective, the notion that each life lesson has many layers, and the idea that we shape our own reality by our thoughts. Looking at a situation from every angle to appreciate all sides is part of the idea, like seeing the beauty and intricacy of a Moroccan rug, which looks different from every angle. Our current situation is a direct result of the way we think. If we want to shift our lives, we have to shift our thoughts.

We have total and complete control over only one thing in life—our thinking. It is not until we change our thought patterns to focus on what we truly desire that we can bring about meaningful and lasting change.

When a painter has an image of what she wants to paint, the image exists in her mind. When it is expressed on the canvas, there is something of the artist there, too.

This law also speaks to what is seen and unseen. So much is unseen: the past, the future, conscious awareness, the spiritual dimension, and the boundless realm of the soul.

The law of correspondence tells us that our outer world is just a reflection of our inner world—as within, so without. As above, so below. Our reality is a mirror of what is going on inside us. Is our inner reality happy, centered, integrated, and fulfilled? If it is, then that's what the world will see.

I think about Gussie, whose thoughts tend to focus on low self-esteem, feeling badly about herself, bitterness, regret, and disappointment. Her outer world is a place of drama and chaos. Gus's life seems like a self-perpetuating situation. She feels badly about herself, and her outer world is unhappy. She self-medicates to try to make herself feel better. The worse the outer world becomes, the worse she then feels about herself, which has a direct impact on her reality. She blames others for the things that are wrong in her life. I believe if Gus could change her thinking, she could change her life. *How to help her do that*, I wonder.

The Principle of Vibration

The law of vibration states that everything in the universe moves and vibrates—people, animals, plants, trees, tables, cars, rocks, thoughts, our emotions—everything is vibrating at one speed or another.

Energy is always vibrating in motion. We can't create or destroy energy, but we can transform it by exchanging one habit for another habit. All the energy that exists now has always been in existence in some form. A wooden spoon was a tree, before that a seed, and before that another tree.

This law says that we draw to us or attract energies similar to our own. Birds of a Feather Flock Together. When you think positive thoughts, you attract positivity and vice versa; like attracts like. What you think about, you tend to bring about. Every thought, emotion or mental state has a corresponding vibration.

I wonder, *How far does this law extend? Beyond this life? If people reincarnate together, is there some element of attraction that lasts beyond life? If yes, what are the elements in the soul that exist from life to life?*

The Principle of Polarity

The law of polarity recognizes that there are multiple dimensions to things. Things that appear as opposites are only two extremes of the same thing, like heat and cold, love and hate, war and peace. It is possible to transform your thoughts from hate to love, from fear to courage, by consciously raising your vibration. I think about viewing retirement as not just an ending but also a beginning, like commencement.

Between two extremes, everything exists on a spectrum with an infinite number of points. The difference between heat and cold is only a matter of degree. There is no place on a thermometer where heat stops and cold begins. The same is true between east and west, light and darkness, large and small, and good and bad.

When I was young in my business career, I felt a need to be "right" and to have things done "my way." I would correct people often. One of my first bosses told me I needed to become less of an asshole. I cringe at the memory; it stung because it was so true.

I consciously worked on being open to other views. As I matured and began to lead teams of people, I remembered teaching young professionals how to handle situations, such as "There is always more than one right way. If the leader you are supporting has an idea of how they want to address the situation, work with it. Find the right way that gives them confidence in their instincts; reinforce that they know what they are doing."

Later, as I had very senior leaders reporting to me, I helped them trust their inclinations and rely on their own ideas and approaches, and I learned that even if I would have done something differently based on my past experience, I held back from saying, "Here's how to do it," because their instincts were good, and I trusted them.

My thinking was, let me not substitute my judgment for theirs if "their way" is a decent option. Often, I would make a small tweak or suggestion. Rarely did I have to step in and say "no." Their values were in the right place, and they knew how to think. Most things don't have to be dealt with in absolutes. There are almost always more options if we look deeply and with enough perspective.

Also, in the law of polarity, we see that within every problem lies the solution, and within failure lies success. Babe Ruth held the world record for the most home runs *and* for the most strikeouts.

A further step in the law of polarity means that all the wisdom we need already exists inside us. Maybe that's why old memories are coming back to me; there must be concepts and themes that I already "know" on some level.

The Principle of Rhythm

Universal principle number five is the law of rhythm. This is the idea that there is a season for everything, a flow and a natural order. Daily, monthly, seasonal, annual cycles influence the tides, our bodies, and all of nature. And there is probably also a rhythm for major life transitions.

In science, they say, "For every action there is an equal and opposite reaction." The pendulum swings in everything. I think about the waves of the ocean, the rise and fall of empires, business cycles, and personal successes and failures. In accordance with this law, when anything reaches a point of culmination then the backward swing begins almost unnoticeably until such time that any forward movement has been totally reversed; then the forward movement begins again, and the process is repeated.

I think about the subtle backward swing and wonder how to be better tuned in to notice the start of that shift. At Canyon Ranch in one of the lectures they ask the audience, "How do you know when you are old?" The answer is when you can no longer rise out of a chair using just leg strength; no arms. I wonder if you notice the day you get old? On that first day, you struggle to stand up, can you catch yourself and reverse it somehow?

The advice from wisdom traditions seems to be that when you feel the law start to draw you back in, do not become fearful or discouraged. Instead, know that you are one with the universe for which nothing is impossible and fight to remain positive. Even if your efforts meet with failure, find comfort that by virtue of this very same law, the upward motion must start again.

The Principle of Cause and Effect

The law of cause and effect tells us that "Every cause has its effect; every effect has its cause." The New Testament expresses it as, "Whatsoever a man soweth, that shall he also reap." This law is often referred to as the law of karma. In Sanskrit, karma is the concept of "action" or "deed." There is a continuity between all events precedent, consequent, and subsequent. A relationship exists between what has gone before and what follows.

You get back what you send out. The choices or decisions you make will set in motion a chain of reactions and give you back a result corresponding to whatever that decision triggered.

In accordance with this law, every effect noticed in the physical world has a very specific cause, which has its origin in the inner or mental world. I marvel at how the laws interweave and support one another. Here again the concept of thought and "as within, without" is interwoven. Every thought, word, or action sets a specific effect in motion, which will come to materialize over time. The implication is that there is nothing like chance or luck.

I have read that in the spiritual plane, cause and effect are instant, but in the real, material world, our concept of time and space creates a time lag between the cause and the eventual effect.

I am intrigued once again with the idea that when you focus on a goal with intention, what you want to create in the physical world is automatically manifested in the spiritual world, and with perseverance, practice, and continued concentrated thought, it will also come to materialize in the physical world.

I think of executives I have worked with over the years. Some had a very clear idea of their ambition. The ones who said, "I intend to be a president of a business unit" or "I expect to be a CEO" eventually seemed to get what they intended. The clearer one can be, the more one puts their concentrated effort on the achievement.

Humans process experiences and react. They label things good and bad. Some understand that we can alter our reality by changing our thoughts. I think of veterans that are now physically challenged with injuries and people who have survived a dread disease or a horrible loss. Some say that the experience changed them in a positive way. For most of those "glass half full" people, they sculpted their own mental transformation; they changed the way they looked at the situation and altered the way they summed it up.

The ones who developed and inserted a new perception overcame their ego in some way. Everything that is happening to us is a signal of the way we are processing the present moment. Our past experiences, memories, and desires create our current experience.

We are able to choose the way we respond to any given life situation. I stop to really let it sink in—*we have choice.* Our ego likes to give up our power to others so it can then become a victim. If we live in spirit versus ego, we can be fearless, immortal, and living abundant lives. I want to look at my current situation from a "glass half full" perspective. I am commencing on the most exciting time of my life with plenty of resources and good health; I can embrace this as one of the most positive things that has ever happened to me.

In ego, we come from lack, from fear. But if we realize we are not our body, our possessions, our personality, or our job title—then we can live a more conscious life.

To live more consciously, we have to witness ourselves becoming the seer who can dispassionately view ourselves making decisions and choices and make it possible to change our thinking in order to alter our reality.

Again, I come back to the "how" of developing this capability, and it reinforces—again—that meditation is a way to repave the neural pathways.

I have read that by aligning our thoughts and actions with the law of cause and effect, we can create abundance, heal ourselves, attract the perfect partner, and manifest the ideal lifestyle.

The Principle of Gender

The law of gender is the last of the seven laws and reminds us that yin and yang are in everything. Everywhere in nature, we see both feminine and masculine aspects of plants, animals, and minerals. It takes both sides to create or to reproduce in nature.

There must be a balance between more masculine energies like assertive action and more feminine energies like reflection and contemplation. People who are in balance with both their masculine and feminine energies move forward with thoughtful action that breeds success.

Within this law also resides the notion of everything happening in its own time; there is a natural gestation period for all things. It takes nine months for a child to develop in the womb. All seeds must germinate before sprouting. Ideas, hopes, and dreams need time to develop.

A lesson for me in this law is to let go of a sense of urgency for things to happen right now. I need to shed my sense of hurry and develop patience and faith.

I believe that if I were living this law correctly and had the right level of faith, I would trust that everything is happening in a divine order. I have been told that through a balance of energy and the necessary gestation time, manifestation will occur. I often try to manipulate situations quickly out of fear that if I don't intervene, I won't get the result I want. I wonder if there really is a divine order to things and think how profound the notion of "let it be" is.

I continued through the last part of July going into the office and spending more time writing random thoughts in my journal.

Today I did downward-facing dog in a tank top and short workout tights. By a mirror. And glanced. This was not a good surprise: ripples of loose skin from top to bottom. Aging. If I were cultivating being egoless, I would not care about this. At all. But I am not yet enlightened enough to be egoless.

Rich and I have lived longer than both our moms. My mom died at age fifty-one. Rich's mom died at age fifty-five. How we would have loved it if they could have gotten old enough to have rippled skin while doing downward facing dog. They both would have loved yoga.

I have never been thin, but I am now at my lowest adult weight. My boobs are tangerines instead of grapefruits. It doesn't matter in the daytime, thanks to my push-up bra. But at night in my PJs, I think, *What happened?*

And while it's nice for my body to be leaner, my face looks a little caved in. In Manhattan, they used to say, "Choose; it's either derriere or face. If you are happy with your face, your ass is too big." I'm sure there is a happy medium there somewhere.

I want to be egoless and to let it all go. Laugh at it. Be the master of my own thoughts. Be grateful to have the chance to age.

As I think about my body, I remember reading that having a body may not be our soul's natural state. If reincarnation exists, then as souls, we might live much of our existence free from encasement.

What is it like to be free of having a body? Identity must be retained in some way. We might have greater freedom of movement and much greater perception. We probably still communicate in some way—maybe through thought. I once read that becoming embodied is like putting on a space suit. Our senses are restricted and muffled, like trying to see with blinders on.

July 20

I talked to my great friend Sandra, who used to be my old boss. I love her. She said, "Aren't you excited? For the first time in life, you get to be a housewife." Housewife? We laughed because it has always been a little bit of a fantasy for both of us.

I continued to ponder the big existential questions during this time of empty hours in the office. Finally, I have time to think. Today, I wonder if other people who aren't monks, rabbis, priests, or nuns think about spirituality as much as I do. I am nearly fifty-eight years old and embarrassed that I don't know more. I tell myself to just enjoy my late-bloomer and beginner status and just take it one step at a time.

I have a lot of questions about God or Spirit or Universal Mind or Divine Source or Creative Force or Great Mystery or Eternal Energy or the Universe or All That Is, or any of the other divine names of God. Though I am partial to "Spirit" or "Universe" I haven't found the name for Him, Her, or It in my own mind. Though I imagine He/She/It to be beyond gender, the childlike part of me likes thinking of

Spirit as female. It is presumptuous to ascribe human characteristics to Spirit, but as I begin to try to grasp the secrets of the infinite, it's what *my* mortal mind tries to do as I come up with and discard theories, guesses, and speculations about Spirit's nature and the meaning of life.

I didn't have enough time to think about Spirit in corporate life. So, I have thirty-six years of pent-up demand to think about Her. The first thing that rings true is that anyone who claims to know the true nature of Spirit is speculating. But I wonder if, after each lifetime, we really do learn more of these secrets? If yes, then maybe there are mortals who at least know more than I do. I believe She is infinite, eternal, and not subject to change. Why do I believe this? Faith? Do I *know* this on some level? Am I remembering something I have known in the past and will learn more about in the future? At the end of the grand cycle of rebirths, if that is even true, will we be able to know the whole truth of being one with Her?

As I ponder questions like the nature of Spirit, part of me feels ridiculous to have such a deep desire to keep questing to find answers. To what end? Is any of what we experience real, or is life but a dream? If it isn't real, then should I go on acting like it's real? Is that the game? To sort of stumble and bumble around and around? Or is it right to keep my mind on the big questions and yet live as though daily life is all real and substantial?

I go back to the advice I have gotten: keep one foot in the ether and one firmly planted in the day-to-day material world. As tempting as it is to live in a world of dreams, the business in this life must be to *live.* We—probably none of us on this plane or very few of us—really know the true meaning of life. I expect that it is not a mistake to try to live to the highest and best potential that is within us. We are all on a path, and my faith or intuition tells me that the road keeps going in an elevated direction with some rest stops on the way.

I emerge from my wool-gathering and start to get excited again about the prospect of retired life. Now I can finally read books and take classes and do exercises and paint paintings and, in the background, keep wondering about the big existential questions. And, as I ponder, I look at my doodles of the day—upward moving spirals.

July 21

I started the day with twenty minutes of meditation, studied Italian, went for a run, did laundry, took a segment of an online class, and stood in front of a blank canvas, pondering how to paint the concept of equilibrium. Can that be done geometrically? I imagine that if the shapes were in correct proportion in relationship to each other, that could convey balance. I made some sketches of the shapes that were rolling around at the edges of my mind, planned menus for the week, and wrote in my journal.

I am reading a book by Deepak Chopra, and what he says resonates with me at some deep level. He would say I am a seeker. Raised a Catholic, I miss going to Mass. I miss singing. I miss Christmas Eve and Easter morning and being part of a congregation, and I miss the ritual and the feeling of connectedness. I used to love the sign of peace. I would actually feel a glow expand around my heart, shaking hands with random members of the congregation. My dad still goes to Mass every day he can.

For me now, what resonates is broader than organized religion. It's about a connection to everyone and everything. Though my view is broadening, I watch with something like envy when I see people walk into their places of worship. So, now I seek. And I study, and I explore, and I take classes and read. And I wonder.

July 23

July marches on. I am biding my time until my last day in the office. Today I jogged to the gym and lifted weights before spending a few hours in the office. There are only days now until my work life is over; I could probably count it in hours. But I feel I can't "start" any big projects until I "finish" at work.

I ran errands in the middle of the day; something I have never had the luxury to do. I called Cherri from the Target parking lot and asked, "Anything going on?" "Nope; no need to rush back at all." Cherri will be fine; she is in line to work with another senior executive, something I am very grateful for.

I came back and doodled mandalas in my notebook. Mandalas are so visually pleasing; I love the symmetry and the sense of mystery and power in the parallel shapes, above and below, within and without mirrored.

July 24

They finally made the enterprise-wide announcement about my retirement. The outpouring from all the people I have interacted with over the years is nice to experience, but it is also exhausting. I can't wait to get on with it. I am trying to let go of ego in all aspects of this transition. I have been able to pretty much detach from the painful part of letting go in the wounding realization that they won't miss a beat without me.

And so, I will not let myself feel too much pride in hearing people say I helped them and supported them along the way. I had filed these stories away or simply forgotten them. Nice of people to go out of their way to reach out. Cherri and some others wanted to plan a retirement party, but I said please not to. It does not seem right with the exits that will be taking place very soon.

My proudest moment this week: the LGBTQ associate affinity group I sponsored made me an honorary lesbian. I am proud of that, ego or not.

I keep making different to-do lists and here is one more:

1. Get my technology sorted out
2. Organize/archive/digitize years of family photos
3. Go to Capital Area Humane Society to meet some puppies
4. Take Bella to a canine specialist

5.   Search for classes in spirituality, health, fitness
6.   Learn about *feng shui* and numerology
7.   Plan a trip to Europe
8.   Declutter the house
9.   Get my painting studio set up
10. Buy a big easel
11. Get certified as a meditation instructor
12. Find out how to get my own personal mantra
13. Learn yoga
14. Sign up for an Italian class
15. Give work clothes away to Dress for Success

I move from the laws of the universe to the study of chakras. I find old notes in my red notebook. I had a lot of questions in the beginning: Where *are* chakras, exactly? Are they down your spine? Down the front of your body? Inside you? Outside kind of in your aura? I was embarrassed not to know.

I learned that the seven chakras are like swirling wheels of energy corresponding to nerve centers in the body as well as our psychological, emotional, and spiritual states of being. When your chakras are healthy and open, your life flows more smoothly. When any one of them is sluggish, blocked, or has a weak vibration, the imbalance can show up physically, impacting a particular area of your body, or as an emotional or psychological symptom affecting your outlook.

I remember a soul-gazing exercise I did with Rich when I got to the fourth chakra (heart). We were in Miami at the Mandarin Oriental Hotel for the weekend. Rich and I sat face-to-face on the floor of our room.

We began to breathe with our eyes closed, into the center of our chest, the heart chakra. After a couple of minutes when our breathing was steady and in unison, we looked into each other's eyes. It wasn't creepy. The guidance was, "Don't speak, just be." We probably stayed there for ten minutes. He said he enjoyed it. I loved it! My heart felt very full of love for him, for our life. I am so lucky to have a husband who evolves with me and seems to understand my keen ache to go deeper.

I ordered books, and they came today. I want to do a comparative review of different wisdom traditions and begin to understand ideas from quantum physics and learn more about the universal laws. I have no idea whether I am on the right path or not. I'm basically going by the book recommendations Amazon is making; researching one leads to others.

I wish I better understood, for example: What are the beliefs of the Jewish faith, the Muslim faith? What do Buddhists believe? What do atheists believe? How does mythology fit in? Does anyone still follow any of the ancient belief systems? What are they, and how have they held up over time? Who are the most forward thinking philosophical and spiritual teachers of our time? What do they believe? What do scientists believe?

Here are some books I ordered:

- *Bhagavad Gita* translated by Eknath Easwaran
- *The Yoga Sutras of Patanjali,* translated by Alistair Shearer
- *The Hero with a Thousand Faces* by Joseph Campbell
- *The Science of Being* by Eugene Felson
- *God Is Not Dead* by Amit Goswami
- Two reference books on Numerology
- *The Biology of Belief* by Bruce Lipton
- *Sefer Yetzirah The Book of Creation in Theory and Practice* by Aryeh Kaplan
- *God Is a Verb—Kabbalah and the Practice of Mystical Judaism* by David Cooper
- *The Future of God* by Deepak Chopra
- *The Wizard of Us* by Jean Houston

I am going to start with something easy: feng shui. Sasha is going to loan me a couple of her books.

July 25

Sasha, Drew and the girls are here! Our house is in lovely, teeming chaos. Rich and Drew are playing in a golf tournament. Sasha and Drew are great parents. They are patient, they love the girls, and they see humor in (nearly) everything.

The girls are six and almost four. It will be interesting to watch their personalities fully emerge. Avery, the six-year-old, is cerebral, focused, and usually has a sweet nature. Sloane is affectionate, funny, precocious, and willful, just like Sasha was at her age.

Sasha and I took the girls to play in the neighborhood playground. We played "mean old troll" who demanded a toll to cross the bridge about a million times. Lots of screaming and laughter. So fun.

Sloane had a meltdown over her turn on the swings, and I got to see Sasha in action. She swooped Sloane up into her arms and started walking with slow and measured steps the couple of blocks back to our house.

Avery was solemnly holding my hand, and we were walking behind them. She gave me a look as if to say, "I would *never* behave like that." Sloane was screaming and sobbing, *"No,* Mommy!" She made her body stiff like a board. Sasha didn't miss a step; she kept walking and held Sloane sideways in her arms. I had a moment of déjà vu, remembering Sasha at Sloane's age. It was a small moment of karmic payback, but Sasha didn't get frustrated or upset. She just kissed Sloane and comforted her, and soon the tears stopped.

It is amazing to see the range of emotions in these little ones and how they can be laughing and then burst into tears in the next moment. When did we lose this ability to feel and express things so keenly?

We went swimming though Sloane protested that she is *too big* for the baby pool. We colored and "did art" and went to Build-a-Bear. Sloane and I played the Quiet Game. I won.

Avery can focus like a laser. She can also grab hold of an idea and not let it go. At Build a Bear, she wanted the inserted song to be "My Little Pony." Sasha made several other suggestions with enthusiasm. Avery was not swayed. For each alternative, Avery said "No!" I asked, "Avery, are you sure you want a song about a pony in a bear? "Yes!" Emphatic.

So, all the way home, she played over and over again "My Little Pony, my little po-ho-nee." I wonder how long it will take for us to get that song out of our heads.

After much playtime, many snacks, and our house looking like a storm struck, the Goodhearts have left the building. Whew. We are exhausted. It is good that children come to young parents.

As July wound down, I went deeper into my daily meditation practice. I have now mastered the frustration around thoughts coming into my mind. One of the meditation teachers at Canyon Ranch said, "You *can't* clear your mind. Stop trying to make that the goal.

I find meditation to be very peaceful and calming. I have been searching for meditation certifications and courses on line. There are a lot. I also called the Chopra Center and asked them how to get my own personal mantra, and they told me how: I need to take the Primordial Sound Meditation class. So, I will do this soon.

I keep coming back to the quest. What is my dharma, my purpose now? I feel at a loss and have no idea how to even start the process of figuring this out.

I have read that to learn what your purpose is, you have to be integrated so that everything you think and do is in harmony and feels genuine and authentic. So, going deeper in meditation will likely help. Painting will help. Even getting my simple "equilibrium" painting on canvas feels as though, through expression, some innate yearning is being satisfied in what I am trying to convey.

I think it would really help to have a spiritual teacher. Maybe the Chopra Center is a pathway there. Does my teacher have to be physically here with me? Maybe my teachers exist in these books, or I will be led to my teacher by just starting to study.

The third task, learning the lessons I am meant to learn in this lifetime means being open to the "gifts" of learning from every good and painful thing that happens and trying to become wiser and more aware with each lesson learned. I have been trying to do this for the past few years by reflecting on what happened and asking, "What was the lesson for me in this?"

I imagine that so many times the lesson to be learned is to put ego aside. Sometimes I can't see the lesson in real time and have to wait for hindsight. I have also heard that becoming aware of and working through my "shadow side" is part of the learning process.

I have read when someone accepts their three assignments of knowing who they are, knowing what their *dharma* is, and learning their lessons, then they have a responsibility to manifest what they learned. Once we have an inkling about what we are here to do, then we need to find the courage and whatever resources and skills are needed to strive to achieve whatever it is.

This links with the idea of using more of your potential. I've also read that making dreams come true is not in service to ego, but in service to fulfilling your mission.

I once had a colleague who went around talking about his "purpose." He was a good, hard-working, well-intended guy. He made me feel uncomfortable, and I had to work not to roll my eyes every time he started talking. I am having flashbacks and hoping not to become a person everyone else tries to flee. I feel compelled to find my purpose, my dharma. How do I do that and still live life in a sane and balanced way without making the people around me feel sorry for me or want to avoid me like the plague?

This feels like such a private thing. I don't yet know how to talk about it, but it seems to help to write it down.

I think my purpose, or *dharma* or whatever it is, has something to do with being healthier in mind, body, and spirit. It has something to do with accessing my creativity, elevating my personal vibration to assist in positivity in the world. It's emerging, but I can't quite get it. I feel stuck and excited at the same time, like I am on the verge of discovering something. There is something about painting certain shapes, colors, and lightness that makes me feel I am capturing a specific, higher vibration level. I feel it too after I have meditated.

In the meantime, as I am on the quest to become more conscious, when someone parks in the no parking zone at Kroger or leaves dog poop on the path when there are doggie toilet boxes every quarter mile, I still have to remind myself: "They are enlightened. It must have made sense to them at the time."

July 26

Today was my first unofficial day of retirement. I am still technically "on call," but won't be going into the office. My great friend David, the general counsel, came to see me this morning. He has been my best friend at work for years and the only one I could completely confide in because there was nothing too confidential to discuss with him.

He said, "Jane, this is ridiculous. Go home and be on call. You are torturing yourself coming in to the office when everything is coming off of your calendar." Of course, he was right. I would have given anyone else this exact advice. It was so obvious. I wasn't trying to be a martyr. It just never occurred to me not to show up until the last moment of my notice period. For my whole life, I have been wired to show up.

I have not even taken a sick day in over thirty years—what a stupid accomplishment. There were a couple of days over the years when I went home early with a sore throat or called in to meetings because I had a cold, but I had no unplanned days off. I even worked most of the day on colonoscopy prep day and went in the afternoon after my colonoscopy. Now I realize that was beyond ridiculous. Who in their right mind would care about it, anyway?

Isn't it funny when you can be eminently clear about what someone else should do, and yet when you come to yourself, you sometimes need a friend to remind you? So, I left. I hugged Cherri, grabbed my handbag, walked out, and felt a guilty pleasure, like I was playing hooky.

When I got home, Rich was leaving to drive to Cincinnati for a quick appointment, and I asked, "Want me to come?" and he said, "Sure."

I did something spontaneous with my husband on a weekday. Such a pretty drive, with rolling hills, beautiful trees, the greenest grass. When we got home, I went to the grocery store. Can I just mention the awesome wonder of the grocery store on a weekday evening? It was quiet, and there were no lines. Amazing. I wonder when I will stop rejoicing at the mundane. Hopefully never.

While we were in the car, I studied feng shui. Rich asked, "You don't really believe that stuff, do you?"

"I don't know enough yet to have an opinion. But it's fun to read about it. Something this ancient has to have some basis, and I respect that. When I was in China and Korea, feng shui was taken very seriously. It's a little hard to understand, but now I realize that, of course, there's an app for it."

I was intrigued that our house might be situated in an inauspicious way, but it turns out (now that I downloaded the app) that our front door faces northeast, which is our fourth best location. The way the roads curve in our neighborhood is excellent. The pond across the road is good *chi*, and our fountain might be decent *chi*, but right now, the fountain is barely pumping water. Is it bad *chi*?

I am a rooster, and he is a goat, which isn't the most compatible pairing. Now I find this out after more than thirty-seven years together?

Rich started arguing that the feng shui compass app was wrong! I didn't have the energy to tell him about the animal couple pairing. At least our lucky number is the same—eight.

The book said that decluttering is important in clearing *chi*. I decluttered the pantry before trash pick-up and got rid of old items where the freshness date had expired. I kept yelling up to Rich, "Honey, we moved this from New York ten years ago!"

I learned that there are numerous ways to improve quality of life from basic feng shui steps, such as good airflow and good light to slightly more advanced ones, such as facing your best directions. Your best feng shui directions help you attract the quality of energy that is most nourishing, or suitable, for you.

Since we are both eights in feng shui, our luckiest direction (southwest) is not the one we actually face (northeast), but it is not the worst we could have, and there are "cures."

The fountain guy came to fix it today (it just needed more water), and I realized that the current flow of the water is away from the house—bad *chi*. So, I asked the guy if we can reposition the basalt columns—yes we can. Here is the important life lesson in that: ask for what you want. He will send someone.

I painted more on my geometric "equilibrium" painting. I am using acrylics on a huge 48 x 60 canvas with reds, oranges, blues, and purples. Somehow it feels that these shapes reflect some deeper, inner wisdom. It is shaping up. I am covered in paint. Hours slip by and seem like minutes.

I am decluttering the library so the shelves are less packed. I gave boxes of books and CDs away. It feels good to let things go and have more space.

I did "Songs of Tara" chanting meditation today; Tara is revered in Tibetan Buddhism as a protector and savior. She offers practical help. Her primary mantra is *Om Tare Tuttare Ture Soha,* which means something like "Om, I call upon you who carries us over, swift one, hail."

One of the tracks on the CD is recorded by His Holiness, the Dalai Lama. I see that people call him HHDL. Cool. It was very peaceful.

Tonight we had steak, a wonderful salad, and baked potatoes with an excellent Spence Howell Mountain cabernet. No one makes a steak like Rich Ramsey. I wonder as I go deeper into spirituality if I will want to or need to become a vegetarian. I have not seen anything written about this yet, but I suspect I will. Each sentient being has a nervous system. If I think too deeply about this, it won't be long before I think I'll have to call it quits on meat. If that was one of my last steaks, it was a good one to go out on.

I painted and went for a walk around the pond after dinner. I took a break from my geometric painting and tried a Pollack type of painting in the unfinished part of the basement where I can be very messy. I put tarps down and started flinging paint around. It was as though my inner child was freed and having the time of her life. I have paint all over my ankles and shins. The painting has a deep orange background and ultramarine blue paint blobs and lines. I like it, and so does Rich.

He seems to understand, at least on some level, that I have an impulse for creative spiritual expression, and he is supportive. He sometimes asks me what a painting means to me. I treasure that he tries to understand, and yet I am usually at a loss to explain. I paint things I sense are trying to emerge. There seems to be some mystical idea that creates an impulse and somehow communicates "red" or "blobs" or "geometric symmetry." Sometimes there is an idea like "equanimity" or "balance" or "polarity" and sometimes it is just impulse after impulse where my hands just seem to go to the right tube of paint.

July 31

I went to the office to turn in my badge and computer and pay for my phone. Before I went in, I gave away my work clothes to Dress for Success. No turning back now!

It was emotional but good. I am mostly relieved and excited. It has been nice to ease into the transition over the past couple of weeks.

I wrote final handwritten notes of gratitude for a couple of special people, hugged my closest colleagues, and walked out with good friend Charles, which was very fitting because we have worked together since 1986. He was the perfect person to see at the end. It was like a *Seinfeld* episode. We chatted about nothing as we opened the door and walked out for the last time.

Chapter Two
August

In my first official month of retirement, I settle into a sweet daily routine filled with meditation, exercise, healthy food, painting, studying, and time with friends. The newness of being able to do what I want is something to treasure. Working out, reading, dog training, decluttering, and even running simple errands all fill me with a kind of mystical wonder. I feel compelled to paint. I begin a project to digitize the family photos. I take a quick trip to check on Dad. I become certified to teach meditation and go to the Chopra Center to receive my own personal mantra. I check on Gussie daily. Worry about Gus, Dad, and Raleigh are like tethers that ground me and keep me from experiencing complete contentment.

August 2

I bought feng shui plants and got a retirement haircut: shoulder length layers. I now have bangs for the first time since grade school. It feels different, which is somehow right.

I am starting my Certification in Meditation course online.

After a morning of rumbling thunder, we had a glorious summer thunderstorm with a soaking rain. Bella and I did training on not barking as people and their dogs walked by, using a clicker and salmon treats to reward good behavior. She lay by my feet and huffed and moaned as other dogs passed—but no barking. A good girl.

"Whatever you can do, or dream you can do, begin it. Boldness has genius, power, and magic in it. Begin it now." I love this quote, whether Goethe actually said it or not. I think, *I have now begun it! My one-year 'sabbatical' has begun.*

I felt inspired to continue painting geometrics and started a new 40 x 40 canvas, using acrylics in primary colors. I vacillated in my feelings about the canvas as each shape emerged.

It is so funny how I can look at a painting and say, "I *love* it!" and then two hours later look at it and say, "I *hate* it!" Why does that happen? And when Rich comes in and says, "Wow, I would hang it," somehow that means the world to me.

August 4

I read a quote from futurist Eric Hoffer. "In times of change, the learners will inherit the earth, while the learned find themselves beautifully equipped to deal with a world that no longer exists."

This makes me feel more hopeful about being a beginner and on a steep learning path. I began to research massive open online courses (MOOCs). There are so many, and a lot of them are *free.* How does their business model work?

A few are EdX, Coursera, and Udemy. I want to take the Science of Happiness class from University of California at Berkeley when it is next offered and an exercise physiology class. Both have a free option.

August 5

I meditated, did four hard miles on the elliptical, and made a healthy smoothie with mostly veggies. I had coffee with Rich and a walk with Bella. I took a class at the Apple Store and parked right in front of the store, with no searching for a parking spot. When I drove by the office, I had to stifle a chuckle.

I went to Whole Foods; I have never before seen it virtually empty. I met with the house painter to do some touch-ups around the house and then checked in on Gus. She was slurring her words and seemed very down. I didn't know whether to scold her or love her, so I did some of both.

I try to make sense of Gussie's situation from a spiritual stand-point. Everyone is on their own path, but I also believe that paths must be intertwined. When you love someone, and they are hurting themselves, it can't help but impact you. So, on some level is her struggle my struggle, too? What are the lessons I should be learning? Compassion? Nonjudgment? Try to save her? Detach? Set clearer boundaries? Tough love? Hold space? For the past few years, I've read books on how to help family members who have addiction issues. There are no clear answers. And Teresa, Bethany, Joe, and Emma felt at a loss also.

As I was reflecting about the law of polarity and the wisdom already existing deep inside us, another old memory came up for me. Maybe there is something wise I need to learn from my seven-year-old self.

This could be pretty universal with kids who were raised Catholic, but when I was in first and second grade, I became obsessed and lit-eral as I was learning catechism. I made myself sick. I was fine for the first few concepts, but learning about original sin made me sleepless and afraid. We recited the Baltimore Catechism every day in religion class. Sister Phillip was our teacher. She asked the questions, and we answered, using a little pamphlet to help us with the responses:

Who made the world?
God made the world.
Who made you?
God made me.
Why did God make you?
God made me to know Him, to love Him, and to serve Him in this world, and to be happy with Him forever in heaven.

Where is God?

God is everywhere.

Does God know all things?

God knows all things, even our most secret thoughts, words, and actions.

How many Persons are there in God?

In God, there are three Persons: the Father, the Son, and the Holy Ghost.

So far, so good. Here's where it began to break down for me:

What befell Adam and Eve on account of their sin?

Adam and Eve on account of their sin lost innocence and holiness and were doomed to misery and death.

What evil befalls us in the disobedience of our first parents?

Through the disobedience of our first parents, we all inherit their sin and punishment, as we should have shared in their happiness if they had remained faithful.

This was the part where it became unfathomable to me. I didn't have the words to articulate it, yet I could not stop obsessing about it. Doomed to misery and death? *Why* did God allow Adam and Eve to sin? Eating an apple doesn't seem like such a big crime. Was the punishment really proportional to the crime? And why should *we* inherit their sin when we had *nothing* to do with it?

I couldn't articulate these feelings verbally as a second grader. I didn't have the internal vocabulary to lay out the argument in sentences. But it did not square up with how I thought about God. Like an achy tooth I could not leave alone, it haunted me especially at night. And really scared me that the adult, authority figures in my life believed this story when I didn't. I thought I was a sinner for sure because I could not make myself believe it. Sister Phillip knew the idea of sin, and especially original sin, upset me. I remember she tried to put it in perspective for a seven-year-old. "It means you should always obey your parents and obey the law."

"And God sees everything?" Yes, she said. I started to obsess over things like the stop sign way down at the end of our street. The law is to stop. If I don't stop walking in our yard when I see the sign, am I breaking the law and sinning? And God sees me? Am *I* doomed to misery and death? I saw a commercial on TV with Smoky the Bear, and he said, "Only you can prevent forest fires!" *Only me?* But I am just a little kid, and I don't even live by a forest! So, is every fire my fault if I am the only one who can prevent them? Every action I took I saw as a potential sin. My poor young mind was overwhelmed by thoughts.

I couldn't fall asleep. Mom and Dad rocked me as I sobbed. They kept asking me what was wrong. I remember trying to explain, and they said, "Honey, God is good. He loves you. What you did wasn't a sin. No, you aren't responsible for forest fires, I promise."

I am so grateful to have been born to loving parents who wanted me. And they were good parents, but they also had a lot going on, and I wasn't the only one they were taking care of.

I got so sick with worry I developed an actual ulcer. They took me for an upper GI. So, at seven, I started drinking Maalox. I had completely forgotten this old memory. Why is it coming up for me now, I wonder?

Maybe it was to remind me not to become too engrossed in thinking about spirituality and to stay balanced and sane, questioning things but not obsessing. And that instinctively, I might know the right path for me and not to believe something just because someone else does, or someone tells me to.

August 6

Today, Rich and I talked about Bella. When we adopted her, the Humane Society explained she had been abandoned in a foreclosed home. She was so skinny when we got her, her ribs were sticking out. She is afraid of wind. She is aggressive with some dogs. She has been in a funk since Beau died. We wonder if it would help her to have another dog in the pack.

Today I spent hours sorting photos and slides for the digitizing project. I will use scanmyphotos.com. I enjoy the tedious work of tossing all duplicates and all landscapes, following the advice I found in *Real Simple*. If there is no person in the photo, toss it. I will get the digitized discs back in four to six weeks. The dining room table looks like a mountain of sepia and Kodachrome.

There are some family photos I have never seen. My eyes well up as I discover them. I can't wait to digitize them, so I can send them to my sibs. I found some of Mom. She was beautiful with a wave in her dark hair and pretty brown eyes, and she is slightly smiling in this photo. Maybe this was her engagement photo.

I am grateful to have the time to do this. After I get the digitized discs back, there is no need to keep the actual photos, but it's hard to imagine throwing them in the trash.

I am getting many headhunter calls. Some just want to know the real scoop of why I left. Some want names of candidates. There are a couple of huge corporate roles they try to entice me with, encouraging me to "just go on the interview." But the calls really serve to solidify my desire to be done with corporate life—at least for now.

I finished my geometric painting. I used ultramarine blue, cadmium red in medium, and cadmium yellow and then mixed other harmonious greens and purples and oranges from those original shades and added shapes—more triangles, circles, and squares.

I did a few hours of meditation training today studying the work of several great teachers including following the breath, visualization, somatic meditation, kundalini meditation, and some call-and-response meditation.

August 7

My favorite day of the week is Thursday—trash day. I might have a trash obsession, a trait I inherited from Dad. I feel compelled to get every bit of the trash out on that day, and when I was working, I was too rushed. Now I can gleefully check the refrigerator, pantry, and every wastebasket in the house. I found more expired freshness dates on things in the pantry. Every Thursday is another reason to continue decluttering, which is amazingly satisfying. The primary feng shui lesson that will stay with me is how freeing it is to get rid of clutter. Everything in your environment can either advance your goals or work against you. Letting go of what no longer serves you creates space for the things you want to achieve.

In feng shui, our homes are considered to be sacred spaces. The idea is to maintain our homes, just as we maintain the hygiene and health of our bodies.

As I clear clutter, I find things to be repaired, such as a beautiful old art-deco electric fan with lovely rounded blades, a drill I can use in my studio, and a light fixture. I want everything in the house to be functional. Broken items are symbolic of a broken life, and who needs that?

I'm working out our travel for Europe: we will go to London, Paris, Tuscany, Rome, and Barcelona, and we may meet our friends who are renting a villa in Umbria.

When I get quiet in meditation, I have been trying to check in and ask myself if I feel bored or depressed. I honestly don't. I am so surprised. I don't miss work. Maybe I will at some point. So far, I am amazed how quickly the days fly by. Every day at six when Rich turns off his computer and ends his work day, I am shocked that it's that late already.

Today I studied mindfulness meditation, a meditation for health and happiness and a relaxation body scan meditation. Moment by moment, we all have thoughts and body sensations. We have a choice; we can think of the sensations as "me," or we can detach from thoughts and sensations as though they could be someone else's. One way to slow down the overactive mind is to become more aware of the present moment. In meditation, thoughts subside, and something else arises that is a kind of awareness to be present.

August 8

Dad is doing poorly; the sibs have been texting about it for a few days. I keep telling myself that worry is a useless emotion.

I took two fitness classes this morning: a weightlifting class to music called Body Pump and then a class called YPM (yoga and Pilates mat). The first one seemed too easy, and then I realized there were ten million repetitions, so it got hard even with light weights.

Spending time at home on a weekday still seems novel. For the first time, I see that there is a whole humming daytime rhythm to the neighborhood that I didn't ever know about. People are out on the paths all day; happy kids play at the pond across the street. The mail person comes at a certain time. An army of landscapers descend on the lawns and the public areas. It is so fun discovering this. The gym is on the second story and looks out over the path and the pond. So, I see the village pass by and notice the way the sunlight showcases different parts of the pond during the day.

August 9

I am now in Carrollton. I threw some things in a bag, went to the airport, and got on a flight. I am grateful I now have the freedom and resources to do that.

Dad is in the hospital, and we are thankful. He was in poor shape at home: unable to walk, with swollen legs and mental confusion. Joe stayed a few days here, and then Gus did. That was scary because I'm not sure who was more impaired—Gus or Dad. Joe and Gus both had to go to work, and Marie was unable to lift him, of course. Late yesterday, Marie said he was very confused and unable to walk. Home health service came by to see him, but no way was that sufficient.

I took a 5 a.m. flight, gained an hour, drove from Kansas City, and arrived this morning before the home health nurses came.

When I walked in, it was devastating to see Dad confused, unable to walk or stand, sitting in his underwear in his chair in the living room. I was shocked to see my intelligent father reduced to this undignified state. He was not cogent when he is normally sharp. He was uncharacteristically grouchy and in lots of pain. Dad was determined to stay home, but he could not get out of his chair on his own. Gus left a canvas belt to tie around him to help him get up, but using it required strength and leverage. He didn't have the strength to assist. He needed to get to the bathroom, so I used the belt to try to help him up. Marie had hold of his arm, and I used the belt, but it took several minutes to get him standing. He was teetering, and I didn't think we had him. Finally, we got him standing and to his walker, but in the process, I severely strained my back. I am strong, but I don't think I could have pulled him up again. When he was in the bathroom, Marie was in there with him, and the home health nurses arrived.

I told them this situation was not safe or sustainable. They agreed. I conferred with Marie, and she agreed. They called an ambulance, and now he is settled in the hospital.

A few days ago, I wrote about being old when you can't stand up; seeing Dad unable to stand today was almost too much of a coincidence to comprehend. I also really hurt my back. There's no need to bring this up. I'm not being a martyr—I just don't see how that information would help right now.

When we got him to the hospital, they immediately drained off fifteen pounds of fluid, and his edema is better. He is already sharper and less cranky. His sodium and potassium were all out of whack. His heart rate is very low. His good friend Doctor Pete thinks he should probably get a pacemaker. Our goal is to have him stay long enough to qualify for the swing bed program in which they will do therapy to see if he can get stronger.

I am struck by how many people here love him. He has had lots of visitors. Dad was on the initial board of directors for the hospital, and it was his idea to build a regional hospital. All the nurses and staff know that and treat him with reverence and great care. There is a lot to be grateful for.

I have made sure to talk to all of our allies in the hospital and thank them for all they are doing for us. They assure me that he will qualify for the swing bed program, and they will keep him as long as they need to.

Meanwhile, Gus is a wreck. With Dad in the hospital, she is worried he will die. I talked to her for a long time today. I told her that he's nearly ninety years old. She needs to accept that his health is declining, and he will die someday.

August 10

Dad is stable and guaranteed to be transferred to the swing bed program. I flew home and got back to my routine. Meditation class today focused on loving-kindness. This is a familiar practice, yet I learned some different phrases. Loving-kindness is also called *metta* meditation and uses words and feelings to evoke friendliness toward oneself and others. With each recitation, the seeds of loving wishes are planted.

The instructions are to sit comfortably and relax. Let go of any preoccupations. Breathe gently, and silently recite the phrases directed to your own well-being. You begin with yourself because without loving yourself, it is almost impossible to love others.

May I be filled with loving-kindness.
May I be safe from inner and outer dangers.
May I be well in body and mind.
May I be at ease and happy.

When you feel you have established some stronger sense of loving-kindness for yourself, you can then expand your meditation to include others. After focusing on yourself for five or ten minutes, choose a benefactor: someone in your life who has loved or truly cared for you. Picture this person and thoughtfully recite the same phrases: may you be filled with lovingkindness, and so forth.

Then the practice is to move onto other loved ones, people we feel neutral about, people that have been difficult for us and finally to all sentient beings. Simply continue to plant the seeds of loving wishes, repeating the phrases gently, no matter what arises.

This type of meditation always makes me feel grateful for family and friends and can even take me to a place of equanimity for those who have been difficult in my life. I am particularly grateful Dad is being cared for today.

August 11

It is Sloane's birthday today; she is four years old. We sent her princess gloves and a princess birthday card.

Today's meditation study taught how beneficial meditation is for your brain and described the other health benefits, including decreased heart rate, normalization of blood pressure, quieter breathing, reduced stress hormones, and strengthened immunity. These benefits come from the shift into restful awareness.

We met our great friends Tom and Abigail in Yellow Springs for a late alfresco lunch. Knowing we would likely have wine, we had a driver take us and drive us home. All foodies, we took our time reading each menu item. We reminisced about a great bike trip we all took together to Provence a few years ago and talked about joining them in Umbria in October. It is wonderful to have the freedom to just say "yes."

August 12

As I continued to pore through my red notebook, I was reminded of the talk I used to give to newly appointed vice presidents at the company in their onboarding session. I was there to point out that they were now in a leadership role, in charge of the direction of people.

I told them, "You have a big title on your business card but check your ego at the door. Your job is to serve the people you lead and remove obstacles for them. Develop them. Teach them to make good decisions, and teach them how to run the business profitably, yet always within our strong values."

The retail industry has a reputation for being tough and leaders being harsh and demanding. Happily, in the enterprise where I worked, we were improving culture and changing that old story. I asked the new leaders: "How many of you have ever had a broken bone? Does it still hurt today?" Heads shake no. "How many of you have ever had a leader say words to you in anger? Does it still hurt today?" Heads solemnly nod yes. "Don't allow yourself to speak or decide in anger. Find ways to keep your equilibrium. And always strive to do what's right for the business and your people."

Thinking about this made me reflect on what was most fulfilling to me at work. In a retail enterprise, talent is everything. Hiring and firing decisions, succession, culture, who to develop—and how—can make or break a season, a year, a brand. I have always thought people were fascinating. A leadership role gives you an inside view of what motivates people, how they look when they are at their best (and worst), and how ordinary people can sometimes do extraordinary things.

Most of the time, I loved my role and felt honored and grateful to have it. I was very grateful for my boss, who had strong values. Change was constant, and standards were high. They put an emphasis on a thriving culture. Though change was ever-present, if the change impacted people, they were treated fairly. I had been treated fairly.

Some of the most fulfilling things I did in my career involved shaping a good culture. With the help of the Senn Delaney consulting organization, we taught concepts like be here now, assume positive intent, thinking shapes your behavior and results, and gratitude is the fastest way to elevate your mood. These ideas began to permeate the organization. Concepts of "win/win" instead of "win/lose" began to be articulated. Business continued to improve.

I think the work was powerful because it helped people in their personal lives as much as it did in their work lives. Thousands of associates participated in a multiday culture-shaping workshop where, through shared experiences, the enterprise had a common language and understanding of concepts. On the first day of class, the concept "be here now" was introduced. The idea is simple: pay full attention to the person you are with. In today's world, with technology calling, this is rare. Facilitators gave workshop participants a homework assignment. Go home tonight and be here now with a member of your family for fifteen or twenty minutes and then come back tomorrow and tell us what happened.

I was facilitating a session for forty people from the information technology function. For some, English was not their first language. I debriefed: "So, tell me what happened last night when you practiced be here now? A few minutes into the debriefing, one reserved gentleman raised his hand. "Yes, tell us what happened for you."

He described going home and spending focused time with his six-year-old daughter without any interruptions. He talked about playing on the floor with her and how they laughed. At this point, he had tears in his eyes. He said, "My daughter, she hug me and say, 'When Daddy happy, whole family happy.'"

Those were the best moments, when I was able to facilitate an insight that would make someone happier and more effective.

August 13

I am reading a book Teresa gave me called *Spiritual Literacy* that reminds me how much I treasure our daily rituals.

I hope I don't take them for granted—ever. When we wake up, we say a happy "good morning" to each other and ask how the other one slept. Rich gets me a cup of decaf coffee.

Rich keeps up his chatter: "Bella, would you like some food? A good girl deserves a good ration. Today is hump day. Let's get you a good hump day ration. Bella, I need to make some money today. We have to be able to buy more dog food." And then he tells her which companies announce sales and earnings and which investor calls he will listen to.

Yesterday we went for a great bike ride. We were starving by the end and made mushrooms, onions, and eggs for breakfast. I started a dark-and-light painting, depicting yin/yang that has been whirling around in my imagination. I decluttered our closets by the back door, packing up jackets and baseball caps to give away.

I found a page of some favorite quotes in the red notebook. Every time I found one over the past few years, I wrote it down.

"If a man does not keep pace with his companions, perhaps it is because he hears a different drummer, let him step to the music which he hears, however measured and far away" (Thoreau).

"All men naturally desire to know" (Aristotle).

"Walk with those seeking truth … *Run from those who think they've found it*" (Deepak Chopra).

"We all have the extraordinary coded within us, waiting to be released" (Jean Houston).

"All transformation is an inside job" (Mitch Behan).

"When you change the way you look at things, the things you look at change" (Wayne Dyer).

August 14

It was fifty-nine degrees this morning, and I was able to jog a little despite my achy back. Dad is improving. I send him a card or letter every day. He is now able to walk again. Today, when I talked to him, he chuckled, getting back to his normal upbeat personality.

I had an art college board meeting, took a drawing class on Udemy, and sent a note to a friend today: "Retirement is great so far. I have been in major decluttering mode. I gave my work clothes away and have been setting up my painting studio. Bella is getting skinny because I have taken her on so many walks. I am doing meditation every day. I'm meeting my high school girlfriends for a weekend trip."

I love doing the twenty-one day Deepak and Oprah meditation in addition to my meditation course.

Rich and I took Bella to the Humane Society today. The team brought a whole parade of dogs out on the lawn, one by one, so that they could do a dog-to-dog evaluation to see how Bella reacted. We looked for signs that she would be excited about any of the sweet pups on display. She yawned, licked her lips, and did slow tail wags but seemed bored and didn't invite anyone to play. I nearly lost my heart to each one. But from hounds to labs to golden retrievers, none seemed like a match for Bella. There was no connection. On the way home, we talked about it with her: "Bella, we love you. We *loved* being a pack of four when Beau was here, but it looks like we will be a pack of three now. That's OK; it's not the end of the world."

Though Bella is looking svelte, I have put on a couple of pounds. I track every workout with a heart monitor, so I know I am burning a ton of calories. My stress is lower; I am enjoying all our meals and probably celebrating this new stage of life too much.

I am haunted by a time in life when I felt out of control and weighed much more than I do now. We were living in New York. I was working crazy hours. It was after 9/11, and one day I went into my closet to get dressed and none of my pants would zip. I very reluctantly pulled the scale out from under the bed and dusted it off. When I stepped on it, I was shocked: up fifty pounds from my ideal weight! It had crept up and crept up, and now I was out of control. And there was something about that timing of the week after 9/11. I said to myself, "Damn it, you can't control much in this world, but you can control yourself."

Through exercise and diet, I got back to my fighting weight and have kept it off for more than fifteen years. I am hyperaware of staying in a range of healthy weight.

August 15

It's fifty-nine degrees again this morning—heaven! Is this really August? I did easy elliptical, and then we took Bella on a long walk. My back feels a little looser.

I took a class at Apple to learn how to make a movie. I downloaded sketchbook for drawing. Mastering technology is still a challenge. Yet, through persistence, I made the movie and got sketchbook up and running!

I took an online landscape painting class. Our neighborhood is so pretty; I have been snapping photos of this lovely summer and thought, "Why don't I try to paint it?"

I put Bella and Rich into three of the paintings. They look a little blobby and not proportional. These are in a sort of Grandma Moses primitive style, but who cares? It's fun.

Dad continues to have wonderful visitors. He walked—with nurse, belt, and walker, but it is still walking. Dad called me today to laugh about today's card I had written: "A great man once told me if you act enthusiastic, you'll be enthusiastic." One of his trademark lines, and it reminded him to be more cheerful. Raleigh is back in the hospital, too, for his surgery next week.

Gus seemed upbeat and clear today, joking and happy. She seemed sober and swore she has stopped drinking.

August 17

Meditation is good. I feel joyful and peaceful just listening to Oprah and Deepak every day. Rich is now starting to meditate with me! Bella loves it. Earlier this week Deepak said, "It will surprise you when you discover how wise you are."

Today's meditation was about a contented feeling of peace that gives us steadiness when life may be confusing and when times are happy and fulfilling. This is interesting because I notice that I have been trying to stop and enjoy whatever I am doing—to "be here now" and notice throughout the day that feeling of peace and appreciation.

I never got to watch daytime TV, but I would have loved watching *Oprah*. I got to see her one time in person at an event to benefit inner city kids in New York where a colleague was given an award. At the end, she wrote a personal check for $10,000 and talked about the importance of helping where help is needed. I don't think there was a dry eye in the house.

I remember seeing her in *The Color Purple* in 1985. I went to see it with my friend, Judy. I had read and loved the book. We kept hearing about this young phenom named Oprah Winfrey before we saw the movie, and after her first scene, Judy and I looked at each other and said, "Wow."

So, like zillions of people, I feel I watched her grow up and that her talent and success lifts us all up. I see her as a force for good in the world. Like so many, I feel like Oprah is one of my people.

And I have a fantasy about meeting Deepak someday. Isn't it funny I feel so close to him that I just call him "Deepak," like he is a friend? He has millions of people who feel this way about him.

What I did today: ran before coffee, Pilates, hit tennis balls with Charles, lifted weights, went on a 5K walk with Rich and Bella. It was spectacular day: cool in the 60s in the morning with a high of 75, blue skies, wispy clouds, and a little breeze. It's so nice to just be able to slow down and notice. Whole seasons would go by when I was consumed by work, and it barely registered.

Today I sat on the patio with Rich and Bella in the daytime; it was heaven. I just laid back and watched the clouds for a while. I think I have not done that since I was about seven years old.

My huge new easel is so great! The guy who made it wouldn't accept any money for it, so I gave a donation in his name to the art college. It is so massive that I will be able to paint four large paintings at once.

August 18

Today's meditation was about being playful, which was perfect since I am heading off to Kansas City to meet great life-long friends: Joanie, Vivian, and Clara. Hopefully we can relax and play together.

"We don't stop playing because we grow old; we grow old because we stop playing" (George Bernard Shaw).

I get excited on the flight to Kansas City. Joanie, Vivian, and Clara are close friends I can confide in completely. Vivian is an entrepreneur—she owns a thriving flower shop in Carrollton. She works her ass off. She is hilarious and irreverent. Vivian and I have shared experiences throughout our whole lives. It takes about two minutes to get in the groove when we see each other again. Her dad was my dad's big brother, so we are cousins as well as friends. Vivian is curvy and cute and has a huge, engaging, outgoing personality. She's never met a stranger, and she knows how to make people know she is interested in them and she cares.

When we were about fifteen, Vivian and I worked together as waitresses at the Wagon Wheel restaurant and sale barn where auctioneers would sell pigs, cows, and sheep. It smelled earthy and real—like manure and hay. At the end of the night, we would compare tips. Vivian would routinely make $150. I didn't know what was wrong with me at that moment in my young life. I didn't have a term like "introvert" to blame for my lack of success. With almost no eye contact, I could barely mumble, "Can I take your order?" and Vivian would be sitting down, leaning in, order pad in hand at the table with the farmers in their dirty overalls saying, "Frank, how's that new baby girl?" "Bill, can I heat up your coffee?"

I always marveled at Vivian's easy way with people. The fact that I was a success in business later in life was a shock to both of us, given my waitress experience.

Vivian and I both had identical pink Schwinn bicycles. We would ride around Carrollton, talking about boys and about being nuns. In high school, we both played the organ at Mass, and would "trade" Saturday 6 p.m. and Sunday 8 a.m. services, depending on who had a date. One Sunday after prom, Vivian had the Sunday 8 a.m. mass and fell asleep right onto the organ keys after being up all night. Father had a chat with her. We have thousands of stories and memories like these.

Clara is a beauty. She always has been, and even in her late fifties, she is still gorgeous. She is blonde and blue-eyed, and her skin is luminous like a film star. Her mom was Dad's oldest sister, so she, too, is a cousin as well as a friend. Clara married Wayne right after high school. She was always one of the smartest kids in class, but college was not her ambition. Wayne's family had a thriving farm, and Clara was ready to be a wife and wanted to be a mother. So, Clara raised a family and ran the farm with Wayne. She is tough, resilient, and strong. Clara is a devout and vocal Catholic, so I sometimes have to work to find common ground when the conversation turns to a more spiritual nature. Vivian complains, "Clara, you are so fucking holy. Knock it off."

Clara and I once spent an afternoon in a hot tub talking about the Holy Trinity and the communion of saints. Vivian and Joanie protested but hung in there.

Joanie was my best friend in junior high, high school, and college. We are no longer in close touch, and when we are together, it gives me some pain because I remember how sweet it is to have a best friend you see every day who knows absolutely everything about you.

Joanie is exuberant, engaging, and curious. She is friendly, interested in people, naturally gregarious, athletic, and funny, with an easy sense of humor. She loves animals and nature. She is striking: tall with short, curly dark hair. In junior high, Joanie had very long, lovely hair, and she used to get a ton of compliments on it. One day in high school, Joanie cut it really short; it suited her, and she has worn it that way since. She is the mother of two incredible sons, and she is married to another close high school friend, Bruce.

Being together again was so sweet. What a gift to be with old, close friends. We giggled and reminisced. We laughed at our aging bodies and how they have changed. When I put my PJs on, they laughed at my now-little boobs, and we laughed at Vivian's still-huge boobs. They reminded me of our last high school reunion, when a guy came over, pointed to my chest, and asked sadly, "What happened?" We talked about their kids, grandkids, siblings, and other old friends. We watched a movie, and Joanie, Vivian, and Clara all cried while I rolled my eyes. They said to me, "You wouldn't understand. You've never been a mother." But it didn't bother me. It was good.

August 19

I am reflecting on our girl's weekend. The weather was perfect. We stayed at the Intercontinental on the Plaza; everything was walkable.

It has been eight years since we last had a girls' weekend. Everyone looked great and seemed pretty happy in life. We could not believe we are way closer to sixty than fifty.

It felt like high school again where we had sleepovers nearly every week. Friday night, we walked over to Seasons 52 and then heard a great live band in the lobby. On Saturday, Joanie and I did the Deepak and Oprah meditation together and had a fun breakfast in the hotel, and then we all went to spa appointments.

We had a great lunch at Gram and Dun, a fun gastropub. It was a pretty day, and the restaurant had a cool vibe. We sat half in/half out and people-watched and showed old and new photos.

On Saturday afternoon, we hung out by the pool and listened to the band and talked and laughed about old memories. Another cousin, Keith, and his wife Erika met us for a drink on Saturday night. After dinner at Capital Grille, we walked around the plaza and poked in and out of shops before heading back to the hotel. On Sunday morning, we hung out at Starbucks. We heard the plaza church bells ringing as we walked along, looking at the fountains and statues. Then we ate a last breakfast and went home. When we said goodbye, we promised to do something special for our sixtieth.

Dad came home from the hospital. When we took him a couple of weeks ago, I wondered if he would come back home. I'm so grateful that he is strong enough to come back to the life they love.

August 20

It was cool enough to run with Bella after coffee, and we loved our early meditation. It is so remarkable that we have cool mornings in August. Some leaves are already changing, and today we heard the geese during meditation. I wonder if they are coming back already.

I painted today, adding light in my geometrics; I want them to be luminous, to almost glow. I happily moved from landscapes back to my normal expressionist painting and used some of the new techniques to make my abstracts more powerful and make the color pop.

August 22

"The most wasted of all days is one without laughter" (e.e. cummings).

Meditation today talked about lightening up. We laugh with Bella every day. She can be so goofy. She is coming out of her funk and now will do a play bow to try to engage us. And when we say, "Let's go for a walk," she gets excited and jumps around.

The weather turned hot and rainy—much more seasonable. I had a golf lesson because Rich has been encouraging me to learn to play. I want to be open to learn new things that Rich likes, in appreciation for him being open to doing things like meditate with me.

I love the way my studio is set up in an even more organized way where I have all my materials as I need them. In Manhattan, I had to travel to my painting studio, taking the subway from the Upper West Side down to SoHo. The shared space was stifling in summer and freezing in winter. I had to set up and tear down each time I painted. It is so wonderful to have my studio in the house with everything in place so that even if I only have twenty minutes, I can make progress on a painting.

August 24

Rich is with his dad, who is in the hospital for another procedure. I painted today on my light-filled geometrics, trying to capture some of the images I see in that fugue state between awake and asleep: gauzy, luminescent shapes that are in slow motion and beautiful patterns and colors, like beings filled with light.

I opened the book *Sefer Yetzirah: The Book of Creation in Theory and Practice* by Aryeh Kaplan. This is a translation of the Kabbalah and its ancient, mystical, and magical aspects. It is ancient and hauntingly beautiful. The first commentary on this book was written in the tenth century. It seems both magical and meditative. Some ancients say it was written by Abraham, but others argue if it had been, it would be part of the Bible. Kabbalah or Cabala is the Jewish word for "tradition" and is the body of mysticism and magic. The Kabbalah seeks to explain the nature of reality, the levels of being, the origin of evil, and the ways of attaining knowledge of God. Kabbalistic teaching focuses on the Sefirot, the ten qualities or powers of God, the infinite, who is described as undifferentiated, absolute perfection. The Sefirot seem to simultaneously be the emanations of God's power, the names of God, the realms or planes of God, and the inner foundation of every creating being or thing.

Beautiful images include the ten Sefirot arranged in a tree of life pattern. It contains the inner significance of the Hebrew alphabet and also incorporates ancient astrological teachings. The complexity of numbers, Hebrew alphabet, names and qualities could supply years of study. The images are almost haunting, and it's easy to imagine they contain mystical powers.

As I try to make my way into this book, I realize I am way out of my depth. It would take many years of study with a gifted scholar to understand this beautiful translation. I hope to come back to it with a teacher, but I need to put it aside for now. I realize that the idea of going back to the most ancient teachings is very appealing to me. What did people believe before Christianity? How did they think the world worked? For those people who think you must believe in a specific deity to get into heaven, what do they think happened to all the people from the centuries before Christ or their chosen view of redeemer?

August 25

Something fun is happening to me. Somehow, I can, for the first time, understand song lyrics. I have finally slowed down enough to start to pay attention. I realize anew how beautiful music is. The stories in lyrics draw me in and make me feel emotion. Rich caught me weeping to Jay-Z's "Empire State of Mind." I think about the parallels between music and painting: theme, repetition, variety, intensity, rhythm, dialogue, balance, and unity. I think about Teresa, who can actually hear color.

Before, music sometimes seemed like background noise. This new ability to discern lyrics feels like some kind of progress. Music makes painting feel mythic and majestic.

I painted a quick nude today as I was waiting for another canvas to dry—mostly blue with red windows in the background. I really like her; she is very strong and fit with big, defined biceps.

I found another old 48 x 60 canvas I didn't like, painted a coat of gesso over the old work, and started a work of two abstract nudes on the same canvas. It will be two women sitting near enough to touch hands, and they will be in a busy city. The images of the buildings and the skyline will be part of their bodies, and they will be hard to distinguish from the cityscape. I named it "City Girls"; the idea will be that it is nearly impossible to separate us from our environment, as we are part of our environment and it is part of us.

August 25

I overdid it today: four miles on the elliptical, walk with Bella, Body Pump class, and tennis lesson where I had nothing left to give. Several hours on the photo archiving project. My back hurts. Perhaps I am an idiot.

I sat outside and started to read *The Biology of Belief* by Bruce Lipton. Lipton is a biologist who bridges science and spirituality. He explains the scientific and philosophical rule called Occam's Razor. I have always pretended to know what this means, like some wise scholar. It simply holds that when several competing hypotheses are offered to explain something, the simplest one that accounts for the most observations is probably the correct one.

Bruce Lipton passionately believes that we are immortal, spiritual beings who exist separately from our bodies. I love his story because he went from being a rational "scientist" to being led to spiritual discoveries through his work as a biologist. I can't wait to read more.

I finished my online meditation teacher "certification," took all my tests, and got certified. They are mailing me something official. That seemed way too easy; I don't feel qualified to say I am a meditation teacher. The tests took a total of about two hours. It doesn't feel legitimate.

I called the Chopra Center and got connected with a teacher who can do Primordial Sound Meditation this week. I am going to take a quick jaunt to Southern California to go deeper in meditation and get my own mantra! How fun it is to have a whim and then just *go!* Love that Rich is so supportive. He is a freaking rock star.

August 26

I flew to San Diego on United through Chicago. I am at La Costa. The Chopra Center is a pretty white building with a purple lotus flower logo. I am thrilled to be here. I took selfies and sent them to my sibs. They are all excited for me. I am really looking forward to actually going to a meditation session here. They offer them for free to the community—very nice. My personal meditation instruction will start later tomorrow, so I have time for full workouts, an Ayurvedic treatment, massage, and yoga.

August 27

I woke up very early and called Rich after meditation at 4 a.m. Pacific time. I had coffee at the twenty-four-hour market on the property, and when the gym opened, I did elliptical, changed shirts, got a green smoothie, and then went to a spin class. The guys in the class were sweet and welcoming; many of them are locals.

After breakfast, I went to group meditation at the Chopra Center. There were some older Eastern European ladies who all seemed to know each other and who commandeered a couch along the wall on one side of the room across from the instructor. They generated a very cheerful welcoming vibe. The meditation room was cozy and dark, and everyone sat on either a couch or chairs; there were footstools and blankets. It was very comfortable. Maybe twenty people were there. No one sat on the floor, and there were no mudras or special yoga postures. It was a very peaceful meditation led by a great instructor named Teresa who made everyone feel comfortable. She started out with the four soul questions:

- Who am I?
- What do I want?
- What is my purpose?
- What am I grateful for?

It was a mantra meditation; So Hum was the mantra (unless you had your own), and then we all chanted OM out loud together at the end. I loved the feeling of connection with everyone there. I feel so glad I came, and am very joyful and excited to get my own mantra. They gave away a paper hanger to hang on your doorknob that says, "Silence, please. I am meditating."

I had my 10,000 steps in by 8:45. It's so fun to be on Pacific Time. I went to Chopra Center yoga; it was gentle. The instructor was very encouraging. They do a different yoga practice for every day of the week. Today's focus was karma.

I had my private meditation instruction session with my instructor and finally got my own personal mantra! She came to my suite, and it was nice to sit together with the windows open and look out at the lovely grounds of La Costa. It was very peaceful. She set up an altar on the side table, and then she did a ceremony to give me my own mantra. She intoned a long beautiful chant she had memorized in Sanskrit, thanking generations of teachers for the gift of being a teacher herself. I had tears in my eyes. She was such a peaceful person; I liked her immediately.

She has been meditating since she was a little kid—forty-one years. She studied Transcendental Meditation with the same guru the Beatles had, Maharishi Mahesh Yogi. She started with Deepak Chopra and David Simon in Massachusetts and then came to California when they had the center in La Jolla. Then she moved here to Carlsbad and got certified to teach the Primordial Sound Meditation approach.

I was surprised she was not familiar with the many other forms of meditation I have studied. She has been focused on T.M. and her method. Cool with me.

She explained that meditation takes us to a place of expanded awareness where we remember that we are peaceful, centered, grounded, and creative. She told me that my mantra was personal to me and private, not to be shared because then it would lose its effectiveness.

She also said, not to worry about a certain posture or, mudra. She said I can sit in my bed surrounded by pillows; there is no need to be uncomfortable on the floor. If my back is really bad, it's OK to lie down, but it is recommended to sit for alertness. If I need to shift positions, I should do it. I like that. She said that as I silently repeat the mantra, it may become distorted, and that's OK. I like that this feels quite relaxed without big expectations of physical contortion.

She said I would become more aware of my higher self, which is silent, whole, creative, and blissful. I really, really love this.

My meditation using my mantra was very peaceful, and I saw gorgeous, flowing colors. My back actually stopped hurting a bit when I was meditating. The instructor told me to meditate again this afternoon for thirty minutes.

I love my mantra. I think I already had an experience of expanded awareness. I saw beautiful images and felt Mom with me. Now I am so hungry, a monkey can't see in. My teacher brought me some oranges from her tree, an orchid bloom, and a little quartz crystal as a "congratulations on getting your mantra." She set up a whole altar with incense, a candle, a picture, and her chime.

Very cool. I ate the oranges; I hope that was OK.

August 28

I got up at 3:45 and meditated. Then I had coffee, a treadmill workout, and a shower. I washed out my gym clothes and hung them out to dry in the beautiful Southern California air. Then I went to yoga and

Chopra meditation and used my own mantra! I love that they ask the four soul questions to begin.

Later I had an "Odyssey" treatment at the Chopra Center, an Ayurveda treatment. Ayurveda is an ancient health system. I want to learn more about it. My very skilled therapist was Justin. The treatment started with a dry brushing of my skin, using silk gloves I got to keep. Then he used sesame oil and covered my body and my scalp with it. He then did a kind of deep tissue massage and ended with marma points—interesting and cool.

In my class with my teacher today, she talked about the idea of slipping into "the gap" in meditation when you disengage and suspend from thoughts. I think this has happened to me; it's not falling asleep, but afterward there is a feeling of having been somewhere else—almost like a shift in time.

Charles and Sarah were at Aviara with their companion puppy in training, Lane. They had a late lunch with me at La Costa and then drove me to the Meditation Garden in Encinitas. It was a retreat and ashram center where Swami Paramahansa Yogananda lived for many years. I noticed a synchronicity; he is the Yogi I read about in *Autobiography of a Yogi.* The center is beautifully situated high above the Pacific Ocean, about twenty-five miles north of downtown San Diego.

The gardens were breathtakingly gorgeous and so serene. There was no talking; people sat silently, with their eyes closed in meditation. The gardens end on a high cliff, looking over the blue water of the Pacific. As we looked at the view, we saw the water dotted with surfers.

I did afternoon meditation when I got back; again, it felt like there was a connection to some kind of supportive energy. It was very peaceful and uplifting.

August 29

Another early workout. I bought some books and gifts and got information on the next Chopra Center class I want to take, which is called

Synchro-Destiny. I also want to get certified to teach Primordial Sound Meditation someday.

My teacher came at 1 p.m. She covered a lot of what I have already learned in my other meditation classes. She reaffirmed things like the idea that AUM is an ancient universal sound, and when scientists have checked the sounds of the universe (I wonder how?), it sounds like OM. She said my personal mantra was the vibration of the universe at the moment and place of my birth. Let me just accept that idea because I really love my personal mantra, and this idea seems beautiful.

I looked it up, and AUM is an ancient Hindu mantra—the sacred sound of the universe. Composed of three soft tones, a-u-m, the sound is a never-ending vibrational energy, reminding us that the universe is constantly in motion. You can hear it in the sounds of a forest stream, inside a seashell, and in the mistral wind. The visual symbol that looks a bit like "30" represents the meaning of AUM and consists of three curves, one semicircle, and a dot. The large bottom curve symbolizes the waking state, A. The middle curve signifies the dream state, U. The upper curve denotes the state of deep sleep, M. The dot signifies the fourth state of consciousness, *Turiya*. The semicircle at the top represents Maya and separates the dot from the other three curves.

Chanting Om is a reflection of how the whole universe moves, the setting of the sun, the rising of the moon, the ebb and flow of the tides, and the beating of our hearts. As we chant, it takes us for a ride on this universal movement, through our breath, our awareness, and our physical energy, and there we begin to sense a bigger connection that is both uplifting and soothing.

She encourages meditation twice a day for thirty minutes. Twenty minutes is probably more my level now, but I will try it. I told her I also wanted to do the Oprah and Deepak meditation with Rich and Bella every day, and she said it's fine but not to overdo it. She also said to meditate in silence, and I told her that Oprah and Deepak use music. She said sound is not recommended. OK, I will try it her way.

She said meditation more than twice per day could make me a bit loopy. I laughed when I thought about all the hours I have meditated in the past few weeks with my classes, and I realized she is right.

I had a great sense of being connected to some force or vibration again when I meditated tonight. I also saw beautiful colors, light, and motion behind closed eyes.

My teacher talked about a painting metaphor and said every meditation is a blank canvas; of course, I liked that. She said it is important to bring innocence to each meditation and not to have an expectation. I told her about the colors and motion I saw, and she said there are lots of experiences people have, but not to have any expectation of that going forward. She said it was just the release of stress. I tried to argue with her a bit because I have seen the color, light, and motion images before, and so each time would I have the same experience with stress release? But she was clear. Don't look for any particular experience in meditation; each one is different. Okay. She is my teacher, and I respect what she says.

I thanked her so much; it was a great experience. She gave me a booklet and CD of the primordial sound meditation practice led by Deepak. We set a time for a Skype follow-up the next week where she will cover the higher states of consciousness. That will be great!

I flew on the red-eye home and managed to doze.

Rich's flight was a little delayed, and he got home late/early, too. Bella was so happy to see us both. Rich's dad took a turn for the worse last night after he was in flight; Raleigh is now in the ICU. It sounded like rough procedure. Our poor dads. We talked about this stage of life when we have to worry about our parents like they worried about us when we were kids.

August 30

"We can be serene even in the midst of calamities and, by our serenity, make others more tranquil" (Swami Satchidananda).

Deepak says the world seeks peace in the midst of violence. People seek inner peace in a tumultuous world. There is no way to peace; peace is the way. If you want peace, be at peace.

I told Rich he is the paragon of restraint because he can make his morning coffee last two hours. I still need to learn to savor mine as part of a slower, more relaxed life. I did an active recovery workout, coffee, sniff walk with Bella, and played college fight songs for Rich because football starts today.

The luxury of a sniff walk is remarkable. We let Bella stop wherever she wanted (which was every tree and post). Her nose is a miracle. I read that a dog's sense of smell is millions of times more sensitive than a human's. Dogs smell pheromones; they know if the last dog that passed by was a male or female, what they ate, and what mood they were in. Dogs smell individual ingredients and can move their nostrils independently. What a joy in slowing down and noticing.

The Deepak and Oprah meditation series is coming to an end; Rich and I have loved it. My new routine is to do my private primordial sound meditation just before Rich wakes up, and then we do the Oprah and Deepak meditation together. I do another private primordial sound meditation in the afternoon.

I continue to sense images in meditation. This morning I saw a breath-taking swirly magenta image about twenty minutes into my meditation, and I was so startled I opened my eyes for a moment, hoping it would still be there when I closed them again. I was sitting up in bed with my back propped against the headboard for support. The image stayed with me until the end, shimmering and moving gracefully like lava in a lava lamp. I felt completely peaceful and didn't want to stop meditating because I was so enthralled. It was as though the image had been just beneath my consciousness and was now able to come to the surface. I wonder if this is because I am now using my personal mantra, as though that opened a portal somehow.

I know my teacher would say to release my focus on the image and gently bring my attention back to the mantra. But I am going to see if I can capture the image on canvas.

In afternoon meditation, I saw lovely, light-filled images again. This time, they were in more colors in addition to magenta, including cool yellow and light-filled orange. They were misty and flowing like a sheer veil. Again, I brought my attention away from the images and back to my mantra, but I loved the feeling of connection to something larger than myself.

Other than Gus drama and Dad's health issues, what a great August we have had. I really am so grateful, peaceful, contented, and joyful, and I'm appreciating our time right now.

Chapter Three
September

September brings a new dimension to the Ramsey household. In my daily journal, I stop cataloguing in detail every workout, every meal, and every meditation as my precious daily routine becomes less of a novelty. My new meditation practice deepens, and studies continue with a Soul Beliefs class that provides insight into different wisdom traditions. I come across a startling new paradigm as I wrestle with the question of free will versus destiny. My expanding experience of daily joy and wonder continued in the midst of real life.

Teresa, Bethany, Emma, Joe, and I are in regular touch, trying to find the right pathway related to Gussie. Each of us is trying to find the balance between being loving and supportive, setting boundaries, and keeping our own emotional equilibrium through the experience of loving a person with addictions. We struggle through questions of when to believe her, what types of help are beneficial, how much to help, and when it is right to say no. Our emotions cycle between sorrow, hope, guilt, shame, anger, and feeling helpless. None of us think we were getting it right, but we find solace by being in it together.

Gussie texted us almost daily; we took turns being the main responder.

September 1

Rich, Bella, and I are off to meet a chocolate lab puppy named Chip. I feel nervous and excited.

On the drive to meet Chip, Rich said, "You know we're coming home with a puppy," but I did not dare believe it could be true. Mary and Jerry, the current dog parents, have a lovely, huge homestead in Heath, Ohio. Mary has a newly discovered health issue and can't keep the puppy.

As we drove down the long driveway onto their massive property, Rich and I were immediately aware that we have less than an acre on an active road, where Chip would need an electronic fence, so we were hesitant because this would be a big change for him. I prayed that if he came home with us, we could keep him safe.

Bella met Chip on a leash in the driveway. She was perky and very interested; her tail was wagging side to side, and she was moving toward him. Chip seemed tiny next to her. He was timid and submissive with lots of play bows and little engaging barks.

After they had sniffed each other on leash and seemed ready to play, we all went inside to a dog play area Mary and Jerry had created in the basement. The dogs bonded immediately. Bella and Chip seemed to love each other. Zigging and zagging, they played hard, jumping on and off the old furniture in a game they both understood. When one stopped to catch their breath, the other was egging them on to get back in the game. It seemed like they both were smiling. Rich, Mary, Jerry, and I bubbled over with laughter.

Rich was right; we did bring Chip home. I wasn't quite mentally prepared, and neither was Mary. With tears in their eyes, Mary and Jerry gave us a container of his food, his teddy bear, a pad for him to lie on, and his duck decoy. I imagined how difficult this must be for them. Jerry was hugging Mary while she cried and waved in the driveway.

Rich needs to leave town in the morning to take care of his dad, so I made a rushed trip to the pet store to get puppy supplies: a crate, a bed, and puppy toys and chews.

Today was the final "bonus" meditation in the Oprah and Deepak series. Here was today's message:

Life is infinitely more than we realize. Every cell in our body is made of cells, atoms, and atomic particles. Quantum physics says that you can trace your body to the entire universe. There is an invisible source to the mind as well; it draws upon infinite reserves of energy, creativity, love, beauty, truth, and compassion.

I love this: Deepak said each of us is like a millionaire with amnesia because we have forgotten that in reality, we are very rich. We become convinced we are limited, but we know no boundaries. We participate in the infinite of the universe. The soul rejoices when it wakes up. The mantra was Aham Brahmasmi.

I love this mantra. I want to study quantum physics, but now I have a puppy to raise.

September 2

We survived our first night with Chip. We put the new crate in our bedroom lined with the pad Mary gave us. Chip has tons of curiosity and *tons* of energy. Rich took him out for the last potty, and I went to sleep early. I got a little sleep before he needed to go out at 12:30. After he went, I got him and Bella settled back in their beds. At about 12:45, he started barking insistently, and I was lying there thinking, "Could he have to poop, too? Surely, he would have pooped if he needed to. We were just out!"

I took him back out and Bella went with us, and amazingly, he had to poop. After getting settled back in bed *again,* he started whining and barking. I went and got his stuffed bear that Mary gave us, and he settled down a bit and finally went to sleep again about 1:30. I tossed and turned and Bella jumped up in our bed with her head right by mine, as if to say, "Is he *staying here?*" Then at 4:30, I heard him stir, and I tried to get him up and out before he started barking because Rich needed some sleep before his flight. I took them both out, he peed and pooped *again,* and we got back to bed about 4:50. He then barked continuously, and so I took him in the gym with me at about 5. I leaned over to put my hair in a clip, and he grabbed the clip out of my hand and ran with it across the room. He explored the gym while I ran on the treadmill, including shredding what was in the wastebasket and destroying the lucky feng shui bamboo plant.

He kept coming up to the treadmill, sniffing at it, sniffing my running shoes, and trying to put his nose and paw on the treadmill. I would say, "Back, Chip," and he would jump back and bark at me.

Somehow, I managed to get in three miles, though now I feel as tired as I am at the end of a flight to Asia. After my run, I was bending over and stretching, and he leaped onto my head. And yet, when he finally tires out, he sleeps like an exhausted angel.

Chip and Bella are playing a lot; she play-bows and invites him to wrestle and run. When she's had enough, she puts her chin on him, and he turns over and rolls onto his back.

I did my afternoon meditation and got through about ten quiet minutes and then another five while I tried to ignore the puppy cries, but it was a lost cause.

Gussie:
What I wanted to say is the following. I am drinking again, and I know I need to stop. I really hate myself right now. And I'm trying not to, but the point is that rehab can only do so much for you. Before you all inundate me: rehab does NOT WORK for me. Sibling love DOES!

Bethany:
Gus, get a drink of water and go to bed.

Gussie:
Already there, Bethany.

Bethany:
Sweet dreams then.

Then Bethany wrote to us (minus Gus):

I know this is a hard idea. But what if we all just stopped applauding and stopped being afraid of what would happen to baby sister if we stopped supporting her. What if we just said, "Enough is fucking enough, Gussie. Sorry things didn't work out." At some point, are we to blame for enabling her addiction with our "Yay! Gussie" for every meager step forward? Where does the line get drawn between compassion and get yourself together?

What if we say, "NO, we are not paying for you to go to rehab again"? And "NO, we are not sending you money for your (whatever) bill because you haven't figured out how to make your budget work and still get your vodka and cigarettes."

It's hard. It's sad. We all want to save her. We can't save her (I don't think). Gussie knows how to game the system. She can stay sober enough to keep the job that pays the insurance that keeps her alive enough to drink enough to work enough to stay sober enough to keep the job to pay the insurance.

Bottom line: it is Gussie's choice. If any of you have a better approach, let's hear it.

Jane:

You make great points, Bethany, and I wish I knew the right answer. The other day she made me feel like I/we had to be there for her anytime she is in crisis—because if we weren't, she might drink. Trying to hold us hostage over her own choices is something I don't want to participate in anymore. But I often say to her, "When you feel vulnerable, call one of us." So, I am a hypocrite. There is a part of me that wants to help her from a distance, but I hate being pulled into her daily drama. I set some kind of boundary by telling her I will only talk to her when she is sober.

September 3

I am home alone with Chip and Bella. Rich is with his dad, who is in the hospital in Missouri. It has been a challenging day.

Chip requires constant watching when he is awake and uncrated. He chews everything, including my office chair, Pilates straps, electrical cords, outlets, vents, stairs, shoes (even when they are on my feet), and Bella's collar (while she is wearing it). When he tried to chew a metal weight this morning in the gym, I said, "Dude, if you want to chew that, go for it!"

Yesterday I found a frozen yellow teething ring in the freezer from when Sloane was a baby and thought that might feel great on Chip's gums. He *loved* it but destroyed it in ten seconds. Now I am trying ice cubes.

Bella is being great with Chip, and he annoys her constantly. I try to give her some "time out" breaks where I crate him. He chews her ears, tail, and feet and jumps on her, runs between her legs, and sniffs her backside a lot.

Last night was fairly tough. We were up at 12:30 and 3:30, and then at 5:30, we just stayed up. Sarah told me to curtail his water for a couple of hours before bed, which I did and was good advice. He only cried and barked for about ten minutes when we came back in each time. I tried to ignore it, which is hard.

There is a logistical problem with two dogs and one human; Bella went out each time we went out, and she went exploring, so when Chip was ready to come back in, Bella was out and wide awake. I need to leave her inside.

This morning, I took them both into the gym for my workout, and it was fine. I would have been grateful for ten minutes, and I actually got forty! Each minute was like a bonus, and they both sat like angels and watched me puff along. Maybe the lesson is that I should just live my day and enjoy it. I asked for it, after all. Right now, I am hating myself for telling Rich, "I want another dog. I have more love to give!" I am an idiot. Be careful what you wish for.

I have been trying to stick with my meditation practice and find that I can do it when I am wide awake in the middle of the night. I am not as successful in the afternoon with puppy cries to distract me.

I had my follow-up call with my meditation teacher today. I apologized for the puppy cries. She is a dog person, so it was OK. The focus was on higher states of consciousness, which I have always wanted to learn more about. First, she checked in to see how I was doing in my daily practice, and she seemed pleased that I have stuck with it and enjoyed it. She said I would know when meditation is working when I could see changes in my daily life and see that my desires were manifesting.

I told her about the light images I am seeing, and she said it is important not to look for any experience in meditation. She said other people have seen things like this. It isn't unusual, but I shouldn't get attached to the images. They will likely pass. The important part of meditation does not occur while you are actually sitting in the practice. OK, I get it.

I liked her key points today. She said things like "You are not in the universe; the universe is in you," and "If you don't like your situation, then change it."

I told her that I have always said to people, "You are holding the remote control to your life. If you don't like the movie of your life, then change to another channel." She liked that and said that in meditation, you realize it is your universe, and you can change it.

My teacher explained that there are seven states of consciousness, and everyone can experience them on their spiritual journey.

She gave a high-level overview of each state starting with waking, dreaming, and deep sleep. Then she got into the more abstract discussion of four more states of consciousness that are experienced as you continue to meditate and begin to feel the presence of spirit in everyone and everything. She said the expression "Namaste" when we put our palms together and bow means "I recognize the divinity in you that is also in me."

She said enlightenment is sometimes compared to the drop of water that is experiencing itself as the ocean, knowing that it was the ocean the whole time. You and God are now one because there is no you left any more. You are not the drop in the ocean; you are the ocean in the drop.

She wrapped up by talking about the importance of integration—having the experience of slipping into the gap and then integrating it back into daily life.

Meditation is a tool we use to enrich our lives, and we go from the deep rest of meditation to activity. It is important to have the integration of meditating and then going about your life. Meditation opens the door even more to the higher states of consciousness and the field of infinite possibilities.

Head spinning to process this new information, I thanked her so much for the teaching.

September 4

Rich got home last night. Chip woke up three times in the night, but he didn't whine as much, and Bella stayed in with Rich. Progress.

Today I had a board meeting, so Rich was in charge. And I managed to get in my full meditations, so my overall sense of serenity, gratitude, and humor came back. I could not stop thinking about all I heard about the higher states of consciousness lesson.

When Chip is awake, I typically keep him on a long leash tied to my belt loop. But he still chews constantly and needs to either be watched like a hawk or crated.

Now I know why Mary called him "devil dog." "Why do you call him that?" would have been an excellent question. Even when he is attached to my belt, it does not deter him from jumping up to get any item not nailed down or to get in the sniff-and-crouch position that makes my hustle him to the door to go out.

He needs to go out every couple of hours. I am grateful it is not winter, and I try to remember in my sleepy stupor to look at the night sky and the quiet neighborhood and appreciate it.

Today, spending time with Chip and Bella, I kept thinking that humans are unique because we have the gift of being able to become self-aware. If you believe in reincarnation, then you might believe that each person was once a rock, a mineral, a plant, or an animal and that we humans can change our lives and reawaken our true state of consciousness.

We call them higher states, but my teacher said yesterday that these states are really our normal state of consciousness. Most of us are experiencing a less-than-normal state. It's our true divine right to remember those things that are available for us to know and to reawaken our true state of higher consciousness.

Most people only use a fraction of their potential; they live in constricted awareness. When we slip into the gap, we go beyond memories and desires and can break out of our habits and get a glimpse of the soul and bring it back into our lives.

I feel a sense of wonder to be learning this. And it seems funny that I can experience the mundane daily life of dogs and sleep deprivation and Gus drama and working out and meal prep and errands and yet be very conscious that there is so much more to life than we experience with our senses. I have one foot in the material world and one in the ether.

Gussie:

I'm going to dry out this weekend. Mason is being a turd, but I understand why. He drove me to work and told me not to come home tonight. I've done this before. I've lied. The best thing you guys can do is not scold, but support.

Emma:

Given that circumstance, any chance you would consider professional help with your detox this weekend? Someplace safe to go and be cared for?

Gussie:

I can do it by myself. My PCP prescribed some anxiety meds.

Bethany:

Gus, there is no shame in getting help.

Teresa:

We can help find you a place to go. This is not a rescue. Don't let this drag on any longer.

Gussie:

Give me twenty-four hours. That's all I ask. Please. I can do this! Please stop intervening! Believe in me!

Jane:

Gus, if you are sober and want to talk, call. Love you.

Gussie:

Need to get through today. Not currently sober. *I can't go back to rehab!* Please—one more chance, I'm begging. Somebody— call Mason and get him off my ass! He's the main reason for all of this!

Bethany:

Gussie. Here is the truth. Mason is not the cause of your alcoholism. Quit lying to us and, more important, quit lying to yourself. I say this with love.

Gussie:

I'm safe at Anna's. Could not stay home. Please don't call me. I absolutely refuse to do an inpatient program. No one can force me. Detoxing. Going back to sleep now. I'm in a safe place.

September 5

I am sleep deprived. Chip is a challenge. Just when I get the last mess cleaned up, it seems like we have another one. We have tried the crate everywhere in the house and now finally got two crates because he can't stand to be separated from his pack.

When he comes out of the crate, even though he is on a leash on our belt, all hell breaks loose. I keep trying to see it from a puppy's perspective, thinking how much change he has gone through: leaving his mom and siblings, going to Mary and Jerry's pack, and then coming to us in a strange new place. I can't really blame him, but man, I hope he sleeps through the night soon.

I tried to paint my light images. There is no way that's happening right now. He can't stand to be in the crate when I am in the studio and whines pitifully. It's always the worst when I am covered in paint and can't respond quickly. Maybe we need a third crate, but that seems crazy. I tied him to my belt to have him with me in the studio. He jumped up on the easel and a wet painted canvas crashed down on his head. As I was cleaning him and the floor, he snatched a tube of purple paint. Luckily it had the cap on.

I know other people do this. Parents cope with actual human babies and survive. I feel frustrated and mad at myself for insisting on this puppy idea. I must have been completely out of my mind.

But this afternoon I took him with me into the gym because it is the safest room in the house with tile floor. I lay down on the stretching mat to just close my eyes for a few minutes. He snuggled next to me and looked up at me soulfully with his sweet brownish green eyes and started licking my hand. And then I fell totally in love with him. We're not taking him back.

I had not seen my light images in days, but they came to me again in afternoon meditation. Again, mostly magenta-pinkish, but there was a dark center and swirls of white and gray. I tried to keep my mind focused on my mantra and not the beautiful iridescent color and the fluid movement, like fireworks in water. The brightness and elegance shifted slowly, slowly into different shapes. Again, I brought my attention back to my mantra. The time flew by, and before I knew it, my Insight timer gonged, signaling the end. And still I sat, feeling peaceful and connected, like my heart was expanding. I felt tears leak out from behind my closed eyes.

Is it exhaustion? I hope it's a message from my higher intelligence: "It's all going to work out. This little guy will finally sleep through the night."

I want to try to paint what I see because words are failing me as descriptors. I wonder technically how to do it. Oils would allow me to blend colors. Liquid acrylics might provide the sense of translucence. How to get the sense of glowing flow? It feels daunting, but I am compelled somehow to express what I am seeing.

September 6

Our great college friends, Don and Mary, are visiting. Last night we got a puppy nanny and went out for a couple of hours, which felt like breaking out of prison.

I can't let Chip cry with friends in the house, so I got up with him at 1:30 and 4:00. At 1:30 when we were out, it started pouring, and Chip was too wound up to poop, though I knew he needed to. So, I got an umbrella and stood out in the rain. He loved the water. He let rivers wash over him, shaking it off every few minutes. I tried to breathe and just enjoy being out in the pretty rainy night. Lesson: grab any moment of peace you get.

As I stood sleepily in the rain, I wondered if the essence I see in some meditations is some kind of guide. Or if I am just connecting somehow to a vibration of my true self. Is my true self a guide? Are guides real? Teresa believes in guides. If I understand the concept, guides are there to watch over us, kind of like a guardian angel.

While we are encased in a mortal, human body, the idea is that we have some experts to call on who love us and are there for support. Teresa told me that she believes we have several guides who have specific expertise. They work like stage hands behind the scenes, so most people don't even know they exist. Like many kids, I had an imaginary friend when I was about five years old named Tom. I wonder if Tom was a guide, or if I am so sleepy, I am making all this up. Then I started to daydream (nightdream?) about a spirit guide job description.

Wanted: Jane's Spirit Guide

Must be able influence subtly and with synchronicity: for example, clock times, numbers, radio songs, email messages, and sections of books and magazines Jane randomly flips to. Must be able to convey, "You are on the right path!" through her sympathetic nervous system. Must be able insert messages into her dreams and meditations, using compelling imagery that will capture her imagination.

Must be able to hold space for her as she stumbles through life. Support her. Allow her to make idiotic decisions like getting a puppy. Help her know the right next step to take in helping Gus.

Finally, Chip did what he needed to do. We went in, I dried him off, and we both slipped into blessed sleep.

September 7

Chip is getting cuter. He has insatiable thirst and therefore has to pee every ninety minutes. He has been out twelve times today (including middle of the night last night.) This is not an exaggeration. I am keeping a log. Today when I was doing TRX and weight workout in our gym, he would get between me and the floor on pushups, jump on me for tricep dips, try to eat the Pilates and TRX straps, and generally made the workout more challenging.

I have started an online class from Rutgers University called Soul Beliefs with Professors Daniel Ogilve and Leonard Hamilton. Should be interesting.

In the first part of the Soul Beliefs class one of the professors laid out the case that almost all wisdom traditions believe in something like the soul and believe the soul survives us.

The MOOC shows the lecture hall with the students actually attending the live class. It looked like a few hundred students. They all look so young. Online learning like this is perfect for my personality type because I just want to learn; I don't need the in-person interaction.

The professor asked students to come up to the stage and say what they were taught to believe. Not what they believe now, but what their parents and religious leaders taught them from childhood.

He asked the class to raise hands: Any Catholics? Protestants? Any Jews? Any Muslims? Any Buddhists? Any Hindus?

He said he wanted to focus on beliefs about the afterlife in section one.

He called volunteers from each category to say what they were taught. Some contradicted each other. When he got to the Catholics, I was surprised no one recited the Baltimore Catechism or the Nicene Creed where they were taught very specifically what to believe.

So, it was anecdotal but fascinating.

The Catholic students said they were taught about heaven, hell, and purgatory and that there is a soul, but you must be baptized to get into heaven.

The Protestant students mostly agreed that people are born sinners with original sin and can't get into heaven unless they are saved. Some said they can't get to heaven unless they are saved, baptized, confirmed, and also Protestant.

The students talking about Islam were interesting. They talked about Allah, the one God; and Muhammed, the seal of the prophets; and that the Koran is the most widely read book in the world. They believe the soul is eternal. They don't believe in original sin; they said sins don't count until puberty. Muslims know where they stand with God; they know their obligations, and there is clarity. The creed is simple: believe "There is no God but Allah, and Muhammed is his prophet." Be constant in prayer, which keeps life in perspective. Pray five times a day: on rising, at noon, mid-afternoon, after sunset, and before sleep at night, lifting your heart in gratitude. Be charitable. Fast during Ramadan to become sensitized to compassion and to remember man's dependence on God, and journey to Mecca at least once in life. Like Christians, Muslims believe that the present life is to prepare for the next realm; this life is a test. On Judgment Day, all people will be rewarded by God according to their beliefs and deeds. Those that believe that there is no true God but Allah will be rewarded with life in Paradise forever.

The Jewish students were not at all aligned. This made me laugh, thinking of some of my Jewish friends and colleagues who love nothing more than discussion and debate. They seemed to agree there was no hell, and heaven was a more recent concept and that all life can be seen as a reflection of God so that we should enjoy life's goodness. Traditions preserve the memory of past generations. They believe Jews have been chosen to serve and suffer the ordeals that service requires and that the preservation of the tribe is critical. There is no central doctrine, yet faith, observance, culture, and nation kept coming up. They talked about a Book of Life that reveals what you have done and how you have lived your life. They talked about the importance of having a personal relationship with God and said that the soul comes in at conception and lives on after life.

The Hindu students said that Hinduism is not a religion and that the soul is a spark and is immortal. They believe in reincarnation and that the next life depends on karma, which is your duty or purpose or lesson you must learn. They said the goal is to get out of the circle of life and get to the next level and, in each life, to try to gain more enlightenment.

There were only a few Buddhist students. They did not speak of the soul per se; it was more like a "chain of being," but they did talk about karmic deeds and reincarnation. They talked about striving for enlightenment and the end of the cycle of suffering.

This is very interesting. We will see how I balance class with a puppy.

I managed a lovely afternoon meditation and felt completely peaceful and joyful after even though I didn't see any "light beings." Good thing I am not attached to them.

September 8

I got more sleep last night than I have had in a week, and I almost feel human again. What a good husband I have; he took middle-of-the-night puppy duty. I spent some more time on my soul class today.

The professor pointed out that given widespread agreement about the importance of the soul, it is amazing the topic is so rarely discussed. Maybe, he says, the subject is too sacred, too personal, too sensitive, too controversial, or too elusive, or people are so sure about their afterlife beliefs that talking about them would be stating the obvious. They might risk challenging their own belief systems, which can create too much dissonance.

In learning more about soul beliefs, I can't stop thinking about the higher states of consciousness. I have started to read a book on quantum physics, and I have heard a few times that everything we perceive with our senses is in space time.

I keep hearing the term *nonlocal*. Our souls are beyond limitation. The higher states are nonlocal. I am having a hard time grasping this. What does it really mean? Nonlocal pure awareness: what is that? My teacher said it is the *potential* for all experiences. When we slip into the gap, we slip into the space of nonlocal awareness. We are not our thoughts, we are not our minds, and we are not our bodies. We are the experiencers. I need an example of what this means.

One explanation is that nonlocal pure awareness is like radio waves. The Chopra website features a lecture by Roger Gabriel. He compared it to the CNN news signal. The signal that CNN sends out is nonlocal. When you tune in on your TV, you give it attention, and that localizes the nonlocal into the experience of CNN news. The TV is the instrument that localizes the nonlocal signal, like our mind and body localize the nonlocal spirit and convert it into the localized, limited events of our daily life.

OK, maybe I am starting to get it. We are not our thoughts, minds, or bodies. Our attention localizes our nonlocal experiences.

September 9

Rich has to go to the dentist today. His smile is gorgeous and perfect, and could light up the heavens. Once I saw him twist a cork off a bottle of wine using his teeth, and I nearly leaped across the room. *No!* I beg you not to use your beautiful teeth on that. I am grateful that he takes care of himself.

Last night, amid dog-related momentary crises, we realized it was our anniversary. We laughed and said we will celebrate on Friday.

In class today, the professor covered the earliest known, ancient religions, which believed in multiple gods and spirits; they were egalitarian power-sharing tribes and rigid, top-down societies with rulers. He talked about the importance of tribe cohesion for cooperative hunting, food sharing, and success in battles. Tribes survived when members were so committed that they were willing to die for the group.

Rituals increased bonding and group identity and were used for the full spectrum of life events: feast or famine, rainfall or drought, birth and death. Dancing, singing, blood-letting, animal and human sacrifices, and other rituals were performed to bring about good fortune to the tribe.

Ancestor worship and seeing deities in nature were common— seeing spirits in trees, in the sky, under the ground, on mountaintops, occupying the bodies of various animals, or existing in different realms.

Rituals, sacrifices, and gifts were used to influence the spirits to cure illnesses, increase the supply of food, defeat enemies, and preserve the existing social order.

I described today's lesson to Rich. He nodded thoughtfully. "That's very interesting. Bella, can you go to the refrigerator and get me a sparkling water?" Bella continues licking herself. Rich looks at me. "Does she provide any utility?" he asks. "Chip, you are young. Can we train you to go the refrigerator and bring me a can of sparkling water?" He squeaks in reply. Rich, "No? Not even from the newest member of the pack? Wow."

After much drama and communication, Gussie has now agreed to go to rehab in Santa Fe. She and I spent time together on the phone last night, and she had a breakthrough. I asked her to just stay open to hanging in with me through a whole conversation, and she agreed. I calmly tried to reflect back to her a sense that she could harness her higher intelligence, make better choices and get out of victim mode.

We talked about some of her deeper fears about her upcoming divorce, moving out of the house, and potentially losing her current job. As we talked through each fear, she somehow became more receptive to the idea of going to rehab in Santa Fe where she will be close to Teresa. Her co-pay is $7,500. Rich and I will pay that (bless him), and he has already wired the money. Joe and Emma bought her plane ticket. Teresa will pick her up and take here there.

I have been working on detachment, not from her but from the emotional roller coaster of deep fear, despair, and surging hope. Meditation is helping. I remind myself that she is a forty-seven-year-old adult on her own path, making her own choices. I am happy she is trying rehab again but know from past experience that it may take more than one more stint in rehab for her to stay sober.

September 10

Whew. It was a rough night. Chip got me up at 12:50, 1:30, 4:00, and 5:30. He pooped in the gym during my workout despite my staying outside with him for thirty minutes *right before.* Happily, he pooped on tile. Now, that is a gratitude perspective.

In class today, the professor covered more on the history of afterlife beliefs in ancient civilizations. Tribal dancing and drumming produces exhausted delirium and trance states, which lead to a sense of tribe identity. It is not known whether the hunter-gatherers believed in a personal soul with an afterlife.

I think I am living in a trance state right now. Certainly, exhausted delirium applies.

Now in email, I am starting to receive ads and offers from meditation-related organizations; I must now be on some kind of spiritual seeker list. I bought, downloaded, and experimented with some brain catalyst tracks from I-Awake and Holosync that are designed to deepen meditation practice.

My silent primordial sound meditation is more effective for me than the brain catalyst tracks, but I'm going to buy some of the tracks for Gussie; I think they could help her.

Images are still coming to me in some meditations. To me, they almost feel like presences who come to visit. They morph now: first magenta and orange, then grey/yellow and white, and then pulses of dark into light colors. The light gently shifts. They are so lovely, I almost stop breathing, but I keep trying to shift my attention back to my mantra and away from the images.

At the end when I am saying *Namaste,* I almost always now get an image of teal/turquoise that melts into almost purple: a peaceful ghostly outline of a person sitting in meditation. I love to stay there and rest a few moments to relish that deep feeling of peace and calm. It's almost as though I am outside of my body, seeing myself sitting there.

September 11

I always exchange notes or calls with a few beloved former colleagues on 9/11. Jenn and Charles write each year. We will always have a strong bond. It was a horribly emotional, gut-wrenching time to be in New York on that day, taking care of lots of associates, many of whom experienced one of the worst times of their lives.

Chip had invisible fence training again and then was so tired he went into his crate on his own and took a nap. I have been singing him to sleep. I lay right by his kennel, stroke his nose through the grate and very softly sing, "You are my sunshine."

Last night, I sang to him. He seemed to be asleep, so I tiptoed to bed. Then, I heard him sit up and softly begin to squeak. I held my breath and prayed, "*Please* go back to sleep." Then he started to whine. Then tiny barks. Then big barks. People have advised, "Put his crate in the garage, so you don't hear him." I am almost ready to do it. I do realize on some level that I love taking care of him, and I may be making it harder than it has to be. I took him outside and then, unable to fall back to sleep, I sat up in bed and meditated, and it was very peaceful.

Class today focused on the establishment of agricultural communities about 15,000 years ago.

As roles diversified, shamans and priests emerged—special designees entitled to communicate with the gods or spirits. These spiritual leaders were typically close to the ruling elite. The time horizon of work and life also changed because farming requires planning and forward-thinking. The point the professor made is the more one engages in future thinking, the more likely one is to ponder about the fate of the self after the body dies.

The earliest written accounts of the emergence of a concern about the next life were the story of Babylonian King Gilgamesh and stories out of Ancient Egypt at around 2700 BCE.

So, the earliest *written* trace was 4,000 years ago. I think there must be artistic and oral traces that can be found before writing was common.

September 12

I received the first DVD of over 1,600 images from my digitized photo archiving project. I sent the sibs photos of Mom. This is going to be hours of work, but to me it is fun. I am going to open each digitized photo and tag with names and dates as close as I can determine. Three more DVDs will come after this one.

In soul class today, the professor covered more concepts from Ancient Egypt and Greece. In the eighth century BC, Homer wrote the

Iliad and the *Odyssey*, and new concepts emerged, such as the notion of psyche and Hades. Psyche, or soul, was believed to be breathed into the body at birth and breathed out at death. Psyche travels directly to Hades, a desolate place, where it exists as a shade.

In the seventh century, Hesiod described the Isles of Blest: an afterlife with good crops, no suffering, no sorrow, and eternal life. This good life was only available to soldier heroes killed in combat in the wars at Thebes and Troy. This is the first known use of paradise as recruiting tool for armed services, later echoed in Norse and other philosophy and teachings.

In the sixth century, Pythagoras taught the notion of resurrection where psyches could disengage and reengage from their bodies. The idea of "transmigration" from one body to another body (including to the bodies of animals) is attributed to Pythagoras.

In the fifth century, Plato made some important declarations about the soul.

- The soul is a divine creation.
- The soul is immortal.
- The body and soul are separate entities.
- All souls preexisted in other bodies.
- The soul is perfect, but perfection is contaminated by having to be encased in the body.

The tension between desires of the body and having a pure soul later became a central feature of Christian and Islamic religions.

I am very satisfied to have found this course at this moment in time. It seems like it came to me at the perfect moment when I wanted grounding in ancient, foundational belief systems.

September 13

Chip slept for six solid hours last night; we are thrilled and grateful. He and Bella had a big play session before bed, Rich kept him up until

10:30, and he did all of his business right before sleeping. We will try to replicate this going forward.

Last night we celebrated our thirty-seventh anniversary (to be technically accurate, this depends on how you count and if you include the divorce break). We got a puppy sitter and took Lyft to 3rd and Hollywood in Granville and had great salmon and spinach and herb salad.

Class today focused on Hinduism. Our professor apologized in advance for the high-level view and said we need to understand that there is much greater complexity than we will cover in this class.

Though Hinduism speaks of spirituality and God, it is not an organized religion. The word *Hindu* is not religious. It is a geographical word, referring to those who lived close to a certain river as Hindus. It has no single, systematic approach to teaching its belief system. There is no founder.

There is no bible or simple set of rules to follow like the Ten Commandments. Local, regional, and caste practices influence the interpretation and practice of beliefs throughout the Hindu world.

Hinduism is an open book and is always evolving; it adapts with the times and is open to examination and diverse thoughts. So, Hinduism is not easily defined. Some say that it is an ever-changing ancient tradition, and some say it is a way of life. Yet there are some common threads:

Truth
Hindus pursue understanding of the truth: the essence of the universe and the only reality.

Brahman
Hindus believe in Brahman, one true God who is formless, limitless, all-inclusive, and eternal.

The Vedas

The Vedas are scriptures that contain revelations received by ancient enlightened beings and sages.

Dharma

Dharma is a concept that does not translate easily to Western thought or the English language. Dharma can be described as purpose, right conduct, righteousness, moral law, and duty. Anyone who strives to live their dharma tries to do the right thing, according to one's duty and abilities, at all times.

Immortality

A Hindu belief is that the individual soul (atman) has been, is, and will be. It cannot be created or destroyed. The consequences of actions performed in a life are reaped in the next life—the same soul in a different body. The process of movement of the atman from one body to another is known as transmigration. The kind of body the soul inhabits next is determined by karma (actions accumulated in previous lives).

Moksha

Moksha is freedom or liberation: the soul's release from the cycle of death and rebirth. It occurs when the soul unites with Brahman by realizing its true nature. Several paths can lead to this realization and unity.

Fascinating. I love learning this. I have always wanted to learn about the differences between wisdom traditions. This is the perfect class for me at this time.

I have consciously done things to be healthier in mind, body, and spirit today. My soul beliefs class and Italian lesson are helping my mind, and a good workout and healthy food help my body. Chip, Bella, and meditation are good for my spirit. Well, sometimes Chip is good for spirit.

September 14

Chip has discovered the joy of toilet paper. He sneaks in and grabs some whenever we forget to close the door to the bathroom. I was on the treadmill, and he streaked by with a whole roll snaking behind him by the time I leaped off the treadmill and got it away from him.

It was actually lovely taking him out into the cool, starry night with a half-moon at 2 a.m., and today is another crisp fall-like sweater-weather day. I am so grateful it is not snowy and icy during this time of late night and early morning sojourns.

The segment of class I watched today talked about moving from believing in many gods to one deity. *Monotheism,* belief in the existence of one god, or in the oneness of God is distinguished from polytheism, the belief in the existence of many gods, and from atheism, the belief that there is no god.

Modern Judaic, Christian, and Islamic religions feature one God.

The Christian and Islamic religions were derived from Judaism, so theoretically, the idea of having one god is the same for all three faiths. The worship of only one god, monotheism emerged in about the third century BCE, but took centuries to become widespread.

In polytheism, the deities worshipped depended on the culture and include wind, rain, and ocean deities; gods of happiness, doom, death, and destruction; gods and goddesses of love, war, fertility, health, and every part of nature as well as major deities that existed as sun gods; and minor deities, such as the Egyptian deities that oversaw lungs, liver, stomach, and intestines.

Some gods were thought to be moody and difficult. Others were considered open to negotiations and offerings. The shift in belief from multiple deities to one deity is traced to the beginning of a belief system of a single Israelite god named Yahweh. This was a monumental shift in the landscape of beliefs and became the foundation of modern-day Judaic, Islamic, and Christian religions.

It is fascinating to better understand the history of belief systems and to realize how much hope, fear, and superstition have played a part throughout history. It makes me realize I need to step back as part of my spiritual journey and keep asking, what do I believe and why? I know what I was taught. It's also interesting to note the belief systems that attribute spiritual power or at least a connection to sun, moon, sky, mountains, trees, and wind—a recognition that spirit is in everything.

Do I now believe in some homemade blend of new-age spirituality? I am amazed that I cannot clearly articulate what I believe other than a general belief in Source or Spirit. Why do I have faith that a higher power exists? I just can't believe it's all random. I am filled with wonder at everything from the magnificence of how our bodies work to trees coming to life in the springtime. Pine cones. Sea shells. When I think about nature, our amazing bodies, and the cosmos, I believe there has to be some grand design in play. Like Einstein said, "Either nothing is a miracle, or everything is a miracle." I vote for everything.

I feel compelled to keep thinking and studying. Maybe by looking at the spectrum of wisdom and belief systems, I will find more answers. I think that exploring is healthy, but I also think that when your core beliefs are challenged, a person can feel unmoored, seeking a place to land. I see why people who grow up in a belief system don't allow themselves to wander too far afield. It's a little scary out here. I am loving this exploration, but I feel kind of jealous of people who are solid in a belief system.

September 16

It is a cool fall-like day, with the whole pack a bit sleep-deprived due to Chip's overnight desire to play. I told Rich I am amazed how quickly the days fly by; I am pleasantly busy and mentally challenged without being too stressed. Today I got up with Chip at 4:30, ran on the treadmill, did Pilates, and stretched before coffee. I took a spinning class, did Italian, had breakfast, wrote to Gus, took Chip on a walk around the pond, helped Rich pay bills, worked on my photo archive, and did a segment of class. It feels good, knowing Gus is safe in rehab and hopefully healing. This afternoon, I will walk Bella and watch some more of class, paint, and work on photos. What nice days—I am so grateful.

Today's class focused on Judaism. Judaism is the oldest monotheistic religion in the world. The basic ideas and moral values of Western civilization are based on Judaism.

The professor said that there is no universally agreed-upon "Jewish" belief system. It's not really possible to find out the answer to "What do Jews believe about the afterlife?"

The professor used writing from Mendenhall (1992) and Goldenberg (1992) as primary guides.

He said one reason for the vagueness of Jewish positions on immortality and the afterlife is because these matters are not dealt with in the Hebrew Bible. The topic does not exist in the first five chapters of the Old Testament.

However, this does not completely square with what I have heard, so I checked another source, and it said that Judaism teaches that there *is* immortality to the soul, and that life doesn't end with death. It teaches that raising children and having a family is a blessing of life, that people are responsible for their actions, and that reward and punishment are a part of life and the afterlife. Jews are meant to be the influential moral force in the world.

One consistent theme that also was apparent from the Jewish students who, on the first day of class, described what they were taught to believe: that what matters most is this current life.

The professor noted that there are Jews who care deeply about afterlife, but most Jews faithful to their traditions are not living a just life to assure themselves of a comfortable afterlife but to preserve a tradition that they consider to be more important than their personal fate.

Individuals come and go, but the Jewish tribe and its traditions are to be preserved at all costs. The book of Daniel became part of the Jewish Bible late in its evolution. Biblical scholars note that Daniel contains the only passage in the Old Testament that refers to afterlife, to wit: "And many of them that sleep in the dust of the earth shall awake, some to everlasting life and some to reproaches and everlasting abhorrence" (Daniel 12:2).

The professor noted that most past and present rabbinical scholars avoid dogma, pointing out that speculations about afterlife are only that—speculations. Nobody speaks from experience.

And I keep coming back to this point again and again. No matter how many years I seek, I won't actually *know* until this life is over.

September 17

Jane:

I had a long voicemail from Gussie. She said she is grateful to all of us. She says she is healing and emotionally and spiritually ready to get better. She is working hard with the therapist on three things: (1) never relapsing, (2) experiencing emotions without self-medicating, and (3) learning to love herself. She went hiking with a group and finished last, but she did it. She sounded clear and excited like I have not heard her in years. She won't call again until next week. Love to all.

September 18

It got into the forties overnight and is a crisp, cool morning; it should get to seventy today. We have a fundraiser tonight. Chip was up four times last night; something's got to give! Maybe it's time to follow the vet's advice and just let him bark and whine. He had lots of playtime and exercise yesterday, so it's not that. We cut off his water after supper, so it's not that. Rich got up more than I did. It's good there are two of us, because when he gets frustrated, I can talk him off the ledge, and he can do the same when I am ready to tear my hair out.

I got my next 1,800 photos; now the project is starting to seem overwhelming with more DVDs to come. I can see this lasting for a year. It is fun to send photos to people I haven't been in touch with in a while, though. I found one yesterday of Mom and Dad cutting their wedding cake, and one of my gorgeous Aunt Sharon.

Class today focused on Christianity. Interestingly, the essential features of Christian afterlife beliefs cannot be found in the New Testament.

Our professor relied on the work of Keck (1992) who said, "The New Testament contains not a single chapter that summarizes the Christian view." In fact, since chapters in the New Testament were written by many people over centuries, the book contains many contradictions.

Catholicism was the dominant Christian religion through the Middle Ages. Protestantism emerged at the end of the Middle Ages, largely due to protests against certain practices of the church.

The Protestant Revolution begat many Protestant denominations. However, Catholics and Protestants alike seem to agree on the following:

They believe that people are born sinners. St. Paul dealt with this topic in the Bible. From his writings, God originally created humans to be pure, innocent, and immortal. But Adam, with the assistance of Eve, disobeyed God's explicit instructions to avoid eating the fruit from the Tree of Knowledge of Good and Evil. Adam's sin polluted the world forever, and death became mankind's fate. The belief is that everyone is a sinner at birth because of Adam's Original Sin.

I already know how I feel about this. It is interesting to study original sin in a class where it is just described factually in a comparison to other belief systems, without the terror of personally experiencing the catechism thrust on me as a youngster.

The ritual of baptism is designed to cleanse the soul from inherited sin. But baptism alone does not guarantee salvation.

This belief system says that the only way to salvation is through Jesus Christ. Although the "wages" of sin is death, John declared, "For God so loved the world that he gave his only son, that whoever believes in him should not perish but have eternal life" (John 3:16). The belief system generated by this is that people who accept Jesus as their personal savior are reborn.

Keck (1992) stresses the idea that rebirth in this life involves transforming the "old self" into a "new self' that is committed to the teachings of and resurrection of Christ.

Day of Final Judgment: There are different versions of beliefs about the final day (or days) of judgment. For instance, in Apocalypse according to John (the book of Revelation), Christ will return for a final thousand-day battle with Satan. After Satan is defeated, all the living and dead are gathered and final heaven or hell, judgments are made.

Not being redeemed results in eternal damnation. There are two deaths. The death of the body is definite. The second death, it is believed, can be averted by faith in Jesus. Biblical interpreters vary in their extremes of the second death from being excluded from the presence of God to the fiery pit of hell.

The Christian belief system says that the result of salvation is everlasting life in heaven. Heaven is the final destination for Christians. Some churches preach that the soul rejoins the body at resurrection time, though some take the position that the final form of an immortal being will be a "spiritual self."

September 18

We had an adventure this morning while taking out the trash. Chip and a bee had a squabble, and the bee won. He got stung, and his poor face immediately started swelling. He was running, whining, and rubbing his face on the rug, the tile, and the hardwood floor. I gave him half a Benadryl and took him to the vet. She gave him a shot and said he would be sleepy all day. His face is so swollen that he looks like a Sharpei. We have to give him a steroid pill today and tomorrow. Bella seems worried about him; she keeps going over to lie by his crate and whine.

Today's class focused on Islam.

Islamic and Christian afterlife beliefs are similar in several ways. The existence of heaven and hell are underlying beliefs in both religions. The existence of a Day of Reckoning is prominent in both belief systems. Muslims believe:

- There is no God but God.
- Everything in the universe was brought into existence by God.

- All things that have come from God will return to God.
- The only people who will be resurrected will be those who believe in him and conduct their lives, according to his teachings as recorded by Muhammad in the Koran.
- A difference between Christian and Islamic belief systems is Christians believe that heaven is open only to people who accept Jesus Christ as their savior. Muslims believe that Jesus was one of 120,000 prophets, but that Muhammad is the final prophet sent by God.
- God's message was recorded in the Koran (frequently spelled Qur'an). Another difference is Muslims do not share the Christian belief in original sin.
- God created human beings to share the wondrous bounties of existence. He endowed each human with unbounded potentials.
- When a soul has realized its true nature, it faces a loving and compassionate God upon resurrection.
- Those who have ignored their responsibilities will come into the presence of a severe and wrathful God.
- Body and soul are independent after death until the Day of Resurrection when they are reunited. Some teachings imply that the Day of Resurrection lasts for a thousand years, and at the end one group goes to the Garden of Paradise, and the others go to the Fires of Darkness.

September 19

Yesterday, after the vet visit with Chip, he was drowsy and slept in his crate. I thought, "Great; maybe he will just nap all day." Then, I gave him a steroid as directed at 2 o'clock, and he became a crazed, Cujo-like maniac. He burst out of his kennel, raced through the house, and pooped and peed everywhere as I ran to catch him.

When I finally got him outside, he ran through the electric fence and onto the road. People stopped and got out of their cars to help me round him up. I thanked them profusely, picked him up, and lugged him back home as he squirmed in my arms. He was safe, but I was nearly hysterical.

I think the combination of the Benadryl and steroid was too much for his little body. I crated him and started cleaning the messes. New rugs are definitely in our future after we get through the puppy phase. It is unfathomable to me that that much content could have come out of a thirty-five-pound puppy. I will never, ever purchase expensive rugs again for as long as we have dogs.

I filled three poop bags and took them to the park to put in the doggie trash can after Rich got home. Last night, Chip's swelling went down. He was starved for dinner, and we elected not to give him the other steroid. He only got up twice in the night, so we are hoping he is back to normal today. He looks like a sweet angel now, but we know that deep inside, there is the evilest devil dog.

I was relieved to sit down for class and meditation once he was settled.

In class today, the professor talked about human beings placing importance on tribal membership throughout the ages. He wrote a paper summarizing a partial history of afterlife beliefs and invited criticism. He makes the point that millions of people hold that their personal belief system about God is the only correct one. We will study more examples of hatred and warfare waged in the name of defending sometimes amazingly similar views of God.

We have to write a paper for class. We are also going to hear from four atheists; that will be interesting. We are not going to delve into Buddhism in this class, so I have already found a class to take from Princeton.

Teresa:
Just got home from an emotionally draining two-hour visit with Gus. She was shaking badly and does not look well physically. We met with her therapist; I like him. Gus said she is through lying. At one point in the session, she got very angry, raised her voice, got red in the face, and said she wanted to leave rehab now. Her therapist said there is something deep in her that is causing anger

and resistance, and we began to explore it. We talked about her marriage, her relationship to all of us, her shame and guilt, and all the hurt in her life. She sobbed through much of the session. I hugged her, but the therapist said she doesn't need family to rescue her or to fix her; she needs to make healthy coping mechanisms her default behaviors, and it takes time to learn them. Gussie is trying to let herself feel pain without drinking.

It was hard to see her like this. We are all invited to family therapy day next week. You can dial in, and I will be there in person.

Love you all, Teresa

More family discussion about Gus all day. Emma wrote her a good letter:

Hello, my sweet sister!
Joe and I are thinking of you every day. We are proud of you for making the tough decision to go to treatment. We truly believe that your health (even your life) depended on it.

Teresa has updated us on your family therapy sessions. It sounds like difficult, agonizing, work. I'm grateful that T. is there for you and able to do this. It has to be so hard on you, and I'm sorry you are going through such a rough time. You sound terrific on the phone and seem like you are getting some of the help you need.

Give yourself time to heal and get strong.

We all love you so very much. If we could love your pain and addiction away—it would be gone forever! But it is up to you. You have to have the desire to get well. You have to have the determination to do the hard work it takes to get there. We believe you can do it. I hope you believe it too.

Love,
Emma

September 20

I had a glorious bike ride at sunrise to get ready for Tuscany; I was the only one on the road for a long time. I got back in time for Rich to go play tennis. Chip had gotten away from him and pooped under my easel again.

I roasted vegetables from White Barn organic and left a plate of roasted peppers on the counter to cool while Chip and I walked around the pond. While we were gone, Bella got up on the counter and ate all but three measly peppers. But we had beautiful cherry heirloom tomatoes for dinner: yellow, red, and green. We have been so lucky to have great produce this summer.

Today's Soul Beliefs class was a video of the Four Horsemen of Atheism sitting around a table talking for two hours. They are Richard Dawkins (evolutionary biologist), Daniel Dennett (cognitive scientist), Sam Harris (neuroscientist), and Christopher Hitchens (journalist). They were annoying, charming, arrogant, and irreverent as they talked over each other and passionately made their points. Basically, they are alarmed by certain ways of thinking, particularly when people are zealots about their chosen beliefs.

They know they offend people, but they also feel it's wrong that people are offended. People should be willing to have their views challenged. I actually agree with this; it's painful to listen to some of the things they say but important to hear it.

One said, "You have wasted your life on the glorification of something that's a myth!"

I can imagine the horror they must feel observing faithful people doing unspeakable things in the name of a belief system. It's interesting to watch, and I keep having to remind myself to have an open and expansive mind.

Two hours with atheists was not the most enjoyable part of class, but somehow, I feel more informed and that my thinking is broader. They seem to believe societies are likely to destroy civilization because of religion.

There was a separate lecture from Richard Dawkins. He is witty, with a charming accent. He wrote a book called *Unweaving the*

Rainbow. In the YouTube video, he read some moving, poetic lines he wrote that he wants read at his funeral, saying basically that we are going to die and that makes us lucky; most people won't die because they will never be born.

I keep thinking that there is some aspect of spirituality threaded through some of their beliefs. I will do some more research about atheism.

According to a poll, 12 percent of Americans do not believe in God. In Europe, it is often higher; in Sweden, as much as 85 percent of the population does not believe; France, 54 percent; Great Britain, 44 percent; and Japan, 65 percent.

Daniel Dennett, the next atheist featured, wrote a couple of books that sold very well. One was *Darwin's Dangerous Idea*. He takes on creationists and fully explores the theory of evolution.

Christopher Hitchens was a journalist who died a couple of years ago. He wrote *God Is Not Great*. He criticized those who are certain their version of God is right. He said, "It's a choice between civilization and religion." He particularly focuses on religious zealots.

Sam Harris studies religion and philosophy. He is very articulate and pretty likable. He wrote *The End of Faith* and *Letter to a Christian Nation*. He seems to recognize and honor spiritual and mystical experiences. He said in the video that he recognized that there is range of rare, transcending experiences that people have in life, like feeling at one with nature.

Then they seemingly agreed that organized religion is not the only game in town when it comes to being spiritual and implied that you can be an atheist and be spiritual.

Interestingly, I found a reference to this in Deepak Chopra's book *The Future of God*. He says that in a Pew Research Survey, 21 percent of Americans who describe themselves as atheists believe in God or a universal spirit, 12 percent believe in heaven, and 10 percent pray at least once a week. I always thought atheists did not believe in God at all. The range of belief systems is really boggling.

Here is the definition from Wikipedia:

Atheism is, in a broad sense, the rejection of belief in the existence of deities. In a narrower sense, atheism is specifically the position that there are no deities. Most inclusively, atheism is the absence of belief that any deities exist. Atheism is contrasted with theism, which, in its most general form, is the belief that at least one deity exists.

So, there is a wide spectrum in what atheists believe, and some of them are spiritual. They seem to converge around disliking organized religion and particularly fundamentalists. I see their point.

I'm glad to be studying this. Maybe it is expanding my mind. At least, it is satisfying my curiosity to know more about what wisdom traditions and atheists actually believe.

September 21

Chip woke us up every two hours last night, but this morning, there was revenge. Bella wore his little ass out running him through the hedges. She ran like the wind. He kept up pretty well, but he squeaks when he runs, and he likes to hide behind the bushes and jump out at her. It was hilarious, and we loved laughing; it cleared the air after the last few days of wanting to kill him.

I am studying Italian, and I tried painting today while Chip whined in the crate; I am getting excited for the Europe trip, and especially biking in Tuscany. We had family therapy with Gus today. It was much as Teresa described last week—long and heartbreaking to see her struggle so hard.

September 22

In class, we had an interesting lecture on the role that sectarianism played in recent crises. I have a paper on intergroup conflict due next week. Since we will be gone, I wrote it today. I wrote about the Sunnis and Shia because I am embarrassed to say that I could not articulate the difference.

Sectarianism, according to Wikipedia, is bigotry, discrimination, or hatred arising from attaching importance to perceived differences between subdivisions within a group, such as between different denominations of a religion or factions of a political movement.

I cited recent articles that explained the contrasts between the two Muslim groups. The division originated in a dispute soon after the death of the Prophet Muhammad over who should lead the Muslim community. Members of the two sects have coexisted for centuries and share many fundamental beliefs and practices. The differences lie in the fields of doctrine, ritual, law, theology, and religious organization. Their leaders often compete for power, and many recent conflicts tear communities apart. In the paper, I outlined the subtle differences between Sunni Muslims, who regard themselves as the more traditional branch of Islam, and the Shia, who believe in the right of Ali, the son-in-law of the Prophet Muhammad and his descendants, to lead the Islamic community. I outlined some of the Shia history of loss and martyrdom. Though their overall numbers are only about one-tenth of all Muslims, Shia Muslims are in the majority in Iran, Iraq, Bahrain, Azerbaijan, and, according to some estimates, Yemen. There are large Shia communities in Afghanistan, India, Kuwait, Lebanon, Pakistan, Qatar, Syria, Turkey, Saudi Arabia, and the United Arab Emirates.

I recounted the role sectarianism has played in recent crises. Part of this history includes the Iranian revolution of 1979 where Shia challenged conservative Sunni regimes, particularly in the Gulf. Tehran supported Shia parties beyond its borders, while the Gulf states supported Sunni governments. In Pakistan and Afghanistan, hardline Sunni militant groups—such as the Taliban—have often attacked Shia places of worship. The current conflicts in Iraq and Syria also have sectarian overtones. Young Sunni men in both countries have joined rebel groups, many of which echo the hardline ideology of al-Qaeda.

Here's what I think: the subtle differences between these groups make it nearly impossible for an outsider to pretend to understand the nuances.

September 23

We are taking only one suitcase apiece to Europe, including all of our biking gear—a packing challenge. Chip will go to obedience school while we are gone. And, even though she is "an old girl," Bella will, too. I love thinking they will be mentally and physically challenged and will have interaction all day, every day, with lots of attention.

I feel somewhat restless with the end of my Soul Beliefs class but feel unable to really start something big until we return from Europe. So, I want to try to wrestle to the ground the question of determinism versus free will.

I also want to take a deeper dive into Vedanta. My beloved Primordial Sound Meditation came from Vedanta, and of all the soul beliefs we have covered this month, I am intrigued to explore more about what the Vedas teach. I'd like to know more about what I am here to do—my dharma—so I can get on the right path with learning the appropriate lessons and being of service.

Similarly, I have been amazed how many times I find myself thinking about whether there is really "a plan" for us humans on earth. I am always horrified at calling hours before a funeral when a well-intended person says to the grieving family, "Everything happens for a reason." Or, "It was God's plan." Or, "It was his time." Are these people idiots or enlightened? I have always believed strongly in free will. Are these ideas mutually exclusive?

My thinking is circular, and I can't seem to make progress. Is there really a plan? If there really is a plan, it would follow that there is a deity or a mechanism driving it all. But what about free will?

Aristotle implied in many of his lessons that things happen for a reason and are predetermined. He is the first person I can find this concept attributed to. I read something that said that he believed that every experience in your life was designed to shape you and form you into the ultimate and greatest version that you could ever imagine yourself to be. The only thing that prevents this is having the wisdom to see it.

September 24

Thank you, Nikkie Gray. This is from her blog where she talks about the notion that we *do* choose our lives, and we come to this incarnation with a plan that we have agreed to—a contract, so to speak—that balances predetermination and free will. Finally, this is something that makes sense and resonates with me. She says:

> A "Pre-Birth Plan" is set in place but free will gives us the ability to create any reality we choose. There are certain things we are meant to experience. There's a lesson to be learned, an experience to be had for growth, healing or balance.

I am intrigued by this idea of a pre-birth plan. If I understand what she is saying, both notions could be valid: there is a plan, or at least a blueprint, and there is also free will.

I called and talked to Abigail. We are talking about logistics for Umbria, but I wanted to see what she really thinks about this. She said it can be comforting to think that there are no accidents and that what happens reflects an unfolding plan.

"So, if there are no accidents, then do we imagine the world is fair, since what happens is just part of a bigger plan?"

"Hmmm. I have to think about fair. That might be a stretch."

"If you suffer from a terrible disease or live in poverty in a war-torn country, is that just part of your plan? Or did you do something to deserve it?"

"Hmmm ... there has to be more to it than this. Maybe we have to look out beyond one lifetime." I look to see what atheists think, and I go back to my four horsemen from my soul class.

Richard Dawkins wrote that the universe exhibits "precisely the properties we should expect if there is, at bottom, no design, no purpose, no evil, and no good, nothing but blind, pitiless indifference."

That is kind of depressing. Ha. I take a few minutes and imagine Richard Dawkins' plan is to be a renowned atheist in this life, and Richard is doing exactly what the Universe intends. I sort of like this idea.

I do online searches on this topic for the different wisdom traditions.

The Jewish faith stresses that free will is a product of the intrinsic human soul, but the ability to make a free choice is via the part of the soul that is united with God. OK, so this wisdom tradition believes in free will, but do they believe that there is a plan on which you exert free will, or just random events with no design? More digging is needed.

Free will, according to Islamic doctrine, is the main factor for man's accountability in his or her actions throughout life. All actions taken by man's free will are said to be counted on the Day of Judgment because they are his or her own and not God's. OK; same question as above.

In Christian theology (and the Protestant sects differ on the degree to which they believe this), God is described as omniscient, omnipotent, and omnipresent—a notion that some people, Christians and non-Christians alike, believe implies that not only has God always known what choices individuals will make tomorrow, but he actually has determined what choices they will make. That is, these people believe that God, by virtue of his foreknowledge, knows what factors will influence individual choices, and, by virtue of his omnipotence, he controls those factors.

People in this belief system might believe that God *does* choose the Super Bowl winner, and to them, praying to God before a sporting event makes sense.

I found an author, Robert Schwartz, who wrote a book on the notion that we plan our own lives before birth. This idea blows me away. I downloaded it and can't wait to read it.

The Amazon review says, "Would you like to understand the deeper spiritual meaning of physical illness, parenting handicapped children, drug addiction, alcoholism, the death of a loved one, accidents, deafness, and blindness? *Your Soul's Plan* explores the premise that we are all eternal souls who plan our lives, including our greatest challenges before we are born for the purpose of spiritual growth and that suffering is not purposeless, but rather imbued with deep meaning. *Your Soul's Plan* helps readers awaken to the reality that they are transcendent, eternal souls."

We plan our own lives? Wow. My logical mind says this is nonsense. There can't be rational evidence for this. Yet my intuition strongly resonates with this idea. I'm sure this notion is way out there for some. Rich will surely roll his eyes. But I am on a spiritual vision quest of exploration with an open and curious mind, and I can't wait to read it.

September 24

I stayed awake for hours last night reading *Your Soul's Plan*. My intuition is fighting with my rational mind, and I am favoring my intuition. This resonates. For the first time, I might have a reasonable explanation for why Gus's life is the way it is.

Jane:
Teresa, download this book: *Your Soul's Plan* by Robert
Schwartz. Read chapter 5 on "Alcoholism and Drug Addiction"
and call or text me when you are done. Blown away. xoxoxoxoxo

Teresa:
Downloading now. Can't wait to read.

For me, this book provided a major paradigm shift. I have wondered for years about the question of whether the circumstances of our lives are preplanned and if there are agreements or contracts between souls prior to incarnation. This book offered me an elegant explanation of why human challenges might exist. I feel I have stumbled onto a possible profound truth, and I can sense my mind expanding. I think that now an important piece of the spiritual puzzle I'm trying to construct may have fallen into place. Am I ready to completely believe it? I am ready to ponder it, to hold it up, and weigh it—but it's clear that these ideas resonate with me on some deep level.

The author worked with several gifted mediums channeling guides who accessed the Akashic records. In the chapter I focused on, the author and medium were talking to an alcoholic, Pat. The medium, Staci, could see the karmic lessons he had chosen to work on in this incarnation.

Staci got information about Pat's pre-birth planning session. In this session, agreements were made with others who would walk the lifetime journey together. In these relationships, there is a great deal of love at the soul level.

Staci tells Pat he drank to cover up anger and fear, and she brought up reasons in his current and past lives why this was so. Pat had planned not only the alcoholism but also to overcome the challenge and become sober. Pat chose his family members. He planned the life experiences that would set up the alcoholism and then lead him back to a connection with God, with his own divine nature. Alcoholism was his road to discovery, and it was his choice.

In the session with Pat, the author talked about free will. Pat could have chosen never to drink, but a choice for a less painful life would have led to less growth. I was fascinated thinking of the millions of recovering alcoholics who viewed their drinking with self-loathing. If you looked at it from the larger perspective of many lives, what if their addiction in one life had accelerated their spiritual growth? I also read with great interest about the family members in Pat's life and what their role had been; did they choose to have an alcoholic husband and father? In each case, the family member interacts with Pat and agrees to play a role in Pat's life. The book details the different family members coming in to say what their roles are for Pat and mentions their own upcoming choices and lessons: for example, learning shades of gray, learning balance, and learning to stay focused.

I focus on the notion of *choices*. This dovetails perfectly with my questions about free will. So, maybe it is true that a person does make free will choices in life, but there is a roadmap that has been outlined with choice points along the way. I read somewhere that we are completely responsible for our present condition, and we will have exactly the future that we are now creating. That it isn't about chance or luck; our decisions are freely arrived at. We may be dealt a particular hand, but we are free to play the hand in a number of ways; we always have the opportunity to make a choice.

September 25

Good workouts today. I am studying practical Italian like food and directions because that's what I think we will need on our trip.

I am reading more of *Your Soul's Plan*. I haven't talked to Rich about it yet; I am still digesting this new paradigm. I am devouring the other chapters, and I can feel my horizons expand as I consider the chosen life challenges that are featured in this book: physical illness, parenting disabled children, deafness and blindness, the death of a loved one, and accidents. And he wrote another book as well, which I have downloaded for the trip.

This book inspires me to think. We are not our physical bodies; we are eternal. Everything has a higher meaning. Maybe there is a blueprint for our lives, and surrendering to whatever the plan is may bring the most profound learning of all. Maybe there *is* a divine order to life—a reason we are here and a plan for our lives that will help us remember who we really are. As I write these words, I realize these are some of the things I have heard in metaphysical feedback, but "discovering" these truths for myself helps the lessons really sink in.

This takes me back to the four soul questions I learned when I got my own mantra. Who am I? What do I want? What is my purpose? What am I grateful for?

Because these four questions seem foundational, it makes me feel even more compelled to now study more about the belief system of Vedanta. Part of me is afraid to continue to explore. Now that I have found a few tentative "footholds" of resonance like reincarnation and the notion that our lives have a certain destiny, I am afraid to shatter them with conflicting evidence. I will keep going because I now really believe I am supposed to be on this vision quest.

I also continue to wonder about the presences that sometimes seem to come to me now. Who or what are they? Guides? My guardian angel? My true self? My soul? Some other inner guru? What do the Vedas say? I don't know. Certainly, the idea of "true self" must be part of Vedanta because Deepak talks about the true self often in the meditation series. I realize that my deepest desire may be to learn why I am here and to serve in a way that fulfills my purpose in life.

As so often happens now, the Oprah and Deepak meditation of the day completely dovetails with the question that is bubbling up in my mind at that moment going in to the meditation. It's almost eerie. But I will choose to think of it as the Universe sending me a message right when I need to hear it.

Oprah starts out by reading a quote from the author Sue Monk Kidd who said, "The true self is not our creation but God's. It is the self we are in our depths. It is our capacity for divinity and transcendence."

Oprah goes on to explain that it is our choice to connect with this awareness—this cosmic energy force—or not. It is always there waiting for us to tune in and connect. The more we allow the energy of our true self to rise up, the more attuned we will be to our life's divine plan.

Deepak says, "Your true self wants to see you expand, thrive and grow every day. To have this in your life, you must first desire it. Once you consciously connect with cosmic intelligence, your desires will be fulfilled at exactly the right time and place. Your needs will be supported by the universe. This is one of the great secrets of the world's wisdom traditions."

September 26

Chip is growing so much every day; I wonder if he will look different when we get home. I will miss the dogs very much, but I'm excited to go on our trip. This is the longest time we will have ever been away. I am glad Gus will be safe in rehab while we are gone. We had family therapy with her again today; it was gut-wrenching to see her struggle so hard.

I am ready to start studying Vedanta. I found a wonderful teacher to follow: Pandit Vamadeva Shastri (Dr. David Frawley) who some say is the best Vedic scholar, or *acharya,* in the West. He teaches internationally and at the Chopra Center. I need certain texts. I already have several of these (though I have not read them yet), and so this seems like a synchronicity (or at least a confirmation that I am on the right path).

The Vedas

The Vedas are the oldest Hindu scriptures, prayers, verses, texts, and hymns of the ancient Himalayan Rishis from more than 5,000 years ago. Most important of the Vedas is the Rigveda, which is the largest and oldest of the Vedas.

The Upanishads

The Upanishads largely consist of a collection of dialogues and teachings from great Vedic sages some centuries before the time of the Buddha. The term Upanishad refers to "sitting near the teacher," or dwelling in the presence of the inner self. They are famous for directing us to ask the fundamental questions of life, such as, Who am I? What is God? and How can we go beyond all sorrow?

Bhagavad Gita

The *Bhagavad Gita* consists of the dialogue between Lord Krishna and his friend Arjuna on the core issues of life. Each chapter of the Gita reflects different yogic teachings. The Gita teaches us to follow our dharma in life regardless of outer circumstances and challenges. It shows that life is a battle for the light, and we must be firm in our motivations, convictions, and intentions to find the truth.

The Yoga Sutras

The Yoga Sutras are a compilation of short axioms, called sutras, on yogic teachings by the sage, Patanjali. The Yoga Sutras is the main authoritative textbook of Yoga Darshana, or the "yoga school of Vedic philosophy." The sutras are required reading for many yoga training programs and provide a great deal of knowledge on meditation and samadhi as well.

Shankara's Crest Jewel of Discrimination

This is a text from around 1,500 years ago by the great teacher Shankara. I have heard Deepak call Shankara the greatest of all the yoga teachers. The *Crest Jewel of Discrimination* is written entirely in verse. I have a translation by Swami Prabhavananda and Christopher Isherwood.

September 27

In my meditations today, the dogs got very quiet, and even Chip was still during almost the whole afternoon meditation. I did not quite get to thirty minutes because he got restless at the very end, but it was still peaceful.

I am excited about my next subject of study: Vedanta. I can't wait to get to it. I realize my brain travels with me, so I can keep reading and thinking while I am gone.

I am packed. Miraculously I fit everything in one bag; a black-and-white wardrobe with pops of color and my biking clothes.

Today I was thinking about karma and getting excited to learn even more about this concept that I have misunderstood all my life. When Rich is at the dog poop box by the pond, he pulls an edge of the green complimentary sack out of its little holder for the next person because it's time-consuming to find the edge—kind of like finding the edge of Saran wrap. And he says "See, Bella, this is good karma. We're leaving the poop box better than we found it."

Some people describe karma as "cosmic debt." It has also been described as a lack of balanced experiences. *Your Soul's Plan* references karma, describing, for instance, a life where you are a now a caregiver for a person with a physical disability, and maybe in a prior life, you had a physical disability and the person you care for cared for you.

Or if you abandoned someone in a lifetime, then you restore balance by experiencing abandonment. So, along this line of thinking, karma is not necessarily balanced by "doing good" for someone else. Maybe it's about what you experience yourself. I've heard Deepak say we can get addicted to trying to focus on good karma.

And there also seems to be a distinction between balancing and burning or releasing karma. Karma is balanced when the soul has experienced the full perspective of an issue—all sides. Karma is released or "burned" when the underlying causes of the original imbalance are resolved.

Because, this thinking goes—until you heal the issues that are underlying the karma, you can create new karma even after the original karma was balanced. OK; I am intrigued and can't wait to learn more.

September 28

Chip is a chewing nightmare. It's like he is part goat. We keep him on the indoor leash tied to our belt when he is not crated. It doesn't matter. He sneakily finds and chews everything from paper towels, Kleenex, napkins, or newspapers he finds in the trash. He chewed paper money out of Rich's wallet as well as the money clip itself; my Kindle charger; (the cord *and* the part you plug into the Kindle). He chews our wooden stairs, pens, bracelets, napkin rings, spoons, water bottles, Rich's glasses, coasters, rocks, sticks, the plastic covers on the sprinkler system, the metal legs of the table, my hair ties, panties, and headbands. If my back is turned for ten seconds, he has something in his mouth for sure. He lets me pry his jaws open and take out the "prize," but he always seems sad to let it go.

Mary told us "he likes rocks," but I didn't imagine he would take a rock the size of a hot stone massage and pick it up and chew it; he even chewed and carried around a six-pound weight from the gym.

As I read blogs about puppy-raising, it makes me feel ashamed that we "allow" him to get all of these items but even if you are really, really, really paying attention and then take one tiny break to take a phone call, all chaos breaks loose. Thank goodness for meditation where I can crate him or know that the delta or gamma or theta waves I am producing make him nod off.

I have long suspected that my even-tempered, balanced temperament that the world seems to see is veneer for an enraged, frustrated bitchiness that bubbles up when he does something really bad, and it scares me but kind of amazes me, too. Like maybe I *am* capable of a broad range of emotions.

Today I spent hours researching the concept of karma. Karma is an Eastern concept based on the Eastern belief of reincarnation.

Karma means action, or the energy created from an action. Energy is neither good nor bad—so karma is also neutral.

Maharishi Mahesh Yogi said, "Everything is set, but everything can be changed."

There are three types of karma:

1. Prarabda Karma, which we are processing during this lifetime
2. Sanjita Karma, which is added karma we are storing to be dealt with at some later time
3. The new karma we are creating every moment

Interestingly, in some of my research there was a mention of a contract. Vedanta teaches that between human incarnations, the soul rests in the astral plane. When the soul is ready to reincarnate and work through some of its karma, a contract is agreed upon and two other souls agree to be its parents. As the incarnation begins at birth, the contract is activated.

The seeds of the karma exist and must be released, but through our choices, we can minimize its effects in our lives.

This takes me back to the notion that we plan our lives. It follows that all of the situations in life and everyone we meet are as a result of our karma. We have, on a cosmic level, asked for situations to enable us to release that karma.

If we struggle against situations, it makes me wonder if we recreate exactly the same karma over again by our attitude.

This makes me think about forgiveness, acceptance and gratitude. If everything is a release of the karma we asked to experience, we should be grateful for everything in our lives.

I also read with interest about the new karma we generate. We create karma with every action, word, and thought in our lives.

By living consciously, we can minimize new karma which will have to be released at some later date.

I also read that meditation is the single most powerful tool we have when addressing karma. I want to understand more about this.

September 29

We took Chip and Bella to the kennel this afternoon before we flew out. I sent all of our area rugs out to be deep cleaned, and we have scheduled deep cleaning for all the hardwood floors while we are gone. It will be good to come back to a sanitized home. Hopefully Chip will be even more house-broken when we return.

We are now in flight and I am ready to think about some core teachings of Vedanta. I am seeing if I can grasp each idea conceptually.

Core Teachings of the Upanishads

I am Brahman (*aham brahmasmi*)—The self within me is the same as the self within God.

Everything is Brahman (*sarvam khalvidam brahma*). Everything we see is pure consciousness in manifestation.

The self is Brahman (*ayam atma brahma*)—the principle of self-being in the universe is God or the divine presence.

Thou art that (*tat tvam asi*)—You in your true nature are that as the cosmic reality.

Om is the entire universe (*sarvam omkaram eva*)—The entire universe is rooted in and comprehended by pranava, or primordial sound.

The Upanishads were created from dialogues between the great gurus and their disciples, and dialogues among the gurus themselves. The ancient teachers encouraged their students to take nothing on faith and to question everything. They examined questions including Who am I? What is the meaning of life? What is the one thing being known, through which everything is known? What in us endures death, and What is the ultimate reality?

They looked for the answers to these questions through inner observation and meditation.

The Upanishads teach the way of self-inquiry, self-knowledge, and self-realization. They guide us to go beyond our conditioned mind, with its many opinions and beliefs, and experience our true self, which is pure presence and pure consciousness. They also show us how our true self is reflected in the entire universe. The Upanishads are practical, systematic teachings that aim to help us develop concentration, discrimination, and detachment.

The Upanishads and the wisdom of Vedanta are the foundation of the Primordial Sound Meditation practice, the practice where I learned my own mantra, which offers a way to open to the infinity within and around us. The goal is to develop meditation as a practice of self-inquiry and as a path for cultivating direct knowledge and awakening to your inner self. This is about cultivating direct knowing through meditation. I like this much more than accepting some other person's teachings.

Get direct experience for yourself. They don't say "believe this." They say, "If you do this, this, and this, you can confirm it for yourself."

September 30

We arrived in London early; we had a massive tailwind, and the flight arrived about 6:30 this morning. It is a pretty day here, in the sixties and partly cloudy.

We got through immigration quickly. Our hotel is in Covent Garden. Our room wasn't ready, but a slightly upgraded room was; we took it and laughed because though very nice, it is so small we can't unpack. I would hate to see the smaller room we were supposed to have.

We took a long walk up and down the Thames, saw Parliament, Big Ben, and the London Eye. We came back and had a small nap and then went to lunch in Covent Garden. Today all we want to do is get on the right time zone. So, an easy day.

Rich had never been to Covent Garden's central square before. It was fun going together to see the marketplace and all the street performers and food stalls.

We loved meandering down side streets with cheese shops, pubs, and art galleries and walked to charming Neal's Yard this afternoon where we got a healthy green juice. Later we had dinner at a restaurant in the theater district. We walked Waterloo Bridge after dinner to see London lit up after dark, gorgeous and memorable. We took a lot of photos.

This is the first time we have been to London for pleasure. Rich has a great sense of history, so London is particularly meaningful for him. He knows a great deal about European history especially the two World Wars.

I imagine lively medieval London as we walk the streets, with markets and horse racing, dancing in the open spaces at festivals, and archery, wrestling, and sword fights.

I think about friars preaching, public executions, and how cruel life was in many ways in the thirteenth and fourteenth centuries. In medieval London, streets were sometimes named after the trades carried on there. Bakers lived on Bread Street. Cows were kept in Milk Street.

In 1381, in the Peasants Revolt, the rebels broke into the Tower of London and killed the Archbishop of Canterbury and other royal officials. At least a third of the population died when the Black Death struck in 1348–49. Peeking into a side street, sitting in a pub, strolling along the Thames, the history washes over us.

Chapter Four
October

October brings a trip Rich and I have dreamed about for many years. On the trip to London, Paris, Rome, Tuscany, Umbria and Barcelona I experience wonder, pleasure, incredible food and wine, soul-filling views, and time with great friends. I also study ancient Vedanta texts, which makes the experience even richer, more meaningful and memorable. Returning home, Rich and I take care of Raleigh, rejoice in being back with the pack, and I explore Buddhism. At the end of the month, Gussie returns home from rehab and has a difficult time.

October 1

You are what your deep, driving desire is.
As your desire is, so is your will. As your will is, so is your deed.
As your deed is, so is your destiny.
[Brihadaranyaka IV.4.5]

I am savoring the Upanishads. It is not lost on me that traveling and exploring are metaphors for desiring to understand. The desire to see what else is out there—to explore not just new countries but consciousness itself. The desire to prove there is more to life that what we experience every day.

The Upanishads make a distinction between pleasure and joy. Pleasure, which comes mainly through the experience of the five senses, is fleeting. Joy arises from being in harmony with the creative forces of the Universe; it is more permanent and limitless. I appreciate the many pleasures I am experiencing on the trip but also realize that my deepening spiritual practice is bringing me daily joy. From joyful days, a joyful life is built.

I am grateful that Rich agreed to do the bike trip now; grateful we have the means and the time to do it. And I am struck again and again how I can immerse myself in the pleasure of mundane daily life and also feel pulled to spend more time in that expansive place beyond senses. And how time spent "away" in meditation seems to make my experiences in the world sweeter and more profound.

Heavenly sleep—over eight straight hours. We meditated, and then I worked out in the hotel gym while Rich caught up on the markets. We had a lovely breakfast and then walked for hours; eight miles so far today. One of the best stops was Fortnum & Mason, maybe my favorite store in the world. In the produce section, they had the perfect sign in the middle of the arugula

PLEASE HELP YOURSELF TO WHAT YOU FANCY,
AND WE'LL WEIGH YOUR CHOICES AT THE TILL.

In their flower market, every bloom was perfect; the display was like an artwork intricately balanced in color and proportion. The candy department featured brightly colored marzipan fruits and vegetables.

Then, we stopped for a pub lunch in Knightsbridge and loved being immersed in day-to-day London. We decided to be tourists, riding a double-decker bus and taking a boat down the Thames. On the bus, the tour guide would tell a story and explain some history and then say "Riiiight." Every sentence he ended with "right." It was so quintessentially British.

From the top of the bus, we saw the installations of red poppies falling like tears from the stonework at the Tower of London. I wanted Rich to experience a cab ride where the driver called him "Guv'ner." So, we took three rides, and finally it happened.

One last night in London. In my afternoon meditation, I fell asleep at the end, still adjusting to the time difference. We had dinner at Axis with a special bottle of Pauillac 2007 Chateau Batailley. Tomorrow we take the train to Paris.

October 2

Another nice night of sleep and a sweet meditation as the sun came up. We ran along the Thames and through Covent Garden. I had my hair blown out at a salon across the street from the hotel. I love the way they fixed it. So much better than navigating European plumbing, and we are off to Paris in an hour.

It is so wonderful to truly be on vacation, with no urgent emails, no conference calls, and no guilt or worry that I should be taking care of something. It is also so lovely to go to sleep and wake up at the same time. I particularly love our morning meditations together.

I have been studying Italian. I always think it is respectful to be able to say, "Thank you" and "Good morning" and "How are you" in the native language. I studied Mandarin and Korean and could say at least basic greetings before my Asia trips. But I realize with our upcoming stop in Paris my "direction and menu French" is a little rusty. I hope it will come back to me when I am immersed in the environment.

The Upanishads are so inspiring, poetic, and hauntingly beautiful. I feel grateful to be reading them while traveling. The feeling I get when I read them is that even if all your daily needs are more than fulfilled, there is still a hunger to seek and to know the meaning of life. This doesn't diminish the happiness of being on his long-anticipated trip; in fact, feasting on new tastes, sights, and sounds, *and* contemplating inspirational ideas make this moment unforgettable.

Take the example of a man who has everything; young,
healthy, strong, good, and cultured, with all the wealth that
earth can offer; let us take this as one measure of joy.
One hundred times that joy is the joy of the Gandharvas, but
no less joy have those who are illumined.
(Taiitiriya, The Upanishads 8.1)

October 3

He who sees all beings in his Self and his Self in all beings, he
never suffers; because when he sees all creatures within his
true Self, then jealousy, grief and hatred vanish.
(Paramananda, The Upanishads)

The train trip through the Chunnel was much faster than I imagined. The whole ride was only about two and a half hours, and we were in the Chunnel itself for only about twenty minutes.

We were seated across from a sweet elderly couple from Peru who had about a gazillion Apple devices; they each had a phone, earbuds, iPad, and a laptop. We were amazed by their many gadgets. They were probably in their late seventies. Despite our language differences, we communicated a little. I love old couples who are still obviously in love. I did my primordial sound meditation on the train, a perfect place to meditate. And I read more from The Upanishads.

The kennel sent photos and an update of progress for Chip and Bella. They are doing great. I swear it looks like Chip has grown in two days.

We went out of St. Pancras in London and came into Gare du Nord in Paris. We are staying on the left bank.

Our hotel is great in the common areas, but our room, the most expensive of the whole trip, is a matchbox. I talked to the front desk and they actually moved us to a "bigger room" but if that is true, it must be about a millimeter bigger. I thought because of the price and the great review that this would be the best hotel of the trip, but no. There is a bed and a tiny nightstand. With our two suitcases, there is no room to move except a deep window ledge that looks out over Paris. So, I stay roosted in the window when we are in the room.

At a great seafood restaurant last night, we tried to decide whether the couple at a table near us was a father and daughter or a Parisian gentleman and his mistress; we finally decided with no question: mistress.

We walked Paris, had a romantic and nostalgic lunch at Brasserie Lipp, where we have been a few times before, and then I booked a massage.

October 4

Who is better able to know God than I myself, since He resides in my heart and is the very essence of my being? Such should be the attitude of one who is seeking.
(Paramananda, The Upanishads)

We are getting ready to leave Paris and fly to Florence. Last night we walked through the streets of St. Germain and popped into galleries and fresh markets. I took several photos for painting inspiration. We walked more than ten miles yesterday. I read the Upanishads until I fell asleep. Forever in my memories, I will link the Upanishads to this trip.

This morning after meditation, we ran along the Seine before dawn and saw the streetlights flicker off. The street cleaners were out, and there were a few joggers but no big crowds.

It was a good, romantic workout. We were reminded how much we love Paris and glad we stopped here on the way to the bike trip. Last night, we had a bite to eat at an outdoor cafe near our hotel on the left bank; it was a beautiful night in the seventies. We sat next to a couple of professors from University of Oregon who are here on sabbatical. Rich was grumpy that we saw Americans, but he got over it. He always hates it when we run into Americans in foreign travel. We spent the evening talking about getting to Florence and beginning the Tuscany bike trip.

October 5

The little space within the heart is as great as the vast universe. The heavens and the earth are there, and the sun and the moon and the stars. Fire and lightening and winds are there, and all that now is and all that is not.

(Prabhavananda, The Upanishads: Breath from the Eternal)

I read the Upanishads on the flight. I kept reflecting on the parallels of reading something breathtakingly poetic while we are in beautiful, memorable places. We arrived in Florence in the evening. There was a demonstration blocking some streets, so the cab driver wasn't sure he could easily get us to the hotel, but we arrived without incident or too much delay.

Rich says this region looks like Napa Valley on steroids: rolling hills, vineyards, and beautiful scenery. Our hotel has "the best rooftop bar in Europe," overlooking the Arno river, and we got here just as the sun was setting. We sat out on the roof and had a glass of Tuscan wine to celebrate being here; it is gorgeous.

Our room is a suite; enormous, comfortable, and contemporary with a view of the Arno. We laughed because this is the best room we have had on the trip so far, and we got here late, so there is no time to luxuriate in all the space. We took a short walk through the streets around the hotel. I should have realized the restaurants would be fully booked. We ordered room service and sat by the window and looked out at the romantic river Arno and all the people walking by. We are so glad to be back in Italy.

We woke up extra early and meditated. I got a chance to lift weights in the really nice gym before we met our fellow riders and started biking to heavenly weather in Trequanda. We rode through the Appenines to tiny Montisi, where we had a rapturous lunch, which felt well-deserved after some excruciating hills.

I felt nervous riding today; there were hairpin turns with traffic, including big trucks whizzing by on what felt like very narrow lanes.

We were in the bike lane on the extreme right with sheer cliffs off the mountain right next to us. It felt like the cliff edge was only inches away. If we needed to swerve, we would be toast.

Riding hills made my lungs feel like they were on fire. We couldn't train on hills because our area of Ohio is pretty flat. So, this feels extreme. But it started getting easier after the first hour, and I began to relax on the bike.

Our lunch was in a cozy trattoria on the edge of an olive oil estate. I dawdled walking in the olive groves, just savoring their deep green leaves that look silvery in some light.

We will ride our bikes to the next chateau every day and leave our luggage for the guides to transport. It's a great way to see a lot of different places, but somewhat tricky to unpack, repack, and have our luggage ready to go before we bike. I brought my oldest bike jerseys and ancient, disintegrating workout bras and plan to just discard them along the way.

Some of the riders in this group are elite riders, and they will ride a century—100 miles each day. There are also a few people on the trip who are older than we are, and they are using e-bikes. So far, we are holding our own with the youngsters in the group, except for these couple of incredible athletes. After lunch, we had more hills, some wonderful blessed downhills, and a hotel so gorgeous I had tears in my eyes when we got to our room and opened the shutters, looking down at the green valley below. Centuries old *Locanda dell'Amorosa* in Sinalunga means "lodging of romance." We are going to be here two days. It will be nice to sleep two nights in the same bed.

At the hotel, I took a walk around the property, and I met Robert, a seventy-seven-year-old artist in residence. Through my basic Italian and him knowing some English, we managed a conversation. He knew of the art college where I am on the board. His paintings were beautiful landscapes, almost impressionistic with gorgeous yellows, oranges, blues, and greens.

Last night, we attended a little cocktail party in the hotel courtyard— great prosecco, Parmigiano-Reggiano, sausages, and prosciutto—and then a tremendous group dinner in a restored part of the hotel that was originally the stables.

Rich and I stepped away from the others for a few moments during cocktail hour and sat together on some ancient stone steps with our wine and a plate of cheese and prosciutto and savored the sweeping view looking out over the cypress trees, smelled the sweetness of the air, and listened to the bells chiming in the tower.

We had incredible food, fun company, and awesome Tuscan wines while hearing about everyone's riding experience with much good-natured complaining about the hills. Part of dinner was handmade tortellini with sage sauce—heaven—and no guilt because we had definitely worked it off.

Human beings cannot live without challenge.
We cannot live without meaning.
Everything ever achieved we owe to this inexplicable urge
to reach beyond our grasp, do the impossible, know the
unknown.
The Upanishads would say this urge is part of our evolution-
ary heritage, given to us for the ultimate adventure: to dis-
cover for certain who we are, what the universe is, and what
the significance of the brief drama of life and death is we
play out against the backdrop of eternity.
(Anonymous, The Upanishads)

October 6

Dreams are real as long as they last. Can we say more of life?
(Anonymous, The Upanishads)

This morning for breakfast there were fresh figs, sweet just-picked cherry tomatoes, sharp and creamy cheeses, and great crusty bread—fuel for today's ride, which will be through the incredibly lovely Val d'Orcia. We slept very soundly with the windows open and feel amazingly ready to ride.

We got another photo update from the kennel about the hounds; they both look happy and healthy.

We rode through rolling countryside this morning; charming villages like Borgonuovo and Farneta. In Borgonuovo, I got to exchange "buon giornos" with several ladies out for their morning walk, which I particularly loved.

The ride was long with fewer hills than yesterday but one huge one that seemed to go on forever. I kept looking up, thinking that the next hairpin turn would be the top, and maybe it was good I didn't realize that there would be about twenty of those before we got there. It was all the workout we needed.

We were thrilled to see the blue van our guides were driving and all the e-bikes that signaled we were finally at our lunch destination.

It was an incredible picnic. We parked our bikes and walked into a bountiful lunch prepared by Sara, an Italian grandma in her lovely home with a huge, lush back yard which had two enormous festive wooden tables under a grove of trees. One table had blue and white gingham table cloths with yellow plates and the other a red and white tablecloth with blue plates.

The whole bike group was there—even the century riders who had miraculously covered 100 miles while we rode sixty—and we had a fabulous party complete with music and dancing. There was a guitar player, and Sara's granddaughter sang some traditional Italian songs including "Bella Luna" and "O Sole Mio." After quite a bit of wine, we did an elaborate ring around the rosy kind of dance and a conga line in biking shoes. I love a party in the daytime.

I took some great photos of Sara proudly showing off her kitchen. The lunch was bountiful: tomatoes, peppers, eggplant, salami, prosciutto, incredible cheeses, and fresh bread with local olive oil. And of course, lots of pasta—and Sara's irresistible tiramisu.

As the wine was poured, the songs got a little saltier. It's a fun group. The short, eight-kilometer ride after the festivities was on a route with no traffic and all downhill. It is perfect weather: seventy-three degrees and sunny; if we had ordered ideal biking weather this is what it would look like. When we got back to the hotel, we took hot baths in our huge ancient tub and then sat at our open window, resting, reading, and looking out over incredible Tuscan scenery.

After a short nap with Rich, I meditated and thought about this sweet day. I love the view, fresh air, and exercise. Tonight, we went to the neighboring town of Bettole for dinner. We had incredible pasta with truffles and more Super-Tuscan wine.

More of The Upanishads until heavenly sleep.

October 7

As by knowing one tool of iron, dear one, we come to know all things made out of iron: that they differ only in name and form, while the stuff of which all are made is iron—so through that spiritual wisdom, dear one, we come to know that all of life is one.
(Eknath Easwaran, *The Upanishads: Translations from the Sanskrit*)

We had a light breakfast because we have a steep sixteen-kilometer hill climb as we begin the ride today; everyone is dreading it. Yesterday as we arrived on the long, sweeping downhill, we said, "Wow, we are so glad we are riding *down;* it would be a real bitch going *up.*" And then this morning, the guides, Po and Remi, told us we had to go up that hill to get to our route.

Everyone is saddle sore after two hard days of riding. We have had fun getting to know some of the other guests; there is a whole extended family from Canada. I got some great photos and videos of the group from our picnic yesterday: candid shots of everyone in their bike clothes singing traditional Italian songs and eating with abandon because of the calories we are burning. Today we ride to Siena.

We saw some of the most stunning scenery of the week as we pedaled through the *crete* (cray-tay), the clay hills leading northwest to

Siena. We left our bikes at an organic winery just outside of Siena and took a taxi in to town, avoiding all of the traffic.

This was our hardest day of biking yet; I burned over 1300 calories in three hours. Demanding, long hills with gorgeous scenery.

We love Siena. We are staying at the Grand Hotel Continental, where our room is big and gorgeous—about four times bigger than our room in Paris. Rich often reminds me that the power of a twenty is universal; and as soon as we checked in, I put a twenty-dollar bill in my hand and asked the concierge to find me a blow-out bar because my hair was "eesgusting," as Avery would say. Seeing the twenty, he not only found and booked one immediately, he walked me there! It was a couple blocks away. The salon was great, though strangely they were playing American Christmas music, such as "Santa Claus Is Coming to Town"; however, this might be true, as I feel like a human again.

The food shops are great, with whole salamis for sale. Street artists are everywhere. Rich got a photo of me in front of a sidewalk chalk Mona Lisa, and I got one of him in a shop with hanging salamis.

After I meditated, we had a walking tour before dinner of the city's most famous sites with a local historian; glimpsing inside Siena's striking thirteenth-century cathedral and visiting the Piazza del Campo, location of the famed Palio horse race.

We had a memorable and delicious dinner on our own at Tullio Tre Cristi in Siena. We had sea bream, pasta and salad, a wonderful Brunello, and some surprise grappa from the waiter for dessert.

It was nice to be on our own, away from the larger group. Another couple in the restaurant was celebrating an anniversary, and they brought their well-behaved dog, which made us miss Bella and Chip.

A gay couple from Wales discussed the merits of different wines in great detail with the sommelier, "We're a couple of naughty chaps and we're going to order the 2001." When the wine came, they said, "This is *much* better than the wine we had with lunch!" Ah, vacation.

More Upanishads tonight.

October 8

As rivers, flowing down, become indistinguishable on reaching the sea by giving up their names and forms,
so also the illumined soul, having become freed from name and form, reaches the self-effulgent supreme self.
(Mundaka Upanishad)

We started biking outside Siena and had a long but easier day of biking overall. There were some challenging hills, especially the last one to our lovely hotel La Fontanelle in Chianti. We rode through beautiful vineyards, saw gorgeous vistas, and went to Brolio Castle for lunch. The estate is still home to the descendants of the Baron Ricasoli, who discovered the blend of grape varietals that make up the now-famous Chianti Classico appellation. We sampled some of the reds while ravenously devouring a delicious lunch of homemade pasta with *cinghiale* (wild boar), the regional specialty.

The afternoon ride to the hotel was relatively easygoing until we got to the last monster hill.

I don't know the grade of the hill, but it was so steep it was very hard to even walk it, let alone try to do it on the bikes. The guides told us to just secure our bikes beyond the property gate, which was a quarter of the way, and walk the rest of the way up. But one of our fellow riders just left his bike abandoned in the ditch before he even got to the property gate. Later, he said he just got exhausted and couldn't push it anymore. We won't say he feels entitled. Perhaps he is enlightened.

I put my bike in the lowest gear possible and somehow, through sheer will and pasta energy, made it riding to the gate but there were moments when I felt like I wasn't making any forward progress. My quadriceps were on fire. We rested at the gate, and then, huffing and puffing, we trudged up the long, steep hill. We are delighted with the property. The sweeping views of the green valley below are incredible. Once we got to our room, we got out of our wet bike clothes, put on our swimming suits, and jumped in the pool.

Later, when Ian and Matt, the two elite riders, ended their century ride, they raced their bikes up that incredibly steep hill. They had to walk for a bit but got on their bikes and finished together, clasping hands at the finish line. They are amazing athletes and fun to watch. The rest of us waited with cold beers for them.

Rich and I both love great food and often relive our food memories. We had a glass of wine and a lively discussion full of laughter poolside as we remembered each meal we have had on the trip and tried to top each other's descriptive words for rapture at a meal.

This requires the use of all our senses: appearance, texture, smell, and taste. Rich calls the appearance of a plate "Vitamin I" (vitamin eye). Presentation is important to him. He says the appearance of food is everything because we all eat with our eyes.

We test out the expansion of our food description capability:

"Ambrosial epicurean delight"
"A savory spread"
Our Canadian friends come over to chime in:
"Toothsome, divine, tempting, lip-smacking"
"Tantalizing, luscious"
"Briny, piquant, celestial"
"Flavorful, tangy, herb-scented, spicy"

Then we get into a discussion about the wines and beers we have tasted: "Full-bodied, heady, lusty, mellow"
"Redolent, rich, strong, well-matured"
"Honeyed, succulent, thirst-quenching"
"Lush, opulent, sumptuous, luxurious"
"Nectarous, peppery, pungent, tasty, yummy"
"Is nectarous a word?"
"It is in Canada!"

Tonight, we regrouped for dinner at the hotel's restaurant overlooking the extraordinary Tuscan countryside and continued the sensual foodie discussion. Our new shared vocabulary and fragments of foodie descriptors could be heard in the midst of other conversations: mouthwatering zucchini flan, savory pecorino cheese fondue, earthy summer black truffle, briny Sicilian red king prawn carpaccio with citrusy orange sauce.

I had fresh baby arugula salad, a *kamut* linguine pasta with scampi, breadcrumbs with dried tomatoes and basil and, for the main course, sea bass fillet confit with sautéed spinach and baby squid, tomatoes, and black olives. And lemon sorbet for dessert.

I am so glad my meditation teacher said that no lifestyle changes were needed as I began my deeper meditation experience. I would hate to give up my foodie passions, and I have now started to silently take a moment and bless my food at every meal. This food is worthy of blessing, for certain.

October 9

From food are made all bodies
which become food again for others after death.
Food is the most important of all things for the body; there-
fore it is the best medicine for all the body's ailments.
They who look upon food as the Lord's gift shall never lack
life's physical comforts.
From food are made all bodies.
All bodies feed on food, and it feeds on all bodies.
(Taiitiriya, The Upanishads 2.1)

After that fun dinner, camaraderie, laughter, and a nice night of sleep, we are ready for our last day of biking. The trip has gone by quickly. We are saddle sore, physically tired in our quads and hamstrings, and not sure how much we will be able to do today.

We laugh because Rich did not realize until yesterday that he had one lower granny gear after all this mountain riding, so he will probably find it much easier today.

At one point yesterday, my heart rate monitor showed my heart rate at 223; that had to be an error, but there is no doubt that these are *hard* workouts. We are so happy we did this trip before we got any older; it is really challenging. We were looking enviously at the few people on the trip, who used e-bikes with a motor. They would zoom by us as we struggled up hills and say, "You're doing great; see you at the top!" Using e-bikes is not a bad thing to consider as we age.

Today is a loop ride described in the route notes as the "rolling" hills of Chianti. They say "rolling," which is code for "steep as freaking hell."

The towns around Chianti are shady with wooded groves and hilltop vineyards with lovely views of the valleys below. We stopped a lot to take photos, wanting to remember the views. We visited the well-known villages of Gaiole and Radda, both postcard-picturesque.

I got lost from the group in Gaiole. I was having trouble reading the road signs, given my blurry vision, and I missed a turn. So, it took a few kilometers to find them again, and I had to bike through the busy business district full of traffic that the group had bypassed. Rich was waiting for me at a coffee bar. The locals helped me, seeming to like that I was trying to speak Italian. With a few "*grazie mille*" I was back on track.

I made a big cultural mistake in Radda. I actually know better, but somehow, I forgot my training. There was a huge farmer's market bursting with fresh produce displayed in colorful rows, and I wanted some cherry tomatoes. The protocol is to wait your turn until the market owner notices you and then point out the produce you want without touching it. They put on disposable gloves and pick it out for you, bag it up, weigh it, and then tell you the cost. As I was pointing out the tomatoes I wanted, I mistakenly actually touched one and got a very heated scolding. I apologized profusely (*Mi dispiaci*!) and felt like an ugly American.

We decided not to eat in Radda but to ride all the way back to the villa and have a late lunch outside on the patio by ourselves. We wanted to enjoy the last beautiful afternoon of this part of the trip and have some time with just us. Lunch was incredible. I had a prawn salad, and Rich had a local fish. They brought out olives, crusty bread, and creamy, salty butter with our just-picked salads. We drank a crisp, nap-inducing white wine.

We talked about how amazing it is that we finally got to be on this much-dreamed-about bike trip while looking out over the expansive green valley of cypress trees, olive groves, and vine-covered hillsides. Mostly, we were thrilled to have made it through the steepest challenges and proud of ourselves for hanging in there.

Tonight, we went to a private tasting and dinner in one of the region's top wineries, complete with a million euro-view across the Chianti landscape.

I was cranky. We had a lovely nap, and then I tried to wash and dry my hair because it was a dress-up night. The hardest thing about a trip like this is hair. The shower was just a head you use while sitting in the bathtub. I'm sure there is an effective way to wash hair, but I have not learned it. The hairdryer blew only a tiny puff of air, and it was connected to the wall in a way that made it hard to maneuver. It took about an hour to get ready, put makeup on, and find the least-wrinkled dressy thing to wear.

My introversion caught up with me, and I begged Rich to blow off the dinner. "Rich, I have peep overload; please let's not go and just stay here by ourselves tonight."

"Babe, come on. We have to go. It's the last night and special for the group."

"We have seen a gazillion freaking wineries, and we know how wine is made. I can't take one more winery tour!"

Rich finally talked me off the ledge. I did a twenty-minute meditation and then was in a much better state of mind. And, okay; he was right. It was a very nice, fun, and memorable evening.

October 10

We left La Fontenelle at about 9 o'clock to get to the Florence station in time for our train to Rome.

I talked to a couple of our new friends, and we decided on 10 percent of the cost of the trip for a tip for our guides and hoped that was right. So, we put it in an envelope and gave it to the guys as we got on the bus.

We almost missed our train. After our driver maneuvered around two roundabout wrecks and got a little lost, we ended up sprinting through the terminal and jumped on board as the train pulled out like something from a movie. One last workout in Tuscany! Because of the mad rush at the end, we didn't get to say a real goodbye to our new friends.

Thank goodness, we only had one bag apiece and that I had on flats, or there would have been no way we would have made it. We enjoyed the peaceful train ride to Rome, which gave me a chance to study and meditate.

We checked into our hotel in Rome, and Rich was giving me the evil eye as we waited in line. I could tell what he was thinking: this is a *tourist* hotel! I hate it! It was his turn to be cranky.

Soon his mood improved because we got an upgrade to an awesome, expanded room with an amazing wide terrace with views over Rome. We had so much fun on our balcony, overlooking a pool of tan smoking Italians. There is a kickass gym and spa, complete with steam, cold plunge pool, and hot tub. We are both fighting the sniffles, and so we spent an hour in the sun, knowing that rain is coming tomorrow.

After the pool, we went to the steam, cold pool and hot tub. It was so fun because there were lots of Italians in the baths down in a blue grotto-type cave below the gym. We laughed because we were in Roman baths in Rome with Romans.

The baths were coed. There was one heavy-set cranky, loud baggy bathing-suited grandma who scolded her skinny, handsome grandsons who were wearing speedos. And she complained dramatically to her husband with many hand gestures, including pointing fingers and swearing, which we loved. We love to observe a little human drama when it's not directed at us.

We could actually stand up in our shower, which had an actual installed shower head with great water pressure—and a *real* hair dryer that actually worked.

I had a headache and no aspirin, so I walked to a pharmacy a few blocks away and had an engaging conversation with two pharmacists who were intent on giving me exactly the right medicine.

I said, "*Buona sera, ho mal di testa.*" This spurred such a rapid reply I had no idea what was said. Then I finally figured out through hand gestures and them speaking very slowly that they were asking if it was a big headache or a small headache. I imagine a big headache would be a migraine, so I said, "*Mal di testa piccola.*" Ah! Si, si. So, I got my aspirin, but most importantly, felt like I had a successful conversation in Italian.

I made an amazing discovery today. The eczema that has plagued me for several months is completely gone. No bumpy rash. No itching. It's amazing. It must be a combination of the relaxation, fun, sun and the olive oil. Rich teases me and says, "Maybe it's the wine?"

I ask him, "How will we survive when we get back to reality and don't have wine with lunch?"

We sat in bed together with our laptops. I did some more research about The Upanishads and their place in philosophy. I found a source online: http://oll.libertyfund.org/pages/upanishads-and-philosophy.

"In these ancient documents are found the earliest serious attempts at construing the world of experience as a rational whole. Not only have they been of historical importance in the past development of philosophy in India, but they are of present-day influence. 'To every

Indian Brahman today the Upanishads are what the New Testament is to the Christian.'

"In the case of Arthur Schopenhauer, the chief of modern pantheists of the West, his philosophy is unmistakably transfused with the doctrines expounded in the Upanishads, a fact that might be surmised from his oft-quoted eulogy: 'It is the most rewarding and the most elevating reading which there can possibly be in the world. It has been the solace of my life and will be of my death.'"

October 11

After meditation, a workout, and breakfast, we went to the Rome airport to meet our friends, Tom and Abigail, and another couple, Mike and Paula, to travel to Umbria to the villa we are renting. Our driver/guide, Francis, is fluent in Italian.

A hurricane has blown in offshore, so it is rainy. At the airport, I had time to read about the Rig Veda while we waited. I pulled up Wikipedia and learned that the Rig Veda, a collection of Vedic Sanskrit hymns, is counted among the four Hindu religious texts known as the Vedas. Likely composed between 1700–1100 BCE, it is one of the oldest texts of any Indo-Iranian language. Preserved over centuries by oral tradition alone it was probably not put in writing before the Early Middle Ages.

We found our friends easily right outside customs and knew it would be a great week when our guide, Francis, greeted us; he seemed confident, competent, cheerful, and very knowledgeable.

Francis took us to some of the major attractions of Rome, including looking through the keyhole of a nondescript door on the Aventine Hill, neatly placing the dome of St. Peter's right in the center. It was pouring, but we all gamely got out and peered through the keyhole.

We had lunch in a tiny panini take-out restaurant on a crowded street where we had to take a number, like in a deli. I ordered a panino for each of us (pointing to each and saying: "*Questo panino, per favore*").

On the ride to the villa everyone else was drowsy. So, I talked to Francis who was driving. He is fascinating as well as happy, charming and handsome. So, talking to him was not tough duty. He was born and raised in Africa, speaks five languages fluently, and does the tour guide thing for a week or so at a time and then rejoins his family.

He loves to learn and knows a lot about history. He is very familiar with Italy but says he studies every night to familiarize himself with facts and details as he prepares to help people get the most out of their visits.

We got to the villa about 4:30 in hard rain. The villa was built in 1033; in lovely Benano. I marvel that we are staying in a place that was constructed before the Middle Ages and imagine that this was about the time that the Rig Veda was finally put in writing.

Rocca di Benano is the official name of the villa. It has stone walls, terra cotta floors, and hand-hewn wooden beams. It is a four-story villa with five stunning bedrooms, a fully-equipped kitchen, and a living room with a wood-burning stove.

Abigail found the villa and made all the arrangements in advance. Alex, the houseman, was there to greet us. Francis, familiar with the villa, got everyone settled in.

We chose a twin bedroom at the base of the house because there is a big functional shower and a laundry room. I am almost giddy at the thought of doing laundry and having clean clothes again. There are big yellow-ochre terra cotta tiles on the floor and colorful throw rugs. Outside our room is a kind of office area which leads out to the patio.

Tom and Abigail have a pretty room and bathroom up a level, and Paula and Mike have a great bed and bath on the level above that. Francis is in the bedroom at the top of the villa. So, we all have private space.

A lively chef named Simona came to cook for us; she made tomato bruschetta for an appetizer, local sausage in grape sauce in an ancient grain pasta; with a delicious simple salad and limoncello cake for dessert.

We all agreed to make it an early evening.

October 12

After we meditated this morning, Rich wanted to sleep a little more. I got up and made coffee for everyone. I began to dive into the Rig Veda; it's huge! Rich got up, and we went for a hilly run where we had a view looking down at the villa from the road above. As the sun was rising, we looked back and saw the whole expanse; it is enormous; like a whole village contained in one building. We could see that our big villa was just one of many apartments in the massive edifice, and from that view, we could see the layout and all the different residences throughout.

We saw meadows full of sheep with one wearing a cowbell in each pasture, the shepherding dogs keeping them in line. We jogged along the rutted path looking at the cobalt sky and thinking that there is nothing in our sight that gives us a clue what century we are in; we could be time travelers back to the Middle Ages.

The air smells so sweet. We realized we were starving and turned back.

Francis made us all breakfast. He is a treasure. We decided to explore some towns nearby and went first to Civita, which is an artist's dream with steep, narrow streets and alleys washed in history; each footpath, carved door and staircase is a feast for the eyes, with lush rosemary growing in pots, ivy draped over arches and climbing up walls, and potted flowers on balconies and windowsills.

We next go to Bagnoregio, another ancient Etruscan city that is decaying. The main entrance is a huge stone passageway, cut by the Etruscans 2,500 years ago. Rebuilt in medieval times, it feels enchanted. The complete absence of cars makes it easy to imagine walking through the portal and going back in time.

Then we drove to Orvieto. Francis explained some of the history. Populated since Etruscan times, Orvieto was annexed by Rome in the third century BC. Because of its site on a high, steep bluff, the city was virtually impregnable. It was last conquered by Julius Caesar. Three papal palaces had been built there.

We saw the *Duomo* in Orvieto that was built from the thirteenth to the seventeenth century. It is massive and elegant with deep blue and white marble laid in horizontal stripes across the walls. The cathedral is slender with incredible artworks on the front and inside.

I remember Ken Follett's *Pillars of the Earth* where a master builder painstakingly plans how to build a cathedral and solves the architectural and building complications of erecting such a tall structure without modern cranes. I have reverence for the design, the effort, the financial obligations, and the continuity that is needed when a structure takes centuries to build.

I loved the large rose window (a gorgeous example of sacred geometry) and three huge bronze doors. I was enjoying the history and ancient artworks and was ready to hang in for a long tour of the cathedral if everyone was up for it, but I could sense the mood shift in a different direction—lunch.

I love Abigail; she is one of my most favorite people. She is slender and tiny, barely five feet tall, but she can pack away the food. And she savors every morsel like me and takes photos of food.

Our two new friends, Paula and Mike, were the same way. They are well-read, thoughtful foodies who are compassionate, interesting people who have dedicated their lives to helping others: so good. We had bread and olive oil and two pizzas before we even had our main course. I had pasta (*umbricelli*) with wild boar.

I'm not allowing myself to focus on the calories I am consuming. Last week we worked it off with the intense biking; I don't see that happening this week.

After the drive back to the villa, we took a long walk and a nap, and then Rich and I meditated. Then we drove back up the steep cliffs of Orvieto and went to dinner at Le Grotto del Funaro in a medieval grotto in the center of Orvieto, a cheery, casual, elegant place specializing in pasta with *tartufo* (Abigail's Umbrian go-to meal) sausages, *salumi*, bruschetta, and polenta made with gorgonzola cheese and prosciutto. I had mussels, which were delicious. Francis navigated our van through amazingly narrow streets as we held our breath.

It's fun getting to know Mike and Paula. They are funny, liberal, and very much in love. Mike keeps saying "I love my wife" and throwing his arms around her. It might have a little to do with the wine consumption.

Tonight, I found the Gayatri Mantra, which is the most important hymn in the Rig Veda. It is captivating.

The Gayatri mantra occupies a unique place in Hindu tradition, due to the fact that it has both the power of *prarthana* (prayer) and of mantra. It was written in Sanskrit about 2,500 to 3,500 years ago, and this powerful mantra may have been recited by sages for many centuries before that. The mantra is chanted by a spiritual devotee to remember the higher purpose of life, and it can also be a prayer to the Supreme God to lift our consciousness upwards. Gayatri is seen as a divine awakening of the individual soul. Simply loving the essence of this mantra is believed by many to be one of the fastest ways to touch and experience God.

I then went on iTunes, found a recording of the Gayatri Mantra in Sanskrit, and downloaded it. I played it over and over to start to memorize it. And now forever, Benano and this part of the trip will be associated in my mind with this beautiful Sanskrit chant.

October 13

We ran intervals with Francis this morning. He is much younger but kindly ran with us at our pace.

After another great breakfast, we drove to Bagno Vignoni to thermal waters that have been used since Roman times. At the heart of the village is the sixteenth-century "square of sources," a huge rectangular tank that contains the original source of water that comes from the subterranean aquifer of volcanic origins. We took off our shoes and soaked our feet in the warm running stream.

Then we went to Montechiello and had an amazing lunch at Osteria La Porta, a restaurant just at the village gate on a balcony where Francis proposed to his wife.

Abigail (OK, all of us) got shushed by another table as we got louder. That was after we discovered how much we loved the Bramito Umbrian chardonnay; Paula and Rich, who are the white wine experts, gave it two thumbs up.

I had an incredible vegetable stew. It had chunky, tender carrots, spinach, kale, mushrooms, onions and a hearty tomato broth, followed by pasta, fish, and wine.

Francis then drove us to Pienza, which stands high atop a hill, dominating all the Orcia Valley with extraordinary views. He told us that this charming village was transformed into what was widely considered the "ideal city of the Renaissance." Street performers and musicians made the town memorable. As Francis told us the history of Pienza, Abigail asked, "Isn't this the city of *cheese*?" The pecorino of Pienza is cheese made from sheep's milk, renowned worldwide and delicious, which can go from a delicate flavor to tangy, based on how aged it is.

The streets are full of charming shops selling various types of pecorino, spices, *pici* (handmade pasta), and sausages. We visited Francis's favorite: a fragrant and busy shop. Even though we protested that we could not eat one more thing, we sampled many selections of different ages of pecorino and salami and bought some to take back to the villa.

October 14

After meditation, Rich, Francis, and I went out for a jog and got drenched. No problem—we have an actual shower and blow dryer!

We had lunch in Lago di Bolsena, looking out over the water, then drove to Torre Alfina to visit a beautiful castle. We walked through the town and had coffee and gelato. It was fun to be there and watch "real Italian village life": playing cards, arguing politics, and drinking coffee. I bought a local newspaper to practice reading Italian.

I feel content hanging out in a coffee bar and listening to locals or wandering through a town and imagining living there. I would rather do that than see many of the tourist sites. I know Rich is the same way, and so is Abigail. But we don't want to disappoint Francis, and so we do some of both.

We had dinner in Orvieto at Numero Uno, and we had incredible four types of crostini and pasta after they brought out mounds of veggies cut in spirals.

We all shared. Someone ordered *cinghiale all'arancia*, which was luscious and juicy. Of course, Abigail had pasta with truffles. The desserts, tiramisu and a ricotta and almond dish, were *so* good.

I got a message from Bethany: "All is well with Gussie." I am grateful for the message; she is always on my mind.

October 15

We were in Assisi all the next day. A beautiful village, of course linked to St. Francis, with festive red flags hanging from the stone walls. We teased Francis that this was his city.

Assisi was hit by two devastating earthquakes in 1997. Francis said the restoration has been remarkable.

Rich was the tune master on the way. We brought the iPad, connected it to the stereo, and sang songs in the van, taking requests and alternating between current hits, Italian songs, and seventies hits.

The duomos were many and varied, dominated by two medieval castles.

We went to Saint Mary of the Angels cathedral and the cathedral of St. Claire. Francis was leading us to the next one, and Tom said, "OK, Francis, we've seen a lot of churches. Let's take a break." We ate lunch at a little sandwich shop as the rain poured and then went to the cathedral of St. Francis of Asissi.

We have been stopping at the main supermarket nearly every day. I could spend the day watching Italians in their natural habitat, so I always volunteer to go to the store.

Today, I made another produce error. Francis had explained to us that before you touch the produce, you must put on disposable gloves they have hanging from little stands. So, I faithfully did that and marked the bag with the correct code as Francis had taught me. But I did not weigh and tag the bananas in the department. Somehow, I assumed bananas would be exempt. There was a huge line behind us as we checked out, so the people behind had to wait while the checker went back to the department to weigh the bananas. I turned to the people behind us, held my hands in prayer position, and said a heartfelt, "*Mi dispiace.*"

We cooked at the villa that night and made Abigail, Paula, and Jane pasta from ingredients we had on hand in the villa. Tom baked a juicy, moist, tender chicken—perfecto! It is so nice to just take it easy with good friends.

October 16

I have gotten up early the past two mornings after meditation, and it has been great to study a bit and look out over the valley as the sun comes up.

After a walk and breakfast, we got in the car and stopped in Allerona and walked up several hilly streets to search for a store that was open. We needed Bramito! We finally found a store that was open. They had it! Tom made a profound observation: "The reason there are no fat people in Italy is because they have to walk up all these fucking hills."

We took a cooking class today with Chef Simona at her gorgeous home. We made fresh pasta with sausage and pumpkin and a chocolate torte with whipped cream, mascarpone, and coffee beans.

It took a couple of hours to make the pasta and let it dry. After all our hard work, we had wine, music, and dancing outside in the beautiful sunshine. We ate indoors at a huge square table lighted by a chandelier from Simona's grandmother.

Rich and I took a walk after dinner and saw a neighbor with a friendly golden retriever, which made us miss the dogs even more.

October 16

After morning meditation, we crawled under the covers and went back to sleep. It is so nice not to be rushed. We went for a long walk and then came back to another wonderful Francis breakfast.

We went to Orvieto to shop, eat, and taste wine. Abigail and Tom, and Paula and Mike bought lots of presents for kids. Rich and I poked into galleries and shops before lunch.

We went to a little supermarket in the square, and Tom bought figs and basil for the pasta dish he will make for us tonight. We are using the noodles we made yesterday with Simona. We bought chestnuts from a street vendor, and I got to say, "*Buon pommerigio!*"

We had another afternoon walk today. I got to spend some private time with Abigail; it was amazing we had not had a chance to do that. I got caught up on her life and what was going on with her work, kids, and grandkids.

I told her about the studies I had completed so far, and what I was planning. She was very interested in my soul class, my meditation experiences, and my desire to study Vedanta and Buddhism. And, like me, she was blown away by the idea that we might plan our lives. I gave her the names of the Robert Schwartz books.

I told her about painting and keeping this journal and that I was trying to figure out who I am in this new phase of life. I confessed all the things I am afraid of—that I am not really a true artist and that maybe I am just a dilettante, playing at a surface level of being something that I am really not.

She reminded me that people had bought my paintings, and I said that maybe people are just being nice to me. I told her that my mom, who was creative, used to dismiss whatever she was working on and say, "Oh it's nothing; I am just playing." I don't want to disparage my work, and so I am trying to be confident about it, but so many days I think I really have no talent.

I told her I was afraid that I would miss my leadership role, and I wanted to somehow figure out how to still make a positive impact on humanity, and how much I love meditation and about getting my own mantra. She wants to do that, too.

I said I had given myself a year to figure things out, but I hoped that I would not have to go back to corporate life.

I thanked her for including us on this great trip and for being such a great friend. She is a gift in my life.

We got home and met outside on the patio, our last day in Benano. It went so fast.

I took out my laptop, and we started to record some of our favorite memories, such as the clean metallic taste of the great tap water that must come from some deep aquifer, our daily walk where we smelled the fresh air when we saw the sheep with their sheep dog, listening to the bells of the cathedrals, the taste of fresh figs and pecorino cheese, the supermarket, and the views.

We marveled together how easy and fun this trip was. Francis made everything stress-free. Abigail was a master planner. Our new and old friends were easygoing, with no one insisting on any itinerary or agenda.

We toasted being with friends and the awe of being in a place this ancient. We got Francis to admit we were his best guests ever.

October 17 Barcelona, Spain

As we waited for our flight in the Rome airport, I read more of the ancient hymns of the Rig Veda and then started on the Bhagavad Gita. Before starting to read it, I found a summary written by Roger Gabriel of the Chopra Center:

"The Bhagavad Gita, often referred to as the 'Song of the Lord,' is part of the Mahabharata, which is an ancient Indian epic that tells the story of a great struggle between two branches of a single ruling family, the Kauravas and the Pandavas. They are fighting over the fertile and valuable land at the confluence of the Ganges and Yamuna Rivers near Delhi, and their conflict ends in an awesome battle.

"Before the battle, Arjuna, the head of the Pandava army, is asked to choose to be supported by either Lord Krishna's army or Lord Krishna himself, who will not fight. Arjuna chooses his friend Lord Krishna to act as his charioteer.

"The 700 verses of the Gita, arranged in 18 chapters, are a conversation between Lord Krishna and Arjuna before the battle begins. Krishna represents the supreme soul, Arjuna represents the individual soul, and the battle represents the ethical and moral struggles of human life.

"Realizing that his enemies are his own relatives, beloved friends, and revered teachers, Arjuna is filled with doubt and despondency on the battlefield and refuses to fight. He turns to his charioteer and friend, Krishna, for advice. Responding to Arjuna's confusion and moral dilemma, Krishna explains to Arjuna his duties as a warrior and prince, and through the course of the Gita, imparts to Arjuna wisdom, the path of devotion, and the doctrine of selfless action.

"The Gita is a training for the body and mind, including all four paths of yoga, with a particular focus on karma yoga, the performance of work as yoga for liberation.

"The Gita is often called 'the Upanishad of the Upanishads.'"

We meditated on the flight and arrived in Barcelona at about 5 p.m. We are staying at the Hotel Arts, a contemporary hotel near the *Barri Gòtic* ("Gothic Quarter"), with a view of the Mediterranean. Barcelona is an active, vibrant city full of young people walking, running, biking, and rollerblading.

Many of the buildings date from medieval times, some from as far back as the Roman settlement of Barcelona. I read to Rich from a guidebook about the architect Antoni Gaudí. His best-known work is the immense but still unfinished church of the Sagrada Família, which has been under construction since 1882.

Completion is planned for 2026.

October 18

It is better to live your own destiny imperfectly than to live an imitation of somebody else's life with perfection.

(Anonymous, The Bhagavad Gita)

I woke up before Rich and continued reading the Bhagavad Gita. After morning meditation, we took a walk along the beach. We saw people coming out of the Opium and Catwalk clubs. Some were dressed in elaborate costumes. We laughed because we had been up a while, and the clubs were just closing. Bars on the beach are open until 3 a.m. or later. Clubs stay open until as late as 6 a.m.

This is an ideal city for dogs. Nearly everyone on the beach had a dog, and they loved playing in the water. It made us excited to go home. We had breakfast and then walked more than eight miles to see most of Barcelona, including the Sagrada Família.

We had a 10 p.m. dinner reservation, but after appetizers, we decided to go for a walk and then turn in for the night.

I read Bhagavad Gita until sleep overtook me. We heard the club music thumping every time we woke up; there are probably six clubs in the block around our hotel. At 3 a.m., I teased Rich, "Let's go out dancing; Opium is just now opening."

October 19

Today was our last full day in Barcelona, and we walked more than ten miles. After meditation, we had a great breakfast looking out over Port Olimpic. We hopped on a city bus for a while and then walked for miles after.

In one of the museum gift shops, I found my one souvenir of the trip—a postcard that said in big pink letters "Make Art, Not War." It will go on my easel.

I read the Bhagavad Gita this afternoon, meditated, and then we took another evening walk as the sun set. We packed and got ready to go home; excited to sleep in our own bed, get back in our routine, and see Chip and Bella.

Tonight, we made notes of the trip as we looked out at the Mediterranean.

London—Right. Favorite memory was hearing Big Ben bong while running along the Thames.

Paris—Best memories, sitting out at Le Deux Magot and lunch at Brasserie Lipp.

Florence—We should have spent another day there.

Locanda Amorosa—We would go back; loved the artist in residence and the views.

Siena—We would definitely go back and stay in Grand Hotel again. Two days would be perfect.

La Fontanella—We would definitely go back in a bigger room with a real shower and a real hair dryer.

Rome Cavalieri—We would definitely stay there again—great gym and amenities.

The Villa—We would highly recommend it. Francis definitely helped make the trip.

Barcelona—We were glad we came but can check it off the list.

October 20

A gift is pure when it is given from the heart to the right person at the right time and at the right place, and when we expect nothing in return.
(Anonymous, The Bhagavad Gita)

On the ten-hour flight home, I do prep work for an upcoming consultation with a medium referenced in the Robert Schwarz books. As part of the work, I try to come up with a sentence that describes what I am pursuing in life now.

I answer assigned questions: my happiest moment and why, whom I admire and why. My motto. The causes I support. Recurring dreams. What is freedom; enough money, enough time, enough peace—or? What do I want to be remembered for? If I had one gift to give to everyone, what would it be? When am I most at peace?

I struggle to capture a good sentence; writing with many crossouts. It's close but not there yet.

Evolve to be your best self. Live a full, conscious and joyful life—filled with creativity, learning, continuous improvement of mind, body, and spirit. Use your unique gifts and talents. Thrive.
One sentence:
Thrive—evolve to be your best—in mind, body, spirit

I reflect on the things I love and my simple daily joys: meditation, exercise, fresh air, being with the pack, and journaling with gratitude. Learning. Making a perfect salad. Walking with Rich and the dogs on a beautiful day. Breaking through and achieving a new level of understanding; using my mind in a more expansive way. Or in performance like painting my first "good" nude. When I feel full of vitality, strong—like during a great interval workout. The feeling of expansion, peace, and equanimity. Every day when I feel balanced by "exercising" mind, body, and spirit.

I am inspired by ideas that spark illumination. Living a free, full and joyful life. Creativity. The arts. Incremental discovery and improvement. Healthy food. The freedom to learn. Living life well. Having a fresh and open mind. Inspiring others to reach their potential and live a full spectrum life in mind, body, spirit. The idea that we have the power to create our lives.

On the flight home, I had a great talk with Rich. "Honey, thank you so much for this trip. It was the best vacation of my life. We finally biked Tuscany, a dream we had together for more than a decade. I'm so grateful for our life and so grateful for you."

"You are welcome; I feel the same way," he said. "I want to compliment you; you seem to really be handling retirement well. I was worried you wouldn't."

"You were a great role model. And you know, in my mind, I am not really calling it retirement. I'm calling it a year off—like a sabbatical. When I think about it, I get freaked out that I am no longer earning."

"Babe, you have earned so much—way beyond what we ever expected to achieve in our lifetime. We have so much abundance. You don't ever need to work again."

"How it that possible?"

"You earned a lot of money. So did I. We were incredibly fortunate in timing. We have no tuitions. No debt. And you have the best financial manager in the history of the world. If we don't do something crazy or have some terrible crisis or live to be well over 100, we're going to be just fine."

"I still feel like I want to earn some money. I'd like to have my own stash that I don't have to even discuss with you."

"What do you want to do that you haven't done?"

"I want to take more classes, even if they charge a fee. I want to get certified to teach Primordial Sound Meditation at the Chopra Center. I want to go to the Seduction of Spirit meditation retreat and Perfect Health. I want to go study with Jean Houston. I may want to travel to some seminars, especially ones about spirituality. I still have to answer the big existential questions. I want to take my sibs to Canyon Ranch next year. I want to help Gus if she needs it."

"Well, then let's set aside some money for you; you earned it. Just mentally count on it. How much do you think you need?"

I named a figure. "Wow. OK, done."

If it is possible to fall even more in love with your husband, I just did.

October 21

The man who sees me in everything and everything within me
will not be lost to me, nor will I ever be lost to him.
He who is rooted in oneness realizes that I am
in every being; wherever he goes, he remains in me.
When he sees all being as equal in suffering or in joy
because they are like himself, that man has grown perfect in
yoga.
(Anonymous, The Bhagavad Gita)

We were ecstatic to see Bella and Chip when we got home last night. Christina picked them up from the kennel, and it was incredible to come home and have them here. Bella did her excited dance and song and pressed her backside into us. Chip is now huge! I want to believe he remembered us; he certainly got excited. His tail wagged hard, and he jumped all over us. It is wonderful to be a pack again.

There is a mountain of mail. This week will be hectic. Raleigh comes tomorrow to get treated at the cancer hospital. We have a fundraiser every day if we go to them all. I have board and committee meetings at the art college. This means I have to put on make-up and "real" clothes and high heels every day. Back to reality from vacation mode.

The trees have changed. We are thrilled that we didn't miss the fall leaves. They are beautiful gold, red, and orange.

I took tons of photos of leaves and dogs today. I got a bit of reading time in after our walk and my afternoon meditation. I am now craving very simple food and want to take a break from wine. This is a perfect week to start.

October 22

You have the right to work, but never to the fruit of work. You should never engage in action for the sake of reward, nor should you long for inaction. Perform work in this world, Arjuna, as a man established within himself—without selfish attachments, and alike in success and defeat.
(Anonymous, The Bhagavad Gita)

Chip slept over seven hours. After going out with me at five, the dogs both jumped in bed with Rich; Chip curled into a tiny ball near his feet. They settled down quietly until we finished meditating.

Tonight, we have to stop by another fundraiser, and the hounds will just stay with Raleigh.

My Buddhism class started, and I can't wait to get caught up. Buddhism wasn't covered deeply in my Soul Beliefs class, and I want to make sure I have been exposed to a full range of major belief systems.

October 23

The nonpermanent appearance of happiness and distress, and their disappearance in due course, are like the appearance and disappearance of winter and summer seasons. They arise from sense perception, and one must learn to tolerate them without being disturbed.
(Anonymous, The Bhagavad Gita)

We had a gorgeous walk this morning. My back is sore, so I took it easy. Wearing high heels yesterday did not help. I am out of practice wearing heels; amazing that I wore them every day for decades. In New York, I could walk ten blocks in stilettos. Those days are over. The trees are just gorgeous with fall color; the reds and oranges get prettier each day. We have so much gratitude to be home.

It is always a pleasure to have Raleigh with us. He gets dressed and comes down to dinner every night even though we know some days he feels like complete crap. He eats whatever we put in front of him. The docs say he should have extra protein, so we have fish or chicken most nights and grass-fed beef once a week, and at least one vegetable, and usually sweet potatoes, brown rice, or quinoa. He would like beef or pork every day, but he doesn't complain.

When he is with us, I make him a healthy smoothie every day with frozen banana and mixed berries, along with kale, spinach, celery, carrot, and broccoli. The coolness of the frozen fruit feels good on his throat after all the radiation, and I am glad he is getting the nutrition.

I started my online Princeton Buddhism class today. The professor, Robert Wright, explained the premise of the class: the Dalai Lama has said that Buddhism and science are very compatible and has encouraged Western scholars to examine meditative practices and Buddhist ideas about the human mind. This course reviews scientific data that has been compiled including brain scans of meditators and philosophic examinations of Buddhist doctrines. There will also be discussions of Buddhist descriptions of the mind in light of evolutionary psychology. I'm looking forward to it.

I ordered a new duvet cover and blanket for our bed today. White linens are not conducive to dogs in the bed. Rich is embarrassed we let the dogs in our bed, but I don't care. I love the feeling of being surrounded by my pack.

October 24

We had a nice weekend. Raleigh wanted a steak, and he needs protein. Suddenly meat is much less appealing to me; I don't know if it is a result of going deeper in meditation or something else.

Last night, he and Rich watched football, and I had a few wonderful hours to paint. Raleigh always seems cold now, so we got him a big blanket so he could cover up to watch the game, and we are trying to be conscious to turn up the heat. The weather has been amazing, with cool nights for sleeping. The first fall in thirty-six years that I will get to notice and appreciate.

In class, the professor gave us an overview of the teachings of Buddhism. Basically, the teaching of the Buddha is that it doesn't make sense to get upset over things that can't be controlled. Every human life contains suffering. Our choice is to have a certain mindset about the things that happen to us and try to live life with a healthy approach. This really resonates with me.

In Buddhism, there are four noble truths.

The first noble truth essentially says that while pain is inevitable, suffering is optional.

The second noble truth says that suffering has a cause, and the cause can be known. Clinging causes suffering. The Buddha said, "Everything dear to us causes pain." Things change; our relationships to things we care about change, and we feel the loss of pain and separation.

Buddhism makes us more aware of the constant negotiation between passionate appreciation of life and experiencing things with less attachment.

The third noble truth says that liberation is possible—peace of mind and happiness. So, the Buddha taught that the end of suffering is possible.

The fourth noble truth lays out the eightfold path or circle offered to help make progress toward enlightenment. These eight things are highly linked.

A traveler on the way to enlightenment thinks about having the Right Perspective and Right Intention. The idea that it might be possible to be content even when we are not pleased brings up Right Action and Right Livelihood to make a lot of Right Effort to develop even more Right Perspective.

And if you decide to practice Right Speech, avoid gossip and mean talk, and aspire to make sure what you are saying is both truthful and helpful, it can't be done without Right Mindfulness. This requires Right Concentration. It's all connected.

October 25

Today we started a new Oprah and Deepak twenty-one-day meditation series about the energy of attraction. They talked about desire being essential to our spiritual evolution. Through desire we create more love, joy, and vitality. I want to learn more about this—especially about setting powerful intentions and having them fulfilled.

When we do the "pack" meditation, the dogs both get in bed with us. With Chip on one side by me, and Bella on the other side by Rich, I hit "play" on my iPad, and they settle down. They hear Oprah's voice and then Deepak's. Rich and I silently repeat the mantra. Maybe there is something about those big alpha or gamma or theta waves or whatever they are that get generated; the pups are peaceful. Then, at the end, when Chip hears Deepak's voice saying to release the mantra and reminding us of the thought for the day, he starts thumping his tail hard on the bed. When we say *namaste* in unison with Deepak, he moans, gets up, and put his face up near Rich's face. We are convinced he believes that *namaste* means "breakfast."

Ran, walked, and lifted weights today. Raleigh requested Steak and Shake in his room tonight. It is the first time he has not come down for dinner. I had fish, broccoli, and quinoa prepared, but that didn't appeal to him. So, we got him his burger and then brought up some ice cream for him later. I was not upset about it; he should have what he wants.

I had time to do a bit of Buddhism class today and focused on the concept of "not self."

In the Buddha's second sermon to monks, it is said that the monks who attended were instantly enlightened. We were given an assignment to read from the *Discourse of the Not-self Characteristic* translated by N.K.G. Mendis. We read that the Buddha reviewed the five aggregates, form, feeling, perceptions, mental formations, and consciousness.

For each, he asks the monks if the aggregate is permanent or impermanent; for each, the answer is impermanent. For each, he asks if it is satisfactory or unsatisfactory; for each, the answer is unsatisfactory, and for each, he reviews, "this is not mine, this/these I am not, this is not myself."

I have to say that I'd like to go to a discourse and be instantly enlightened. Okay, non-self is a hard concept. I need to delve in to understand.

October 26

Raleigh seems exhausted, but he only has a few more days of treatment this round. He has requested ice cream every night, so Rich and I make sure to keep plenty of Graeter's and Jeni's around.

I read part of *The Foundation of Buddhism* by Rupert Gethin for class. Gethin explains that there is a physical world (form), mental activity responding to various physical stimuli (perceptions) producing pleasant, unpleasant, or indifferent feelings (mental formations), which can provoke desires or wishes, and finally a basic awareness of ourselves as thinking subjects (consciousness). I looked up several more references to not self.

In his book *What the Buddha Taught*, the Theravadin scholar Walpola Rahula said:

> According to the teaching of the Buddha, the idea of a self is an imaginary, false belief which has no corresponding reality, and it produces harmful thoughts of "me" and "mine," selfish desire, craving, attachment, hatred, ill-will, conceit, pride, egoism, and other defilements, impurities and problems.

Another scholar said the question of a self is unanswerable and that when the Buddha was asked point-blank whether there was a self he refused to answer and later said that to hold either view that there is a self or is no self can lead to wrong views.

Then I read a complex Buddhist teaching that beings are a flow of mental and physical phenomena where a constant "self" does not exist; there is only a causal "connectedness"—the way that one thing links to another. Events occur, according to Buddhist teaching, in certain specific clusters and patterns which are relatively stable over time.

This causal connection does not cease at death. At "rebirth" a new pattern of events, connected to the old, may be of a different kind. Causal connectedness is the basis of continuity in life, and between lives. Death is not an interruption on the causal flow; it is a reconfiguration of a new pattern.

I have questions about what led the Buddha to his path. I look it up and find that the Buddha began by rejecting ancient Hindu ritual and mystery, even the notion of a personal God.

And like so many other wisdom traditions, Buddhism has divisions over fundamental questions that seem to come to every tradition: Are individuals independent or interdependent? Is the universe helpful and friendly or indifferent? What is more important—compassion or wisdom? Is Buddhism a full-time job or is it accessible to ordinary people? I google this and find many explanations of Theravada Buddhism, Mahayana Buddhism, Vajrayana Buddhism, and Zen Buddhism. These branches seem to converge around core beliefs about the Buddha's teachings but divide over how they believe Buddhism should be practiced in daily life.

I'm sure if I was a theology major or a philosophy student, or I had studied comparative religion, the answers might be in a textbook I could pull out of my bookshelf. But there is something I like about posing the question myself and having to search to find answers on my own. It's not elegant, fast, or deep scholarship, but it is my own process. I spend a minute being grateful to be at this juncture of my evolution when it is so easy to pose a question and go online to search for answers. After I wrote this, I found a couple of books on Buddha's life, which look fascinating. I am going to do more reading tonight.

October 27

We loved meditation today. They talked about the activation of desire at its source, which directs our thoughts and actions to lead toward actualization.

Raleigh goes home Monday. He has had a lot of radiation. I keep trying to tempt him to eat with the smoothie of the day. He has little appetite. Today's focus was peaches and strawberries, with veggies for more nutrition; it had ten ingredients. I also went to Trader Joe's for new frozen fruit to add some variety. Gussie is home from rehab and seems quite fragile. We are taking turns checking on her each day.

As a follow-up to class, I read about the Buddha's life. One of the best books about him was written by Deepak Chopra. I was so engaged reading, I stayed up until two this morning. The thing that came through so strongly was that he had his own experiences and came to his own conclusions. To make a fascinating story short, he was born a prince, renounced his life, became a monk who endured tremendous trials and suffering, and finally reached enlightenment six years later while sitting under a tree. Then he lived another forty-five years, traveling around India as a renowned and beloved teacher.

He taught from some simple principles about being. Life is unsatisfactory. Pleasure in the physical world is transient. Pain follows. Nothing is permanent. We cling to illusions; whatever can be seen, heard, or touched is unreal. Reality is purely itself. But what inspires me most about reading his story and philosophy is that he lived the ultimate soul journey that ended in enlightenment.

His followers may have some differences depending on their interpretation of his messages; but they are inspired to live a spiritual life; they meditate and create an atmosphere of peace. They focus on compassion and nonjudgment, striving to be kind and loving and having a reverence for life. They work to break free of ego attachments; like status, belongings, money, and achievements.

October 28

Today's mantra was Ahrah Kahrah, which means something like, "My desires have the power to manifest." I love that mantra because it reminds me a little of *abracadabra*—make the magic happen!

Today was my hardest workout day this week. I ran 3.75 miles, did elliptical, and lifted weights. I took a long walk with both dogs and then read outside at midday, with Bella stuck to one side and Chip on the other. My cup runneth over.

I have been thinking more about "Right Speech" as part of the Buddhist eight-fold path. "Speech that does not add pain to the situation" would presumably include not saying hurtful things and certainly avoiding lies and gossip.

This makes me think about my mom. I wonder what it was like to live her life with five kids in a small town. She was not perfect, but one thing I admired about her then and now is that she did not gossip. Not engaging in gossip is very unusual in a small rural town, where life is slow and not that fascinating. Everyone knew everyone else's business. She and her friends would meet for coffee in the city park a couple of times a week in nice weather. We would play nearby. I was always interested in adult conversation, so I listened in. And I would hear the other ladies talk about people in town: illnesses, indiscretions, wild teenage kids, teenage girls who were "boy crazy," rumors, and speculation about marriages.

There were times when I knew Mom knew "the real scoop" about a situation, but when others would bring up the topic, she just never engaged. She wasn't sanctimonious about it and never said, "I don't gossip" to her friends. I remember her being thoughtful about the words that came out of her mouth. She was not an idle chatterer. She responded to gossipy comments with things like "Oh, I don't know if that's true but if it is, I wouldn't judge her." And then she would change the subject and say something like admiring Jackie Kennedy's hairdo or Audrey Hepburn's outfit.

Emma:
I talked to Gussie. She had a panic attack at work and went home. Her doctor told her it is unlikely he will be able to operate to fix her stomach hernia. Even after all of the work

she has put in to get sober, she is in extremely poor physical health. She has now been diagnosed with "end-stage liver disease." They are worried about infection and uncontrolled bleeding if they were to do surgery. She is dealing with a great deal of physical pain, and she realizes she can't undo the damage she has already inflicted on her body.

It is difficult to follow her in a conversation because her thinking and speech are not clear. So, it was a bad day for her, but I'm not sure there is anything specific we can do.

She told me wanted to kill herself. She didn't sound serious—in fact she said it in a joking way—but this is disturbing. She told me she was going to meet with her therapist; I told her to please update me after.

Love you all, Emma

Bethany:
I am going to fly there next week to see her in person.

October 29

Our meditation this morning was about abundance; happiness, and fulfillment that are our essential nature. Today we had Rich's favorite mantra: *shreem kleem namah*.

We had community things today: board work and children's hospital. My "by-myself" meditations were joyful, but I had to cut my afternoon one short. Still, I am grateful in the midst of a busy day to go to silence. I am learning that the benefits of meditation are cumulative, and even if you don't have the full time, it's better to go ahead and meditate for the time you do have.

As we said goodbye to Raleigh, we confirmed a special trip with him for Thanksgiving to take him to Napa Valley. He is quite excited. So, we will see him in a few weeks.

Today someone asked me if I was bored not working. I laughed. My days feel so full; I have so much more I want to do.

Today I was musing about the Buddhism course, and I thought about all the attachments I have in this life. I am attached to our pack. My relationship with Rich, which I once lost, I am beyond grateful to have back. Every time we have an intimate moment, or that feeling of partnership, I treasure it all the more because I remember what it was like to be without him. Bella and I are completely bonded. Chip is an incredible pain in the ass, but he has stolen our hearts.

The idea that change happens and I won't always have them or they won't always have me—brings pain. I am attached to this sweet time of life. I am probably too attached to my daily workouts. I can justify it by saying that having a healthy body allows me to go deeper in my spiritual practice, and it does, but truthfully, I want to look decent, be healthy, and I want the high energy that fitness brings. I don't want my body to feel slow and sluggish. I am attached to my family and friends. I feel I am detaching from the house and possessions. In fact, Rich and I talk about just completely decluttering; getting rid of nearly everything and downsizing to a much simpler life. While we are so grateful for abundance, we don't need this huge house. I would like something very manageable that I could easily clean myself. We don't need two cars; it's almost silly.

I detached amazingly easily from corporate life. That is a nice surprise. But now am I too attached to this idea of being on a journey—to thinking and pondering?

I think some more about Buddhism. It's so—open. It's a DIY project. There is more than one right way to practice; you can be live a spiritual lifestyle as a monk or a nun, or just live a kind, compassionate, truthful, nonviolent life and love without judgment; or you can take a mystical path and keep working to break the bonds of attachment and focus on nondoing. You don't have to obey commandments or worship a specific God. If I am understanding it, you just have to keep trying to find answers for yourself, to wake up and keep moving toward wholeness.

I love having this grounding and respect this approach. I'm going to keep studying and pursuing my own DIY project. I will come back to the study of Buddhism and learn about the different schools of thought that have grown from the original teachings. What's next to study? As synchronicity so often happens, I got an email today that there is still one opening to study with Jean Houston in her home, a salon with a small number of participants with three months of coaching as a follow-up.

Today was my day to check on Gussie.

Jane:

Gus didn't go to work today; she has a fever. In our call, she kept saying, "I am not worthy, I am such a burden to all of you, I am just a fuck-up," and so forth. And she mentioned killing herself. I reminded her that she told us in family therapy that she had never contemplated suicide and that she thought it was selfish and horrible for loved ones. She agreed with that. I reminded her that she has a fever and is not thinking clearly; I said she is loved and worthy.

She said she is exhausted, and she just wants to sleep. She promised she would stay in bed and asked please not to text or call her anymore today. She said please call her at 9 a.m. her time tomorrow. She asked me to update everyone and say she is sorry for being a pain. I will call her in the morning.

October 30

Today Gussie said she was going to kill herself. She sent a text that sent us into a frenzy of activity.

Gussie:

Siblings, this is it. It is impossible to be a burden upon you. And so, I am going to end it to make sure that none of you have to care for me. If it doesn't work, please don't send me to a psychological facility. What I need is for one or all of you to take me into your care. I know that it will be horribly difficult, but I think I deserve it. My knife won't even cut into my skin at this point.

She was home alone. After Teresa and Joe talked to her, we felt the threat was serious enough to call the police. This was a team effort with everyone playing a role to keep her communicating with us until they got there. Joe did a great job, getting her to think and talk about the future.

She kept saying that she was worthless, and it would be much easier for her to be out of all of our lives.

The police got to her in time and took her to university hospital. She had a blood alcohol level of .399; five times over the legal limit. The hospital said that this was a dangerously high blood alcohol level and that they would need to clear her medically. The policeman said we probably saved her life today.

We called her doctor, Mason, Mia, Mark, and Dad.

Gussie kept texting us; she thought she was in the psych ward, but she was in the regular hospital. She kept begging us to come rescue her. It was heart-breaking.

Jane:

Guys, Gussie is in the family wing in 4 West; she is *not* in the psych ward. The nurse said they are even more concerned about her medical condition than her emotional state, and they can't treat her medical condition in the psych ward. They are taking precautions, so she is in red PJs, and they will have someone with her at all times. Her social worker comes in at 8 a.m. I have left a message, asking that she call me.

It's stunning how coherent she is, given her blood alcohol level. They do not have a phone in the room because they won't allow a cord in there. They took her mobile phone and locked it up for the night. The nurse took his phone in to let me talk to her, but she was sound asleep. I told him, "Great. Don't wake her."

Let's all shut off our devices and get a good night of sleep. She may not be happy, but she is alive. Great teamwork today; love to all.

October 31

Gus is still in the hospital: emotionally calmer today, but detoxing and physically miserable. They are running tests to get a clearer diagnosis of her many medical issues. She apologized for the drama of yesterday. The sibs seem traumatized, but I feel pretty calm. I think about the sad arc of this learning curve, loving someone with addictions. Before the first round of rehab, we had euphoric hope and crushing disappointment. With each successive attempt at sobriety, it seems both my hopes and disappointment have been muted. It doesn't take away the sadness, though. Bethany is going to travel to be with her; I'm grateful for that.

Chapter Five
November

In November, I attend a salon with spiritual philosopher Jean Houston. I meet an intriguing, powerful new friend. I begin to absorb even more new concepts, from the notion of life path and destiny to the concepts of entelechy: interdependent co-arising, spiral dynamics, becoming a generative force, using archetypes, and seeing the larger story of my life. I am inspired to stop boring God and to use my gifts. I gain clarity that pursuing painting is part of my immediate purpose. Gussie is back home after a suicide threat and hospital stay, fragile but holding her own. I take an exercise physiology class, and we have a memorable family visit at the end of the month.

November 1

Though I have been doing monster workouts since we got home from Europe, my clothes are tight, and I am up a few pounds. As I read through my journal about all we ate and drank, it's no wonder. So, I'm going to plan "spa at home" time before my trip to Oregon. I am finished with my Buddhism class as of today.

I ran, painted, and lifted weights. I walked the hounds; lots of people were out enjoying the sunshine and breeze. This afternoon I did stretch/yoga/abs class. Instead of wine with dinner, I had tea. I pulled out my "to do" list to see how I am doing on the things I wanted to accomplish in the "sabbatical year" I have given myself.

Though my weight is higher than I like, my fitness level is improving; I am noticeably stronger and able to lift heavier weights. My technology skills are improving. I'm well into photo digitizing; there is no rush to finish. We now have a pack of four; Bella is much better. I love my classes and will take more. I learned enough about feng shui and I am ready to learn about numerology. We had the trip of a lifetime to Europe. I am decluttering. My painting studio is set. I meditate every day, got certified as a meditation instructor, and got my own personal mantra. Yoga stays on the must-do list. I love doing daily Italian and will do Spanish next. I gave my work clothes away. I honestly record what happens and how I feel about it in my daily journal. I am exploring soul beliefs and the major wisdom traditions. I still need to fully figure out who I am now, what I want, what my purpose is, and what lessons I need to learn. I am still seeking to find answers to the big existential questions. I want to keep improving my painting ability.

OK: numerology, purpose, existential questions, and painting. I started reading some of Jean Houston's books to get in the groove before attending her salon.

November 2

Another spa day. I do not miss having wine. Good! I want to make sure I am addiction free and after all the wine we had in Europe; it's good to abstain for a while.

For the numerology reading I sent the medium my birth certificate name, my date of birth, and the name I go by now. I told Rich I got the feedback, and he said, "You don't believe in that, do you?"

I said, "I have an open mind. Numerology is ancient; I want to know something about it. I want to have an expansive mind that does not automatically close at a concept that seems foreign."

I learned that numerology studies the significance of numbers. Observers of numerology have found correlations between a person's nature from their birthdate and name.

The belief is that birth is a moment of total transformation. Interesting. When I got my own personal mantra in Primordial Sound Meditation, it was based on my birth date, time, and place. Maybe a birthday *is* a big metaphysical deal. I stop to think about that. The belief is when someone is born, they have their own unique character that will unfold. Everything exists as potential; the curtain goes up, and life's play begins.

Why is it believed that numerology works? A few possible explanations are psychic energy, a universal force, or the vibratory effect of numbers. The field of numerology is ancient. It can be traced back to the centuries old Hebrew Kabbala and was given new life by Pythagoras in Greece 2,600 years ago.

The first number shown is Life Path, which gives a broad outline of the opportunities and lessons in this lifetime. My Life Path number is eleven.

An eleven-life path, the report says, has the potential to be a source of inspiration and illumination for people, a channel for information between the realm of the archetype and the relative world. There seems to be a bridge, or connection, between conscious and unconscious realms that can open up a high level of intuition. Many inventors, artists, and prophets have had the eleven prominent in their chart.

It said that elevens are blessed with a specific role to play in life but must develop sufficiently to take advantage of that opportunity. Elevens seem to develop slowly. Thus, real progress may not begin until later in life.

Peaceful and harmonious environments, relaxing music, and a healthful diet are necessary in order to achieve balance and peace.

It is quite interesting and freaking me out a bit since elevens and ones come up for me so frequently. I read and find out that the life path number is derived from finding the sum of the month, day and year of birth and reducing that date to a single number.

I calculate Rich's life path number; it is four. The big themes for a four are limitation, order, and service. Fours are aware of limitations. Practical, they produce order out of chaos. They are hard workers and good with difficult problems to solve as well as honest, sincere, and responsible.

Hmmm. I can't wait to find out more. But now I am off to Oregon.

November 3

Bethany is with Gus, who is out of the hospital and fragile but seems to be on the mend. I am in Ashland, Oregon, to attend the salon with Jean Houston. Known for the Oregon Shakespeare festival, Ashland is artsy and vibrant and has a kind of a Woodstock vibe.

On the flight, I read the Jean Houston book *The Wizard of Us.* Jean's dad wrote for Bob Hope. She was mentored by Abraham Maslow, Margaret Mead, and Joseph Campbell, and she met Albert Einstein and Helen Keller. Wow.

Deepak wrote the forward in the book. The book references Joseph Campbell's *The Hero with a Thousand Faces* and uses the *Wizard of Oz* to explain more about a hero's journey that is in the common psyche.

I stop for a little fantasy; is my sabbatical year a mythic journey? Could my call to adventure have been the sudden gift of a year to go on this vision quest? Is it a refusal of the call each time my cynical mind deeply questions what I am learning? Are my magical allies coming to me through classes, books, and my meditation presences? The Guardian of the Threshold might be my own ego saying, "Don't take the risk; become a wimpy version of yourself!" I might be in the belly of the whale right now, trying to emerge into a better, more complete version of myself and letting go of old habits that are no longer useful. Coming up is the Road of Trials, trying to figure out how to make my way. I will need resources and allies to succeed. The next phase of "Meeting with a Beloved" is to have an authority figure recognize me. This may be my pull to come to this session with Jean Houston. Or, my beloved might be those higher-self aspects within me—my own soul.

I read more of my Numerology report. The next important number is the Expression/Destiny number; it reveals my inner goal, the person I aim to be. The calculation of the name is derived by finding the number value of all the letters in each name on my birth certificate, reducing this sum to a single digit or master number and then adding the sums of all the names together and reducing that total to a single digit or master number. My destiny number is one. I found the next part of the report fascinating:

"For those for whom reincarnation is an accepted philosophy, the vibration of one's full name at birth can be seen as the totality of their personal evolution, the experiences, talents, and wisdom accumulated over many life times. Every experience, no matter how great or small, along this evolutionary path has influenced their development and brought them to their current state of being."

The report says expression ones are leaders: ambitious, original, and courageous with executive abilities. Ones can be opinionated, have great concentration but tend to be self-centered and can be highly critical of others.

Rich's expression number is eight. Eights have organizational and financial capabilities. They have good judgment with money and understand how it is accumulated and handled. They are energetic, self-confident, and dependable, and they seek material comfort.

It's interesting to see how different my life path and expression number are; eleven is focused on matters on a spiritual plane. Ones are focused on achievement and leadership in the material world. I think back to the metaphysical feedback I have gotten where I was told that I have one foot in the material world and one on a higher plane. Interesting. Maybe I am making too much of the connection between feedback sessions. But I like the idea that at least this information is not in conflict with what I have heard before.

November 4

Bethany reported in; her visit has been good for Gussie, who seems to be in a much more stable place for now. She helped Gus and Mason agree on some terms for their amicable divorce that will happen next year, talked with Gus about coping mechanisms, and went with her to doctor appointments.

I am excited for the salon to begin. I tell myself to just be open and experience everything without preconceived notions or judgment. I have read in the welcome packet that we are going to "sing, dance, see dramatic skits, read poetry, hear inspiring thoughts, meditate, do exercises, and touch on quantum mechanics, myths, epic journeys of the soul, purpose, states of consciousness, epigenetics, and neuroplasticity."

This morning after breakfast, I explored Ashland. I saw a woman with long gray hair doing tai chi. A spiritual-looking dude with a man bun was playing "Somewhere over the Rainbow" on his harmonica. The town is very hilly with charming streams and bridges, very leafy and verdant. Tame deer wander everywhere. It was cold enough to need a sweater. I went to Starbucks and got a coffee.

My prearranged ride came to get me. We picked up two other passengers and went to Jean Houston's home on a mountaintop overlooking beautiful vineyards. It was sunny and seventy-five degrees when we arrived.

As I walked in, I felt intimidated. I had not thought about the people who would attend or the interactions that would take place. I felt like a complete beginner among more seasoned and experienced people who had been on a spiritual path for much longer than I had.

Jean's home was filled with palpable energy. Three huge dogs greeted us. The invitation for the salon had clearly stated that animals would be present and nicely said if that was a problem don't attend or take allergy medicine. Habibi is a large, white standard poodle, Jada is an Airedale, and Thunder is a German shepherd. There is a male cat named Monkey. I felt a lot of welcoming chi and energy in the home.

The animals were loving and funny, greeting each person and allowing themselves to be petted by everyone.

Artifacts from Jean's travels to 108 countries were present throughout: a mummy, colorful mythical statues of beasts, Hindu figurines, primitive art, feng shui animals, a menagerie of other animal statues, and oriental rugs. She has a devoted, long-tenured staff who adore her.

Jean will turn eighty soon. She is tall and commanding and looks at least twenty years younger, with a regal presence and long, curling russet hair. She said she decided not to age.

There are about fifteen participants. We will each have a chance to go on the "hot seat" to ask Jean something about our own journey. We were seated around Jean's living room in comfortable chairs and couches. I sat in a plush rocker, and each dog and the cat came to sit with me for a while.

The day started with Connie Buffalo, Jean's colleague, welcoming everyone and covering housekeeping details. Jean introduced her business partner, Peggy Rubin and talked about the agenda.

As I meet the other participants, I wonder if these are some of my "birds of a feather" who are all on a spiritual path—all seekers of one kind or another. This is the first time I have gone to an event that is spiritual in nature.

I feel a connection with each person as though we were all meant to be together. I feel a very strong kinship with one person in particular—Robin. It's as though a special strand of energy has bounced between us all day. Robin and I are seated across the room from one another, but we glance at each other and smile. I feel we resonate similarly with each part of the day. I am excited to connect with Robin at the break.

The theme of this conference is "Elect Yourself." The idea of an election makes me feel repelled, but I know what Jean means; it is time to do more than watch the news or turn off the news in my case. You can't shut out the world forever. Everyone has gifts and talents that are there to be used.

Jean gave a rousing talk about how everyone is called to do more and said that we all feel the yearning to discover "what is my purpose, how do I respond to the call." Heads nod around the room. She is touching a nerve.

Jean thinks her purpose has something to do with helping people hear and act upon the call, to tune into their evolutionary awakenings. She wants us to feel the larger story of our lives, to have a vision of capabilities and capacities without cynical dismissal.

She talked about the scope and urgency of issues facing mankind and the planet and said we all have responsibility for the evolution of the world. She said the extraordinary is now the ordinary. We are feeling a push from the past and a call from the future. None of us are innocent of history.

I am taking copious notes with many underlines and question marks. My pen is flying across my notebook trying to capture what Jean is saying.

Jean wrote an autobiography called *My Mythic Life*, and she has had an amazing life. Margaret Mead, Jonas Salk, Joseph Campbell, and Buckminster Fuller were all friends and allies. Margaret Mead lived with her for six years. These friends and mentors were unique because they sustained creativity over their lives.

They all had access to different modalities of knowing. They had different realms of consciousness available to them, and they accessed them; they had visions and ideas that were independently co-arising. They had help from allies seen and unseen. I am captivated.

Jean said we only use a fraction of our capabilities. I am completely dialed in; this is something I think about every day. Jean talked about why genius happens and quoted someone who said we hear a call coming from generations yet unborn, begging us to remember. Magnificent.

She talked about the entelechy connected to Aristotle's distinction between the potential and the actual. Jean said these are from another domain of reality that can give us access to more capability and assist us. I remember hearing this term years ago when I was studying the Enneagram, something about the notion of the innate desire to continually improve and grow. Jean says it is the dynamic purpose encoded in each of us; it is the entelechy of an acorn to be an oak tree; it is the entelechy of a caterpillar to be a butterfly. We can call upon this principle within us for inspiration, motivation, help, and support.

Jean talked about her friend Teilhard, who she knew as a young girl; he talked about the Omega point and how he believed we are all pilgrims of the future. I realize she is talking about Pierre Teilhard de Chardin, a French idealist philosopher and Jesuit priest. Wikipedia says he conceived the idea of the Omega Point (a maximum level of complexity and consciousness toward which he believed the universe was evolving). During his lifetime, many of Teilhard's writings were censored by the Catholic Church because of his views on original sin, but recently some of Teilhard's work has been praised by the pope.

I am stirred; another synchronicity is that he wrote about disbelieving in original sin. I put him on my "to-read" list that I have started in the margin of my notes.

Jean said that we are at a time of rebirth in the world and then led us in a meditation where we affirmed to the universe that we are ready to step up and do more, to answer the call. Jean is a great orator, and her voice is commanding, compelling, and strong; she is exhilarating, inspirational, and powerful.

She did Q&A. There are people in the group who are troubled by the state of the world and are focused on lack and scarcity. She tried to open them up and stop them from being overwhelmed and to realize that progress can be made by taking simple steps. She said His Holiness Dalai Lama asked, "How do you create peace? Smile at your neighbor."

She mentioned a book *The Power of Now: A Guide to Spiritual Enlightenment* by Eckhart Tolle about paying attention to thinking.

I furiously scribble notes. Clearly Jean is a brilliant spiritual philosopher, passionate, with an incredible education and life experience. I have never met someone like Jean before.

I am certain that Jean has seen mystical things she would never publish or talk about; you can tell she has had deep experiences, and she seems to be choosing her words to convey information that can actually be absorbed by a typical human.

Jean explained that patterns of expectation change. When bikes were first invented, most people couldn't ride them, but by the turn of the century it was a capability most people had.

Someone asked her what she was reading now; one book is *The Intention Experiment* by Lynne McTaggart. I pull up the description and order the e-book as Jean talks.

The session ended about five o'clock. Robin and I finally got to meet. As we were talking, Robin told me she was a shaman and a successful published author and a coach to powerful people around the globe. She had been awakened in one fell swoop one day in her thirties, when an immediate outpouring of spiritual information was downloaded into her consciousness. I was blown away. I told Robin about my long business career and my vision quest.

Jean's caterer friend brought in dinner. Everyone sat down and talked about the day. The food was great and the conversations enlightening. Just meeting everyone and listening to them talk about their lives, I realized there are huge resources available to seekers like me. I scribble every suggestion for more learning, Daily OM, Gaia, Sounds True, Shift Network, Hay House, Chopra Center, and all kinds of books. I asked the person sitting next to me, "Have you ever heard of the idea that our lives are preplanned before we incarnate?" "Of course," she answered, kindly. "Have you read the Carolyn Myss book, *Sacred Contracts*?" Someone overheard the conversation and recommended a children's book by Neale Donald Walsh: *The Little Soul and the Sun*. I write them down.

November 5

My brain was brimming with new concepts. I got a few hours of sleep but was wide awake at two, so I meditated and then went to the fitness room and ran before the start of day two.

Robin and I sat next to one another. We started the day reciting a poem together: "The Journey" by Mary Oliver. Another synchronicity, I had just sent my friend Donna a copy of this poem.

In response to some discussion, Jean started telling the group more about her family history. Her great-great-great grandfather was Robert E. Lee.

Jean has written a book in the past about the *possible* human, and now she is going to rename it the *required* human; humans who are creative, active stewards of self, society, and world.

She encouraged us to assume our existence as broadly as possible, to imagine that everything must be possible in it. There are lots of questions, discussions and an occasional poem throughout the day. One of my favorites is "Outwitted" by Edwin Markham.

Paul, in charge of music, played his guitar and sang an original song from the Mystery School "Seven Steps." This is the notion that if you take one step toward the gods, they take seven (or ten) steps toward you.

One of the participants, a producer, described an incredible show she produced for disabled athletes. She is seventy-one but looks forty-five. I have noticed that there is a youthfulness that seems to be associated with people who have found a clear spiritual path.

Connie Buffalo talked about how we so often stay confined when we don't have to, using a story about the caged tiger who, when let loose out of his cage, *stayed* in the 9 X 12 space.

Jean has a hysterical sense of humor, perfect joke timing, and can mimic any accent. She told a joke with perfect accents about being in Brooklyn on Friday night when the Jewish neighbor was barbecuing steak, and it was driving the Catholics crazy.

And the one about Marcia Rosencrantz. God assured her she would not die when she went in for heart surgery, so she had bunch of other cosmetic surgery done, too. When a bus smashed her dead, she was mad at God, but he said, "I didn't recognize you."

Jean said comedy changes the world. *You* can change the world!

Serve as imaginal cells; be an emergent property. You are
deeply required. As above so below. Don't go back to old stuff.
There is now complex unpredictability in the world that none
of us have been trained for. If you get stuck, shift your environment. Listen to music, laugh, exercise, dance, and travel!

Jean talked about some of the influences in her life. Albert Einstein
said it takes a different consciousness to solve a problem than that
which created it. He talked about imagination being his most important trait. His advice: read fairy tales. He solved the theory of relativity by
imagining riding a wave of light. The imagined life can take you further.

She also met Helen Keller. Jean talked about mythology and some of
her travels using statues of Athena, Aphrodite, Hera, Persephone, and Ptah.

She talked about her long-standing relationship with Margaret
Mead. Jean gave the encomium at the UN when Margaret Mead died.

Jean and Peggy did some training in seeing imagery. Jean said this
was to develop the "hooks and eyes" to catch energy.

Then we did a powerful, long meditation. There was something
about being in that environment that made it very vivid. I saw my floating light essences in color, motion, and light. Entelechy? True self?
Spirit Guides? Angel? Archetypes? Just stress release? Another kind of
cosmic partner I haven't learned about yet? I still don't know, but I
have the deep feeling that these entities are supporting me and there
to help.

Peggy did an imagery exercise, having us picture the colors of the
rainbow. Jean asked us to go *below* the rainbow and allow the connection to the universe.

Peggy talked about the importance of activation of the inner sensory systems. Sensory receptors located in the inner ear, muscles, ten-
dons, and joints that use internal stimuli to detect changes in position
or movement of the body or its limbs are called proprioceptors. Color,
form, and structures—all manner of things—are involved in sensory
capabilities.

Jean said if you are studying the art and science of manifestation, simple guided imagery sometimes is not enough. Some people can't visualize that way. I resonate with this; I have heard that some people see actual movies and clear images behind closed eyes as though in a dream state. But not everyone visualizes the same way. Adding the kinesthetic dimensions helps—the *body* needs to be engaged for many people to connect to higher dimensions.

They talked about the world we experience with our senses and the quantum world "underneath the rainbow." The bottom half that is not visible. Jean had us stand, close our eyes, sculpt the bottom of the rainbow with our hands, and then visualize it. Using body and hands helps to get the image and sensation into the neocortex.

Jean referenced the concept of interdependent co-arising, which makes something more real in both worlds. She said, "Go to the treasures of unseen generosity."

I had only a vague notion of what this is, so I looked it up. One of the cornerstones of the Buddha's teachings is the concept of interdependent co-arising. The Buddha explained: *"This is because that is. This is not because that is not. This comes to be because that comes to be. This ceases to be because that ceases to be."*

I find an article by Thich Nhat Hanh, who explains that considering a teacup can make one realize the countless causes and conditions that gave rise to it—the clay, the kiln, air, and water, as well as events in the solar system that caused the earth to be created. Clouds and air and sun produced the rain that gave the water. A person made the cup, which causes us to consider his or her parents, and on it goes, and soon we realize that the entire universe is present in this one little cup. Taking away even one element from any of the interdependent causes and conditions: the clay, the water, the potter—and the cup would not exist. The final element that must exist is awareness of the cup, and so the observer is also part of the endless chain of interdependent co-arising.

We heard from several of the participants next: a woman from Texas who had started an innovative school and wanted to take it in a new direction and an entrepreneur and healer from Connecticut who works in elephant sanctuaries and is generating funding for the elephants. Jean identified Ganesh as her archetype.

Then I had the hot seat: an actual "throne" that was facing Jean. Jean asked me to describe what was going on in my life and ask my question.

I said, "After thirty-six years, I recently retired. I have given myself a sabbatical year to seek answers to some of the big existential questions. I believe like everyone here I have the potential to make a difference in this lifetime, but now that corporate life is over, it's a time of redefinition. What am I here to do now? It may have something to do with thriving: being at my best with an open, expansive mind; being healthy, using creativity; finding joy; evolving. I want to get clear on my calling; my question is what do I focus on? I feel compelled to serve, be useful, or give back in some way. How can I do this?"

Jean sat across from me and bowed her head in concentration. Then commanded in a very loud voice, "Hold your hands out! Stand up! Close your eyes! Your left hand represents your creative life! Your right hand represents your former solid skill set in business. Put out your future hand; from inside your chest! What do you see?"

At that moment, some of my "light beings" came into my vision.

I said, "I see balls of pulsating light. I feel essences in the light; they are happy, joyful, loving; I see a field of energy around me."

Jean urged, "*Speak up!* Let it fill you! The third hand is from the cosmos itself. Destiny has called, the beloved of your soul! *Act it out! What is happening?*

I said, "I feel great joy; I have the ability to make a choice."

Jean commanded, "Let it become a story. *Act it out!*"

I started to move my hands and said, "I see beautiful, colorful, light like vivid fireworks in slow motion, like they are in water. The colors merge and flow into each other, like they are dancing together. It is like a beautiful painting."

"See the picture; *step into the painting*! Be the picture!"

"Now I see colorful rings; they are organizing into different patterns; now a circle; now an oval like an eye."

Jean pressed, "Drop into it; *embody it*! Describe it!"

I said, "I see teal, red, orange: the colors are filled with light and energy. The colors are there for me, to help me. I can feel them vibrate."

Jean said, "*Very good*! You have the capacity to create something through art that is a transfusion of energy. Those who experience it are changed and participate in your deep connectivity. It's who you are right now. Paint, meditate, and write about what you are discovering."

I felt exhausted but excited. I had a vivid vision in afternoon meditation about a piece of my art hanging in a public gallery or museum. Robin and I met for dinner after the session. I wanted to hear about Robin's work and what she meant about being a shaman.

Robin explained that she is a contemporary shaman and that a shaman is one who has access to (or "walks" in) two or more worlds, one who is not bound by ordinary reality. A shaman works on behalf of the health and well-being of members of their community, a messenger or facilitator of information between the worlds. This is not a religion; it is a path—a healing modality. Robin studied with contemporary shamanic teachers, though shamans have been found in every culture and throughout every time period.

Shamans are healers. Shamans can walk in lower worlds, middle worlds, and upper worlds. It is her job as a shaman to go where needed to get at underlying issues and impediments and "turn over the rock" on behalf of her clients to help their potential unfold.

Robin explained that she is comfortable with the irrational way. When she journeys, she enters a nonordinary state of consciousness and is able to communicate with guides.

I asked where she goes when she journeys. Robin spends time in all three worlds but said she came from the upper realms. She tells me that she senses I also came from the upper realms.

Robin explained that every shaman is different. She often journeys during dreamtime and goes into a state of consciousness that is similar to a meditative state; in that state, she travels and gets in contact with guides and gets information.

Robin is a healer. She said that there is an aspect of our core being that craves contrast and experience: meaning, purpose, story, drama, and richness. It does not want only the good, perfect, culturally appropriate things; it wants the smorgasbord of life. Most people have a capacity to recognize uplifting emotions like joy, beauty, awe, and gratitude. She said your ability to do that is proportionate to your spiritual health.

If someone feels held back, has limiting beliefs about their abilities, is self-critical, worries a lot, or has fears that keep them from realizing their potential, this can be an indication that there is something that can be healed. As a shaman, her role is to help understand the story and to heal that story. So, a shaman goes in and looks around to see what emerges and then restores integration, vitality, creativity, and wholeness.

I am intrigued and a little in awe of Robin, who treats this ability in a very matter-of-fact way. Robin says, "Lots of people have this ability. I suspect there is a shaman in you, Jane."

I ask Robin if she might be able to help heal Gussie. Robin explains that she will not do anything without permission. She offered to go in, based on my request and look around to see what she could sense about Gus's situation. But she would not *do* anything without Gus's permission.

I have a million more questions for Robin. But it's late, and we agree to talk more tomorrow.

Again, I had trouble sleeping; I felt very keyed up with energy, and my mind was busy absorbing new concepts.

November 6

Again, I woke very early, meditated, and worked out before going to Jean's. Today Jean described epigenetic shifts. I had read about this in meditation classes; there is new research showing rapid alterations in gene expression within subjects who do certain kinds of meditation.

We did a big, exuberant happy dance to high-energy music. It felt great to get up and move, and we were all breathless by the end.

Then Peggy led us on an active river meditation and said things like. "Be the river; be the tributaries; families come to picnic on your shore. Flow into the ocean; other rivers come to join you."

Jean said "think of yourself as a creative storyteller. She said we—each of us—is a fulcrum of creativity. This is a time of phenomenal deconstruction and opportunity. The reset button of history has been hit." Jean has a sense of history and said we all should have a sense of history. There is no excuse not to know history with internet access.

She did a little comedy bit as though she lived in the eleventh century. She acted out all the parts and did all the voices like she was performing a one-woman play.

She played the part of Sicilian farmers who went off to the crusades in Byzantium and Jerusalem. And she said at the end that once you get them to Byzantium, how are you ever going to get them back to the farm?

She reminded us of all the struggles we have witnessed in just our lifetimes; the world has become more seismic and multilayered with crusades for women, minorities, marriage equality, anti-war, occupy movements, save the whales, and save the planet.

She talked about Spiral Dynamics based on the pioneering work of Clare Graves. I looked this up: The idea is that the psychology of the mature human being is an unfolding process marked by successive waves or levels. His or her feelings, motivations, ethic, belief systems, and so forth are all appropriate to that state.

Jean said, "There is a new paradigm of psychodynamics; always a spectrum of possibilities and improbabilities. Things are as they are because they were as they were; sometimes no matter how advanced we are, those old historical behaviors still remain."

She asked us to ponder: "What is the expectation factor you live within?" A shift in consciousness requires a change in language. To shift the expectation—hold the intention. Think in terms of Abbondanza equals Abundance."

Jean says that the Italian language has much more capacity for expression. When you shift language, hold it with intensity. Put "in tense" into your personal city—the civilization inside you. "Here is what you do with your intention!" (She stands up and acts it out with dramatic words and gestures):

"Give it *flavor* and *life*! Dance and *sing*!

It makes your electrons move in a different way!"

At this point, Jean breaks into an exuberant one-woman song in Italian, and everyone claps and dances: *"C'è 'na luna mezz'u mare, Mamma mia m'a maritare ..."*

I marvel at Jean. She opened her home to fifteen people, has staff all around, planned the entire salon from music to meditations to meals, performs nonstop for days, and is still emotionally available for her students, many of whom have been studying with her for years and want private time with her.

I can imagine Jean collapsing in exhaustion at the end. But no, she is even scheduled for things during breaks and in the evenings. She is coaching leaders, writing a play, coauthoring books, and has a multitude of events and travel in the pipeline. Truly, she is an extraordinary person with extreme energy and resourcefulness.

I have noticed this about Deepak Chopra also; there seems to be a source of energy some people have access to, where extraordinary abilities can be tapped into—to speak, teach, travel, and write books.

I wonder if those who meditate or have access to this source create more abundantly, have more youthfulness, resilience and energy, and live a fuller life.

That night most of the group went to see a play during the Shakespeare festival in town. I went back to the hotel to connect with Rich, check in on Gus, and then take a long walk to process all I experienced today.

November 7

Again, I barely slept, rose early, and did my morning routine before going to Jean's.

Today's first exercise was to *energize your intention*!

Jean inspires us. "Thinking in myriad mindedness, in joyous merriment, creates a different and stronger energy to make a *bigger* shift. Cook it up, add a lot of spice, and even more music to feel the vibration; this wrenches us from the questions of millennia."

She admonishes us to become miracle-literate and believe in the God stuff. Look at the qualities in you that are manifesting during this time; it is a massive shift in identity. She and Peggy urge us to be polyphonic, asking, "Who are your inner staff members?"

Peggy does a fun routine: she has Anastasia, her "self" who is an accountant who loves numbers and pays her bills, and Olga, her "self" who does housekeeping. She calls them playful polyphrenia. Become them! She encourages us, "Use them to do the things you don't like to do and add a sense of playfulness and fun. This is the planet of drama. Let them go to work for you!" I love this idea; it is something I resonate with and have never thought of before.

Peggy further explains, "We have many personas. Expand your personae! You have an innate band of characters inside you who have everything. We have very leaky margins; use that to capture all the aspects of yourself." She said that we are tuned into the emotional landscape around us. Social relationships have a huge impact on us; they are a melding of yourself and another.

We can be remotely impacted by another's happiness. If a happy person is in your house, you are 90 percent impacted. She and Jean agreed that dogs are essential!

Happiness is the cracking of the personal code. The reason for the entelechy exercise is to gather the excellences of others and to know yourself as the universe, becoming an energetic presence.

Activate your own optimal template and activate it in others; help them release their hold on negative energy.

Then there was a discussion of the power of one with many quotes:
"Believe in yourself. Believe in your own potential for greatness. Believe that you can change the world."

Jean broke in with jokes from time to time: "Will you be a Nebbish or a Mensch?"

Peggy and Jean led us through an inspiring exercise and said to embrace the energy of entelechy and exhorted us to prepare for responsible power.

How do we interface with creation? Every microsecond the universe renews itself; it is a stupendous mystery. Superb synchronicities abound. A serendipity of happiness exists from inner and outer sources.

They explained transdimensional breakthroughs and having access to the microdimensions. They talked about amplifying receptivity and understanding and discovering our optimal template, and about soul-driven living and moving to a higher order of consciousness and the seeding of another society. They said that now more than ever, it is required.

They inspired us with the idea of awakening as a form of mindfulness and talked about our superb evolutionary brain, kundalini rising, cocreating the universe, bringing together the worlds we are coded for, and discovering how to govern our own neuroplasticity.

They described Erik Erikson's stages of development and getting to the stage of generativity when we reach the age of fifty and beyond. At that point, we've given back to society through raising children, working, and through community activities and organizations. Through generativity, we develop a sense of being a part of the bigger picture. The idea is to find a meaningful way to contribute, or we become stagnant and feel unproductive.

Then they talked about the idea of living well after fifty and having the capacity to activate teaching/learning communities. They inspired us with stories about the impact of elderly people in the classroom and reverse mentoring, calling it a "presence-ing" that is available to others—a program of "sage-ing" generatively.

They traded inspiring ideas: "We are being pulled by the generation forward—impelled! We are corresponding to the passions of turning time and aligning with the mystery of a world in transition—it quickens around you wherever you are! Using the power of your creative imagination, grow new patterns for individuation and world spirituality!"

"We have the needed inner capacities to deal with the complexity of the world. We are capable of the art and science of developing creative capacity."

"Make your vision a reality. Become a generative force. Listen for opportunities! There is now emerging a new world spirituality with profound mythic underpinnings. What lies beneath? What is trying to emerge? Listen! Bring your soul into alignment, create safe havens for growth, and become transparent to transcendence. Remember the suchness of we!"

We recited a moving Whitman poem. Peggy referenced the quantum mechanics tenet that in the midst of horror, something is always being created.

And ended with the happiness prayer by Rabindranath Tagore often used by His Holiness the Dalai Lama.

November 8

We started the next day reciting a poem in unison: "What to Remember When Waking" by David Whyte

Jean gave a lecture on the route to transformation proceeding through each decade of life, from your twenties through your eighties. It is common for beliefs to shift as one ages. Jean says, "If you observe your life this way, it may look novelistic."

We did an exercise, making notes of beliefs from each decade of life, and then debriefed each generation. I noted that for most, their twenties, thirties, and forties were about raising family; for me, it had been all about work. I am intrigued with the participants in their sixties, seventies, and eighties who are still blossoming. The eighty-somethings said:

In the eighties, you bless the world and declutter. You realize that life is an art form; you find balance, bring potentials into manifestation, and find a richer, deeper role as magus or shaman, but make sure you don't go unnurtured.

They said things like, "A kingdom is in the midst of you. From the quantum fields, you find allies willing and able to bud forth and assist. We are all cocreators with the cosmos. We have the powers of world-making, self-making, and life-making."

To understand this, they said to use archetypes; they allow you to make your life grander. When we reframe our life story and find new metaphors, we then greatly strengthen our personal identity. We discover higher orders of identity through myth.

Jean talked about some of her anthropological work. When she goes into a new culture, she finds the greatest myth from that culture and then uses that language to talk about stories. Myth is life, which changes our mental structure.

In the 1980s, people became more mythically conscious. Joseph Campbell was interviewed by Bill Moyers. Jean said, he was speaking the zeitgeist. Something was trying to emerge, and he inspired countless people: artists, writers, and filmmakers. Myths sustain our attitudes.

Myths energize our everyday existence. Remythologize your daily acts; when eating cereal and berries for breakfast, think about how you are nourishing yourself. You then realize you are cocreating your life and it opens you to see the larger story of your life.

Mythic actions realign us with the cosmos and the depths of self. What does the hero do? The hero always asks for guidance—maybe from Athena or Glinda or another archetype. The hero is not alone, even when she thinks she is. When you begin to know yourself, you can push the boundaries of your own story. Call in the archetypes!

Archetypes can be saints, gods, or goddesses and can also be something generic like healer, crone, mother, scribe, teacher, or artist. Archetypes are major organs of the psyche. Join in with spirit, nature, body, and the organs of the universe. They are part of the cosmic blue-print of how things work. Archetypes are part of a substantial meta-physical system.

We did an exercise to find an archetype for a partner. During the meditation, I visualized Joan of Arc. As she appeared, I somehow knew who she was; I saw her on a huge white horse with a flag behind her, holding a long silver sword. Then I saw an image of a goddess with fire around her and somehow understood this was Kali. My partner in the dyad saw Leonardo da Vinci for me. Jean and Peggy explain that you find your archetype by focusing at the spirit level; this helps to create something tangible from your own imagination.

Jean says this takes practice. Read *Search for the Beloved*. Court the attention of the archetype; be in dialogue with your archetype. Canoodle together!

She advised us not to talk much about this because the world does not understand, and you will feel the pain of the world more deeply if you do. Ask the archetypes to help you, and you will be in deep home.

Then we did a study of rhythm: beat, pulse, pattern, vibration, and frequency. You are a rhythm transmitter, charged by heart, located in the emotional center of the body.

Paul played a song of African drums, and Jean talked about how the world functions as an echo transmitter. What you are transmitting comes back amplified. What is coming back amplified to you? It's part of independent coarising—the conscious artful transmission of intention. Be in love with and consult with the universe; ask for help to achieve an amplified life. Put it in a ritual, and it gets turned on; the drum beat synchronizes with your heartbeat. Dance to transcend space and time. Use symbols and storytelling to put it in place with tra-dition and to inspire to make a better world. Become an artist, creating your future destiny.

Connie told the Native American story of star woman at the origin of the world, a story of regeneration. When you want to illumine your transition, make a story of it.

Rendezvous with a heightened frequency—meet with the archetype—allowing the higher destiny to unfold. We are walking magnets. We are able to orchestrate the emotional energy and spiritual energy to bring about manifestation.

Peggy did a very moving scene from the one-act play *The Women of Troy*. After ten years, the Trojan War is over. All the men of Troy are dead, and all its women's fate lie in the hands of their conquerors: a future filled with dread, punishment, and humiliation. In a prison, as the women await their fate, they struggle to keep alive their dignity, their humanity, and their memories of a civilization soon to be lost forever. Two thoughts keep them alive: to see their prince survive to found a new Troy and to see the punishment by death of the woman they blame for all their suffering—Helen.

Peggy remembered it word for word and performed it expertly, even falling to the floor at one point. The power of drama and art deepen our radical empathy.

Robin and I met outside the Shakespeare theater that night for the music festival. She told me more about her life, her kids, and partner. She talked about her business, her dreams, and her ambitions. She told me that she will not be able to help Gussie. I realize Robin is choosing her words carefully, but I get the sense that Robin has seen that Gus does not really want to heal.

We decided to be friends and stay in touch.

November 9

The last morning of the salon, we began with another poem: "The Swan."

Jean said that we are crafted to be creative; we have to find how to create and sustain ongoing creativity. We are filled with ideas and associations. We are all works in progress. Most people are dull—Jean exhorted us to "Stop boring God!" Eighty percent of what we think today is what we thought ten years ago.

Take on a different persona and change modality: dance, paint, do yoga. Be available to the possibilities of newness. Always have a notebook with you! Geniuses are prodigious in what they notice.

Creating works of art grow out of the human psyche. Peggy talked about the palace of memory; before paper was abundant, ancient Greeks remembered their theater lines by fixing passages with place. This reminds me of associating what I am studying with the place I am in—like the Gayatri Mantra with Umbria.

Take pen and pad with you—the universe is at every hand, trying to give you information. Notice! Write! Spawn a whole new level of creativity!

Set an intention and then touch it, intuit it, taste it, hear it, and activate your intentions. Life will have mutual passion for you. It is possible to cocreate an intention that is useful for the world—where the paranormal shakes hands with the infinite. We all have remarkable capacities; our visions, joined to courage, will leap up at us.

You can shift society and be a light force incarnate. Things will begin to happen; move out of local humanity and into the genesis. Creation in its first form moves into the lifeblood and the bones.

Then came the closing ceremony of the salon. We stood in a circle and called our patrons: entelechy, friends of the soul, angels, and archetypes. We each anointed the person next to us with oil and said to one another, "Go; do good and caring work." We each got a special blessing. Connie gave each of us a star candle, and everyone departed.

That night, feeling energized and motivated, I wrote notes from the salon while it was all still fresh in my mind. The number of new concepts I am absorbing makes me feel like I am a freshman in college again. This salon was a profound experience intellectually and emotionally, and I feel sparked, inspired, and so grateful to have had the opportunity to participate and learn.

November 11

We got back into our morning routine and meditated together with the dogs, starting where we left off in the Oprah and Deepak series. The last three meditations talked about developing awareness that is unbounded, focused, and fluid. This supports intention from beginning to fulfillment.

It seems I just wrote in my journal that I wanted to learn how to focus on an intention to bring it to reality, and now after the salon with Jean, I feel much more convinced this is possible.

In my private meditations, when images come to me, circles of color now often change and become an oval of yellow/orange like a sunburst or fire surrounding a circle of blue, almost like an eye. They are in a vast field of lights, like stars. It no longer seems remarkable. I try not to focus on the images and just go back to thinking my mantra. But I still want to paint them.

Deepak talked about living life in a certain way: optimistic, low in stress, full of confidence, and humble in the face of anything the universe sends you. Live consciously rather than unconsciously. He said self-awareness is our most precious birthright; we only have to choose to live by it.

I love the idea of living consciously and being more "awake." And now that I have studied with Jean, I feel I have had glimpses of what that means.

Spa week, which was interrupted by the salon, now continues. On our walk, we saw the huge leaf-sucking truck in the neighborhood, so we jogged back and started raking, blowing, and sweeping our leaves to the street—racing time to get them out before the truck came. The dogs kept jumping in our leaf pile; they thought it was a game. The truck pulled up, and the workers helped us rake the leaves the final distance.

I return to the study of Vedanta and begin to read Shankara's *Crest Jewel of Discrimination*. The basic teaching is that God is the all-pervading reality, the individual soul is the universal soul, and ignorance of our real nature causes suffering and pain. The desire for happiness is essentially a longing to awaken to who and what we truly are. The book is written in the form of a self-teaching manual like a dialogue between a student and spiritual teacher. The text discusses the discrimination between real (unchanging, eternal) and unreal (changing, temporal).

I read what Roger Gabriel wrote in his explanation of Vedanta:

Vedanta is the awakening from unreal to real, from ignorance to bliss. It teaches that anything we can experience with our senses only exists in our mind. And yet, in realizing that nothingness, Vedanta opens the door to a freedom beyond anything we can imagine. Vedanta is our journey home. Vedanta doesn't pretend that the journey is easy—it calls it the "razor's edge"—but offers us four paths to enlightenment and tells us "to set our resolve, our ideal and fill our mind with nothing else."

- Jnana: the path of knowledge, understanding, and self-inquiry
- Bhakti: the path of love and devotion
- Karma: the path of selfless work
- Raja: the "royal path" of meditation and mantras

I wonder about the four paths; they are all intriguing. I imagine Jnana is for true scholars. Bhakti sounds wonderful; I love to spend time in devotion, singing and chanting. The karma path sounds noble. Raja is the path of meditation, mantras, and techniques. This is the path I presume I am on. I would like to dive more deeply to understand more.

November 12

In today's meditation, Deepak said as your consciousness awakens, you become more self-aware. Encountering your soul happens without effort because your soul wants to connect.

I find it interesting that Vedanta does not seem to shun external rewards in the path to deeper spirituality. I imagine this is particularly true if you don't have strong attachments to those external things like house, car, title, bank account, and so forth.

I worked on "City Girls" today. And a new painting of a golden oval with a blue center, in a field of stars that looks like an eye. The art college connected me with a student, Tori, I can hire to help me animate some of my meditation paintings.

The sibs are communicating daily; we take turns checking on Gussie, who is working, not drinking, and going to her therapist.

November 13

I did more work on "City Girls" today and started some paintings of the Villa at Benano for Abigail and Paula.

I talked to Tori and outlined the animation project. She probably thinks this is nuts but kept her opinions to herself, and we agreed to start tomorrow. I will pay her $20 per hour. She has already graduated and is doing freelance work while she interviews in Silicon Valley.

We built our first fire of the season tonight. It was lovely. When we moved from New York, we wanted a real fireplace. It smells so good.

Today a lady said to Rich, "I think you have some dog hair on your sweater."

He said, "Yes, ma'am. I have dog hair on every article of clothing I own."

I started to read *The Yoga Sutras of Patanjali*. I have a hard copy that was translated by Alistair Shearer. It's small enough to fit in my handbag, so I can read it often.

Shearer talks about parallels of Buddhism and Vedanta, something I have wanted to understand. I see similarities in the causes of suffering, the four virtues of friendliness, compassion, happiness, and equanimity. It is likely that both sets of texts drew on a common body of knowledge. Both wisdom traditions focus on Yoga, which is from the Sanskrit root YUJ, "to join," and means "unity." In this context, "yoga" means union of mind, body, spirit, and environment.

November 14

In meditation today, we learned that the energy of attraction is most powerful when you want the highest and best outcome. Everyone's spiritual path is perfect. This makes an impression on me; I feel a strong urge to help raise the vibration level and serve in some larger way as a force for good.

Tori began teaching me Adobe After-Effects to animate my paintings. A 2-D painting doesn't convey the life in the images I see. Simple keystrokes that take nanoseconds for her take me minutes. She is patient and deserves every cent. I take my flat 2D paintings and describe the motion I want to see: Light and color flowing like a lava lamp. Colors morphing from magenta to teal. An oval of brilliant fire surrounding a blue circle. We photograph the paintings, upload the photos, and then start to animate.

I felt silly saying, "This is what I see in meditation," but she wasn't judging me.

I imagine what she says to her friends: "There is this kooky lady who sees things in meditation, and she is paying me to help her animate them. Ha!"

In my study of the Yoga Sutras today, Shearer says that all religions use techniques of yoga to lead the mind inward to silence. The ritual movement of Sufism, the "Jesus prayer," and the martial arts technique of the Taoists all are ways of stilling the mind and reaching the silence within. They differ in expression, but in essence they are one.

I think about different wisdom traditions and the many ways individuals go toward the silence and seek their version of the face of God. What if they are all valid, if they just open a different door to the same room? I ask myself, if the path doesn't matter, why do I still seek? Should I just pick something and stick with it? Am I looking for a religion?

As I wonder if there will be an "ism" for me going forward, it makes me wistful. There would be something comforting about saying, "I am a Buddhist." It's too soon to land; I have barely begun to know and experience. I like learning from those who are farther down the path. There seems to be a new process for me now: understanding a concept intellectually, understanding it experientially, and then noticing how it resonates.

November 16

The meditation today taught that a life lived in grace is a merger of self and soul. Our perspective shifts from personal to universal.

I continue reading. Shearer says:

The Yoga Sutras are the most lucid and authoritative of all the texts that serve as maps for the inner journey. The results of many hundreds of years of experience, the sutras are not necessarily the work of one author. They were compiled by Patanjali, about who we know nothing except he lived in India, probably in the third century before Christ. In just under two hundred crystalline verses, Patanjali codified a teaching of such translucence that he created one of the most remarkable works of spiritual literature in the world.

November 17

Meditation today focused on co-creation. I am a co-creator in my life. I have the power to shape my response to the universe. I am the captain of my soul.

Deepak says that our highest role is to help collective consciousness to evolve; it only consists of fulfilling the desires I want—naturally.

I find myself in overlapping thought loops: I meditate, I journal, I think, I study, I reach for the next topic, and it is like following some kind of map or the map is finding me. Recently, I was yearning to find a way to serve through meditation and today the meditation touched on helping collective consciousness to evolve.

Shearer says:

The first four sutras of chapter 1 contain Patanjali's entire message in a nutshell. Yoga is the settling of the mind into silence, and only when the mind is silent can we realize our true nature: the effortless Being of the Self. The remaining one

hundred and ninety sutras are an expansion of this brief intro-
ductory statement.

I also read about the Yoga Sutras in the material I was given by the
Chopra Center: "Patanjali's book can be thought of as a handbook for
enlightenment. The central idea is that we all have a spark of divine
light within us. For most of us, this divine light is obscured by stress,
doubts, and conditioned beliefs."

The 196 sutras are aphorisms that contain vast wisdom. The Sanskrit word *sutra* means "thread" and is the root of the word *suture*,
which means "to stitch together." The Sutras are therefore a collection
of small threads that weave together an enormous body of wisdom.
In Patanjali's day, most teaching took place through the oral tradition.
The teacher would give the students a sutra and then expand on its
essence, meaning, and interpretation.

November 18

Today's meditation said we each have the power to be a beacon of
light and tranquility. Enlightenment is something you become, not
something you possess. *Being* is more important than *doing*. Grow,
live, prosper is the ultimate spiritual secret.

Today I read more of the numerology report that addressed
challenges.

Each of us is born with strengths and weaknesses. If life is viewed as
an educational process that is meant to develop talents and strengths
and address weaknesses, then the job of becoming whole *is* a "be all
you can be" idea.

The report said the First Challenge usually lasts from birth until
approximately age thirty-five. My First Challenge had to do with sur-
mounting my own demons of self-criticism, self-doubt, the suppres-
sion of creativity, and the fear of social interaction. I think of my severe
introversion and fear as a child and young adult, and this resonates.

The Second Challenge usually lasts until the age of forty. Similarly, this challenge had to do with being hyperaware of other's expectations and stifling individuality.

The Third or Main Challenge is felt through the whole life. For me, this challenge is to stand up for my beliefs, develop a clear sense of what is right, and don't go against my values.

November 19

Today was the last meditation in the series. We loved it. Today's lesson was, there is no separation between what is in us and around us; we are one with the universe. Today was a favorite mantra: Aham Brahmasmi. I am the universe.

Our walk was cold and sunny: thirty-one degrees. I worked on "City Girls" and the villa paintings, went to lift and worked on animations. At the gym, I was lifting heavier weights than most of the guys; that was fun.

This afternoon I met with art college faculty and staff and got their feedback about our president candidates.

I read more of the *Yoga Sutras of Patanjali* and learn that there are eight limbs of yoga. I would like to study with an in-person teacher to understand more; I wonder if the eight limbs of yoga are supposed to be sequential stages on the path. Shearer says: "The sequence of asanas, pranayama, and meditation comprise any daily routine of yoga. It is also true that total samadhi is the result of the other seven limbs being fully developed."

I have heard the term *samadhi* several times. My favorite explanation is that as a laser beam is to normal light, samadhi is to normal thought. I still think of myself as truly a beginner on the path, but I like thinking that each meditation is cumulative. My teacher said that no meditation is ever wasted.

November 20

Today we started the first Oprah and Deepak meditation series again. Each time we listen, we hear another nuance that we missed before.

This afternoon, I got to see one of my most favorite people, Danny, for a studio visit and see his newest paintings. They are colorful and inspiring, and it was great to see him. He is battling cancer and has a dire prognosis but is funny, philosophical, and upbeat. I love him, and he gave me some painting tips.

News in the world is depressing. I see why the clairvoyant at Canyon Ranch told me not to watch the news if I could help it. When we were in Europe, especially at the villa, everyone seemed to be talking about current events. It's hard to avoid. At Jean's salon, the news was foundational to many conversations. She was whipping us up to get out there and do something to make the world better.

In some ways, I'd like to push away the world and live in a little bubble with my pack. I used to feel I had to bone up on the goings-on of the world to hold my own in conversations. I have had a recurring hermit fantasy where I dream of separating from the world. Rich always has the news on in the house. I am ashamed to admit I want to tune it all out.

November 21

The grounding in Numerology has given me things to think about. Amazingly much of it rings true. I keep thinking how powerful it would have been (or maybe dangerous?) if I had known some of this at an earlier age. Would I have more easily recognized my challenges? Or when you are going through something, maybe it is hard to get enough distance from things to hold them in perspective.

Here are some things I am going to keep thinking about, particularly as I meditate because these ideas made me feel inspired:

- I can be a channel or portal between the archetypal realm and the material world.
- I want to contribute to the well-being of humanity.
- How do I do that? I don't have a clue. It will be fun finding out.

November 22

After meditation this morning, we donned boots, hats, and gloves to take the dogs out in the snow. Rich does not like cold weather, and it seemed to come very quickly this year.

As he grumbled, I suggested that we could move to a warmer place; in fact, we could move anywhere in the world! We only came to Ohio for my work. My work is over and done. What's to stop us? So, we had a dreamy little fantasy about where we would like to be.

November 23

I had art college meetings the past few days. We are making an offer to the new president: I'm thrilled it is a woman! Because I ran the search committee, I've been the point person in meetings with faculty, staff, and student representatives, and I have been communicating with our candidate, finalizing offer details.

I also volunteered at Life Town today. It is a facility built like a real town to teach kids who are physically and cognitively challenged how to do things like go to the bank, the movies, the salon, the art store, and the pet store. I volunteered in the art store and the pet store. I am going again Monday.

Rich gave platelets and blood today. He always believes he is saving a kid's life, and he has been very faithful about it. He also mentored his soldier who served in Iraq again yesterday. I think it is just in Rich's DNA to want to quietly give back to whatever community he is a part of. He is such a good guy.

November 24

A gorgeous, sunny, and cold day. I had two great walks with Bella and a slow one with Chip, jogged on the treadmill, and lifted weights.

I started a new painting technique with acrylics, using "poured" paint. I had to go to the art store to get the new supplies. The paint is a bit expensive. The pouring technique is *so fun* but incredibly messy. I have to paint in the unfinished part of the basement where it doesn't matter if paint goes everywhere. I splashed paint on my painting shoes and ankles. Being covered with paint is my idea of heaven.

Tomorrow we are going on the trip to Napa, so I took some time out from painting to pack and get ready to take the dogs to the kennel.

Before bed, I did the second pour on my newest painting, using quinacridone crimson, quinacridone magenta, and some black. It looks great so far. The colors of this liquid paint are like stained glass: very transparent.

November 25

We bundled up hounds, beds, treats, food, and toys, took them to the kennel, and flew to St. Louis. We got to the hotel mid-morning, and our room was ready. On the flight, I studied the Yoga Sutras. Each sutra is worthy of hours of contemplation.

The mind does not shine by its own light.
It too, is an object illumined by the Self. (4.19)

We are going to spend the day and night in St. Louis before we charter a jet to Napa Valley for Thanksgiving with family. Raleigh is feeling OK enough to travel after all of his recent procedures. He is now eighty. His older sister, Aunt Betty, who is eighty-eight, is going, too. After a recent broken shoulder, hearing loss, and other physical challenges, she can no longer manage a commercial flight.

This trip was Rich's idea, and a brilliant one. His jokes that his biggest fear is that we die with money. He really wants to do this for his dad and aunt, and I am grateful that he is generous.

We are invited to Thanksgiving dinner at Rich's cousin's home. Betty's son Abel and his wife, Jocelyn own a winery on Howell Mountain above St. Helena. Brook, Betty's daughter and our dear friend, will also be there.

We fly out tomorrow. In the meantime, today, I get to see one of my oldest and dearest friends, Paul.

Paul and I have known each other since kindergarten. He always had a game plan for the day, like "Hey guys, let's put on a play!" His family moved away from Carrollton, and twenty-five years later, we found each other again in Manhattan.

We reconnected in the mid-1980s. We were just learning about AIDS and living through many of our friends getting sick and dying. Witnessing the emotion of that time together made our friendship even stronger. With Paul, it has always been easy to just be myself without working to preserve ego or try to make myself look better. It is just—all real—all trust—all out.

I wonder if there is likely a soul group connection between Paul and me that goes *way* beyond this lifetime. There is no emotion other than pure happiness when I am with him. We don't see each other often enough, but we have stayed emotionally close. Paul is the one friend I write actual letters to. Often when we connect, we find that we have just read the same book or seen the same play.

We had an amazing lunch with that great feeling of kinship where we are so excited to be together; we interrupt one topic to get to the next. I told him about my spiritual adventures and got caught up on his life. Three hours flew by like minutes. It was so great of him to drive over to see me.

November 26

This morning we meditated, worked out and then met Raleigh and Betty at the Spirit of St. Louis airport for the flight. Raleigh looked pale and wasn't walking easily. Betty needed help walking, too, but was very excited and animated. They loved the plane. Betty kept saying, "This is really nice."

On the flight, I worked on a slideshow "movie" of all of our past Thanksgivings with this crew that I will show when we get to Abel and Jocelyn's.

Betty and Raleigh loved the catered snack we had for them, and Betty was thrilled they had Diet Coke on board. We landed in only four hours at the Napa airport. It is a beautiful, sunny seventy-degree day here. Abel and Jocelyn picked us up. They are lending us their Jeep while we are here. They are so excited Betty is back with them one more time in Napa.

The trip was easy, the way a commercial flight never would have been. Because of the time difference, we got here midmorning.

We are staying at Villagio in Yountville. Even though he probably feels crappy, Raleigh is excited to be in California. It is his first time. We took him on a drive before lunch to St. Helena, one of our favorite towns in the valley. Raleigh is not a wine-drinker, but he recognized Beringer Vineyards and Charles Krug Winery. He liked driving down Main Street and looking at the shops. We drove up to the Culinary Institute of America at Greystone and told him about cooking classes we have taken there. He was very interested in the agricultural aspect of the vineyards we passed.

We met everyone at Mustard's. It is so great to see tall, elegant Brook. She still lives in New York, working as a senior executive in advertising. We got a great table in the back and then dove into the menu.

All foodies, we were in rapture poring over the menu. We decided since this was the main meal of the day, to do it up right with appetizers, a main course, and a dessert or two for Raleigh and Betty, who both have a sweet tooth.

November 27

Today was a nearly perfect day in Napa Valley. We woke up early, meditated, got coffee, and then went out for a jog under the starry sky—forty-six degrees and no wind. When dawn broke, hot air balloons were flying over the valley. It was a bright, sunny, crisp morning with fog coming off the swimming pool. We had breakfast with Raleigh—perfect omelets and luscious fruit.

I had one of the most self-indulgent spa treatments of my life: a 100-minute deep-tissue massage with Mario. It was a perfect Napa

Valley day: seventy degrees and sunny—such a nice change from snow and polar vortex.

We all met for a delicious lunch at Market and drove to a couple of picturesque wineries.

I read more of the Yoga Sutras at the pool, focusing more on the eight limbs of yoga, but I ended up with even more questions for a teacher someday. Another long walk, meditation, and then soup and salad across the street at Bistro Jeanty. A peaceful day.

Raleigh did not want to walk over for dinner, so we brought him soup and bread. He wanted to sit by the fire in his room and read. He seems to be doing okay, but he is always cold and covered up with a blanket.

November 28

Today is Thanksgiving Day. We woke up early and meditated. We got coffee, and then I went to the hotel gym to do elliptical and lift. We walked outside when it got light and saw the balloons again. It was cool but sunny.

Raleigh ate with good appetite this morning. He was excited to see the colorful hot air balloons dotting the blue sky. We drove him through Yountville; he wanted to see The French Laundry because he has heard us talk about our memorable meals there.

We drove to Oakville and Rutherford past the Robert Mondavi Winery. We stopped at the legendary Auberge du Soleil. He admired their artful arrangement of heirloom pumpkins in the entry way and loved seeing the way the property is terraced into the sunlit hillside and nestled in an olive grove. We sat on the terrace, looking out at the sweeping vineyard views.

We took him into the Oakville Grocery where he lingered, marveling at the array of picnic food: cheese, olives and pickles, bread, mustards, and sausages. We bought things for lunch. While Raleigh took a nap, I meditated, and then we hung out on our terrace and took a moment to be grateful for our lives. We called my dad, Gus, Rich's brother and nephew and texted other family and friends to wish them a happy Thanksgiving.

We took a car service up the mountain. Abel, Jocelyn and Brook greeted us. Both Abel and Jocelyn are talented and capable. They restored the farmhouse that was on vineyard land, and it is now a gorgeous homestead. Pottery Barn has used their home for catalog shoots. Abel built the winery outbuildings. Their home is warm and inviting with a pool, fountains, a huge stone table, bocce court, and acres of vines.

After a great walk with their dogs and a flurry of last-minute preparation, we sat down to a beautiful table and incredible Thanksgiving dinner with the last bottles of their first vintage, some of the most precious and nostalgic wine in their cellar. It was a memorable feast with beloved family.

Raleigh was tired, so we called the car service and headed down the mountain soon after dinner.

November 29

One last Napa Valley walk this morning, a big breakfast, and then to the airport to fly back to St. Louis on the jet. We had a great tailwind and made it in a bit over three hours.

It was amazing to get them home so quickly. We said goodbye to Raleigh and Betty and then went to Lambert Airport to get on Southwest Airline to go home to Columbus. As we went through security and waited at our gate for our Southwest flight, Rich said to me, "Wow, I guess we are back to reality." I laughed, "It's hard to get them back on the farm once they have seen Byzantium."

On the flight, I finished an exercise physiology class I have been taking for a few weeks. With earbuds and my phone, I have been able to listen/watch at the gym during cardio. Though multitasking seems to be frowned upon these days, learning while exercising seems like a great idea to me, and it makes exercise time fly by. The class reinforces what I have learned at Canyon Ranch.

The summary is that teams of scientists have shown that high-intensity interval training (HIIT), coupled with weight lifting, is the most beneficial way for healthy people to exercise. HIIT involves alternating between very intense spurts of action and a more leisurely pace during exercise. This is great news because I love doing intervals.

HIIT helps rejuvenate our protein-building ribosomes and boosts the energy-producing capacity of mitochondria. As we age, the ability of our mitochondria to generate energy dwindles. This study suggests HIIT can help reverse the age-related changes seen in mitochondria.

The class went through studies of three groups of healthy exercisers from eighteen to eighty. They took health and fitness measures before and after the twelve-week study.

They concluded that different types of exercise offer different benefits. HIIT boosts mitochondrial activity, and weight training improves muscle strength. The NHS recommends that adults do 150 minutes of moderate exercise a week (or 75 minutes of vigorous activity), plus strength exercises.

If people are healthy and cleared by their doctor, they recommend people do thirty minutes of moderate exercise, such as a brisk walk, five times a week. It isn't necessary to do HIIT every day; two to three times a week is a good balance. It is critical to incorporate a flexibility program, such as stretching or yoga several times a week. This is great information—just what I have been seeking. I make the recommended tweaks in my exercise plan.

November 30

It is freezing today—an arctic blast. We are in for a horribly cold winter. Rich feels the cold more deeply than most people. I took advantage of his misery and convinced him to get on my scheduled call with an astro-cartographer to find out where our optimum locations would be; maybe there is a warmer climate for us. He reluctantly agreed.

The paths were not icy, so we bundled up and walked. The dogs like the cold; they are very frisky when they go out. The trips in the middle of the night are not so fun now because I have to take time to put on boots, hat, coat, and gloves.

Chip loves Rich so much. He is growing fast and needs to stretch several times a day. His favorite way is to climb on Rich when he is sitting in his desk chair, put his paws on Rich's shoulder, and then reach up to give him many kisses. He always wants to snuggle against Rich, especially now that it is getting colder. Chip loves to be right on top of Rich's feet.

I was thrilled to paint today. I did the third pour on my first painting and started two more big works; they will be about 40 x 50 when framed. The trick is finding drying space for everything. I love this new paint. It is so different to just pour, see what emerges, and then problem-solve the next right step, as opposed to planning every stroke I put on canvas. Maybe there is an analogy there: just see how life unfolds and react to it.

Chapter Six

December

December brings an astrocartography reading that creates a small bump in the road of our marriage and an exciting new possibility for us. My Synchro-Destiny course opens new vistas for me; the class is beautiful, enlightening, and inspiring. I learn even more about setting clear intentions in order to co-create with the universe, gain confidence in my new painting medium, and experience two more metaphysical readings. Sad news about a friend and worrisome news about Gussie's health remind me that in life, we can experience every emotion. Challenges prompt me to consider that within us are all the tools and courage we need and that sometimes perspective is needed to see the magnificent story of every life.

December 2

I had a good HIIT workout this morning and a wonderful meditation with the pack. Very cold again, but no snow: it was in the twenties when we walked.

Today is our meeting with the astrocartographer. He lives in South America but is originally from Kansas. Rich is being weird about it, almost passive aggressive. He complained about taking time for the call, and I said, "No problem, I will do the session without you." He asked, "How much is this going to cost?" I told him, "$400, but I am taking it out of the stash you set aside for me." He is sulking, seemingly offended that I would do it without him and said he would be there. I know what this is because I have moved with this man sixteen times. He gets rooted to and invested in wherever he lives. He hates the idea of change and disruption. He has a hard time understanding why I get excited to move to the next adventure and complains I have wander-lust. Oh, Jane, why did you do this to yourself?

After enduring stony silence from Rich all morning and through lunch, we did the call at two o'clock. I asked him to come into my office because I had Skype connected on my computer. He brought his notebook and wore his most serious pair of glasses and a scowl. I got the call connected with no problem. The astrologist's name is Dan.

He greeted us and said he had a number of charts to share. He had asked for our birth information and sent charts in an enormous box file: maps of the world with colored lines, strange markings, and nota-tions. An entire set of files for Rich and a whole set for me. He gave us background on the relatively new science of astrocartography. Rich was sullenly taking notes, looking extremely skeptical.

Dan asked what prompted the reading. I said "I've recently retired from a thirty-six-year career. We moved to Ohio for my work, and now that it's over, we could go anywhere in the world. We want to see our most advantageous locations." Rich glared at me.

He went through Rich's charts first, showing each continent on the screen as we peered to see. He said our current location in Ohio was OK for Rich; he had to work hard for what he produced, but it was a conducive location for fulfillment. He went through each continent and pointed to advantageous and less advantageous locations. Parts of Italy were good. Parts of India were good. Parts of China. Rich's eyes were glazing over. I ask Dan to focus; in the western half of North America, where are the most advantageous locations for Rich? South-ern California and parts of Texas. Arizona is not bad.

Then he went through my charts. He pulled up North America and I could see a red, angry line with a strange symbol passing right through central Ohio. He said, "Jane, where you are living is not a good location for you. You are living right on a Pluto line. It's great you are getting out of there."

I tried to tell him, "But we have lived here for years and we have been happy and successful ..." but he kept talking.

He went through every continent for me; parts of Italy and Paris are great for me, and parts of India and China. Most of Africa is not good. One of the best locations for me is Houston, Texas. I asked him to take a look at Southern California. He said yes, that's good; a mercury line passes right through there for you. Arizona is fine. Seattle and Portland are also good. Denver was very good.

Then we started comparing. Colorado is good for me, but not Rich. Parts of Texas are good for us both. Southern California is good for us both. San Francisco is great for me, but not Rich. Arizona is fine for both. New Mexico is great for me, but not Rich. Parts of Oregon and Washington are good for us both. And then our hour was up.

He sent a key that helped us decipher what each symbol meant and asked us to look at the charts and let him know what questions we had. I thanked him, and we ended the call.

It was as if a bomb had gone off in the house, detonating in the midst of our easy, fun daily banter. Rich was uncommunicative. I knew from nearly forty years of experience that when I become the force that wants to initiate change, I have to suffer. I'm sure he was resenting me for sucking him into something he doesn't believe in.

I googled, "Living on a Pluto line." Basically, your life is at risk anytime you get in a vehicle or cross a street. You live in a constant state of seeking with no answers. Wow. If this holds any merit, I really do need to get the hell out of here. My imagination started to spiral. I have been afraid to drive since we moved here. I have been on kind of a treadmill the whole time I've been here. Do I believe it? My rational mind rebels, but I want to be open, and any impetus for a new adventure is welcome.

I start to imagine what it will take to get Rich to open up to the idea of moving. He likes facts and figures. I made a spreadsheet and included Portland, Seattle, Los Angeles, San Diego, Tucson, Phoenix, Dallas, and Houston. I added Standard Metropolitan Statistical Area (SMSA) data: the ranking of the best hospital in each market; notes about public transportation; the number of Apple, Whole Foods, and Trader Joe's stores; annual days of sunshine; and number of golf courses. I find an index of housing costs and put that in.

In meditation, I ask for help. *Please guide me in determining the highest and best next step for us.*

We have a mostly silent, stiffly formal dinner, both talking to Chip and Bella more than each other. I hate this, but I accept it as a necessary step in the process. At some point, we will get back to normal.

After he fell asleep that night, I put my arms around Rich and silently told him how much I love him and that it's going to be OK. "We will be OK. We will go on this adventure together, and it will be the best move we've ever made."

December 3

Good meditation this morning. Maybe Rich's cold front will thaw out. It got up to 40 degrees today. Elliptical workout and walk with the dogs. They were funny this morning, running and playing together. No thawing was evident, though; Rich was still in his remote, punishing persona.

I started thinking about cocreating. Here was the perfect opportunity to test this idea that we are free to dream of new adventures. I keep hearing that the universe truly wants to partner with us to give us our hearts' desires, but we need to be clear about what we want.

I read in a Daily Om email that it's like placing an order—we don't have to beg the waiter to bring us our order or prove to them that we deserve to have it. It is their job to give us what we ask for; we only have to clearly tell them what we want. Once we have a clear vision of what we want, we set our intentions in the silent place of meditation.

Announce the intentions with as much specificity as possible and then release any attachment to the outcome and express gratitude.

So, what do I want in regard where we live? To live in a location that is beneficial to us both, where Rich will be even happier than he is here and where we can live our highest and best life. A safe yard for the dogs. A serene, light-filled space to paint and meditate. A great office for Rich. A large, functional kitchen. A clean, modern, unclut-tered home. Enough space without being too much. I want to see mountains. I want the move to be easy and drama free. I want our house to sell quickly and easily once Rich gets on board.

I spent the rest of the day creating. I took the animations, added music, and an encoded message in each, like "see the larger story of your life" and "raise the vibration level."

I went to the unfinished part of the basement, called on my inner Leonardo, and thought of myself as a conduit for the painting to take place. I put on music and continued with the liquid acrylic paintings, and they dried quickly so I could work on one and then rotate to the next and the next while the other two had drying time. I added layers of color; teal and magenta were dominant in each, and the transpar-ent layers were gorgeous, like a stained-glass window coming to life. As I was painting, ethereal images emerged in the painting. It looked abstract, but within the paintings, light beings were there, under the surface, if you looked at the painting a certain way. I declared one of the paintings "done," and a gorgeous blue light being was embedded in the painting like a shadowy spirit.

December 4

I have been in a painting frenzy the past week. I love my new medium of liquid acrylics. So messy and so fun! The colors can be very vivid if you patiently apply layers and let them dry. Yesterday I had a blotch of red paint on my forehead and spatters of blue on my ankles. I felt very artistic.

Yesterday, the art college announced our new president. She is only forty years old—young for that big role, but she is confident and mature with great experience. Everyone is very invested in her success, so hopefully she will be here for many years. I really like her.

I took part in the communications cascade and made calls to some community leaders to let them know the news and connected with our other candidates to formally turn them down and thank them for being in the process. I am happy to be closing this out with a great outcome. My board term expires in a few months, so I feel even freer to move.

I have had a good workout week. Gus is doing OK: working, says she is sober, and seems focused. Next week she has an appointment at Barnes-Jewish in St. Louis to see if her disease has progressed.

The Synchro-Destiny class today focused on setting powerful intentions, which is so funny, since I just took the step to set the intention to move; maybe that in itself is a synchronicity.

It feels like this class dovetails closely with the meditations we have been doing and where my mind is naturally tuning in. It's almost as if I am getting the message: "You are on the right track here!"

The first important step in setting intentions is to become very clear about what is desired. Deepak guided us through a great meditation to set the stage. He said to write down our intentions in positive language. In the course, they said that the universe is alive and conscious and responds to the intentions. They also advised to be detached from the outcome.

I wrote intentions about the move yesterday, but I want a lot more. Funny, I am hesitant to write these down. Maybe it's the subliminal "I am not worthy" belief.

What do I want?
I want what I have—to be with my pack.
I want love, gratitude, laughter, contentment, and joy every day.
I want the highest and best for everyone I love; for them to be happy, healthy, safe, strong and to live easily.
I want vitality—to be healthy in mind, body, spirit.

I want to know my purpose and use my talents to make the world a better place.
I want a passionate, intimate, loving, fun relationship with Rich.
I want good sleep.
I want a healthy back that allows me to be very active.
I want to maintain a healthy weight.
I want to gain wisdom and open up my intuitive capability. I want to keep learning.
I want to make paintings that inspire people.

And then I included the desires I wrote yesterday for a good location, beneficial to us both, with the specifics about meditation, painting space, yard, kitchen, and mountain views. I added: I want Rich to be as excited about the move as I am and for it to be a great adventure together.

I read my intentions before afternoon meditation and put them in my dresser drawer so I can read them before every meditation.

Then I took several carloads of donations to Goodwill. They have a drive-through and come out to the car to help unload it. And they accept donated paintings! I brought the donation receipts back to Rich for tax planning, which seemed to thaw him out a bit.

Over dinner, I showed Rich the spreadsheets and asked him what other criteria we should include. He seemed impressed with the work and began to open up. We talked about location. I told Rich that I am detached from the outcome; I am open. I would be fine with Washington, Oregon, California, or Arizona. If we can see mountains, I do not care. He can choose. I am thrilled; Rich is beginning to get excited.

Later, I overheard him on the phone with his best friend, saying, "There is no reason for us to stay in Ohio; we could go anywhere."

We talked about the kind of house we want and are amazingly aligned. Rich actually said he's almost ready to have a conversation with a realtor about putting the house on the market!

December 5

The college student art sale was this morning, a good turnout despite the cold. Everyone is so excited for our new president to start. I saw many faculty and staff, and thanked them; their input was invaluable.

I went to the frame store to get the Blue Light canvas stretched and to buy frames for the villa landscapes I finished for Paula and Abigail.

I did more Synchro-Destiny course today. I am deliberately going slowly to absorb these concepts. Embedded in the course are some beautiful bonus meditations. Today I had five meditations. Some were very short, but I am sure my teacher would say, "It's too much; you are going to be loopy."

In class today, Deepak referenced the quote I found from the Upanishads:

You are what your deepest desire is.
As is your desire, so is your intention. As is your intention, so is your will.
As is your will, so is your deed.
As is your deed, so is your destiny.
(Upanishads)

I did more decluttering and trips to Goodwill. Now Rich is cleaning his closet. As we were cleaning, I made a suggestion. *Hey, we have a winter trip coming up; what if we postpone that, take the dogs, rent a place, and look around out West?* Rich agreed. I said I would do the research if Rich would pick a location. He chose the Palm Springs, California, area.

I postponed the trip and started looking for pet-friendly rentals in California. At this late stage, there are no more available this winter. But I found a resort I liked—La Quinta Resort, a Waldorf-Astoria hotel with restaurants on site, a gym, and golf and tennis for Rich. I called the resort itself, and amazingly, they did long-term rentals and had just gotten a last-minute cancellation on a pet-friendly villa, starting in January if there could be flexibility on dates. Yes, dates could be flexible. I rushed in to tell Rich.

December 6

Good sleep, good snuggle, good meditation. I'm so grateful Rich and I are back to cuddling, intimacy, and we are now sharing excitement about our next adventure. We have not yet told anyone outside the pack that we are moving. I did intervals on the treadmill, and then we got the dogs out for a very cold walk.

In Synchro-Destiny class today, Deepak covered what we experience in consciousness: sensations, images, feelings, and thought. Everything that is experienced occurs in consciousness. The qualities of consciousness are called *qualia*. I have never heard this term before; my computer keeps trying to autocorrect it to quail.

He said feelings are the most primordial qualia; they determine the quality of thought, create images in consciousness, and are the source of sensations in the body. Everything starts with feeling. As you become more aware of feeling, you can shift your perception and therefore your reality.

Funny: I know this lesson, except in corporate life we never talked about "feelings," of course. We talked about thinking. I used to teach this lesson in culture-shaping. We called it the results cone; your thinking drives your behavior, which drives your results. If you change your thinking, you can change your life. Gratitude is the emotion that can shift everything to a positive.

December 7

I savored the next segment of the Synchro-Destiny course today.

Today was about appreciating that we are all creating qualia in every moment and to make the experience of life joyful, loving, and fulfilling. To make life richer, feel your connection to the creative source. One of the most powerful ways to do this is in meditation, which gives you the experience of pure potentiality.

Focus on cultivating emotions that increase well-being, including love, peace, joy, and gratitude.

Notice where you are focusing your attention because what you focus on will expand.

I love the idea of continuing to focus on daily joy, nature, laughter, peace, and deep appreciation.

December 8

Snow flurries today but not enough to stick. We bundled up and got out for fresh air. The path was slick, so we walked on the grassy area around the pond. Chip rolled in something disgusting. He was in such bliss, I let him. He joyfully swung his legs, belly up, from side to side, eyes rolled back in ecstasy, and sneezing every few moments as he lolled his head back and forth. When we got back to the house, I wiped down his muddy back, head, and paws and then started on Bella. By the time I finished with her, he had bounded up the stairs, jumped on our bed and he was rubbing his still wet head on Rich's pillow.

Rich came in, and we both gazed down at him. "We are so disciplined." Now we are washing the pillow cases, so Lorena, the house cleaner, won't know.

We continue the daily decluttering, and I take carloads to Goodwill. My goal is for every drawer and closet to be tidy and organized. I am enjoying doing property searches in Portland, Seattle, San Diego, and Phoenix.

The Synchro-Destiny class meditations are captivating. In one, Deepak talked about manifesting true desires and intentions by imagining your wishes are a precious jewel resting in your heart.

December 10

This morning I went to the neighborhood coffee club where we all donated money to help local families. I shopped for some toys for a third-grade girl. One family had their power cut off, so I did research about how to get it turned back on again. There is a lot of need in our community—and happily, also a lot of people willing to help.

Tonight, we are planning to see Danny and Bea; they are going to stop by for a drink. He is really ill, so I hope it can work. I mopped the floors and made appetizers.

Today I did some more testing of brain catalyst technology because Gus really likes the meditations I sent. I read about brain waves.

Alpha Waves are slow. They take place in relaxed focused attention and are conducive to super learning, joy, and happiness. Most meditators produce alpha waves during meditation.
Theta Waves—Advanced meditators have alpha waves with momentary excursions into Theta, which are conducive to dreaming sleep and visions during meditation.
Delta Waves—Delta waves happen during dreamless sleep. Some extremely advanced meditators can make delta waves while awake.
Gamma Waves—Gamma waves exist during certain Buddhist meditations and during inspiration, higher learning, and focus. Gamma waves are always complemented by other brainwaves.

Very interesting. I wonder if I slip into theta waves when I see my motion and light essences.

Danny cancelled for tonight. He had a doctor visit with bad news; he is now eligible for hospice. They want to be alone tonight, of course. My heart sank when I read the text.

December 11

I had an Akashic past-life reading, thinking that learning something about past lives could be an important part of my journey. The medium said that I love the roles of student and teacher. I do not like to stay put; I would rather wander the world. The most successful and happy lives in my past were as a wanderer. Unhappy lives were where I felt trapped and confined.

The medium outlined several of my past lives; I scribbled notes as she talked:

10th Century Hermit Monk—male

In a monastery in France. Politics, bribery, competition and lack of spirituality among the monks made him disillusioned; the monk fled and became a beggar, a hermit. The rest of this life was spent in happy contemplation. The monk lived in the forest and lived well into his sixties, a happy solitary life at the end.

Germany Troubadour—male

A minnesinger: his love songs were dedicated to the Virgin, but the songs were interpreted as love ballads. He had homo-sexual tendencies but did not act on them. This life is where creativity linked to seeking God first showed up.

15th Century Jew in Spain—male

Very happy in early life in a renaissance period of literature, poetry, and inspirational thinking. This was a period of peace when Moors, Jews, and Christians got along. He had a loving family. Then he entered dark period when Jews were expelled from Spain; he took his family to Morocco. Unhappy and disil-lusioned at the end of life.

Denmark 17th Century—middle-class wife

Rich was her husband—a watchmaker. She was married by age sixteen with six kids by age twenty-three. She was unhappy, had no time to herself, did not like being a mother, and became shrewish. Hated her life, town, and neighbors, and became dead inside. She did not find happiness, which was her main challenge in that life. Rich could not understand why she was unhappy; she had food on the table and a roof over her head. She died in her forties because of a mass in her stomach.

18th Century Brahmin woman in India—female

Married to a noble, she was a religious Hindu. She was beautiful and musically gifted, but her husband just saw her as a pretty breeder. After her husband died, she ruled the house in late life, not wanting a behind-the-scenes role.

19th Century England artist—female

Short, unhappy life. She was talented but feared. She did channeling and spirit paintings. Her parents committed her to an asylum. She drew on the walls. They tied her hands, so she could not draw. Gagged her so she would not tell her stories. She committed suicide at thirty-four.

19th Century life in Canada—male

Drudge life in a forestry lumberyard. He dearly loved his wife and children, but he hated killing trees; felt trapped in his life, like a vegetarian working in a slaughterhouse. It was soul-killing work. He had a pretty unhappy life, though there were bright spots with loving family, and died in his sixties.

Philadelphia pharmacist—male

He crafted tailored remedies and homeopathy. His pharmacy was bankrupted in the 1929 crash. He took ingredients and fled. Known as the "doctor man," he found supplies, herbs, and plants in nature to use. He landed in a sleepy rural town in the Midwest and worked there quietly and happily until death in 1953. He died out in the woods under the sky, feeling happy and content—with no fear. Then he was reincarnated in this life several years later as me.

The medium said world healing is part of my purpose now. Meditation, painting, writing, teaching, and finding happiness in daily life is what I am being called to do.

I asked if it was on a large or small stage, and the medium said it doesn't matter. You may have an impact you don't even realize. If you are not on a large stage, you are not doing small work. Forget that question. She said that I am drawn to wander; maybe the next move will be enough to help me settle down.

Painting and expressing myself creatively is a real drive in this life along with spiritual seeking. The medium said—just keep painting. The *process* of painting is what is important—much more important than the end result. The most important thing for me is to just get it out! Keep creating. Do your artwork! Write about it and when you feel the call, begin to teach.

Lots to absorb here. The skeptical part of me wants to reject it; part of me wonders if any of it is true and if there is much value in hearing about past lives. I see a few threads that resonate: creativity linked to spirituality, love of nature, seeking, learning, the importance of treasuring daily joy, and the desire to keep moving. Maybe I do have wanderlust. Interesting that there is so much triangulation throughout various feedback sessions about creating and meditating. I am working to stay open and not reject the information out of hand but have more to ponder.

December 12

I had fitful sleep the past couple of nights, thinking about Danny. We walked the dogs in the cold, and then I went to spin class.

In Synchro-Destiny class, Deepak told a story about a trip where he had "double-whopper" synchronicities. He writes them down in a journal and notes teensy ones, medium ones, big ones, and double whoppers. Mine seem teensy compared to his.

The class facilitator, Amanda, said that even though little coincidences may seem random or meaningless, they are valuable messages that let you know the universe is conspiring in your favor.

December 13

In a restaurant last night, Rich heard the pianist play "Feliz Navidad," and he started singing "New York, New York." I can see where he got it. We laughed hard.

I couldn't sleep but didn't want to wake Rich, so I put in ear buds, hid my laptop screen behind a pillow and watched the next segment of class.

This segment focused on consciousness, which creates all our reality.

> Is our consciousness expanded or constricted? Fear creates constricted consciousness. Enlightenment results in the most expanded consciousness.
>
> Bliss, happiness, creativity, synchronicity, and pure love are related to high states of consciousness. Guilt, fear, anger, jealousy, hostility, and addiction are related to the most constricted and toxic levels of consciousness. Deepak talked about cultivating divine emotions: love, compassion, joy, and equanimity. These get us out of our constricted self and get us out of our ego.
>
> Our natural state is synchronistic. Nature's intelligence is synchronistic: Birds in flight, schools of fish, seasonal rhythms, lunar rhythms, and tidal rhythms.
> He said these natural phenomena are one synchronistic symphony; that's why we call it the Universe. One song.

This segment was interesting and beautifully presented. I learned that all emotions have biological implications, and illness has stress implications. I know my eczema has emotional causes; I have seen it emerge with stress and sadness. I mostly feel very joyful in my daily life right now, tinged with sadness about Danny dying and concern about what lies ahead for Gussie.

I don't think I fear death anymore. Danny and I never talked about anything spiritual beyond meditation. I think we could have talked about spiritual things. He has the vibe.

Rich and I believe there *is* such a thing as a good death. I think Danny has the serenity and wisdom to see death in perspective. But I am sad. I will miss him as will his family, his students, and his community. I think of all the missed opportunity for interaction. I could have talked to him about what he believes: why we are here and what it all means. I feel the loss even before he is gone.

December 14

I woke up at 5:30 and jogged three easy, slow miles after meditation. I made some small healthy muffins this morning, using a Canyon Ranch recipe. They are so tiny they amount to about one bite, but Rich likes them. We took the dogs out for a very chilly walk.

Today in class there was an essay from Deepak about enlightenment.

The essay says that in many Eastern wisdom traditions, enlightenment is the ultimate goal of spiritual transformation. When we reach enlightenment, we realize that we're not isolated and separate but are connected to everyone and everything. This is unity consciousness.

Those who have achieved enlightenment have no fear or worry. Recognizing that they are part of spirit or God makes them lighthearted and joyful. Real enlightenment is much more than an intellectual understanding that all is one. Achieving perpetual unity consciousness is a monumental transformation.

The enlightened states of seers and prophets, including Jesus Christ and Buddha, may seem out of our realm, but we all have the potential to expand awareness of our true spiritual nature and the connection of all. As we become more conscious of that connection of spirit, we see that even small events can have great meaning.

Learning this makes me want to go back and reread *Autobiography of a Yogi* because this was clearly a person who was enlightened. I pull it from my bookcase and enjoy refreshing myself on the life of Paramahansa Yogananda. And now that I have explored the Upanishads, the Yoga Sutras of Patanjali, and the Bhagavad Gita, the book has much more meaning for me.

I think about his amazing life; he knew from childhood that he would travel a mystic path. His dream was to be devoted to God. His life was filled with supernatural experiences.

As his spiritual life developed, he experienced more miraculous events. He became a true swami and monk, and his name changed to Yogananda, with the title of Paramahansa being added to him later. He brought eastern Indian spiritual teachings to the Western world. He developed a following that still exists today: the Self-Realization Fellowship.

December 15

After meditation this morning, we talked about making our marriage even stronger. We want to make sure that every day we take time for fun and love. We talked about the intimacy in our relationship. We have lots of affection every day: hugs, kissing and holding hands. We snuggle every night.

We talk about sex. It has changed for us in the forty years we have been together. Making love doesn't look the same as it did in college because our drive has changed, and the frequency has changed. We are surely not too busy now that I have retired, but we do get caught up in the momentum of whatever we are doing that day. Maybe physical desires just change as we age.

It is embarrassing that I don't know more about sex and how it changes over time. I am sure there are books on this. I could ask Joanie, Vivian, and Clara. I do have kind of a fear of seeming unintelligent on the subject. I know I can be myself with them and ask questions, but this subject in particular seems pretty private. I just want to be the best partner I can for Rich.

December 16

Thirty-eight years ago today, we were married (the first time). Who knew it would be so good? We woke up about 4:45 and meditated together with the hounds. I did elliptical before our walk.

Today in Synchro Destiny class, Deepak taught Mahavakyas. These are pathways to enlightenment and personal transformation. They are an ancient meditation practice. Mahavakyas translate to something like "great sayings" or "great utterances." Because there are seven, Deepak suggests for one for each day of the week.

They are:

Aham Brahmami	Sunday
Tat Tvam Asi	Monday
Sat Chit Ananda	Tuesday
San Kalpa	Wednesday
Moksha	Thursday
Shiva Shakti	Friday
Ritam	Saturday

These are great. He will provide a whole explanation for each of these. I already know some of them from his guided meditation series.

Gussie met with the liver specialist at Barnes. She is stoic and trying to be upbeat, but I think she is petrified. She said she prefers to be optimistic rather than pessimistic, so she is looking for the good in all this.

She now has a MELD score. MELD stands for "Measurement of End Stage Liver Disease." The score is based on zero to forty, where zero is a healthy liver. Gus's score is now in the high teens. In Missouri, fourteen-plus can be a candidate for transplant. Because of her location, she qualifies into the Midwestern Transplant Network.

She has a paracentesis scheduled for next Thursday. Her normal weight is 145, and today she weighed 167; this is all fluid in her stomach. The stomach distension from the extra weight of the internal liquid makes her exhausted, unable to sleep, and makes the hernia in her belly very painful.

Gus knows that she caused her liver disease and is struggling with the ethics of taking a transplant from someone more deserving. She has to have been sober for at least six months to be considered. The transplant paperwork has been submitted. If she gets approved, she can then decide if she wants to go forward with the transplant or not. A committee will review, and she will be put on the list if favorable.

Lots of texts back and forth with Gus and the other sibs this evening after this update.

December 17

I talked to Dad and Marie today; it was below zero last night and too icy to drive to church. It must really have been bad for Dad to miss Mass.

Today in class there was a deeper dive on the first Mahavakya, Aham Brahmasmi, which can be translated as "I am the universe." Deepak said that when we really understand this sutra, everything becomes possible because everything already exists inside us. We are all part of the cosmic intelligence, and that intelligence is the source of all reality, so we are also the source of all reality.

I am going to start to incorporate the Mahavakyas in my daily practice; this will be an easy addition.

My close friends know that I am trying to experience a wide range of metaphysical encounters, and my friend Clark gifted me a reading with his favorite medium: Lesley.

I called Lesley at the prearranged time, and she asked me what was on my mind. But before she even got the first question out, Lesley said, "I see your guides; they are over your left shoulder. They said you are deeply, notably kind; there is lots of love coming from you." Then she said, "I am getting something else; I keep getting 'Deepak Chopra, Deepak Chopra.'"

I was stunned. Lesley said, "How do you know him?"

I said, "I don't, not in person, but I am doing his meditations, reading his books, and taking an online class he is teaching. I have been to the Chopra Center and got my personal mantra there."

Lesley did not seem to think there was anything unusual about this. She asked me what I wanted to talk about. I explained that I have retired and I am most interested to hear about my purpose, or dharma; what am I here to do now?

Lesley checked with her guides and answered: creative pursuits like painting, writing, and meditation. Passion for painting emanates out of me. This is intended to be a very joyful time in life. Art is a way to serve humanity. Art is medicine—it brings beauty and inspiration to the world. Art is a way back home. Meditation is my pathway to Spirit. There is more to learn and also teach.

The guides tell Lesley they want to see me combine meditation, art, and writing. I need to write about what I am experiencing in my life transition. In life, we must teach at least one other person.

She said, this is unfolding to be a profound time of transition for me. My journal is a way to know myself at a deeper level. It has been nostalgic. Examining where you have been helps you discover where you are going. Through meditation, art, and my own seeking, I will have something to offer to others.

I ask Lesley what she can tell me about Gussie—what more could I be doing to help her?

Lesley said she is an early mature soul with drama and a difficult life. Alcoholism is a way to check out; it is slow suicide. She allows her emotions to run her life. She is highly sensitive and feels things intensely, like spending a lifetime as a teenager.

I asked Lesley what she means by an early mature soul. Lesley referenced the Michael teachings and said they may not resonate with everyone but may give me insight. She gives an overview as I take notes.

Lesley explained that these teachings say that souls evolve through five stages of reincarnation: Infant, Baby, Young, Mature, and Old. Each stage has a distinct focus that requires particular learning experiences:

Infant souls focus on *physical existence.* Their life lessons relate to "being a body," including satisfying basic physical needs and drives: survival, physical vulnerability, safety, mortality. These lives are often brief.

Baby souls focus on *social existence.* Life lessons relate to "belonging"—conformity to rules and strict moral codes; order versus chaos; doing right versus wrong; the authority of religion, law and order, crime and punishment; us versus them.

Young souls focus on *individual existence.* Life lessons relate to being "a somebody" with a mind and will of their own—independence versus conformity; individuality versus belonging; asserting personal opinions and personal agendas; competitiveness, self-interest, opportunism; seeking material success, achievement, glory, and self-advancement.

Mature souls focus on *coexistence.* Life lessons relate to being in "right relationship" to self, others, and everything else—interdependence versus independence; heart versus ego; collaboration and compromise versus personal triumphs; positive relationships, self-awareness, sensitivity, integrity, and empathy.

Old souls focus on *being*—fully being themselves as part of all-that-is while allowing all else to be as well. Life lessons relate to autonomy versus identity; authenticity versus respect; letting go, nonattachment, noninvestment; wisdom; and self-actualization and self-transcendence.

Lesley explains that each of these stages actually involves seven levels, from start to finish. And each of those takes *at least one lifetime* to complete.

I ask, so, are there are thirty-five "steps" to the whole reincarnation process? Lesley clarifies that it may take hundreds or thousands of lifetimes to complete the sequence. Souls also progress through further stages beyond the cycle of physical reincarnation. These involve taking on a teaching role.

I said, "I have been told of nine of my past lives. Is it important for me to explore more about these or other past lives?"

Lesley said, "No, you don't need to. You can focus on this life."

I asked, "Who is with me in meditation? Is it my true self? What is their nature?"

Lesley said, "They show themselves in beauty because that is what speaks to you. Think of them as deep friends, as a group who stood up with you for this incarnation and said, 'We will go with you.'"

I persisted. "Are they part of me; my true self?"

Lesley replied, "We are all one; separate but interwoven."

I was taking notes, and I asked Lesley if there was anything else.

She said, "You are entering a time where vocation and avocation are merged. A larger audience is there for you. You will develop the skill to jump into the universe and bring back a talent, to bring back some capability. You have access."

I thanked her for the reading. I am always amazed when people with clairvoyant abilities just think the information they get is so matter of fact. I struggle with the bit of readings that seem irrational, but I tell myself to remain open; I am on a vision quest. I put "Michael Teachings" on my ever-growing "read more about this" list. My mind is filled with impressions and questions, and I have to let this and my earlier Akashic reading percolate for a bit.

December 22

Today is the first day of winter. We woke up and meditated with the hounds as usual. A very chilly day, but no snow on the ground. The dogs were funny and energized by the cold. After our walk, I stayed out with them and let them play together and run through the bushes until they were ready to come in.

Today in class, Deepak said in order to start manifesting synchro-destiny, we try to break conditioning, reframe the way we look at the world, and let old habits die. He led a very peaceful and joyful meditation where he read a series of statements that embody *sat chit ananda*.

Then we did a radiant light visualization while silently repeating the sutra and had the intention of increasing blood flow to hands and face. I felt the pulsing and tingling in my hands and face along with my heartbeat and then sent radiant light to the rest of my body. It was beautiful. I saw light-filled images: warm orange and white and I had a wonderful glowing feeling around my heart.

Rich and I have done our annual planning session together over the past few days. Rich does the bulk of the work and does the writing, but I join in for the discussion. We are going to work on our marriage, health, and fitness. We made giving decisions about philanthropy but put a few on hold to see where "home" will be.

I listened to a lecture on friendship while I painted and learned that friends make you healthier. Journaling and dogs are close seconds; it is important to have a way to affirm who you are and what you are doing, and journaling helps with that. Dogs are the ultimate in accepting you the way you are with unconditional positive regard.

December 23

The dogs were sweet and hilarious this morning. Chip has been so good for Bella. They play beautifully together: growling, wrestling, and play-biting each other's ears. She has as much fun as he does.

In class, Deepak explained that in every moment we are either rooted in awareness of self or caught up in the ego's perspective of the world. Becoming more aware of our internal dialogue is a key component in the process of waking up. Going within and developing our own inner compass is a bridge from here to there.

Deepak said, "What we seek, we already are." When we live in awareness, we feel connected to all that exists. We cease to struggle. We feel free from limitation. We feel safe. We are fearless and willing to step into the unknown. We view ourselves with compassion and self-understanding."

Object referral is when we identify with our self-image or other external factors. If we tie our identity to status, title, possessions, and image, then we will never know our true essence.

If we can shift from object referral to self -referral, we release the struggle for control. We know we are an inextricable part of the field of infinite awareness and are open to experience synchro destiny.

Then Deepak directed us to do a very cool exercise. He said to go to a mirror, look deep into the reflection of our eyes, and repeat these three sayings:

1. I am totally independent of the good and bad opinion of others.
2. I am beneath no one, and no one is beneath me.
3. I am fearless in the face of all challenges.

I looked into my own hazel green eyes and saw they were shining brightly: the seat of the soul.

The next segment of class covered the fourth Mahavakya, San Kalpa. San Kalpa means something like "my intentions have infinite organizing power." It is the sutra for Wednesday.

Through our intentions, we create our reality. When your intentions come from your true self, the forces of nature are with you. When your intentions come from ego, the forces of nature are not behind you.

Deepak led a meditation where we imagine we have the power to help someone else, ease their suffering, help someone else heal.

I always think of Gus and her many sad problems and wish I could help her solve them. I hope the forces of nature are with her.

We connected with family all afternoon and evening. I worry about Gus on holidays; there are all kinds of triggers to drink, and holidays are reminders not only about what is great in life but also what is missing. She seemed OK. She is visiting Dad and Marie, made some fun presents for the kids, and plans to cook some nice meals for them.

December 24

It is not only Christmas Eve; it is trash day! I went to Whole Foods and got mussels, sole, Meyer lemons, and a baguette.

Class today was a guided meditation about the nature of the soul to help us manifest our deepest dreams and desires.

Deepak said meditation helps us reach the level of the soul by taking us beyond the thought traffic of the mind. We come fully into the present moment instead of thinking about the past or future, and our reference point shifts from ego to soul.

The best, most luminous part of our self is connected the rhythm of the universe.

Our mussels all opened. We used saffron and clam juice in the sauce. Rich made crispy, peppery baguette crostinis, and then we made sole meuniere. It was outstanding; the Meyer lemon zest helped make it perfect.

I sent Danny a book. I hope a little cheer or diversion might brighten his day. I heard from Abigail and Paula about the villa paintings I sent them, and they both said they loved them and already had them hanging. I see why gift-giving is fulfilling; it is expressing affection by creating a tangible thing to show love and friendship.

December 28

Tonight, Rich came downstairs and was really quiet. My radar went off.

I said, "What's wrong?"

He said, "Nothing."

"Are you sure? You seem quiet."

Annoyed now, he kind of snapped at me, "Yes, I am fine!"

Then we were driving, and he said, "I can't believe Roku charges us so many times, and could you use a different card, like a Visa, for your Amazon purchases?"

I said "Aha, I knew you were grumpy; you were reviewing the Amex bill!"

"You know I am not monitoring your spending or telling you what to do; I don't care about any of the charges. I just want to make sure all the charges are right."

"OK, thank you, honey; you take such good care of us."

"You know I never question you about how many times you get your hair done or shop at Nordstrom or send things to people on Amazon."

"Thank you, honey, I appreciate that you don't nitpick over the bill."

"That's right, you know other husbands would."

"I know, honey, you are the best."

After a few minutes, he said:

"Do you think you now have all the painting supplies you need?"

I gave him a look, and we belly-laughed for two minutes.

December 30

Today I wrote a blog post:

Have you ever been to a yoga class where they do a pose and say, "If it is available today, balance on one leg? If it is available today, bend from your waist and put your palms on the mat."

I used to think, "Oh, brother. Spare me the new-age speak."

And now, I am humbled to finally get it. Because it is not "available today." Aging is great. Back pain is not great. Things I didn't ever think about before, I can't do some days, like when I drop a spoon on the floor and can't pick it up or need to run an errand, and the stairs to the garage or the idea of getting in and out of the car and walking a quarter of a mile defeats me.

After having been active for many years, this is truly mind-blowing. How often do you achieve your daily 10,000-step goal? I've never not made it, I think smugly. Until now.

Of course, there is a lesson in everything. Maybe to take it all a little less seriously? To be willing to do less and be satisfied with that? To be grateful for the days when it is "available."

December 31

Despite some back pain, we are enjoying a quiet New Year's Eve. We did afternoon meditation together, made appetizers, and had great sustainable fish, asparagus, and rice for dinner. We are sitting by the fire, listening to music, reading, and relaxing. We've been talking about this amazing year and what next year might bring.

I have loved being on my journey. Our daily life is made up of so many sweet moments of tenderness, love, and laughter. Learning, reading, taking classes, and my daily meditation practice all have added so much dimension to life. I believe I am getting healthier in mind, body, and spirit.

A toast, a kiss, and on to a new year!

Chapter Seven
January

January brings new adventures as Rich and I work on our marriage, explore the idea of moving and have a very welcome respite from winter. I learn more about archetypes, finish the Synchro-Destiny class, start the Science of Happiness class, and attend the Sages and Scientists Symposium sponsored by the Chopra Center. My daily rituals of meditation, workout, walks, and healthy meals feel far from routine as I continue to go deeper in my journey toward a healthier, more balanced self and greater daily joy.

January 1

Happy New Year!

We started the year with the gratitude meditation series from Oprah and Deepak. It is our favorite, and we repeat it often. A new year is the perfect time to start from the beginning. Today was about manifesting grace. I love the word *grace*. Gratitude activates grace. I actually now consciously feel that I am living in a state of grace.

We are going to Orlando for the Citrus Bowl. I am trying to do as my dad exhorted us as kids: "Act enthusiastic, and you will be enthusiastic."

We have started working on our marriage; we have agreed that we will have a weekly meeting to check in and had our first one last night.

It is interesting to me that I can't find any good reference books to work on a marriage that is already good in order to make it great. That would be a worthy book to write. All the books out there seem either to be faith-based or focused on what to do when your marriage is falling apart.

First, we sat down, held hands, looked into each other's eyes, and thanked each other for working to have a great relationship. Then we talked about how we want to structure our work; will it be about having more intimacy and communication, becoming more affectionate, sharing gratitude every day for each other and the abundance in our lives, taking more time for fun, developing a hobby together, or all of the above. We agree that meditating together has opened a pathway for the potential to make progress together. We are both going to bring ideas for next week. This should be fun.

Synchro-Destiny class today was about using archetypes.

In Indian Vedic tradition, archetypes are often symbolized as gods and goddesses, symbolic expressions of higher states of consciousness. This is not about "praying" to the gods or goddesses; it is about invoking the *state of consciousness* that the god or goddess represents.

For example, Lakshmi is the goddess of abundance. The notion of abundance is part of us—part of our psyche. Invoking Lakshmi as the embodiment of abundance helps us enliven that part of us; it can help us give rise to the gods and goddesses in each of us.

Ganesh may be the most well-known god as a powerful remover of obstacles. Archetypal deities are representational, with the markings, colors, faces, and objects surrounding them holding deep significance and sometimes abstract meaning. Ganesh is about protection and power, with symbolism related to safeguarding us from life's physical and subtle obstacles. His elephantine head represents strength and power, intelligence and thinking ability. His large ears show that he listens to those who ask for help. His small mouth indicates that he listens more and talks less. His one broken and one whole tusk represent the contrasts of life: joy and sorrow, retaining the good but throwing away the bad. His large stomach shows that he is able to consume and digest all the good and bad in life.

In Ganesh's four hands, he holds various objects, as do many deities. In one hand, he holds a rope, which represents Ganesh's ability to help pull us up toward our ultimate goal of realization and liberation. Another hand holds an axe to cut all attachments with the impermanent and material world we continually grasp for. In his third hand, he holds a bowl full of sweets, which represent rewards for spiritual development. His fourth hand is often shown in a blessing mudra.

Looking at a symbol is a reminder of the states of energy and consciousness. Hera is the goddess of power. Demeter represents mother energy, like Mother Teresa. Athena represents wisdom and a custodian of arts and science. Artemis represents connection with nature and nonconformism. Aphrodite represents sexuality and beauty and love. Persephone represents the underworld, alchemy, and the depths of the psyche.

The suggestion in the course is to develop a relationship with several archetypes that are meaningful and at the end of meditation, invoke them and ask them to be present with you.

Jean Houston talked about archetypes in her salon, but I want to know more. Carolyn Myss has a methodology for defining archetypes, and I downloaded her book, *Sacred Contracts*.

January 2

We are flying to Florida on our way to the Citrus Bowl. I am trying to be positive and have "grace" about it, but I keep thinking of all the things I could be doing: studying, painting, hanging out with the dogs.

We did Day 2 of the Gratitude Meditation today. I am bordering on cranky, but I keep telling myself to stay grateful. The energy of gratitude is transformative. I think of what is good in my life and let the feeling of gratitude rise up. In my mind, I thank Rich for being a great partner and thank Chip and Bella for bringing us daily joy. I feel my emotions lift.

Why do I dislike football? Partly because I don't like that kind of competition; I like collaboration. I have never experienced that passionate feeling of "I want my team to win!" I feel I am separate from the rest of humanity on this issue. I always wish games could be a tie. I hate to see anyone, ever, at the risk of injury, and football seems violent. But this is important to Rich, so I am going to keep my mouth shut and hang in there. He says because I didn't grow up playing team sports, I am seriously flawed. Maybe I need to invoke an archetype of sports to help me.

As we fly, I do the Carolyn Myss Archetype Exercise. It will take me a while to synthesize it with the other things I am learning. It's a lot easier when someone just tells you, "Your archetype is Leonardo." In her *Sacred Contracts* book, Myss provides an extensive series of questions to help you determine your archetypes. I answer them as we fly. At the end of her book, she gives a detailed explanation of each and gives examples from movies, fiction, mythology, and religion.

From a larger list of archetypes, I chose twelve that most resonate with me, including student, scribe, mediator, artist, child, seeker, and teacher. I followed her recommended process and asked myself a list of questions about each, including what events or personal characteristics led me to choose this archetype, and what guidance might this archetype have to offer me?

We got to the hotel. Rich is meeting with some old college friends for a few hours, so I have time for meditation and to finish my class because I am close to the end.

The next lesson is about the sixth Mahavkya for Friday, for the activation of archetypes. The sutra is Shiva Shakti. In the meditation, he instructed us to imagine this: "I am giving birth to the gods and goddesses inside me. They express their powers through me. All mythical beings reside inside me. I can become the heroes and heroines I most admire."

I did the next session of class as well, which introduced the seventh and final sutra or Mahavakya. Ritam, which is for Saturday, is about moving with the rhythm of the universe.

Deepak ended by saying that we can be the author of our own life story. Our genes are not fixed; the expression of the genes can be turned on or off depending on how we live our life. While we can't alter the sequence of DNA, we can alter the expression by creating a lifestyle that includes loving relationships, balance, and meditation.

How we live our life impacts our biology. We can expand joy, kindness, peace, and equanimity. And our choices ripple out into the world. Self-awareness is the key to positive transformation.

This was an intriguing class; I want to find more like this one. I particularly love the notion of influencing our health at the cellular level, going beyond our conditioned responses.

What a great way to end class and to start the new year. And it is perfect timing because my new class, Science of Happiness, starts tomorrow.

January 3

I actually enjoyed the football game. A cousin of mine is the quarterback, and it was fun to watch him and all the other gifted athletes use their talents. No one got hurt, and I was interested to see that knowing someone on the team began to translate into that universal feeling of "I want my team to win." And they did. Maybe I am becoming more human.

Tonight, I started my Science of Happiness course!

One of the first lectures was how scientists define and measure happiness. Dacher Keltner is one of the primary professors for the class.

He said that being "happy" could refer to many things: a sense that life is going well, a fleeting emotion, a trait we possess, or even a sensation. Scientists often focus on the first two aspects: life satisfaction and positive affect, which combine to form "subjective well-being."

Before the late seventeenth century, happiness was considered to be the result of luck or divine favor.

In the seventeenth and eighteenth centuries, there was new thinking about happiness, and it was now declared to be a right, as in "Life,

Liberty, and the pursuit of Happiness" in the United States Declaration of Independence.

Happiness is not the appropriate emotion in all circumstances. Negative emotions are normal and sometimes appropriate. Anger, sadness, and fear all have roles. If a high bar is set for happiness, someone could be disappointed not to achieve expectations.

January 4

Here's what I learned in my Science of Happiness class today; we can increase our happiness.

Scientists have discovered that people have a genetic set-point, which accounts for about 50 percent of our happiness. So, some part of happiness is determined by genetics.

They have found that *only 10 percent* of the happiness level is dictated by life circumstances. I thought that would be a much higher percentage. I am shocked by this, actually.

A whopping 40 percent can be changed by intentional activity. That is pretty amazing; we can change our happiness level though the development of relationships, philanthropy, optimism, savoring, mindfulness, physical activity, spirituality, and goal pursuit. So why doesn't everybody do this?

I spent the afternoon getting ready to go to California, packing for myself and the dogs and getting the house ready so it can be shown while we are gone. Stopping the paper, forwarding the mail.

January 5

In today's meditation, they talked about the true self: the source of grace. I can feel peace and joy rise up inside me nearly every time I meditate.

I am really enjoying my Science of Happiness class. Barbara Fredrickson's research says that a ratio of 3:1 positive to negative interactions is required for thriving. Most of us operate around 2:1, while 1:1 or worse might indicate depression. (This ratio has since been contested by other researchers.) To become more positive, she suggests trying to be open, appreciative, kind, curious, authentic, and sincere. She also recommends keeping track of your positive and negative emotions to monitor your ratio.

Our homework is to spend ten minutes every night remembering three good things that happened during the day. This teaches us to seek out and savor positive things, and it has been shown to increase happiness six months later.

Three good things today:

1. Though it is bitterly cold, the sun is out. The dogs had a huge play session that made me laugh; they chased each other in and out of the shrubs.
2. Christina and I cleaned Chip's ears. This makes me feel like I am learning how to take better care of him.
3. I have phone calls set up with three shamans who teach an apprenticeship.

I resonate with the lesson in this gratitude practice. Noticing daily life, even the simplest of things, creates a ripple of appreciation that radiates out and seems to generate even more abundance.

January 6

1. I got a good picture of our snow dogs in the five inches that fell overnight.
2. I am enjoying my class; learned a new concept about *jen*.
3. We made a large (for us) financial contribution to the library; we are especially excited about their after-school programs and the lunch program.

Science of Happiness class today: There is a term called "hedonic happiness," That is where the saying "no whining in the yacht" must have come from because humans can get used to higher quality of life and stop savoring it and appreciating it.

Professor Emiliana Simon-Thomas explained further:

> Though hedonic adaptation is a real phenomenon, we fail to predict how much and how quickly we'll adapt to positive and negative circumstances—this is called the "impact bias." People are poor judges of what will make us happy or unhappy in the future; our "affective forecasting" is off. We fear breakups, though people bounce back; we pursue wealth, when (after a certain amount) having more wealth doesn't give us a boost. We buy things, when material purchases actually can decrease our satisfaction.

January 7

1. It is frigid, and the paths are slick with ice, but the sun came out for a while.
2. Rich and the dogs drove me on errands because it was icy.
3. A guy came to fix my closet door, so it will close and keep Chip from eating my shoes.

In class today, we listened to an interview with Sonja Lyubomirsky. She said that hedonic adaptation makes sense from an evolutionary perspective because our ancestors had to be alert to danger.

When circumstances are constant, we pay less attention. In the case of negative experiences, it's a blessing. Except for a few horrible circumstances—like severe disability or losing a loved one when you're elderly—we tend to bounce back from everything. From divorce to cancer, humans tend to find the positive in experiences.

One big question that people often ponder is whether becoming a parent will make them happier. Results are mixed; parenting makes certain types of parents happier—those who are middle aged (or older) and married, for example. Fathers tend to be happier than mothers, and parents are happier when they have custody of their kids and their kids are trouble-free.

I have always wondered if parents are happier. We don't regret not having kids, but many people feel sorry for us or feel that something is wrong with us because we didn't.

Lyubomirsky's research suggests there aren't many cultural differences in happiness, although there may be differences in myths about happiness. (For example, having money is more valued in the West.) But that doesn't mean there's one formula for happiness—instead, we have to consider our own situation and personality and choose activities that "fit" in order to see results.

This is also fascinating. Happy people make more money, cope better, and are better leaders and negotiators. Happy people are more likely to get married, have fulfilling marriages, and have more social support; they are more creative, productive, philanthropic, other-centered, resilient, and healthier. All of this research was recounted by Dacher Keltner.

Happiness is associated with greater longevity and health. Happy people have better social relationships: they have more friends, are judged to be warmer, more intelligent, and less selfish, and are more likely to get assistance and trust. Happy people who get married are less likely to get divorced and feel more love and fulfillment. Finally, happiness can boost creativity and innovation for us and our subordinates at work.

January 8

1. I got a refund from the iTunes store on a purchase I mistakenly made instantly with no questions.
2. We are packed, psyched, and ready. *California, here we come!* We will be there for Rich's birthday. Right now, it is 50 degrees warmer there than it is here. *We'll take it!*

3. We had a romantic fire in the fireplace, talked about our relationship, and what we want to do make it even better. We talked about more hobbies we would like to do together. Maybe a sport that we could do together?

From class today:

Happy people are more sociable, energetic, charitable, and cooperative. They think more flexibly and with more ingenuity. Happy college freshmen have higher salaries sixteen years later; happy female students are more likely to be married at age twenty-seven and satisfied in marriage at age fifty-two.

January 9

Today is Rich's birthday, and we are leaving for California. He got three cards: from Chip, Bella, and me. We got him a sun hat.

1. We feel so fortunate that we are able to take the dogs. We looked like the Beverly Hillbillies with all our gear, including two dog beds. Our flight left at 8; it was incredible to wake up in the cold and be in the sun four hours later. I had a few last seconds of bracing cold as I rolled the trash cans up the icy driveway.
2. It was 12 degrees when we left, and the high today here is 72; I got a little sunburned on our afternoon walk.
3. Our villa has an interior courtyard where the pups sniffed, played together, and lay in the grass.

La Quinta Resort is charming and completely dog friendly. Everyone wanted to stop and pet them. They even give dog treats at the bell desk.

From Science of Happiness Class today—What's joy got to do with it?

Barbara Fredrickson says that positive emotions open our hearts, minds, and perspectives to think more broadly and see global differences and similarities. People experiencing positive emotions actually expand their field of vision, can see more possibilities, and be more creative. Doctors experiencing positive emotion make better medical decisions.

Positive emotions may even affect us on a biological level, at the level of cell renewal.

Doing meditation to improve health at the cellular level is exactly what Deepak said at the end of Synchro-Destiny class.

January 10

1. The dogs loved sniffing new smells. We got in a two-mile walk right on the property.
2. This historic resort opened in 1926. Greta Garbo, Clark Gable, and Shirley Temple were regulars, and there are small plaques throughout the property, saying things like "This was Greta Garbo's favorite view of the Santa Rosa mountains."
3. We took the dogs and sat at a fire pit for a relaxing dinner. Incredible to sit out under the stars in January.

Science of Happiness

OK, I think this is fascinating. In today's lecture on money and happiness, Professor Keltner said that money makes us happier—but only up to a certain point. People in poor countries become happier when they have more money, but we don't see much change in happiness as people start earning more than $75,000 a year. These days, wealth but not happiness is increasing in the United States, and 37 percent of the wealthiest Americans are less happy than the average American.

In another segment of class, we learned that the vagus nerve (that starts at the top of our spinal cord and runs downward through the neck muscles) has connections to many key physical functions, including oxytocin networks and immune and inflammation responses. Activity in the vagus nerve is related to feelings of connection and care, so it activates in response to emotions. People with lots of vagal activity show more positive emotion, stronger relationships, more social support, and more altruism.

January 11

1. The dogs love the courtyard and go back and forth between the casita (my "office") and kitchen table (Rich's "office").
2. Today Rich said, "Why don't we look around *here* for a community that would be a good fit?" I added Palm Springs to our spreadsheet.
3. I connected with the shamans who teach the apprenticeship. It sounds intriguing. I am applying.

From the science of happiness class today we learned about oxytocin, "the love hormone" (Dacher Keltner).

Oxytocin is a neuropeptide, a sequence of amino acids that affects the brain and organs. It is increased by touch, and people with a particular gene on their third chromosome produce more oxytocin. A whiff of oxytocin generates more trust, generosity, empathy, and the ability to read emotions. Giving a father oxytocin will cause his baby to show increased oxytocin. Giving oxytocin to nonhuman species increases monogamy and caregiving.

In general, more oxytocin correlates with a reduced stress response in our hormones, cardiovascular system, and amygdala and correlates with secure attachment and peaceful conflict resolution in romantic relationships.

January 12

1. This villa gives me an idea what it would be like to live in a smaller place. The casita is my office, painting studio, and meditation space. It's perfect. The enclosed courtyard is a great feature. I can clean the villa in about ten minutes.

2. It is 12 degrees in Ohio, and they have a foot of snow. Today it got to 78 here.
3. I absolutely love looking at the mountains every day. They ring the Coachella valley, so it feels like we are in a nest.
4. The grounds are beautifully maintained with vivid flowers. Bougainvillea adorn the walls.
5. We went to open houses today; nearly every home has a casita! And most have an enclosed courtyard.
6. Some fun text exchanges between the sibs seems to be giving Gus a sense of connection, love, and belonging to maybe lift her up a little.

OK, it's hard to find *only* three good things to write about.

Today's class focused on marriage—a very welcome topic, since we are working on our relationship. It was fun to talk about this with Rich.

Marriage correlates with happiness, but researchers are untangling whether marriage makes us happier, or whether happier people get married. Some evidence suggests that it's actually happy marriages, not just marriage, that make us happy—and, in fact, unhappy marriages take a huge toll on kids' happiness.

Certain demographics of people are more likely to have happy marriages, like older people and those from a higher social class. Research by John Gottman and Robert Levenson shows that happy marriage is predicted by the way couples interact: couples who exhibit contempt, criticism, stonewalling, and defensiveness have a 92 percent chance of divorce, while happy couples exhibit humor, appreciation, forgiveness, and emotional disclosure.

We looked at homes today. Thankfully, we are aligned; we think the community is more important than the house. We want young families around for vibrancy. We want to be centrally located, so shopping is easy, and we want access to a great gym within walking distance for me, good places to walk, and golf and tennis for Rich. Other things on our wish list: beautiful landscaping, views of mountains, a casita, an interior courtyard for the pups, and a great kitchen. The home should be clean, contemporary, and light. We agree we want to significantly downsize.

January 13

Okay, I get the point of the "three good things" exercise, but I am going back to the way I have been keeping my journal. I concur that there is great benefit to daily recapitulation of what happened; it keeps the good things at the forefront of my mind, and the details help create positive memories.

We had nice sleep and great meditation. Rich played golf and met some new friends. They had lots of advice about where we should live. They told him about a community here in Indian Wells that has an awesome gym and a great, active vibe with lots of biking and hiking. We are going to look at it.

Rich is funny because he got hot today playing golf but would not let himself complain about the heat; it is 18 degrees at home. I sat outside and looked at the mountains against a cobalt sky and listened to some soft, sweet music with a dog on either side of my chair: incredible.

January 14

My class is focusing on touch. I am trying to be very conscious of touching Rich much more during the day. Professor Keltner is an expert on touch.

He said we are physically built for touch, with dexterous hands and skin that is full of information-processing neurons that manipulate our immune response.

Touch can be used to communicate emotion—in one study, even a one-second touch on the arm communicates emotions like gratitude, fear, and disgust with 50 to 60 percent accuracy.

Touching someone creates feelings of reward, reciprocity, safety, soothing, and cooperation. In certain situations, the touch from a romantic partner is powerful enough to eliminate our stress response.

Yet our culture is becoming touch-deprived, particularly in the United States. While friends at a cafe in France or Puerto Rico touch each other over 100 times per hour, we cool Americans touch each other twice. Many babies died in orphanages before caretakers started holding and touching them.

To combat this trend, touch therapy is being used in health care and education. It has (almost miraculously) been shown to increase weight gain in premature babies, reduce depression in Alzheimer's patients, make students more likely to speak up, and decrease mortality in patients with complex diseases.

Maybe it has to do with us touching more, being in California, wearing fewer layers, or consciously working on our marriage, but we have had more intimate time in January than in the past few months combined. There just seems to be more time here somehow, and we manage to find a way to connect in the afternoon. We kind of feel like we are in our twenties again.

I had a good interval cardio and lift session. My back is feeling healthy and good; I am very grateful. We had a fun lunch together in the courtyard, with the dogs looking on hopefully for any crumb.

We absolutely love this time zone. We have settled into such a nice daily routine: early to bed and early to rise. We wake up, meditate, make tea, and go out for our first walk. The dogs are in heaven here, and everyone loves seeing them. They get so much attention. "What a handsome boy," they remark about Chip. And his tail wags. "You are beautiful," to Bella, and her graceful head raises as if to say, "Of course." We come back, Rich gets caught up on the market, and I go to the gym. Yoga, errands, class. Often, I will pick something up for lunch.

When I get back, Rich goes to the gym, and I study, paint, or both. The market closes early afternoon, so he is free for the rest of the day. I meditate around 4 o'clock; we take the dogs out for another walk and then make a simple dinner. Watch TV, read, or sit out and look at the night sky on these mild nights. Lovely.

Rich and I went to take a look at a community in Indian Wells. The location is perfect; near Whole Foods, Trader Joe's, and the nicest shopping area in the Coachella Valley. Lots of restaurants are close by. The landscaping is gorgeous; it looks like Italy with plantings of olive trees, ivy-draped stone arches, incredible flowers, stately palm trees, and breathtaking views of the mountains in every direction.

In the community is a fun casual restaurant with a lounge, covered terrace with an incredible view of the Santa Rosa Mountains, and a display kitchen. There is also a very pretty formal restaurant.

The lounge area opens to a covered terrace with large disappearing pocket doors. The outdoor garden terrace has a great fire pit.

There is a coffee and juice bar with a friendly barista as well as an Olympic pool, a covered pavilion, bocce courts, pickle ball, tennis, organized biking and hiking, an event lawn for kid's activities, indoor and outdoor fitness classes, a Pilates studio, yoga studio, and incredible workout area with state-of-the art cardio machines and weight-lifting equipment. There are thirty-six holes of Jack Nicklaus Signature Golf and a spa on-site—and a dog park! Best of all, there was a very friendly, welcoming vibe and a nice vibrant, unpretentious feeling.

We walked through eight model homes and found several examples that are light, airy, and contemporary. Every model has a casita and interior courtyard. I am getting more and more excited but containing myself because I want Rich to choose the next home.

Rich said, "OK, now we have the benchmark."

January 15

Lovely morning. Rich is playing golf. I went to easy yoga, a good class that is just my speed.

I am now doing "small art" since I don't have a big space where I can be messy with paint. I am drawing small mandalas and painting them. I have tried a few sizes from 6 x 6 up to 12 x 12. I've been trying paint pens, and now that I have the hang of them, I like them.

Mandalas are beautiful. I am experimenting with many patterns, and they are all captivating. I have always been drawn to symmetry and geometry. The name *mandala* comes from Sanskrit meaning "circle." Even though it may have features like squares or triangles, a mandala always has a concentric (circular) nature. The balancing visual elements symbolize unity and harmony.

I experiment with color and find that, for mandalas, I am most drawn to those that have harmonious colors: for example, shades of blue and purple or shades of darker and lighter magenta. I am still very drawn to teal, peacock blue, and aquamarine shades.

There is something almost meditative about creating mandalas. I can see that it could be therapeutic, and I start to wonder if I could be useful in working in a senior center or hospice organization where the patients or residents would want to create something. Maybe I could pre-draw the mandalas, and they could color them in.

I read that mandalas can be symbolic. The shapes and colors you create in your mandala reflects your inner self at the time of creation.

I did a few hours of science of happiness class yesterday and today.

The resort is getting busy with a nice buzz of activity. The locals say that the weekends are busy with people driving over from Los Angeles, and during the week is quieter. We had a delicious tofu wrap for lunch. We are feeling more attracted to plant-based food, and there are such great choices here.

We have a pup sitter coming to stay with Bella and Chip, and we are going to go to Phoenix to take a look at different neighborhoods—mostly in Scottsdale.

I told Rich I feel bad that a realtor will waste his or her time on us when we are just exploring. I said that to a realtor in Scottsdale who said it goes with the territory—an occupational hazard.

I loved class today:

According to professors at UC Berkeley, the voice is another primal way we connect. We are able to make more vocal sounds than other primates—in fact, we can communicate many emotions like interest, disgust, and sadness without even saying a word (hmm!). Our ears are also specially built for hearing human speech.

Dacher Keltner explained that pair-bonding is a human tendency across cultures. Scientists distinguish between desire and love, which can even be observed in primates. Much like humans, primates express desire through actions like pursing and licking their lips, and love through open arms and smiles. Love behaviors, but not desire behaviors, coincide with the release of oxytocin.

January 16

The days are flying by, yet each has memorable moments. I dread going back to Ohio. We found a dog park nearby where we can let Bella and Chip off the leash. No other dogs have been there. Perfect. Every day when we walk, I turn to Rich and say, "Look at those mountains."

I like holding the intention every day that we are working on our marriage. I am trying to be conscious of creating more depth and meaning in our partnership. In the night, when I wake up, I reach out and touch Rich for a few minutes and silently tell him how much I love and appreciate him. During the day, I try to do some things for him that will, through action, express a feeling of love and care. Little things. Making sure to look for his dirty socks before I do a load of laundry. Bringing him a glass of ice water. Telling the dogs something nice about him that I know he will hear. "Chip and Bella, your dad is a brilliant money manager!"

I try not to look for any reciprocal reaction; it's not tit for tat. I am just trying to give affection freely, and it seems like a couple of funny things are happening. I feel more fulfilled because I am aware that I am freely expressing emotions. And it seems like this encourages him to open up to me more.

I realize I have probably lived a lot of my marriage, trying to balance things—the attitude of "I'll do something for you if you do something for me." Maybe I would resent doing some small task if it seemed like the balance was off, such as "I have emptied the dishwasher 99 percent of the time, and you have only done it once this whole month."

Now I wonder if the more you give and express appreciation, the more you yourself enjoy the relationship, even if you don't initially receive a reciprocal response.

The fruit and vegetables here are amazing. Every Sunday, there is a great farmer's market right in old town La Quinta. So far, I love California.

Science of Happiness

Dr. Daniel Siegel looks at how we can use our time so that it supports our well-being and inner growth. He lists seven ways to spend time:

- Sleep time—Getting a full night's restful sleep
- Physical time—Taking time to move and let your body be active
- Focus time—Being alone for a while to concentrate on what matters to you
- Time in—Taking time for meditation, prayer, or self-reflection
- Time out—Setting aside time to simply to be here and rest into existence
- Play time—Time to have fun and enjoy yourself
- Connecting time—Intimate private time between you and those you love and care for

January 17

Chip slept through the entire night! We had veggie soup and black bean burgers for lunch; it feels healthy to add more legumes into our diet.

It was sunny and beautiful out; I sat out with the dogs in the court-yard. I heard from Sheri today; she said Danny is near the end. I did an hour-long meditation this afternoon and just sent him and Bea ease and comfort and love. I hope he is not in much pain and will go easily.

We leave this evening for Phoenix. The pup sitter is coming at five, and we'll head to the airport for the short flight.

January 18

We are staying at the Princess Hotel. When we got to our room, we ordered room service and snuggled all night long; I kept just listening to Rich breathe and kept thinking about Bea and that this might be her last night with Danny. I can't even imagine how she must feel. We meditated this morning and set loving intentions for them. I had a hard run this morning in the hotel gym. It felt good to get some of the emotion out. Before the realtor picked us up, I heard the news; Danny passed. I can't stop thinking about Bea.

The realtor, Doug, was cheerful and knowledgeable. He took us through several neighborhoods and different communities. Some we just drove through, and in some, we looked at homes.

Many of them were a far distance from shopping or even a grocery store, but there are some lovely homes, maybe bigger than we want or need. We saw the Boulders, DC Ranch, Desert Highlands, Desert Mountain, Estancia, Silverleaf, and Tatum Ranch. We drove through Paradise Valley.

Doug knew we were also looking in the Palm Springs area, and so all day he interjected negative comments about California: the taxes, the earthquake risk, the infrastructure, and the crowds, as well as how everyone he used to know in California had moved out. He called the Palm Springs area "God's Waiting Room."

After the long day of house-hunting, we thanked Doug and went back to the hotel and talked through each community.

Some of the homes we saw were stunning. Rich loved one community in North Scottsdale; it was golf and tennis heaven, but it is far from Phoenix and goods and services. That could change in the future as areas get built out, but for now, it didn't seem like a match. Some of the communities had no young families and were missing vibrancy. Some had young families, but the few homes that were available would need a lot of renovation.

Now that we had a benchmark, it seemed that every comparison today was to the community we loved in Indian Wells, and each place fell short.

January 19

We woke up early and meditated, worked out, and then went to the airport to fly back to Palm Springs and got "home" to the villa mid-morning to many happy greetings from Chip and Bella. The sitter said they were perfectly behaved and that she would be very happy to stay anytime.

I continued my Science of Happiness class. The villa was clean; housecleaners had come while we were gone. The dogs had already walked, but we wanted to take them out again. We laughed at how Chip feigns needing to scratch when he gets tired. We relished the sunshine, landscaping, and mountain views and talked about this area being so green and lush compared to Scottsdale.

I felt very content to be with my whole pack, enjoying the pretty day. I realized that this might be the first January of my life I have enjoyed. I talked to Rich to see if he would be okay if I went to a conference in LA in a couple of days. Deepak Chopra is hosting a "Sages and Scientists" conference at the Beverly Wilshire, and they have an attendee spot open. Maybe Rich would want to come? We agreed to get a sitter and go together. Rich will visit some friends and scout some of the areas around LA while I go to the sessions.

January 20

I arranged for the sitter, registered for the Sages and Scientists symposium, and reserved the hotel room. Los Angeles is only a couple of hours away, so we will drive. I am excited to keep learning.

We had our "Monday Night Meeting" to talk about our relationship and what we could be doing to make it better. We both agree that increasing touch has a positive impact on intimacy. I thanked Rich for being open to go on our next adventure and for supporting me in the things I want to learn. Rich thanked me for pushing him—or pulling him to continue to evolve.

January 22

After a nice morning of meditation, working out, and dog walking, we drove to Los Angeles and checked in at the Beverly Wilshire Hotel and got upgraded to a suite.

The fact that the Palm Springs area is only a couple of hours away from Los Angeles is a plus. On the way, we talked about some different scenarios; game plans if the house in Ohio sold right away, or if it didn't sell soon.

Rich said if we were to decide right away, he was leaning toward Indian Wells. I said I felt the same way.

We talked about our concerns about the Palm Springs area: (1) Is it too much of a resort community without enough infrastructure and goods and services? (2) How good is the healthcare? and (3) What would we do in the summer?

And we talked about our concerns about California: (1) high taxes, (2) poor infrastructure, (3) earthquake risk, and (4) crowded.

I said I was surprised at the quality of goods and services we had experienced. Not every major store is here, but all the bases are covered. And LA is two hours away. Pretty much anything needed could be delivered the next day. Rich said he had read positive reviews of Eisenhower Health. We talked about the need to escape the hot summer; we would face this same issue if we went to the Phoenix area. We both want to explore more of the West. We could easily rent a house in a cooler area for the summer; this would satisfy some of my wanderlust.

We talked about concerns about California. Rich said the taxes in Ohio were high in our community. Because we will be downsizing, the taxes would be about the same. I said that I had thought a lot about the earthquake risk, and if we were meant to experience an earthquake, then we would. I did not think this would be the reason not to move. Rich agreed. California has unique infrastructure problems, but every state has its issues. And, parts of California definitely seemed crowded. But after living in New York for sixteen years, that didn't seem like such a big issue. I grinned at Rich. "We are talking ourselves into California!"

I went to register for the conference, and Rich got in touch with friends he is seeing. We agreed to meet for dinner at The Grill across the street.

I had no idea how many people would be at the conference, but when I went to register, hundreds of people were there. However, registration was efficient.

We had a delicious dinner and walked down Rodeo Drive before going back to the hotel. It was a gorgeous night, and the streets were crowded.

January 23

Rich and I meditated early and went to the gym to work out. Rich is driving to Dana Point today to see friends and look around at the area.

The conference starts at eight. I have a big notebook ready and plan to take copious notes. As I look at the conference program, I am amazed at the number of presenters. The format seems to be a number of presentations on a related topic and then a panel discussion.

Organizing this must have been very complex. It is going to be simulcast around the world, so it has to run fairly on time. I am delighted to be in the audience instead of the organizer of the event. It seems like a very international crowd. I see a number of women in saris and men in sherwanis, and I can hear a number of languages being spoken. A lot of the attendees seem to be physicians.

Before the conference started, beautiful images filled the screens in the ballroom—galactic images morphing from color to color. I was fascinated; this imagery is what I've been trying to create as I animate my paintings. It makes my attempts at animation seem painfully pedestrian and amateurish and yet, even though I realize that it would probably take years before my animations could look this professional, somehow I felt an instant kinship with the conference.

Deepak Chopra opened the conference; he first appeared in a beautiful onscreen hologram and joked, "I am here nonlocally."

He opened by talking about the human universe and the mysteries of existence. He told a great story about his grandson asking brilliant questions such as, "Dada, what is dark energy?" and "How did the ocean get made?" And his naming all the planets in our solar system.

Deepak asked him, "Where did the galaxy come from?"

His grandson said, "From another dimension."

Deepak said that being Indian, he started to wonder. Who is this kid? And he began to imagine sages from the past reincarnated into his grandson. And he asked, "How do you know this stuff?" And his grandson said, "It's on my Pokémon."

Then Deepak started to outline some of the big mysteries in the realm of the unknowable that science has yet to fully understand, like the 99.9% of the universe that does not lend itself to observation.

Seventy percent of the universe is made of dark energy. Scientists say that dark energy is the most accepted hypothesis to explain the observations since the 1990s, indicating that the universe is expanding at an accelerating rate. This is a force like the opposite of gravity that rips space apart. Dark matter —another mysterious entity—makes up 24 percent. What is dark matter made of? WIMPs, or weakly interacting massive particles.

Only 4.6 percent of the universe is atomic, meaning made up of atoms or "regular" matter, such as stars, planets, and people.

Because our cosmic horizon is 47 billion light years away, he said the observable universe is smaller than the 4.6 percent; the visible universe, including billions of galaxies and trillions of planets, is probably about .01 percent of the total. So, 99.9 percent of the universe does not lend itself to observation.

Then he went through a history of scientific models through the ages including the divine universe, the classic universe, the industrial age, Einstein's discovery of the relativistic universe, the quantum revolution, quantum mechanics, chaotic inflation, and the big bang. And he reminded us that none of the models explain how we *experience* the universe.

Who is the "me" who has the experience of viewing something? He said, "I don't experience quantum mechanics; I experience sound, texture, color, joy, emotions, compassion, fear, and ecstasy."

The most common word used in the world is "I." "I" is the center of experience, volition, sensations, and thoughts.

So, he said, we have two hard questions:

1. What is the universe made of?
2. What is the biological nature of conscious experience?
3. Scientists have tried to find a material explanation for consciousness. Perhaps we are asking the wrong question, and the universe is made of nothing and consciousness is made of nothing. He quoted Rumi:

We come spinning out of nothingness, scattering stars like dust.

Or, a different worldview is that the universe *is* consciousness. Deepak quoted Rupert Spira, who says, "There is something present that is conscious of these words."

Shift your identity; as a formless being, you cannot be destroyed. You are not subject to birth or death. I am the whole universe—the light of awareness: color and dimensionality, and the light of consciousness.

An ancient teaching that comes from Vedanta describes five causes of suffering:

1. Not knowing the true nature of Reality and not knowing your true self
2. Grasping or holding onto what is illusory or insubstantial
3. An aversion to or fear of something, a revulsion to something that is insubstantial
4. Identification with the false self or ego so we are constricted and limited in our consciousness
5. Fear of death

When you find yourself, you find the universe.

I was delighted. Because of my recent reading, I was actually tracking with at least some of what Deepak said.

The next lecturer was Joel Primack, a professor of physics and astrophysics at the University of California, Santa Cruz. He covered the modern theory of the universe. He showed photos from the cosmic web of galaxies and confirmed our cosmic address as the third rock from the sun.

At the beginning of this lecture, I had a very strange experience. He was showing stars and galaxies on the screens in the room, and I was not only seeing the images that come to me in meditation, I was seeing some of the specific ones that I had painted and animated.

I actually gasped when he showed the Eye of God Nebula because that is the image that I have seen most often lately. Everyone else at my table turned to look at me, and I said I would explain after the lecture. My heart was pounding, tears welled up in my eyes, and my hands were shaking. I tried to continue to pay attention.

He went through dark matter and dark energy and showed the flat rotation within the galaxy, which confirms the existence of immense fields of dark matter that are invisible.

He talked about cold dark matter, tame space, and wild space, and showed the long filaments of thousands of galaxies. He lost me somewhere in the science, but I felt lifted up by the simulated movement of the beautiful galactic images from space, which felt very, very familiar to me.

After the lecture, I showed people at my table the animations I had made that were on my phone, and they were amazed that they mirrored the images that had been shown. Talk about synchronicity. I could not wait to tell Rich what happened.

Following Joel Primack was Priyamvada Nataranja. A professor of astronomy and physics at Yale, noted for her work in mapping dark matter and dark energy and in creating models describing black holes. She authored the book *Mapping the Heavens: The Radical Scientific Ideas That Reveal the Cosmos.*

She talked about how the "pot holes" in space deflect light rays and how the inner planets rotate slowly, and outer plants that are farther away rotate more quickly.

John Horgan, an American science journalist known for his book *The End of Science,* was next. He has written for many publications, including *National Geographic*, *Scientific American*, *The New York Times*, *Time*, and *Newsweek*, and is a "bunk basher." Deepak likes to invite skeptics and critics to events like these so that people can hear opposing views and decide for themselves.

He said there had been no real new scientific paradigms since the big bang theory. And that we should beware of gurus peddling enlightenment. Yet he is not an atheist; he believes our existence is improbable and therefore is a miracle.

Amanda Geffner followed Horgan; she is a young scientist who wrote *Trespassing on Einstein's Lawn*. She and her dad taught themselves physics and set about to find answers to unknowable questions. She told the story of their lives and their book. Her father asked her (at fifteen): "How would you define nothing?" She read up on general relativity and quantum mechanics, as she and her dad began a life-altering quest for the answers to the universe's greatest mysteries. Reality, the Geffners believe, is radically observer-dependent. She said she believes that nothing is actually real and that the world is made of nothing. Things only exist relative to an observer. The observer and the observed cocreate.

Donald Hoffman was next. He is a professor in several departments at the University of California, Irvine. He studies consciousness, visual perception, and evolutionary psychology, using mathematical models and psychophysical experiments. His new book, titled *Do We See Reality?* expands on his TED talks and explains how our perceptions have evolved to hide reality from us. He asked and answered the question: "Do we see reality?" and the answer is "No; we reconstruct reality." He said that one-third of our brain's cortex is used in vision.

After a panel discussion, Bernardo Kastrup spoke about nonduality. He is an expert in artificial intelligence and reconfigurable computing.

He wrote *The Idea of the World: A Multidisciplinary Argument for the Mental Nature of Reality*. He introduced the idea that our universe is in fact fundamentally mental. What we call physical things and events, don't exist independently of subjective experience. If they did, how would one even prove such existence? Conscious experience is the only way that reality can be known.

He also explained the argument that the universe is contextual—the act of looking makes the universe exist.

Neil Theise, MD, followed. He is a stem cell researcher and complexity theorist from the Mount Sinai Beth Israel Medical Center. He talked about the intersection of three domains: philosophy, science, and metaphysics to approach solving the hard problems. These three fundamental principles underlie the self-organizing universe: complementarity, sentience (or "creative interactivity"), and recursion. These features map directly to insights regarding the nature of reality from contemplative practices and philosophical inquiry from diverse cultures and spiritual perspectives.

At the end, he said that he believes there is something underneath all of this—there is a fundamental awareness. He said, "We are walking, talking earth."

Next was Subash Kak, an expert on cryptography, artificial neural networks, and quantum information. He told a great story about Nikola Tesla meeting Vivekananda, one of the leading figures in India's renaissance.

The actress Sarah Bernhardt introduced them, and they had an instant attraction. Vivekananda wrote "Mr. Tesla was charmed to hear about the Vedantic prana, akasha, and the kalpas. He thinks he can demonstrate mathematically that force and matter are reducible to potential energy.

Tesla did not succeed in showing this equivalence of mass and energy. But the equation $E = mc^2$ was published just a few years afterward.

Tesla, in his search of the akashic field, was looking for something more than converting matter into energy. His objective was to harness the primal energy within space for mankind's benefit.

Tesla wrote about the use of akasha and prana to solve mankind's greatest problems:

"Long ago ... [mankind] recognized that all perceptible matter comes from a primary substance, or tenuity beyond conception, filling all space, the Akasha or luminiferous ether, which is acted upon by the life-giving Prana or creative force, calling into existence, in never ending cycles all things and phenomena. The primary substance, thrown into infinitesimal whirls of prodigious velocity, becomes gross matter; the force subsiding, the motion ceases and matter disappears, reverting to the primary substance."

The idea of an akashic field that is the medium of consciousness caught peoples' attention, notably Hungarian scientist Ervin László whose 2004 book *Science and the Akashic Field: An Integral Theory of Everything* posits a field of information as the substance of the cosmos.

Both Vivekananda and Tesla were hoping for a mutual confirmation of Vedanta and physics. But time was not ripe for it then. Physics brought observers into the picture thirty years after their encounter through the framework of quantum mechanics.

Kak said now we may be much closer to explaining the interplay of prana and akasha.

After Kak was Menas Kafatos, an American physicist of Greek descent and a writer on spirituality, science, quantum theory, and cosmology.

He completely captured my attention; I could feel my heart beating as I scribbled every word. I felt a real connection with him and made a note to read his books. I googled him and saw that he was collaborating on a book with Deepak, which has since been released called *You Are the Universe*. He said:

This is you and you are all there is. God lives within you as you. We are already that which we are seeking. You are consciousness and I am consciousness. The universe is conscious. Start from the highest; don't start from the lowest. If you want to build a cathedral, you don't just gather a bunch of stones and stained glass and put them together randomly. You start from the vision; from the highest. The whole manifests the parts. If this paradigm works for you, you are already home.

Science does not really have answers to the big questions. I'm not advocating to get rid of science; I am a scientist. I'm advocating to enlarge it and make it a way of knowing.

Then he launched into a lecture about some of science's fundamental universal principles—the means through which Consciousness objectifies the world: *complementarity*, *recursion*, and *sentience* or *creative interactivity*.

My attention became riveted as I realized that some of the universal principles he was explaining were the hermetic laws that started my exploration—a triangulation or confirmation of linkages with the law of correspondence and polarity.

Complementarity, or integrated polarity, is the law that accounts for the "apparent opposites becoming unified at the deeper level" of universal consciousness.

Recursion (or correspondence), can be simply stated, "As here, so elsewhere"; "as above, so below." Recursion assures that all particles of one kind (say electrons) are similar, all cells in different organisms are similar; all stars share common properties. Without recursion, science and knowledge themselves would not even be possible: the world (and therefore consciousness, which is its foundation) operate through recursive relations.

The third law of nature, *creative interactivity,* states that interaction between objects, between living organisms, and between planets and stars, take place constantly; like universal interactivity through gravitation, interactivity through electromagnetic interactions, interactions between subjects and objects, between sentient beings (in which case it takes on the special form of *sentience*), between objects and objects, and between cells and cells. In particular, sentience is, in a sense, a fundamental aspect of consciousness, that forms the foundation of the conscious universe.

He said the universe is alive and that science is today a most powerful, successful, and continuously changing human activity. An activity that asks "big questions," such as, how did the universe start? An activity that also asks questions that may not be "big" but are, nevertheless, very important, questions that affect our everyday lives and well-being. He ended with: "We came from the stars," and "We only have one quantum world."

Stuart Hameroff was up next. He is an anesthesiologist and professor at the University of Arizona known for his studies of consciousness. He talked about where consciousness arises and which came first—consciousness or life?

He said that life began as primordial soup, and consciousness is derived from the underground. Did primitive pleasures spark the emergence of life? He said, "The deeper you go, the higher you fly."

Then there was a panel discussion on exploring consciousness, and all the speakers joined Deepak on stage. There were interesting questions raised, debate, some polite disagreements, interruptions, talking over one another, clarifications, but no firm conclusions.

Much of the conversation was beyond my experience, but I furiously took notes on things like the Copenhagen interpretation (an expression of the meaning of quantum mechanics that was largely devised by Niels Bohr and Werner Heisenberg).

Questions arose, like "What about the world before there was any life? What is cosmic consciousness? What is cosmic mind? What is objective consciousness? Is the mind separate from the brain? Is the mind outside the brain? Why does changing the brain seem to change the mind?"

Some anecdotes about things like organ donor recipients taking on the memories of the organ donor, which caused the skeptics and even some of the scientists say, "That's just an anecdote, not a controlled study!" And interjections like "talking about brain and mind will never get us anywhere!" Some side conversations like "I cannot be sure that you really exist. Reality is a figment of the mind. My experience is my own."

I got the feeling that these scientists knew and respected each other and that these kinds of debates had been raging between them for decades. There were lots of terms I had heard but would be hard pressed to define, like solipsism (the view that the self is all that can be known to exist), empiricism (the view that all knowledge is derived from sense-experience), and quantum entanglement (a physical phenomenon that occurs when pairs or groups of particles are generated, interact, or share spatial proximity in ways such that the quantum state of each particle cannot be described independently of the state of the others.)

Deepak was trying to control the discussion and allow for questions, but there continued to be interjections like, "Solipsism is the most reasonable and parsimonious perspective!"

Finally, he said, "We are not going to solve these questions tonight," thanked everyone, and wrapped up the day.

I left, mind racing with all the new concepts I was trying to absorb. That night I went through my conference notes with Rich. He was stunned about the image on the screen that matched my meditation presence and very interested in the speaker and panel topics.

We went to dinner at an Italian restaurant near the hotel, Il Fornaio.

January 24

We woke early again and went to the gym. Rich is going to drive to San Diego to meet a friend and look around at the area.

The conference for today started with the great yoga teacher Eddie Stern outside on the terrace of the Beverly Wilshire at 6 a.m. It was challenging but with plenty of easier asana alternatives for the less experienced, which was my category.

Then meditation followed at 7 a.m. with Dan Siegel. I was so excited to see him in person after learning about him in meditation classes, Science of Happiness and Synchro Destiny that I did not notice for a while that Deepak was two yoga mats away from me.

After an Ayurvedic breakfast, Reverend Mpho Tutu opened the day. She is the daughter of Desmond Tutu.

She said we misunderstand the scripture about humans having dominion over earth; that what this really means is that we should cultivate a dominion of care.

She leads a group that plants food gardens for HIV kids outside of Cape Town, trying to provide needed nutrients. She builds raised gardens using recycled soda bottles.

She said, "We are all a part of creation; as we heal our planet, we heal ourselves."

Cameron Russell was next talking about climate and consciousness. She is a fashion model who is a social artist. She believes change can best be brought about by artists and creative approaches to problems. She said artists are capable of changing the world.

She said creativity is low cost and abundant. She and other models show up for earth days and marches and use their social media networks for good. Interestingly, for the conference she wore no makeup, tied her hair back, and wore a plain dress. She looked gorgeous, but she was not playing on her looks.

She said, "Remember why life is sacred. We need everybody. Ask: What can I do? Start with things you have access to."

Next were two climate activists from Kiss the Ground: Lauren Tucker and Finian Makepeace. They talked about climate change and regenerative agriculture.

Dan Siegel was next. He asked, "Is the mind what the brain does or the brain what the mind does?" And answered, "They do each other." Mind is a journey into the heart of being human.

Interestingly, no group has agreed on a definition of the mind. Dan tried to create a definition in the 1990s, but he still does not think it fully represents what he wants to say; the mind is *an emergent, self-organizing process emerging from and also regulating the flow of energy and information within the body and within our relationships.*

The mind is much more than brain activity. Harmony and health emerge from integration, the linkage of differentiated elements. The best predictor of well-being is how integrated you are. What happens if you integrate consciousness and have awareness of awareness?

Dan talked about the wheel meditation, and we did it twice as a large group because some did not go to the early morning meditation. Dan asked for reaction after, and people said they felt "clarity, joy, expansiveness, the infinite eternity, God, love, peace, a sense of being part of the fundamental whole, connected to others."

He said, "Energy is the movement from possibility to actuality; the source of all that is possible, and MWE (me + we) is kindness and compassion."

William Mobley from UCSD followed next. He is an expert on Alzheimer's disease (AD) and Down Syndrome (DS). He talked about how the nervous system works—how neural circuits operate.

He cited a study I learned about in Science of Happiness class where fMRI showed neural activity when someone felt empathetic when a loved one got a shock in the next room. They are studying whether one can learn to be more empathetic.

Rob Knight was next, talking about the microbiome and health. He is the author of *Follow Your Gut.*

He said we are only about 1 percent human; we have 20,000 human genes and up to 20 million microbial genes in our body. Brightly colored food is the language that speaks to our genes. How can we map our microbiomes? If you have a dog or a baby in the house, you definitely share microbiomes.

He asked, "What most impacts your microbiome? The range of plants you ate in the two weeks prior." He stressed the importance of eating a range of healthy fruits and vegetables.

Then, Dr. Shamini Jain spoke. She is a psychologist, scientist, and social entrepreneur. She is the founder of the Consciousness and Healing Initiative (CHI), a collaborative accelerator that connects scientists, health practitioners, innovators, and social entrepreneurs to forward the science and practice of healing. CHI was formed through Dr. Jain's deep desire to bring key stakeholders together to create a coherent and effective movement to move us beyond models of "disease thinking" and the "decade of the brain" into the study of systems-based healing processes, and personal and societal empowerment.

Dr. Jain explained that she studies healing, including ancient forms like reiki, healing therapeutic touch, electromagnetic therapy, and other energy work to combat chronic pain.

She said that subtle energies conspire with consciousness to foster healing in spirit, mind, and body. Their perspective is that consciousness, regardless of how one defines it, is essential to guiding our well-being, and that the scientific exploration of consciousness will lead us to breakthroughs that will impact not only healing and healthcare, but how we understand and appreciate the interconnections between us and our planet.

The next presenter was Ryan Castle. He has started an open access site for integrative studies, ISHAR. The Integrative Studies Historical Archive & Repository (ISHAR) is the world's largest single source for academic information on integrative studies, including Ayurveda, acupuncture, meditation, yoga, Qigong, and everything in between. It is a free searchable index of research information.

Deepak's friend and coauthor Rudy Tanzi spoke next. He is the vice-chair of Neurology, director of the Genetics and Aging Research Unit, codirector of the McCance Center for Brain Health at Massachusetts General Hospital, and professor of Neurology at Harvard Medical School.

I had read *Super Brain*, the book that Tanzi wrote with Deepak, and I was excited to hear from him. He said that "we maximize human potential through brain health, and we must integrate mind/brain health into the medical establishment."

He said that everyone needs brain care. Those that have no disease today need to prevent it. Those that have risk but no symptoms need to do so as well, and of course those with brain injury or disease need to treat it.

AD first hits the hippocampus and destroys short-term memory and destroys sense of self. He asked, "What is self? Who am I? My brain? My mind?"

The core of you is the observer: the witness who observes the mind.

In *Super Brain,* they put forward that "the true you is the observer of your brain activity, the navigator of your mind."

I was furiously taking notes. "There is neuroplasticity in your brain—your neural network is reshaping itself all the time. You can change gene expression; habits are very important. Your mind and body of tomorrow are the results of your habits today. Eat a Mediterranean diet: fruits, veggies, nuts, olive oil, and less red meat. Get eight hours of sleep; do meditation and yoga. Rudy talked about the meditation study he conducted at La Costa. His conclusions: "Vacation is good for well-being. Meditation is even better. Meditation increases expression of telomere maintenance pathway." He said, "Vacation is expensive, but you can meditate for free." And he ended with a hopeful message:

"I believe there is a significant possibility that we will have a solid plan for eradicating Alzheimer's disease by 2025."

Then they had a panel discussion with all the speakers from the section on genetics, epigenetics, and neuroscience. My notes from the discussion include:

We do not know the mechanics of intuition or if there is a cellular substrate for memory. How can you see your mom's face in your mind?

No one knows how you do that. Imagination, creativity, choice: we don't know how they are stored.

There are two paradigms: physicalistic and nonphysicalistic. Deepak's paradigm is that every form is a phenomenon. Everything we think of as a noun is really a verb: atoms, subatomic particles, the table. Every phenomenon arises from that which is formless. Tagore said, "In this playhouse of infinite forms, I caught sight of that which is formless, and so my life was blessed."

They said a goal of this conference is to bring science and tie it into the contemplative traditions that look inward into the mechanics of experience. Much beautiful poetry by Rumi and Tagore was quoted. I love scientists who quote poetry.

The self is who is "aware of being aware" and "conscious of being conscious."

The panel explored the connection between super brain and super genes. Super brain says, "You are not your brain; you are a user of your brain. Even your mind is not who you are. You are neither your brain nor your mind. You use your brain to navigate your mind. You are the self that doesn't go away even in Alzheimer's." Supergenes say, "You are not just the genes your mom and dad gave you; you can't change the clay, but you can sculpt it with how you live your life.

The letters of the alphabet create a language. The letters create a word. The word is the gene. A language is created by sentences and paragraphs and stories.

Your body is a story of the experiences you have had. DNA is the letters. Intergenic DNA is punctuation and also creates the plot because it tells the genes how to interact and communicate.

Your life is a story, and you are writing the story, but it is being transcribed through epigenetics and neuroplasticity and your genes and brain.

Deepak interjected "the one who is writing the story is a formless being, of course."

From a physician's perspective, changing habits is the hardest thing that physicians ask of patients. *Super Genes* and *Super Brain* motivate patients to make difficult behavioral changes.

Next, Satya Hinduja from Berklee College of Music did an Alchemic Sonic Environment Performance. She instructed us to close our eyes and go inside ourselves while she played a composition designed to help us get in touch with the "energy of your heart center." She said, "Silence is the nest; music is the bird."

Nancy Abrams followed. She quoted from her new book: *A God That Could Be Real: Spirituality, Science, and the Future of Our Planet* that pulls together science and spirituality into a radically new Big Picture for our time.

She is a lawyer, a scientist, and the wife of Joel Primack. As she spoke, she showed more images from the Hubble telescope of beautiful nebulas, and once again, I was dramatically moved; these are the images I see, and I had no idea before this conference that what I was seeing was something that existed outside of my mind.

Abrams hypothesized a God who could be real. She summarized what she had gotten out of the conference so far: a whole new origin story for our planet, scientific revolution in neuroscience, and the notion that we might be able to change our children's genes by changing our habits.

She said God is scientifically possible, the chance to redefine God is in our hands, and spiritual passion could be our fire. What if God was an emergent phenomenon? We are human; therefore, we aspire! What if we saw God this way?

Dr. Barnaby Marsh spoke next. A Rhodes Scholar at Oxford, he does pioneering research on decision-making in complex situations. He works with leaders of major corporations, foundations, and philanthropists, and continues academic research at both the Center for Evolutionary Dynamics at Harvard and the Institute for Advanced Study in Princeton. He said, "Science changes over time. We have made a lot of advancement in science, but not in spirituality; we have not made spiritual progress." He asked, "What would spiritual progress look like?"

- Optimal wellness
- Altruism,
- Love
- Compassion
- Interconnectivity
- Gratitude and joy
- Creativity
- Motivation and purpose
- Finding optimal balance and peace

Most people follow a religious tradition or path. Why is the path to knowledge difficult? We are unlocking wisdom. Could science open the door? How do we make progress?

We know we must proceed with humility: "We are like a toddler in a sandbox; we don't know we don't know." We see benefits in:

- Meditation; health benefits
- Gratitude; life satisfaction
- Forgiveness; benefits the forgiver
- Wellness is much more than the absence of sickness
- Love multiplies when shared
- Love transforms
- What is the self?
- What is higher consciousness?
- How do we boost imagination?
- Can society promote balance?

We need to look at possibilities, not constraints. Be open. Walk with top thinkers.

Then there was a lovely concert from students at the Berklee College of Music and then meditation with Deepak on the terrace to the loud sounds of Beverly Hills. No one noticed the noise.

Tonight was a Michael Franti concert. We went to dinner at Avra and then stopped to listen and dance before going up to our room. I have always loved Franti and was thrilled to hear him play "Say Hey" and "Do It for the Love," and I sent a video of him singing to the sibs.

January 25

After yoga and meditation, the last day of the symposium started with a panel discussion on Technology and Wellness. This panel was moderated with each speaker talking for a few minutes.

Deepak said he thinks technology is part of our evolution as a human species. With disruption, there is often discomfort as people get comfortable with change. He basically was saying, "Get on board; technology is here to stay. Resisting what is irreversible leads to extinction."

The panel was facilitated by Poonacha Machaiah, cofounder and CEO at jiyo.com, and the panel members were:

- Simon Leung, Chairman, Net Dragon
- Sridhar Solur, SVP Product Development, Comcast
- Upasna Kamineni Kandela, Vice Chair, Apollo Medical Group (largest private hospital in India)
- Paddy Barrett, Cardiologist, Scripps, Salk Institute
- Rick Stollmeyer, CEO, Mindbody
- Jeffrey Martin, Entrepreneur
- Moira Burke, Research Scientist, Facebook
- Paul Duffy, CEO, ARHT Media
- Rich Mault, Chief Medical Officer, Qualcomm LIFE

Poonacha opened the panel via hologram and said that the goal of the technology and wellness presenters at the conference is to facilitate

Deepak's vision to "create critical mass for a conscious community that will help lead to a 'more peaceful, just, joyful, energetic, healthy and sustainable world.'" They want to do justice to the word *civilization*, democratize learning, and collaborate instead of compete.

Deepak said, "Technology is neutral; it is a tool that can be used for good and to heal the world."

The discussion turned to future potentials. Someone spoke about the powerful implications of interactivity; for example, the Salk Institute uses mirror technology in rehabilitation for patients who are paralyzed; the technology gives them the experience of moving limbs.

If we think about technology enabling being part of a larger mind, someone could get a dopamine or oxytocin hit from another person doing compassion meditation. Not only can our minds and emotions be positively impacted by each other, our biologies are also intertwined. We have to start using body/mind in the same way as we use space/time. Divisions are totally artificial.

We can rewire neural networks to address phobias, inflammation, and eating disorders; the risk factors for all serious diseases are the same.

The panel touched on creating an ecosystem of technologies: hologram, big data, analytics—to bring education and information everywhere, blending online and offline learning experiences, and using virtualization to help connect the unconnected.

Moira talked about intimacy research. Can social networks impact the area of tenderness? She is a research scientist and studies human/computer interactions and is an expert on the role that friendships play in life and in well-being. Having more well-being is linked to social support. If someone has even one friend, it gives them a greater sense of well-being. Friendships are critical and also part of the purpose of Facebook. Facebook is trying to provide tools for positive interactions. Interactions have well-being benefits; when people interact one-on-one, there is increased life satisfaction. So, if you get comments on your posts and you actually interact on Facebook by engaging with friends and liking and commenting on their posts, you derive more satisfaction than if you passively sit back and read but don't interact,

They talked about connectivity in healthcare and the link to improved health as a result.

Once we have driving technology, 11,000 less people will die annually in car wrecks. Smart homes and smart cars are everyday occurrences now, as well as cars that stop your car before getting in an accident. Sensors and other connectivity like blue tooth pregnancy tests or linked inhalers that let parents know if kids have used their rescue inhaler are within reach.

We are entering into an era of intelligent care with disposable patches that measure heart rate and have EKG, and 3D motion sensors.

The whole panel said—don't resist what is irreversible—embrace technology and think about how to use it.

They talked about advances in digital health; genomics and augmented technologies to generate the best outcomes for patients and improve lives in the caregiver community.

Biomarkers can now show when people are approaching burnout. And they are also using biometrics to study the personal metrics of mood and how that impacts patient care; today they are using this in a passive way to identify those at high risk, even up to the risk of suicide.

The well-being of the physician and medical team has an enormous impact on the well-being of patients. They can take the temperature of a whole department and organization.

Upasna told the story of how, forty-five years ago, her grandfather was a cardiac surgeon at Massachusetts General. He left and went home to India to practice there. He had a dream of providing world-class, affordable medical care to India. They now have 64 hospitals, 2,500 pharmacies, 115 clinics, and nine women's care centers, as well as occupational services and their own insurance company.

They talked about the high suicide rate in India and also poor conditions. There are more phones than toilets in India. People work long hours and are very sedentary.

There are a billion lives there. In rural India, they are trying disruptive technology—doctor/patient teleconsults by smartphone; doing intervention in a very low-cost way. They are now in nineteen countries, mostly India and parts of Africa, bringing world-class healthcare through teleconsults to urban and rural areas.

Moira said people might wonder if social media can really help manage stress. What is watching a cute kitten video worth? Her research has shown that social media can provide meaningful and substantive impacts. She measures stress, depression, and feelings of social support. She measured well-being during major life events like illness, marriage, birth of a baby, and compared well-being changes during times like these to receiving two extra "likes" and comments on Facebook and saw that other people's responses to your posts has a measurable impact on well-being, similar to reactions to major life events.

Everyone has been in a doctor's office and felt that the consultation was rushed. Supercomputing power can now augment the role of the physician. A lot of the basic task-oriented data gathering can free up more time for the face-to-face conversation.

Technology can help counselors reach a greater number of people; digital avatars are now in use where people can interact with a digital entity.

Technology is becoming more and more human-like. Microphones are more like the human ear; cameras are like the eye. Instead of wearing something, it will be in you—bionic. So, someday having a chip on your shoulder might be a good thing. Virtual and augmented reality.

The panel talked about the Michael Franti concert last night and the universal feeling in the room of love, happiness and the desire to get on the dance floor and move. Everyone there had taken a video and sent it to a friend.

Augmented realities are useful because they give us a means to connect. The hunger for direct experience and direct communication remains. Synchronized bio signals now link people together in amazing connection technologies, like a ring you can wear with your spouse to feel each other's heartbeat or the father feeling the fetal heartbeat of a baby. Thinking about it from a human connection standpoint, we can't begin to imagine the degree to which we will be able to make gains in empathy, understanding, and connection with each other.

Moira talked about progress in posting. We should question the feeling that we can only share the most artificially happy, positive, and upbeat posts; part of being human is sharing the tough moments and expressing empathy. When people share sad feelings, they get more supportive comments. If you say you are devastated, you will get more comment and empathy than a positive post generates.

The narrative of health and wellness is changing. How will that actually change patient/provider interaction going forward?

For the past 2,000 years, healthcare has been a face-to-face engagement. It is episodic and haphazard with a black hole in between visits. Technology facilitates a continuous-care model so that doctors can see what's going on without the patient having to do much of anything. Doctors will be able to see things before they become a crisis. Systems like mind/body and well-being of practitioners will dramatically change the healthcare system. We are moving from trial and error to intelligent care.

Last on the agenda was a panel on Creativity and Infinite Possibility.

- David Nash, Berklee College of Music
- Jitish Kallat, artist
- Michael Franti, musician
- Satya Hinduja, musician
- Finian Makepeace, musician and cofounder, Kiss the Ground

Jitish Kallat shared *Public Notice 3*, an installation that connected two key historical moments: the First World Parliament of Religions held on September 11, 1893, and the terrorist attacks at the World Trade Center and the Pentagon on that very date, 108 years later. His work comments on religious tolerance across the twentieth and twenty-first centuries. The basis for Kallat's installation is the landmark speech delivered by Swami Vivekananda at the Parliament, which was the earliest attempt to create a global dialogue of religious faiths.

Vivekananda argued for an end to fanaticism and a respectful recognition of all traditions of belief through universal tolerance. Drawing attention to the great chasm between this speech of tolerance and the events of September 11, 2001, the text of the speech was displayed in the colors of the United States' Department of Homeland Security alert system.

Satya Hinduja is a graduate of the Berklee College of Music. She studies the science of frequency. Diagnosed with fibromyalgia, she used sound and frequency to heal herself. Sound is energy; we can create internal shifts in ourselves using sound.

She drew parallels between the Fibonacci spiral golden mean ratio and the cochlear in the ear and the spiral frequencies of color and light she sees in meditation and the curated sound she is writing to help people get to a higher state. I was excited; someone else who is fascinated by spirals and who sees color and light in meditation!

There is, it is said, a kind of spirit music in the world continuously but silently playing.
Carl Sagan

Finian Makepeace, cofounder of Kiss the Ground, is also a performing musical artist. His mission is "we can do this" on climate change. He believes creative people have allowance to flow into new things and experience what is out of our comfort zone. We should all question,where have we confined ourselves? People are becoming more aware; young people are saying, I'm going to only work for companies that are doing really great things, which can shift the world. There is great power in views expressed well. We need a higher quality of art and music used to influence for positivity. It's about using your talent for good.

Michael Franti said, "I make music for one reason; every person should be happy, healthy, and equal." His mother was the piano player for a church. There were five kids in the house, and everyone played a musical instrument. He was the tallest kid, so he stood in the back of the choir and felt the energy when everyone started singing. Harmonies and words made him cry. One of his professors said, "I am going to sit with you and make sure you get an A in writing and you learn to communicate ideas." He takes emotions that are out there and organizes them into a piece of music to create something that will open people's hearts and souls. He said we might feel stress in body and mind and then Bob Marley comes on the radio and we get rejuvenated. That's the power of music. It's not enough just to have talents; you have to share those talents with other people. He wants to tell the stories of people who feel they don't belong; he feels that every single person in the world is significant. He went to Iraq just to walk around, play music for soldiers, and then talk to people about their lives. After 9/11, he and other artists declared San Francisco a hate-free zone and put on a free concert in the park to sing songs for peace called "Power to the Peaceful." Now he has started Do It for the Love to send people with life-threatening illnesses to see any live concert they want. He closed with: "Be your best, serve the greater good, and rock out."

Key messages from the panel in the last five minutes:

- People are always moved by music.
- You must share your talents.
- There is some part of all of us that feels insignificant.
- Everyone is an artist.
- We are all view shifters.
- Connect and shift your view.
- Art helps us shift our view of the world to compassion, beauty, and truth.

The conference ended at noon. As Rich drove us back to the desert, I debriefed the conference. I was moved by the entire experience, loved hearing the latest in science and spirituality, and thought it was impressive that Deepak invited his critics and skeptics.

I was inspired by the idea that we are all here for some larger purpose and that we have gifts and talents to use for the greater good. I told Rich I wanted to get certified to teach meditation at the Chopra Center and wanted to find a way to link meditation and art.

Rich felt that the close proximity of LA, San Diego, and other resort areas made living in the Palm Springs area even more workable for us. We got back in time for a nice walk with our two ecstatic dogs.

January 26

Today we got back to our daily routine with meditation, workouts, and soul-filling mountain-gazing on our walks. I checked in on Gus and Dad. Gus is depressed and struggling, and Dad is holding his own.

I took some time to go back through my notes from the Sages and Scientists symposium and also from the salon at Jean Houston's home. I feel so grateful to have had these two opportunities of accelerated learning. I want to make linkages and think about the meaning behind all I have heard. My shamanic apprenticeship is about to start, so it is a good time to take stock of what I have learned.

I was able to get caught up on the next segment of the Science of Happiness Class, which focused on relationships and social networks.

Friends provide us with a sense of belonging, visibility, and a chance to express empathy. The risks of friendship are jealousy and dependence: we may become discouraged or bitter about our friends' successes or rely on them too much for approval and self-esteem. The best way to handle these is to remember that we want our friends to be happy—and to realize that their success benefits us, too.

Significant others—partners, best friends, or family—provide us with a host of mental and physical benefits. They fall under the category of "bonding capital," providing support in times of need. Continually cultivating new friendships is a pathway for happiness.

Social capital works best when we have a combination of strong and weak ties. That way, our support system doesn't collapse if we lose a single node. But each connection takes time and effort to maintain, so it's our job to prioritize and know when to say no.

Why cross-group relationships matter for happiness (Rodolfo Mendoza-Denton):

Getting rid of prejudices may be good for health. Prejudiced people get stressed in the presence of people outside their group, but three deep interactions with "outsiders" is enough to lower stress levels. To become more egalitarian, we should deliberately expose ourselves to and cultivate friendships with people outside our in-group.

January 27

Rich and I went back to the community we liked in Indian Wells and looked at real estate. We met numerous residents who gave us good advice and seem encouraging and welcoming. We love the unpretentious active vibe and feel this could be our future home.

I called the Chopra Center and completed the application to become a certified teacher for Primordial Sound Meditation. The class starts next week, but the first section is the enrichment portion, which I have already covered. I will be doing the shamanic apprenticeship, too, but think it can all work.

I need to attend the Seduction of Spirt retreat as part of the certification process, so I signed up for the next one, and I am thrilled to see the required reading list includes books I have already read or started: *The Upanishads*, *The Bhagavad Gita*, Shankara's *Crest Jewel of Discrimination*, and the *Yoga Sutras of Patanjali*.

Science of Happiness class today focused on empathy featuring Emiliana Simon-Thomas.

There are two types of empathy: affective and cognitive. Affective empathy refers to a feeling or an action—the way we absorb or imitate the feelings and expressions of others. We begin mimicking others as infants and continue mirroring expressions and body language into adulthood. Some studies even suggest that mimicry helps us understand what emotions other people are feeling. Affective empathy may be facilitated by mirror neurons, which are motor neurons that fire even when we're just watching other people move (although there is some controversy about whether they affect emotions as well).

Cognitive empathy refers to the ability to understand how people feel and to see things from their perspective. Cognitive empathy involves broader parts of the brain.

Empathic concern can make us happier, as long as it doesn't turn into empathic distress (the feeling when we become overwhelmed by others' suffering). In general, empathy increases the sharing of positive emotions and brings people closer together. And if other people are empathetic, we get the benefits of their understanding and support when we're in need.

January 28

As part of our self-imposed assignment for working on our marriage, we each made a list of nonmaterial wishes. Tonight, we had our Monday night meeting, and it was fun sharing our lists. Here is my list:

- Bring me coffee in the morning. Offer me a glass of wine at night.
- Cook together; I love being in the kitchen together and having dinner dates.
- Run errands together.
- Walk next to me when we take the dogs out.
- Snuggle naked.
- Kiss my forehead, my eyes, my cheeks.
- Tell me when I look good.
- Hug me from behind.
- Kiss and hug me hello and goodbye.
- Dance with me.
- Read the same book sometimes.

Rich's list:

- Cuddling naked under the covers.
- Talking in bed.
- Touch throughout the day.
- Saying "good morning!"
- Walking the pups as a pack.
- Expressing gratitude for abundance.
- Saying thank you for big and small things.
- Learning things together.
- Meditating together.
- Being on an adventure together.

Wow, we really are pretty aligned.

Science of Happiness class today, from *The Evolution of Empathy* by Frans de Waal:

> Empathy is useful from an evolutionary perspective because it encourages us to care for our young and work cooperatively in groups. So, it should be no surprise that humans aren't the only empathetic creatures: researchers have observed empathy in domestic pets as well as apes, who console fellow apes who are suffering. Over the course of our lifetime, empathy grows from relatively simple mimicry and transmission of emotions to the more complex ability to take someone else's perspective. Empathy has a role to play in bringing people across the world closer together and reducing discrimination. But to do that, we'll have to figure out how to overcome our innate tendencies to hate our enemies, ignore strangers, and distrust people who are different.

We talked about this; Bella is definitely empathetic. She can always sense sadness and distress.

January 29

Today I confirmed the Canyon Ranch trip for next summer and sent it to Teresa, Bethany, Gussie, Joe, Emma, Sasha, and Mia, which started a nice text exchange. I hope Gus will be well enough to go.

I made a list of some key things I have learned from my reading, classes and experiences so far. I won't say that my existential questions are answered. In fact, maybe now I have even more questions—but I have loved this phase of my life and this vision quest.

Some things that now feel like truth to me—in no particular order:

- We are spiritual beings having a human experience.
- We all contain divine essence.
- God lives within us. We are already that which we are seeking.
- The events and relationships in our lives are not random.
- Our karmic lessons are derived from actions we took in the past.
- We each have lessons we must experience in this lifetime in order to progress.
- Some have progressed further; some are sages, seers, and enlightened beings.
- Pain is inevitable; suffering is optional.
- There are actions we can take to experience union with our divine nature.
- Everyone can increase their intuitive potential.
- Most people go through life without ever knowing the higher states of consciousness.
- We are the authors of our life story.
- We can alter gene expression by healthy lifestyle, loving relationships and balance.
- How we live our life impacts our biology.
- We can expand joy, kindness, peace, and equanimity.
- Our choices ripple out into the world.
- Self-awareness is the key to positive transformation.
- We can increase our happiness by intentional activity.

- Artists have a role to play through creative approaches to problems.
- Subtle energies conspire with consciousness to foster healing in spirit, mind, and body.
- There is help available—teachers; archetypes, spirit guides, angels, entelechy who are on your team, who care about you and want you to make progress.
- Each person has a dharma or many purposes they are to fulfill in life. It is the quest of each person to figure out what they are.
- It is incumbent on us to take the risk of failure or embarrassment and share our talents.

Science of Happiness

The science of forgiveness stems from the insight that the hurts and conflicts we suffer in life take a toll on our psychological and physical well-being. In response to these hurts, holding onto grudges and dwelling on them—what psychologists call "rumination"—undermines our happiness.

Study after study has suggested that forgiveness reduces stress and fosters happiness. For instance, a study by researchers at the University of Miami links forgiveness to increased satisfaction with life, more positive emotions, less negative emotions, and fewer symptoms of physical illness. The same group of researchers also found that forgiving on one day is linked to higher happiness on the next day.

January 30

My Science of Happiness class is ending. The class ends with a focus on meditation.

From "What is Mindfulness?" by Barry Boyce:

Mindfulness is something we already have, a basic human ability. We have the power to stop feeling reactive and overwhelmed, if only we cultivate it. That can be done through meditation, doing activities (like sports) meditatively, or just pausing from time to time in everyday life.

From Jon Kabat-Zinn's "The Stars of Our Own Movie":

One of the great illusions that comes from a lack of mindfulness is seeing ourselves as "the stars of our own movie." Everything is filtered through the lens of I, me, and mine. We get caught up in our thoughts rather than truly experiencing the world through our senses. But when we deliberately start cultivating awareness, we see that it has no center or boundary. Meditation is not the goal; the point of cultivating mindfulness is to learn to live our lives like they really matter now, rather than constantly living in regret or anticipation.

Richie Davidson founded the Center for Investigating Healthy Minds (CIHM) at the University of Wisconsin. His studies indicate changes in gene expression after only eight hours of meditating.

From Shauna Shapiro's "Mindfulness Meditation and the Brain":

Our attitude and behaviors have a bigger effect on our happiness than our external circumstances. Mindfulness shapes our brain by increasing gray matter in areas related to attention, learning, self-awareness, self-regulation, empathy, and compassion. Meditation can have a lasting impact on our brains and thus our happiness.

Shauna Shapiro: Intention, attention, attitude:

These three characteristics are crucial to mindfulness. Intention involves knowing why you're doing what you're doing—having a goal or a north star. Attention means focusing on the present and not succumbing to the 12,000–50,000 thoughts we have every day. Attitude is how you do all of this—ideally, with acceptance, openness, curiosity, kindness, gentleness, warmth, and trust. "What you practice becomes stronger," says Shapiro.

Mindfulness and Neuroplasticity

Mindfulness literally changes our brains, making some areas more responsive, interconnected, and dense. In particular, these are areas related to empathy (the insula); memory, emotion, and emotion regulation; and reward circuitry. In response to distressing stimuli, meditators see more activation in their prefrontal structures (for awareness) and less in their fear-driven amygdala.

Taken together, these changes make us more attentive and less distracted, more in touch with our emotions, more resilient and quicker to recover from stress, and more prosocial, optimistic, and kind—in a word, happier.

January 31

Doing random acts of kindness was part of the curriculum of Science of Happiness. I drive past a senior center nearly every day as I run errands near the villa. Today, I stopped and talked to the activities director to see what is needed.

The activities director said, "We can always use small Bingo prizes such as candy bars, inexpensive jewelry, hand lotions, crossword puzzle and word search books, any recent magazines, or large print books."

I took my final exam for Science of Happiness and got 95 percent.

I bought some large-type books, valentines, candy, and stamps and dropped them off at the Senior Center.

Chapter Eight
February

We relish our last days in California. I begin the shamanic apprenticeship and experience a relaxed feeling of settling down, deeply enjoying the simplicity and present-moment awareness of painting mandalas, going for walks, and preparing simple meals. I begin to feel even more detached from the drama of everyday life, spending quiet time in the casita without the news in the background. Despite the constant undercurrent of concern about Gussie, I feel a nearly constant state of well-being.

I love feeling more centered and begin to experience even more moments of daily joy where my soul feels stirred by a profound sense of beauty and gratitude. I have also felt a natural shift in food preferences, as Rich and I begin to gravitate toward eating more plant-based food. I am excited to begin my shamanic apprenticeship and learn to journey. I see an impact in my dreams as my awareness begins to expand.

February 2

Groundhog Day. Rich watched the Super Bowl yesterday while I painted mandalas, played with the dogs, and watched the commercials. We love, love, love this time zone. I don't think we have ever made it to the end of the Super Bowl before.

After meditation and coffee, we took a long, relaxing, sniff walk. Because it was such a pretty morning, we kept extending it, saying, "Now let's walk down this street."

I did a barre class after cardio, painted, and then we took another walk this afternoon. It is eighty degrees here, nineteen in Ohio. We ordered Thai food—pad Thai with tofu—delicious.

I received my first shamanic apprenticeship assignment yesterday. There are nine apprentices in class. Our teachers expect us to just dive right in and journey to meet our spirit guide allies. Bella was cuddly today and crawled in bed next to me as I sat, psyching myself up to do my first shamanic journey. I don't know how to start so will wait until our class call to get more direction.

We had a nice "Monday night meeting" tonight, held hands, and talked about how we were doing. I can't remember being happier or more excited to keep learning. It is interesting how the Science of Happiness class echoed the things I learned at the Sages and Scientists symposium, the salon with Jean Houston, and the things I have read. I will be fascinated to see how the apprenticeship goes and if it reinforces or contradicts things I have learned elsewhere.

February 3

After meditation, coffee, and a long, sweet walk with the pack, I went to the gym, jogged on the treadmill, and then did TRX.

In the shamanic apprentice kickoff call, the three teachers explained that that our main task for this week is to journey to meet guides. I took notes as I listened intently.

For any guides that show up, ask their relationship to you: are they a lifelong ally, what is your history, when did you meet, when and why they chose you, is this is your first lifetime working together, and so forth.

They gave instruction on how to journey including the drumming track to listen to, how to enter the journey, and to always be respectful to guides in the journey space. Drumming induces a particular state of consciousness. Some like to lie a certain way when they journey, like with one arm down and one arm crossed over the face. You can do a ritual or light a candle or use a specific blanket. Find a ritual and stick with it, so your brain recognizes the pattern and can relax.

The teachers explained the importance of being open and receptive. Journeying allows you to travel to other dimensions. Patience is critical. Ancient civilizations took journeying very seriously; evidence of journeying is shown in cave paintings and carvings. Meditation tells you to drop ideas from your mind. Journeying uses the brain differently than meditation; it's like allowing yourself to daydream. If you were called lazy for daydreaming, that criticism is embedded in your brain. It takes intention to overcome the idea that "I'm just making it all up."

Journeying is a connection to other realms. "As above, so below"; we have internal and external connections so that when we visit places, they are then always inside of us. When you journey, let go of your inner critic and editor; stay conscious of what you are supposed to be doing. Each journey assignment has a task.

Guides are deeper or higher parts of us or access points to a deeper or higher part of ourselves. Normal waking reality is the very tip of the iceberg; the enormous part is below. We need what they know. We want to develop relationships with a handful of guides. See what relationships form. Which ones seem to show up most often? A guide will emerge at some point, who will be a long-term relationship. Don't journey without them. Wait for a guide to show up before you journey.

Interact; be respectful but firm with guides. Be comfortable saying, "No, I can't do that." Develop relationships; get to know them. It takes patience and time.

Let your brain loosen up. If you have always been praised for being logical, the idea of journeying can be threatening. Work with whatever appears; if a red dot appears, work by interacting with the red dot. Use your contrived imagination until your inspired imagination takes over.

We are to keep a separate journal for each of our journeys, notes from the class calls; everything related to the apprenticeship; so, I will not be keeping my notes in this journal going forward. We are to give ourselves a whole year of journeying practice before we judge where we are.

February 5

Bethany's birthday is today; I sent her the sibling tradition of $1 and a card. It is snowing in Ohio today—sixteen degrees. It will be eighty here. As we were walking, I told Rich if we were home, we would be shoveling.

Rich is playing golf. The dogs are calm. Now is the perfect time to try to journey, but I am apprehensive. I queue up the drumming track on my phone, put in earbuds, and lie on the bed. There is no special blanket, tool, or candle at the villa. I have never smudged anything.

I get under the covers, and as I listen to the drumming track, my brain rebels; I feel ridiculous. I start to imagine what people would think about this whole experiment and feel embarrassed. I have told Rich about the apprenticeship at a high level. He hasn't judged me, but now I am judging myself. What was I thinking? I tell myself that this is just my logical, rational mind at work. This is the negative inner chatter my teachers talked about. Developing intuition and imagination are part of my spiritual journey, and what's the worst thing that could happen? I can't journey? As I am lying there listening, the fast drumming begins, which is the call back to say that the track is nearly over. So, I hit repeat and finally begin to relax with the rhythm of the drumbeat. I make it through my first journey, and write my notes in my apprenticeship notebook.

February 6

We had three showings of the house and got good feedback from two; waiting on one.

Chip is full of piss and vinegar today. He put his front paws on the kitchen counter and chewed the top of the blender and a spatula. I have ordered new ones since we need to leave this rental better than we found it.

I went to the dog store and got a "chuck it" toy and threw balls to him and Bella at the dog park. It is windy today; the Santa Ana winds are blowing, and there are some clouds hovering over the mountains.

I am more comfortable trying to journey today, and the light and color beings that I often see in meditation came as I began with the drumming track. Feeling self-conscious, I mentally asked the first presence I saw if s/he/they were a primary lifelong ally, and I clearly heard a mental "answer" yes! And more information came into my awareness as though they were communicating with me; they "say" they are energy, essence, and vibration; and their appearance may morph over time. They are part of me and also part of something larger. Feeling unsure of myself, I continued asking for any and all information that could be used to be in the right relationship with them.

The answers come into my awareness; they said it is important that I continue to take time in my various practices to waken to greater awareness, to stay open, and continue to relearn the lessons I have forgotten. They said they help me gain insights and learn and understand things.

I asked about our history, and they said they have always been with me, but in the last six months I have started to wake up in this lifetime. They said I am now on a path to expanded awareness. As I write this in my apprenticeship journal and post the journey for my teachers to review, I feel simultaneously foolish and yet excited that, even if I am making it all up, it feels like a connection.

February 7

I talked to Dad. Every year we take him and Marie on a trip, and he now has clearance from his doctors who say it is OK to travel. I asked if he wanted to come to California while we are here, but he can't travel until March. We decided to go to Cancun and meet Sasha and Drew.

I spent the day booking flight and hotel reservations and coordinating with Sasha. It's so great this will work out. Every year, Rich and I think it may be the last trip with Dad; it's heartening that he is excited to go. I booked wheelchairs for Dad and Marie's flights and got a hotel room for them next to the elevator and booked a wheelchair there. There is a nonstop flight for them from Kansas City that gets in within ten minutes of our flight from Columbus.

One of my teachers checked in to see how it was going for me so far in the apprenticeship.

I said I was doing the homework but feel faintly silly. I think I am making everything up in my imagination. I wonder if it is all a waste of time. I usually can't visualize sharp images like some of the others in the apprenticeship; I generally only see motion, light, and color. My rational mind is rebelling.

My teacher told me that everything I am feeling is normal and that many people never visualize in journeys, but they still get information. She said, "Let's say this *was* all just your imagination. Did you know, people have been doing imagination exercises for millennia?"

In the ancient spiritual texts, the Vedas, imagination is viewed as both the transcendent power through which the gods created the universe, and the power that joins the human spirit with the ultimate reality. To live your ultimate reality, you *have* to train your imagination. So, if it makes you feel less ridiculous to say "this is just my imagination," then do that. It's OK.

Freud has compared the human mind to the tip of an iceberg. We are consciously aware of only 5 to 10 percent of what goes on in our mind. The other 90 to 95 percent of our brainpower goes into unconscious thought. Einstein said imagination is more important than knowledge. The ability to imagine things influences everything we do, think about, and create.

Making art and daydreaming are both ways to exercise this creative muscle and tap into the other part of our brainpower. If it makes you feel better to think of your journeys as just a daydream or fantasy for now, it's OK. The more you work with your intuition, the more you strengthen it, and the more it grows. In time, you'll know exactly what your intuition is telling you, and you'll know that you can trust it implicitly. In developing your intuition, you want to make it fun, like a game—not like a dreaded assignment or something that could be right or wrong. Intuition exercises can be fun and in turn help you boost your awareness. Intuition works in mysterious ways, and sometimes you won't see that it is guiding you down the highest path until later. That's why you need to just learn to trust and let go.

This is very helpful advice for me, and somehow the linkage to the Vedas and the reference to Einstein makes it feel more legitimate and comfortable.

February 8

We had a long walk; every day the mountains look different. Week two of my class is released later today; I am waiting for it to post. I can see why the teachers say to stay current with the homework journeys. If you get behind, it probably seems overwhelming. I did an elliptical and weight workout.

We fixed mushrooms, onions, and eggs for breakfast; really good. We had leftover vegetarian lasagna for lunch.

We meditated midmorning after the walk; today was the last day of the twenty-one-day meditation on the Law of Attraction, and the mantra was Sarvesham Shantir Bhavatu—"Let there be peace, health, and wellbeing for all beings, for everything in creation."

I talked to the Ohio realtor. He had positive feedback from an open house. He felt positive about the prospect of moving the house quickly. I told him there was a bonus in there if he sold it before March. He laughed.

As I think more about journeying, I have a sudden memory of learning about angels in the Catholic faith. As a kid, the prayer that most calmed me was the guardian angel prayer; I can still remember it:

Angel of God
My guardian dear
To Whom His love
Commits me here
Ever this day
Be at my side
To light and guard
To rule and guide. Amen

I had no problem as a child accepting that angels were real. Are angels, guides, and other nonphysical entities part of the same stream of well-being? Are they all just extensions of us? They must be if we are all one. I put this on my list of things to continue to delve to understand; I have heard that some teachers draw distinctions between guides, ascended masters, and angels. I read once that an *ascended master* has lived lives as a human, and an *angel* has not.

February 12

We slept with the windows open; it was a sweet, memorable night with the cool air, making for cozy snuggling. The birds are singing. Lovely walk with the hounds after meditation. The resort is now busy; we were spoiled with the gym and restaurants practically to ourselves.

We got a pup sitter, and both went to a high-energy spin class with good music. Then I went to yoga, and Rich played tennis. It is thirty and snowing at home; high of eighty here, but it does cool down nicely at night so that a sweater feels good.

I realize that we are going to Cancun in a month, so I switched from Italian to Spanish in my daily language lesson.

I have been staying current with all my apprenticeship homework, faithfully doing all assigned journeys, being open to the irrational way, telling myself that I am strengthening my imagination and intuitive capability, and keeping copious notes in my apprenticeship journal. This week I did journeys to Hawk, Bear, and Black Panther. My regular guides, the swirly, colorful meditation presences, are always with me in my journeys.

February 13

A great snuggly night of sleep. Our mantra this morning was "so hum" which means, "I am." The dogs were in the same bed cuddled together. They bounded into our bed for meditation, and then Chip got right in Rich's face at Namaste and demanded breakfast. At the now-crowded coffee shop, Bella and Chip got tremendous attention from everyone missing their pups. Only two more weeks until we go back to Ohio. I hope our house sells soon.

We are now trying to have conversations *en Español* to get ready for our trip to Mexico. It often ends in hilarity.

In the apprenticeship, I try to get more comfortable with the Irrational Way. I am conscious that my spiritual path could be perceived with skepticism and alienate family and friends. It can unmoor a person to acknowledge that there is an invisible domain beyond our five senses and subtle energies that are not typically perceived in daily life.

Being open to expanded awareness may mean I have to let go of some people, or they may let go of me. There will be people who think I am a kook. Leaving corporate life was a big step; making the decision to move to the mountains is another step. Following my spiritual journey to see where it will lead is another step.

February 14

Rich got three valentines: from me, Chip, and Bella. In mine, I wrote, "Thanks for being such a great partner in our journey of life. The best is yet to come! I went to the gym and did a great incline walk/run cardio interval workout.

We got another sitter and went to spin class again. We did lots of time trials; Rich kicked it. It was eighty degrees and a little cloudy today—just lovely, with a beautiful sky. I did yin yoga; it was so good!

I love all these extra classes. Maybe the busy season is good because they have more staff and more events. It's crowded but high energy.

February 16

We had a nice meditation this morning; the mantra was om bhavam namah, which means, "I am absolute existence; I am a field of all possibilities." We had a great walk, and seeing the mountains made my mood lift even higher.

I can't help checking the weather at home; it is snowy, bitterly cold, with a high of one degree there, but it will be 78 here. We made blueberry pancakes for breakfast. Then I took some candy bars, hand lotions, and large-print crossword puzzle books to the senior center.

I keep thinking about my regular guides and who or what they are. My mind goes through the possibilities again and again; true self? Just my imagination making things up? My teachers say to trust that they are part of me. We are all part of source energy; it's likely they are just the higher vibration of my same energy.

I did some research to try to finally define true self versus soul. I found something in one of the first books I read; *Soul Mission, Life Vision* by Alan Seale that was a good explanation. He said that the higher self (true self) is the aspect of your being that is pure spirit. The higher self creates soul and ego so that it might experience itself in physical form and learn the lessons required for its growth and development. The soul is the *spiritual* component of the higher self incarnated in a physical body. The ego is the *physical* component of the higher self incarnated in a physical body.

February 17

Rich has a golf outing this week. We meditate very early. I get my workout in at 5, and I'm back at 6 before he leaves, so we don't leave the pups alone in the villa. I had an interval elliptical workout and got back just as he was leaving. I had coffee and then took Bella and Chip out for a walk.

I made an omelet (asparagus, spinach, avocado with egg whites), and the doorbell rang for the front gate to the courtyard. I let the lawn guy in, and Chip went with me. When I came back, the omelet was gone! Bella was licking her lips. Chip is an innocent angel; he always gets the blame, and maybe sometimes it's her!

I made Gus laugh talking about Bella and the omelet. I always feel it is a victory if I can get her to laugh even for a second. I wish I could take her pain away. We meditated together on the phone. I told her about the apprenticeship, and she started teasing me and calling me "shaman."

Today I experimented, trying a new lasagna recipe, with spaghetti squash "noodles," tomato basil Ragu sauce, extra firm tofu and basil for the filling, spinach, mushrooms and onions for the other layers, and cashew nut for the "cheese." It was surprisingly good.

I realized that I didn't fully delve into Carolyn Myss's *Sacred Contracts* book after I did the archetypes exercise. I want to find out what Myss has to say about contracts and prelife planning.

I am amazed and strangely gratified to find that Myss says we do indeed create our contract with divine guidance, and it includes many subcontracts to meet and work with different people. Family, friends—even adversaries—are in our life because we made an agreement with them prior to this lifetime. She says your divine potential also speaks to you through dreams. "We are meant to struggle to make right choices and rise above our basic needs. We can enlist the aid of archetypes and spirit guides through prayer, meditation, and other spiritual practices to try to fulfill our agreements." So, a sacred contract is an agreement our soul makes before birth. We promise to do certain things and to discover what we are meant to do. The divine promises to give us guidance through intuition, dreams, hunches, coincidences and other indicators. It is another triangulation.

February 19

In Ohio, the wind chill is below zero, but it is eighty degrees here. Chip killed a mouse in the courtyard, and after it happened, he didn't know what to do. Bella seemed incredulous, like *Bro! You can't just leave it there*! When Chip didn't carry it around in his mouth, Bella made a beeline for it, but I caught her before she got it. I was grossed out. Rich took care of it.

I borrowed a bike and rode down to the village enjoying the fresh air and the blue sky, wearing shorts and a T-shirt in February. I poked in shops and boutiques and found a new restaurant to try.

Several days a week, I journey now instead of afternoon meditation. I like the "bookends" to my days of morning meditation and either a journey or my regular mantra meditation in the afternoon.

I think about the differences in brain waves between journeying and meditation. My brainwaves are likely alpha with a bit of delta or maybe gamma during meditation, and alpha dipping into theta in journeying. I find a Stanford study that shows that drumming temporarily changes brainwaves to theta. The theta brainwave state fosters creativity. It is the same in the state between being awake and being asleep where it feels there are fewer barriers.

In the theta state, the mind is open, aware but at rest. I notice that now I spend more dream time in that space between awake and asleep.

February 21

This morning I had a vivid visualization after my early morning private meditation when I slipped back under the covers and closed my eyes. My teachers said it is typical for us to begin to have expanded awareness and slip into other states of consciousness more often now that we are journeying regularly.

My eyes were closed. I wasn't asleep or entirely awake, and it was different than dreaming.

I was aware that I was in this state and witnessing all that happened. I was in a biplane, doing loop-the-loops over beautiful cloudy mountains, and then a hawk flew up to meet the plane. Then I became the hawk and flew over the mountains and up into the clouds. It was a joyous feeling of freedom and reaching a new level of altitude.

February 22

Good sleep; great walk; spin class; yoga. Rich played tennis while we watched. Every time a tennis ball came our way, Chip tried to grab it. I lifted weights, painted mandalas, and made my new obsession: sweet potato toast. It is delicious.

When I called Gus today, I vowed to stay in active listening mode as she shared everything on her mind. Gus said she was afraid she was dying. I said, "So, you are worried you are dying. So, you want to move out and get your own apartment. So, you are really hoping you will get a teaching job." At one point, I thought Gus would call bullshit on the active listening, but she never did. She seemed cheered by the end of the conversation, started to tell jokes, and I laughed out loud. Then Gus texted the sibs and told them she made me laugh.

I made vegan chili. I fried a chopped onion and tiny bit of garlic in a large frying pan and threw in some salt, pepper, and a hefty sprinkling of paprika. I added a chopped chili pepper, kidney beans, a tin of tomatoes, and tomato puree and left it to simmer for a half hour. I cheated and used premade rice and guacamole. Rich graciously said it was great.

February 23

It is funny to me how very subtle changes in the weather here are noticed and remarked upon. I guess the weather channel person would be quickly out of a job if they said, "OK, it's another perfect day here; it will be sunny and eighty degrees again!" I really wonder if there is a better place to spend winter than the Coachella Valley. It is the first time in my life when I have enjoyed February.

David is here playing golf with Rich. It feels like coming home to see him; I miss seeing him every day. Neither of us want to dredge up old times and talk about work. We met for a nice breakfast, and then he wanted to drive around and look at some of the properties we had seen. It was great to recap everything with a good friend who knows us both well. We went to the community in Indian Wells, and he agreed it would be a good fit for us. We saw one of the new homes just being finished.

I had a nice afternoon meditation, and tonight we went to Lavender with David. The moon was luminous. We sat outside under fairy lights and enjoyed the live music and people-watching.

February 24

In California, partly cloudy means there are a few wispy clouds in the blue, sunny sky. In Ohio, partly cloudy means that the sun might break through the clouds for a moment or two during the day. I love gazing at the mountains and sky; every day I see something new. Some days the sky is pink; some days a few clouds scoot across the sky. I look at the mountains throughout the day; sometimes the sun is shining brightly on them, and sometimes they are in shadow.

Just before dawn, the mountains show up as dark with the sky a bit brighter; there is an outline of light, bright blue where the mountains meet the sky. Late at night, the mountains are barely discernible as a darker gray with the moon shining over them. I will miss all of these views.

Today was another incredible day; it got to eighty yet again. I think about the concept of hedonic adaptation I learned in Science of Happiness class. Where you get so used to something being wonderful, you fail to notice it. I swear if I move here, I will appreciate every single day of winter.

I had a great walk, followed by elliptical and farmer's market. It is minus thirteen this morning in Ohio. We are going home on March 1. Rich played tennis, and I took the dogs to watch; a million people petted them. We loved being out in the fresh air all day. I made some Buddha bowls in mason jars to grab for easy lunches; they look like art with layers of chopped carrots, cherry tomatoes, quinoa, black beans, pinto beans, edamame, steamed broccoli, avocado, and lettuce on top. I found premade vegan ranch dressing that was healthy and delicious.

In the shamanic apprenticeship, I am learning about some contemporary teachers and writers: Sandra Ingerman, Michael Harner, and Eva Bruce.

Shamanic traditions often agree that there are three worlds: lower, middle and upper worlds. There are also numerous levels within each world.

We have focused on lower worlds so far. Lower worlds are usually reached through a tunnel or some other cylindrical path. They often contain forests, deserts, seas, animals, trees, plants, and rocks. Animal spirits typically have lives in the lower world. They are formed by the dreaming of everything in nature.

The upper realm is more ethereal; guides in this realm are the higher gods and goddesses, passionate angelic forces.

The middle world is a dream aspect of the everyday world. There you may find lost and stolen objects. It may include fairies, trolls, and hidden folk, those who existed before the veils between the worlds were closed to us.

We are now given permission to explore upper worlds in addition to lower worlds. The teachers explain that those who come from the stars will be more drawn to upper world journeys.

I learn that fourteen years is about the shortest shamanic education; this apprenticeship is just the beginning of years of study if I feel called to continue.

February 25

Decent sleep, good workout including a lot of lunges. Beautiful walk. Yoga. Spanish. Watched Rich play tennis. Mountain-gazing. Packing. I took a photo of the moon floating just above the mountain. Our time here has flown by.

I got my hair done and a manicure/pedicure. It is so nice getting my toes done where I can wear sandals. Pedicures in Ohio in the winter are rough. While I got my nails done, I read a book by Ram Dass about his spiritual awakening. He said genuine spiritual awakening manifests as a desire to be of service to others. This can take many forms: teaching, parenting, healing, creative work, but the underlying goal is to help others realize their divine potential in some form. Compassionate acts are the physical manifestations of spiritual work.

February 26

Great lift today; shoulders, calves and abs. A bit of cardio. Lovely walk. Soreness in my quads due to lunges yesterday. Pool time this afternoon with lots of mountain-gazing.

Rich met with the accountants by phone today; I am so grateful I don't have to; he is the best. Polenta, spaghetti squash, red sauce with olives, mushrooms, capers and onions, and grilled tofu—not bad.

February 28

Our last day in California—for now. I am so grateful we have had this time. It seemed that every step of our walk this morning was precious, and I wanted to see every view of the mountains. This morning I took our used coffee grounds with us and, wanting to leave some organic trace of us, pinched a bit off and used it to fertilize flowers and trees along our path on these lovely grounds.

After breakfast and yoga, I drove to a hiking trail that goes into the mountains, and I took some leftover J&B scotch that one of Rich's golf buddies left behind. I walked up the highest peak and called my guides. I rested there in gratitude for several minutes, just being present and appreciating the sky, the air, the clouds, the view, the rocks, the way I feel so whole here. I wanted to treasure and remember the moment. I thanked the guides and the universe for bringing us here and asked them to please bring us back to this beautiful valley. I opened the scotch and poured it out on the rocks, saying, "I mark this as a place I have loved where I feel whole. I am grateful to have been here. I give these spirits to you in thanks. When it is right, I ask that you please bring us back to this place we love."

We packed, cleaned out the refrigerator, got badges and keys ready to turn in to the rental office, and turned in the rental car. Even the dogs seem to sense that we are leaving; they want to sniff every rock and bush.

Chapter Nine
March

A family trip to Cancun, decluttering, house showings, the shamanic apprenticeship, and some experiences of expanded awareness make March memorable. Much of my mind-time is focused on Gussie, with the end of the month bringing significant deterioration of her condition. Despite the feelings of fear, grief, and sadness, I also experience daily joy in the midst of coping with real life. I find myself wondering if this isn't the thing we are here to discover: there will always be pain and suffering in life. In the midst of that, can we also feel divine support and find our own courage and with enough perspective find the love, the beauty, and some measure of equanimity and peace in every situation?

March 1
We had a major tailwind and got back to Ohio in less than four hours. Amazing. Grateful.

Thirty-five degrees feels cold to us; we got into the house and turned up the heat. We joked about how quickly our blood turned thin. We took the dogs out to play in the muddy yard. At least the snow has melted.

We leave for Cancun in a couple of days, and the hounds will go to the kennel while we are gone in case there are house showings.

I read *Bringers of the Dawn* by Barbara Marciniak, who channeled wisdom from the Pleiadians, a group of enlightened beings who have come to Earth to help us discover how to reach a new stage of evolution. Master storytellers and humorists, they advise us to become media-free, work in teams, and eliminate the words *should* and *try* from our vocabularies. The book encourages us to move beyond fear. They remind us that we are Family of Light, and that we that we share an ancient ancestry with the universe. We can help "bring the dawn," consciously, creating a new reality. One of the suggestions is to learn to whirl or twirl like a dervish and get to a point where you can twirl ninety-nine times. I'm going to try it.

March 2

Big crashing thunder and lightning. Bella was in bed with us the whole night because of the storm.

I did elliptical this morning. I tried to twirl and got to thirty-three times; it made me dizzy, and I felt like a kid.

I keep decluttering. Now that we have spent time in California (and that's where I think we will be), I see we can get rid of a lot more clothes. The idea of significantly downsizing is even more appealing. How did we ever amass all this "stuff"? I love the convenience of the Goodwill drive-through; the employee I got to know said, "Welcome back!"

I was asked to donate a painting for an AIDS benefit, and a local gallery owner came to look at my pieces and selected "Blue Light." I was thrilled to donate to such a good cause.

We are packing for Cancun. Happily, we don't need much more than swimwear, shorts, and sunscreen. I am excited to be with Dad and Marie, Sasha and Drew.

The house is tracked with muddy paw prints, and there is a house showing day after tomorrow. Luckily the house cleaner is coming, and the dogs are going to the kennel. That worked out beautifully.

I talked to Gussie. Her divorce is final, and she moved out of the house and into her own apartment in Carrollton. She complained about how she feels, the weather, her car, and Mason. I was working to be positive: "Well, good for you! You did it; you are now independent! You moved out like you have been wanting to do forever!" And Gussie got to a better place saying that she had reconnected with old friends in Carrollton and how nice it was to be able to watch anything she wanted on TV and great to have her own place. She is going to start substitute teaching in a couple of days. I probed to see if she was drinking; she claimed she wasn't. I said to please take care of herself, stay strong, and keep the sibs posted.

March 3

We are in Cancun after an easy nonstop flight. Dad and Marie made it without incident; our flight arrived at almost exactly the same time as theirs. When we got to customs, we spotted Dad and Marie ahead in their wheelchairs.

Our driver welcomed us to tropical paradise. As we drove down Avenida Kukulkan through the hotel zone, we saw the lagoon on one side and the Caribbean on the other. Everyone had been here before, though not in many years. The driver pointed out the powder-white beaches and the beautiful aquamarine water and talked about the remnants of the mystic Indian civilizations.

On the drive, we saw parasailers, diving and snorkeling vendors, deep-sea fishing guided tours, tours to the Mayan ruins, bike rentals, and tons of golf courses. Dad peppered the driver with questions, and we learned that the coastline is over five hundred miles long; there are numerous coral islands and the second largest reef barrier in the world.

Dad has a great attitude, and though he needs a wheelchair to get around, he has a great sense of humor about it. The weather is perfect—in the eighties—and we sat outside all day today. The water is the most amazing color of blue; it is so peaceful. I would love to do a tour of the Mayan ruins, but we are content to stay on property with

Dad and just relax with him. There are several restaurants here, so it won't be boring.

Sasha and Drew got here this afternoon. As soon as Sasha walks in anywhere, the mood lightens and the party starts. This is a gift because she always makes Rich happy, and she is perfect with Dad. She is his oldest grandchild, and she has always had a special bond with him. It's fun to see them together, telling each other jokes, talking and laughing.

We are on the concierge level with complimentary food and drinks all day. This is perfect for Dad; it is great if someone can bring him coffee or a snack as opposed to him trying to get up and get it himself.

The wait staff is professional and well-trained. Sasha and Rich have practically adopted each of them and have constructed whole stories about their lives. One charming bartender, Yaneth, is a star mixologist who manages to keep a crowd of people happy, and she has captured their attention; they eavesdrop on her conversations and watch her hands in constant motion, keeping dozens of orders straight and mixing everything from elaborate drinks to pouring a glass of wine.

The wait staff all speak perfect English yet seem to appreciate our efforts in Spanish. Drew comes to our rescue when we struggle, and he jokes with the amused staff about our mistakes.

Being with Sasha and Drew brings up great memories of our travels together, and we appreciate them being here.

I am conscious that Sasha could become more distant as I go deeper down my path of spiritual discovery, but I want to be completely authentic with her, so I don't hide it. I tell her about what I have been studying and the shamanic apprenticeship in a very matter-of-fact way. I am not leaving anything out or embellishing it. She either will or won't accept it; I hope she will. She asks great questions, and I appreciate she is trying to understand.

Sasha asks how I am managing to keep my left brain from rebelling after getting an MBA and spending over thirty-five years in a rational business. A great question. I tell her about working hard to be open to the irrational way and how my mind fights it, but lately I am finally beginning to trust my intuition, gut feelings, hunches, instincts, and synchronicities. I tell her about the importance of using imagination.

Dad is really enjoying this time in the sun. We have been sitting out at the gorgeous infinity pool much of the day, and we pay attention to see when he has had enough sun. Then one or more of us take him up to the concierge level where he can look out at the view of the ocean from the windows. I have appreciated having some great talks with him, telling how inspirational he has been in my life. He has always had an enthusiastic "glass half full" mentality, and I am glad to be able to tell him what an impact he has made on me.

I offered spa treatments for him and Marie. He can't trim his toenails, so I booked a pedicure, and Rich and Drew got him in the chair. I took a look at his hands and asked if they could do a manicure for him at the same time. We got several photos of him surrounded by pampering aestheticians. Sasha teased him about picking out a polish color.

This afternoon we talked about Gussie and how much of the collective family mind-time is spent in thoughts of and worries about her. Sasha and I talked about Teresa's efforts when Gussie was in rehab in Santa Fe. We talked about our fear with the suicide threat. We admired and appreciated Bethany's visit when she helped Gus and Mason agree to an amicable divorce. This brought us to the current moment: Gus's decline in health, leaving her last job, and now moving into her own place and wanting to substitute teach.

Marie came in for this part of the conversation and shared her worries about Gus. With Gus now in Carrollton, Dad and Marie see her nearly every day, and they see firsthand her deterioration, her confused thinking, and erratic behavior. Marie says Gussie's apartment is a mess; she comes over and lays on their couch and then tells people she has been helping them do tasks around the house. I asked them if they think she is drinking; Marie thinks yes.

March 4

Last night I recorded scribbles of dreams and sent them to my teachers because they requested we keep them abreast of any noteworthy dreams while we are in the apprenticeship. One of our classes focused on lucid dreams and taking control in the dream state.

I experienced lucidity and was able to direct some things in a dream for the first time. I was stuck in a huge mall and couldn't find an exit, going through doors and down stairs and elevators but couldn't get out. Then realized "I'm dreaming, and I can decide to go out!" I saw a door, went down some stairs, and was out on the street. It was such a relief to have control. In another dream, I was on the street in New York but could not get a cab to go home. Again, I realized, "I am dreaming. I can conjure up a cab." I walked to the next corner of the block, and a cab stopped for me. Cool.

March 5

I worked out and "twirled" at the end; I can now twirl pretty easily thirty-three times.

We had a relaxed happy day by the pool with leg pillows to prop knees up while sitting by the perfect sky-blue infinity pool. A hunky, dark-haired guy with a gleaming smile named Ernesto came to clean sunglasses. Waiters stopped by to offer snacks like coconut water sorbet.

I had a deep tissue massage. Sasha's stomach was iffy, so I took her place. There was a deep cold-plunge pool that went to my neck, a hot tub, and outdoor shower. I basked in the lovely sounds, smells, and textures, appreciating everything. Later describing in detail the plushness of the towels, the aromatherapy, the wind chimes, Sasha joked that I was a sensual whore, and we laughed hard at that.

Tonight, there was another glorious orangey-gold sunset, and we were dressed for dinner. Sasha, Drew, Rich, and I went to the beach to watch sunset. Sasha and Rich had had a few pool cocktails earlier and were in vacation mode. When we came back to meet Dad and Marie, Sasha poked Rich in the ribs and stage-whispered: "Look, Rich, Yaneth is here!"

Sasha exults, "Let's go sit at the bar; she will be *so happy* to see us!" Sasha leads Rich over and calls out, "Yaneth; we're back!" Yaneth looks wide-eyed at them, obviously wondering "How do I know these people?" Sasha and Rich ask her questions as she makes cocktails: "Yaneth, what happened with your boyfriend who moved?" "Yaneth, how is your mother?" It reminded me of the overly familiar "Otis, my man" scene in Animal House. Drew and I kept looking at each other and shaking our heads.

March 6

Dad and Marie left because their nonstop flight only exists on certain days of the week; they are already home. Drew and Sasha are still here. Teresa is staying with their girls and sent a picture of their snowed-in driveway. It is zero degrees there and eighty here, breezy with a few sleepy clouds; the water is turquoise. Rich, Drew, and I had a beach walk while Sasha is in her massage. The water is wild, with high surf and whitecaps.

There was a lot of Gus drama today with a bunch of texts. Gus has been drinking again. She is scheduled to substitute teach tomorrow. The texts seemed to get sadder and more desperate as the day progressed. Here is one of over one hundred texts:

Gussie:
I am an addict. And I have depression and possible anxiety. I am going to go to a law enforcement office and pass a breathalyzer and balance test. I am not doing this for you. I am doing this for me. I am very grateful for people who love me. I want to thank you again for riding me and making me responsible. I would kindly request you kick my ass when I do something stupid or make a bad choice.

I have a dreadful feeling about Gussie, and I am glad we are heading home. I can feel that my intuition is now more honed, but that may not a blessing.

March 7

The situation with Gussie continues to deteriorate. She was called in by the principal and given a performance warning. Gus then said she quit her substitute teacher job and walked out. Her thinking is not coherent. Her texts are rambling and seem to be divorced from reality. She blames everyone but herself.

She is now driving to Joe and Emma's. All the sibs are nervous and worried. I feel terrible for everyone involved. I am unclear how to help. On the flight after I meditated, I kept praying, "Please help me understand the right next step to take. Please don't let her hurt anyone." It feels like we are watching a slow-motion self-destruction video, and there is nothing we can do to stop it.

March 8

We had a couple of house showings while we were gone and positive feedback from a family that may relocate here. My heart feels heavy with worry about Gus, so I stay active. The sidewalks were packed with ice, and I got a good workout breaking the ice and shoveling. It will get to forty today, so things should start to melt.

After shoveling, I took Bella and Chip to the garage and carefully cleaned all eight paws. It is going to be a struggle keeping the house clean for showings.

Emma:
Gussie's behavior is bizarre. She picked up a strange woman at the bus stop to give her a ride as an "act of kindness." She gave a guy quarters for laundry. The man got a call from a friend who was having an asthma attack. Gussie drove him to pick up the woman and then got lost trying to get back to our house.

She is all over the place in conversations, saying she is flat broke and then later saying she has just received thousands of dollars. When she got back this afternoon, she bought a case of beer for workers in my house—she said it was another "random act of kindness." I confronted her about it, and she got defensive and wanted to leave, but I took her keys because I wasn't sure she was sober.

She must have had another set of keys because when I checked thirty minutes later, her things were out of her room, and her car was gone.

Jane:
Did she smell like she had been drinking?

Emma:
I didn't smell anything on her except Listerine, but her thinking is confused, so I am not sure. It's terrifying, and I have no idea what to do. I hope she stops somewhere and stays in a motel. Clearly, she now has some money. There simply doesn't seem to be any way to explain her bizarre behavior other than her physical deterioration is damaging her ability to reason, use sound judgement, or function in anything close to a reasonable manner. I tried to call her, but she didn't pick up; she is angry with me.

Jane:
I just got off the phone with Gus. She was talking about driving to Chicago and having an adventure. She claims she is sober and wasn't slurring her words, but like Emma said, she can't seem to stick with one thought; she changes the subject in midsentence. She couldn't even tell me where she was. I offered to fly somewhere to meet her, and she told me she wanted to have a fun weekend and to "get off her ass."

I didn't want to distract her further while she is trying to drive. I don't know what to do except pray. I hate this so much. I am not sure if we should call the police and put out an alert? I don't even know what state she is in—Iowa, Missouri or Illinois?

Four hours later:

Gussie:
In Bloomington, Illinois. Too sleepy to drive safely, so getting a hotel now. Super 8. Safe and sober, willing to submit and pay for a breathalyzer, urinalysis, or blood test. I have been admonished by every sibling at this point. I forgive them because I'm an alcoholic and a liar. I do not deserve your trust, but I do deserve every bit of admonishment you would choose to give me. It makes me feel really great—not! Joe and Emma will attest to you my bank account balance. I am also going to have $25,000 in savings. I will send you photos from Chicago. I love you with all of my heart. Thank you very for your support and faith in me. That is what I need rather than concern or admonishment. I promise to let you know the moment I feel unsafe.

Jane:
Thanks, Gus. I know you are mad at us, but we have been waiting up to hear from you to know you are safe. Please get some good rest and text us tomorrow. Good night, everyone.

March 10

Gus drama continues. After the rest of us thought she was safely sleeping, Gus kept driving, and Bethany stayed up all night with her, talking to Gus for hours trying to get her to stop. I had seventy-five unread text messages when I woke up.

Bethany was ready to call the police to pull her over but could never pin down exactly where Gus was. I'm sure the experience shortened Bethany's life. Finally, when Gus checked into a Holiday Inn in Illinois, the hotel clerk called the police because of her erratic behavior, and when Gus asked for a breathalyzer, they gave her one, and she got a DUI even though she wasn't driving at that moment. They impounded her van. We did not get the straight scoop from Gus about this and figured it out in pieces as the day went on. She also made some other wild claims, like stealing a policeman's backpack.

I feel completely distracted, and my stomach is churning though I am trying to just go through the normal routine of the day. In a vivid dream last night, I got a message saying, "Prepare for death." I have not tried to further explore what this means because on some level, I know it is about Gus. I keep wondering if I talked about random acts of kindness with Gussie. I feel terrible, as if I somehow inspired her.

Teresa, Bethany, Joe, and Emma are really pissed at Gus. I don't feel angry. I'm exasperated, worried she will hurt someone, wondering what I should be doing to help, and upset that the family is so upset. After I talked to her yesterday, I meditated, and when I got to "What do I want?" I just kept repeating, "I just don't want her to hurt anyone. I know she is on her own path and as inexplicable as it seems, it must make sense on some level. But please keep her from harming anyone." And I continue to ask for help in my own decision-making to take the right next step for her, to say the right words to her. I asked my higher guidance if there were any messages for me related to Gus, and I got, "Keep a bag packed and be ready to go." So, I am.

Jane:
I read everything I missed last night. Bethany, you should be canonized; are you OK?

Teresa:

Me too; so sorry I missed all the drama; I thought she was in bed asleep. Thank God she did not hurt anyone.

Bethany:

It was a wild ride; I just woke up. I was a nervous fucking wreck. Do you think we should fly to Chicago to get her?

Jane:

The car is impounded, so she can't drive. She has told us to get off her ass. This might be her last bit of freedom. Having said that, my bag is packed, and I can go with a minute's notice.

Joe:

I am still so pissed off at her I can barely breathe. Thank you, Bethany for hanging in with her last night.

Emma:

I am still really pissed off. Her brain is fried.

Teresa:

How will she get home if there is no car? Fly? Do we think she is really in Chicago? Does anyone know how to track where she is via her phone?

Emma:

I got in touch with the kids; they tracked her phone; she is in a hotel thirty miles outside Chicago.

Gussie:

Beautiful morning to everyone! Just awakened and I'm lounging with a cup of Earl Grey tea. Today's agenda is the Frank

Lloyd Wright house, architectural tour, Art Institute, and deep-dish pizza. May we all find gratitude and peace today! Augusta

Jane:
Gus, keep your wits about you walking around in downtown Chicago. Keep your bag across your body on its shoulder strap, and mind the steps going to the architectural tour.

Later:

Gussie:
I am texting to tell you good night. I'm safely in Chicago. I in no way deserve your trouble, nor do I deserve your kindness. I would politely ask that you let me take a break from the family for at least three days. I feel really terrible about myself presently. I feel like an undeserving piece of junk. I do not have a car, so you do not need to be concerned about me drinking and driving. The only thing that I would politely request is that you consider me a piece of shit and that you do not contact me unless there is an emergency. I lied to you. I am a lifelong alcoholic. I have done many stupid things. I do not expect or deserve your forgiveness.

I am not a danger to myself or others. I have extreme gratitude. Joe is my durable power of attorney. If I pass due to my end-stage liver disease, I would politely ask you to cremate me. I would also ask politely that you take my remains and place them at Canyon Ranch. I reiterate that I am extremely apologetic, and I appreciate your unconditional love even though I do not deserve it. I would furthermore continue to ask for you not to contact me unless it is an emergency. May we all find gratitude and peace today! Augusta

Bethany:
She's delusional, but until she is home safely, we need to keep her in communication with us and not have her shut down.

Joe:
Do you guys think she is close to dying? It's like she has a death wish. And this whole thing about asking for a breathalyzer; it's like she *wants* to be arrested. So fucking strange.

Emma:
Lies on top of lies. I agree with Bethany. Let's try to keep her in dialogue with us.

Gussie:
Helllooooo! Just arrived in Kansas City from Chicago. I am safe! Please don't worry about me!

Teresa:
Wait. Kansas City?

Gussie:
Yes. I decided to go ahead and get closer to home. All is well. I am safe and strong.

Teresa:
Did you fly from Chicago to KC?

Gussie:
Yes! $59. Safely in a hotel.

Gussie:
Please feel free to text me anytime, but please also know that I don't need to be further admonished. Don't we all deserve a period of time when we can just simply be by ourselves? I'm not a danger to myself or anyone else at this time. I do not intend to become a danger. I'm simply on vacation and enjoying what I feel that I deserve. I still have plenty of money.

Gussie: text to group 4:29 p.m.

I have a new car—100 percent fully insured and fully purchased. Excellent vehicle! 2009 Ford Escape. The car salesman has kindly brought to it to the hotel for the night. Please do not correspond back but know that I am extremely safe and making very intelligent decisions.

Gussie:

I want to thank you all for respecting my period of great self-hatred and shame. I am three minutes away from my apartment. I love you all, and I am quite sorry for being such an idiot. I hope that one day you will be able to forgive me, but I certainly do not deserve it at this time. Please know that I am punishing myself far further than you ever could. However, I am not a danger to myself or others at this time.

Bethany: (new thread)

I just talked to Dad and Marie. She really does have a new (used) car. I have no idea who would have sold her a car; I can't believe she came across as having control of her faculties. Does she even have a driver's license? I guess she must have one if she got on a flight. Needless to say, Dad and Marie are very concerned about her. They said she smelled like alcohol. They wanted to drive her to her apartment, but she walked out before they could get up.

March 12

Jane: 3 a.m.

Guys, I'm sure you won't see this until morning. I just got a call from Marie. Gus is in jail. She called Marie asking to be bailed out. She is in a town called Henrietta, Missouri. I'm heading to the airport to take the first flight out and will get there midmorning. I called the jail and told them I am on my way. Love you guys. Will text.

Gussie:
Jane, please text me your ETA. I am shivering and freezing, and they will not give me any assistance here. I wet my pants because they would not allow me to go to the bathroom. I'm really scared about resolving this. I know that I will probably never get to teach school again. I'm going to give you my wallet and my keys and ask that you take my car away. If I need to get somewhere, I will walk. I'm having terrible abdominal pain. My only polite request would be that you go to my apartment for my pillow and blanket. Please don't take me away. Please don't talk to me when you pick me up. I'm just too scared. I am scared that you are so mad at me; I am scared what you will say to me.

Jane:
I'm not angry. If you feel sick, tell them you need help. I land at KCI soon. Hang in there.

On the flight and after I picked up the rental car, I prayed for guidance. Please help me know the right next steps to take. I tried to think of what to do next and where to take Gus. She can't come live with any of us; she needs to be near her doctors. Her apartment in Carrollton is no longer viable. I don't know if her license is revoked, but I imagine yes. Either way, she should not be driving, and it's too much for Dad and Marie to take on. Going back to Mason's is bad for everyone, though he has said he will take her.

I got to the jail and talked with the desk officer. She said Gus has been trying to hurt herself in the cell, so they have someone watching her. She said Gus was throwing herself down on the concrete floor. I asked about the charges against her, and they gave me a paper; she got a DWI and a charge for disturbing the peace. Apparently, she went to the school where she had been teaching and started being disruptive during a ball game. Someone called the police, and she was arrested. She was drunk and asked them to give her a breathalyzer, and she "blew" three times the legal limit. They said she was compliant and handed over her keys to the officer, and they brought her to this jail. I asked where her car was; it was towed to Carrollton. Her driver's license has been revoked, and she is not legally able to drive.

I thanked the officer and asked if I needed to sign anything; he said no. So, I took a deep breath and asked them to release her.

She was crying, filthy, and bruised on her face and arms. Her stomach was huge from ascites, and her face, legs, and arms looked swollen. She smelled terrible. I reached out to give her a hug, and she pulled away from me, not saying anything. I gave her a hankie and asked her to use the bathroom and wash her face before we left.

I grabbed her arm as we walked out to the gravel parking lot because she was shaking badly and seemed unsteady. She started sobbing as we walked, and so I steered us toward a bench and sat there with her for a few minutes until she calmed down. She wouldn't speak to me. I said "Gus, this is ridiculous. We have to be able to communicate; you have to talk to me." And then she started in on the "I'm so afraid of what you will say to me; I am not worthy" bullshit, and I just calmly looked at her and said, "I love you; I am not angry. But we need to talk about next steps. I have a water for you in the car. Are you hungry?" She said no, but said she needed a diet coke and a cigarette, and she needed to pick up her anxiety medication at a pharmacy.

After she had had a cigarette and diet coke and got her prescription and I got her in some dry sweat pants, we got back in the car, and as we were pulling out of the parking lot, she turned to me and said with complete sincerity, "It's a beautiful day." And something about that struck me as funny, and we both started laughing, which cleared the air.

It was a beautiful day; I had not even noticed. The sky was blue, and the sun was shining. I said, "Gussie, we will figure this out together. Do you have any ideas of what you want to do?" And she said, "I am afraid to think about it; what do you think my options are?" I said, "I don't think going back to Carrollton is a good idea. You can't drive now because your license is revoked, and it has been very stressful for Dad and Marie to have you in town. You need to be near your doctors so you can get regular paracentesis. You could live with Mason again, or you could go to rehab somewhere near your doctors."

She said, "I want to go to rehab. I've been thinking about what you said about me never embracing AA principles and the twelve-step program even though I believe in a higher power. I am ready to do that." I said, "I think you are making a great choice; good for you," and said a silent *thank you.* I asked her where she wanted to go, and she said Vista Hope. And she wanted to make the call herself. My phone was charged and on Bluetooth, so she got the number and used it to call. When they answered, she said "My name is Augusta, and I am an alcoholic. I have just been released from jail, and I want to come today." And strangely, I was very proud of her in that moment.

They have a bed available and said we needed to be there before 6 p.m. She told them we would be there. I asked her to please text Joe, Emma, Teresa, and Bethany to tell them, and she did. And she called Dad to tell him.

We went to her apartment, so she could shower and pack her things. I threw away the perishables in her refrigerator, realizing she would likely never be back. I found her insurance card, car keys, credit cards, and wallet. I copied the credit cards and insurance cards. I threw away junk mail and took the bills and copies to send to Joe. She wanted to take two suitcases of clothes plus pillows and blankets. I tried to argue with her and finally just let her take what she wanted. We found where they towed her car and asked the garage owner to take it to Dad's.

We drove to Dad's, so she could say goodbye to him and Marie and give them the car keys. I made her get out of the car and go in, thinking this might be the last time they see each other. Then I drove her the ninety miles to get to Vista Hope on time. She was shaking badly and needed to stop to use the bathroom about every twenty minutes. I could see how fragile her health is.

On the drive, I asked what happened last night; she said she didn't remember. I told her I was so grateful she had not hurt anyone, and she agreed. She talked about dying and being sorry for all the things she had done wrong. She talked about her adventures in Chicago and the DUI she had gotten there, but I had no idea what was truth and what was fiction or fantasy.

She got quiet, and I turned on the radio, hit the volume, and we sang our hearts out. There were some nice moments. I think she could feel that I was proud of her on some level, and she seemed proud of herself for finally taking positive action. I pray it isn't too late, but I have the feeling that this is the beginning of the end for her.

As we got to Boonville where Vista Hope is located, she wanted to stop and buy Diet Cokes and candy. I gave her some cash and stayed in the car to text everyone and when she got back in the car, she had been drinking. I said, "Gus, really?" And she said that she had to have alcohol in her system, or they wouldn't admit her. And maybe she is correct, but it is hard to believe after all this, she decided to drink. We found Vista Hope and got her checked in. I had to cosign, but they accepted her insurance. I carried her bags in while she had her admission consultation. I apologized she brought so much, because they have to inspect everything that comes in. They will lock up her computer and phone. We will be able to communicate with her only with supervision for at least the first two weeks. I filled out paperwork for her, and then they told me it was time for me to go. I gave her a quick hug, wished her good luck, and as they took her away, we said, "Love you, see you, bye."

Jane:

Gussie is checked in at Vista Hope. She was extremely shaky
but stuck with me all day as we tracked down her car, cleaned
her apartment, got her packed, said goodbye to Dad. Love and
gratitude to our team. Night, night.

I lay in bed and just said prayers of thanks; thank you for not letting her
hurt anyone. Thank you for letting it be her decision to go to rehab.
Thank you for letting her finally embrace AA principles. Thank you for
having her in a safe place now, so we can sleep.

March 13

I'm home. The director of Vista Hope, Donna, called Joe and me
for background on Gus. We will have a family conference for/with
her each week. She said Gus is embracing AA principles, but she
is being cold and aloof to the other residents; she won't sit with
anyone or talk to them. We apologized and said she can be very
elitist.

The apprenticeship gives me a needed distraction. Our class call
was today. The topic this week is shamanic tools: drums and rattles,
white sage, sweet grass, incense, Florida water, divination cards, crystals, and stones. I took notes but had a hard time concentrating.

We took the dogs out for a long walk, and that helped.

March 14

Dad had a mild heart attack. He is in the hospital in Kansas City but in
good spirits. If it was not for the huge drama with Gus this week, we
would all probably be on a plane to be at his bedside. It's like we all
have family bad news overload.

I have been thinking about death since the dream message said
to be prepared. As I think about death, I try to examine what exactly
I now believe. I think we are eternal, and this life is just a momentary
stop on a much longer journey. I don't believe the most important

essence of us dies. The fear of death is leaving me, but the mystery of what happens between lives remains.

We walked so far yesterday, it made Chip's paws sore. He started whining in the night and I checked him over. When I got to his pads, I could see they were sensitive. We were walking up to three miles in California, but it is the first time in Ohio he has walked that far on the paved path, and it hurt his paws. I feel terrible. He moaned all night in his sweet whiny voice: "Aaaaaaah, sigh. Uuuuuuuuh, sigh." I would wake up and pat him and cuddle and soothe him until he fell asleep, and soon after, it was "Aaaaaah, mooooooan," all night. That lasted until I finally got up and had the bright idea to put Vaseline on his paws and wrap them up in some old rags. Poor sweet puppy boy.

March 15

I talked to Donna at Vista Hope, who told me that she is very concerned about Gus's physical health. I said that she must see this a lot, and she said, "I have never had a resident here who was this sick." That shocked me. She does not know if they can keep her there because they can't provide for her basic medical needs. They are transporting Gus to her paracentesis today. On a positive note, Donna said that Gus seems to really be embracing AA and even carrying around and quoting from "the book."

I began to look into Gussie's legal issues and found an attorney who specializes in DUI issues in Illinois. His fees to represent Gussie are about $2,500; the fine could be $2,500, and there is a possibility of up to a year in county jail. She has been charged with a criminal offense, which is a class A misdemeanor.

It helps that she has voluntarily gone to rehab; the longer she stays and more successful she is, the better. If she pleads guilty, she will have to attend victim-impact panels where she meets with families that have lost loved ones to drunk drivers, and so forth. She will have to do 100 hours of community service; this can be done where she lives, but the court will supervise her work. He will also need the testimony of her professional rehab evaluators on her progress and health status and whether she is seeking ongoing care from substance abuse experts; they will want a holistic perspective on her case.

I put all this in a letter to Gussie.

March 16

We got a last-minute house showing request for today and leaped into action; we took the dogs to the kennel, and then Rich and I cleaned like mad for three hours. I bought flowers and then we lit candles, turned on the lights and music, and went across the street to wait for the realtor to come and show the house.

They were a no-show. I am not kidding. I called Alan and said, "They didn't come." He called and found out the realtor got confused and showed a house down the street. I am trying to stay balanced and not lose my temper, but I am really not amused. This was a wasted day. I really needed my afternoon meditation.

Then we got a showing request for tomorrow, so I called the kennel, and we are leaving the dogs there so that we don't have muddy paw prints throughout the house.

Rich and I did a shamanic ritual in our very clean house. He was a little reluctant but agreed. I lit sage grass. We cleansed each room by waving the smoke around. "Garage, you have done a great job for us. We now release you for the next family." We did that in every room and stopped a moment to relive memories from each part of the house, such as the mudroom where we played with Beau as a puppy and our favorite table where we gathered for so many happy meals. When we were done going room by room, we went outside, faced the house, and said, "You have been a great home. We have loved living here. We release you from service, and you are free to welcome the next family."

Gussie's physical and mental health continue to deteriorate. Physically, she is swollen, uncomfortable, and has low energy. She wants to sleep for much of the day. Mentally, she has periods of confusion and sometimes says things that don't make sense. However, she is working through her twelve steps of AA principles, quoting from "the book," and told Donna she might want to go to a year-long sober living community after Vista Hope. Donna called it a "breakthrough."

Donna said the letter I sent was a harsh wake-up call. I asked her if I should not have sent it, and she said it is reality, and Gus needs to understand the consequences of her actions and focus on getting sober if she is going to have a future.

March 17

Dad is doing better. I slept well, had a great run, and did Pilates. For the first time, I twirled ninety-nine times. We had good feedback from the showing; it is a family who is relocating. The weather is cool again, but the wind is drying the muddy yard, so we'll take it. I took Easter candy and large-print books to the Senior Center closest to our house.

Jane:
Hi, guys; I have the information we need on Gus's DWI in Missouri. I have put all of it in another letter to her. The most important part of the conversation was the lawyer's advice to put a durable power of attorney in place in case Gus continues her mental decline. I asked her to draw up the DPOA. She will send it to me, and we will need to get Gussie to sign it and have it notarized. The attorney said that we may need to make Gussie's medical decisions for her in the future, and this will allow us to do that.

March 18

Chip chased a squirrel and ran out of the yard through his electronic fence. I ran after him like a maniac and stopped traffic as he blithely trotted across to the duck pond and then to the neighbor's yard. We turned up his collar to "nuclear."

In meditation and journeys over the past few days, I have been trying to release my feelings of being stuck, blocked, impatient, and worried. I am ready for the house to sell, ready to move to the mountains. I am worried about Gussie and also, I am somewhat ashamed to admit, resentful that Gussie's situation makes my own life veer off course when I drop my own agenda and attend to whatever new crisis emerges for her.

Today I tried to tell myself to move beyond my own ego to surrender and embrace the concept of divine timing and invited the universe to direct my progress. I asked that my actions be positive, helpful, and attract the highest and best result.

I realize my ego wants to feel in control; I want to direct things. But maybe if I can release my expectations and allow events to unfold as they need to, I will be more relaxed, and my natural feelings of optimism will stay on the surface even through these times. I want to believe that everything will work out in the right way at the right time. I have the sense that I still have some more minor parts to play for Gus, and I am not going to be "released" until I've fulfilled what I need to do for her. So, then I started to feel grateful that I have been close enough to be able to jump on a plane and get to her in a few hours. Let me continue to be there for her in whatever role I need to play.

March 19

I had a "twilight" journey to the monk I often glimpse in my dreams. I was in that state just before sleep, and I asked if the monk was there. Instantly, he said, "I have been here the whole time." I thanked him for coming and asked him to tell me about our relationship. He said he has been my friend through many lives. He was my childhood imaginary friend in some lives, a best friend and fellow monk in other lives, and is present in my intuition; now he represents my inner wisdom. He said that I had broken through barriers, and now I have easy, instant, and constant access to him. He said I don't even have to formally journey to get to him. I asked him why it was so hard to find him, and he said it's not hard at all, but I can't visualize him because he is in me. All I have to do is ask for him. I asked him his name, and he said he doesn't have a human name, but I could call him Buddy. He explained that he is energy, and he is a bit further down the path and is there to help me.

I asked, "Like a Bodhisattva?" He said yes. So I said, "How about I call you Bhodi?" He said that's fine. I asked him about being a monk, and he said that I was in monastic life for many lifetimes, and I love a simple life of routine, discipline, meditation, and working with my hands to make things. I was a scribe in one life; he told me how fulfilling it was for me to make and illustrate books.

He kidded me about loving my daily routine now and how I get cranky if I don't get to do the things I like to do every day, and I said it was from all those years of being required to do things at a given hour. He said that there were times in those lives when I dreamed of the freedom to do whatever I wanted and be spontaneous, and I should relish that in this life. We talked about Gussie, and he said if I possessed the power to "fix her," she would be fixed. It is not because of a lack of desire on my part. He said she is on her path for her own reasons and that her divine plan makes sense, even if I cannot understand it.

We talked about me wanting to move on, sell the house, and get settled in a new place, and he said things were breaking open, and it would happen "soon." I asked him to define "soon" in human terms and he laughed. He told me that he is easily accessed when I am walking outside, doing a cardio workout, painting—anytime I feel a little dreamy. We talked about all the people I have thought were kooky, annoying, and irritating over the years who say things like "it was his time" or "we all have a purpose" or "God has a plan" or maybe they believe in ghosts or fairies or leprechauns. I thought they were nuts, and now I have to rethink everything. He laughed. He told me he is always with me on journeys but to call on him specifically if I ever think I need translation. I asked him, "How many of you guys are out there for me?" He laughed and said, "A lot."

March 20

Chip is ten months old today. He is very tall, but it's all in his legs. Despite the huge amount he eats, he is as skinny as a greyhound.

March Madness is on. Rich is watching lots of basketball. Every time he gets excited about a game, the dogs think he's engaging them, and I have to say, "Bella, he's not mad at you! Chip, calm down; this doesn't mean he wants to play."

Today was filled with hours of Gussie drama. She fell and hurt her knee and was taken from Vista Hope to the emergency room. Her bloodwork revealed low sodium and potassium, and they were working on admitting her in the ER when she got frustrated and signed herself out against medical advice. Joe, Emma, Teresa, Bethany, and I spent the afternoon trying to find her with the help of campus police, city police, taxi companies, and an old friend of Gussie's. We finally found her in Walmart, where she was trying to purchase more than $10,000 of merchandise to send to flood victims. She had seven carts full of merchandise. At the end of the transaction, they realized she did not have a photo ID, and so each item had to be refunded back to her debit card, which took a very long time. Joe talked to the store manager, apologized profusely, and explained Gus's fragile mental condition. She had a $400 cab bill, which Teresa paid along with a generous tip.

Emma finally got her on the phone, and Gussie said she purchased clothes for children affected by the floods, as well as a dog bed, collar, leash, food, and toys for her (fictional) service dog named Scout.

She finally made it back to the hospital where she was admitted.

March 21

I have been having more lucid dreams where I know I am dreaming. In one I saw huge animals as big as houses and made them become tame. In another, I was diving off a cliff into a pool, but realizing it was too shallow, I veered off to the ocean instead, willing myself to breathe underwater. I became empowered in the dream state and directed how the dream came out. This makes me feel more under control, and my teachers say it is a normal step in the process.

March 22

The "to do" list related to Gussie's continuing deterioration is growing. I made a spreadsheet and sent it to Teresa, Bethany, Joe, and Emma, so we can divide and conquer. It has all the follow-ups that are needed from the simplest (what is her iTunes password?) to her wishes about a funeral. It's amazing how a few days of dysfunction can generate so many follow-ups from the DUI, DWI, bills, medical affidavits for lawyers, research for places after Vista Hope, Social Security disability, thank-you notes to all those who helped us track her down, and so forth. She is generating a huge amount of work and is completely oblivious. Again, the feeling of gratitude for the sibs and Emma is washing over me. I can't imagine how overwhelming it would be if there was just Gussie and one other sib. Gussie is mad at us and has said she doesn't want to talk to any of us for a few days.

Meanwhile, Gussie's car was repossessed. We can check it off the to-do list!

Though she doesn't want to talk to us, we are checking on her several times a day with the nursing staff and monitoring her pain level, eating habits, sleep, and mental status. In moments when Gussie feels better physically, she has been disruptive and argumentative. She wants to go outside and smoke, and the staff wants to keep her in their sights and don't want her to leave the floor. So she has been sneaking out of the hospital. Worry that she will escape again covers us like a blanket.

March 23

When I am in my daily routine, everything seems better. I am grateful for the flow of wake up, meditate, work out, twirl, breakfast, class, meal prep, check on family, lunch, paint, afternoon meditation, and so on. This gives me a concrete sense of hitting milestones and allows me to flow into the next activity without feeling rushed or anxious. This sense of daily structure makes me feel more in control. And I think it also makes me more able to adapt when new variables arise.

Some fun synchronicities from the past day:

I have been doing more decluttering and found two copies of Victor Frankl's *Man's Search for Meaning:* one in the basement and one in my bedroom. I couldn't bear to give them away, so put them in the "save" pile. A few hours later, when I was reading the paper, I read an article that referenced this book.

As I did a tools journey, I thought about my favorite lost crystal I always thought had amazing energy. It has been lost for six months, and then a couple of hours later, I found it on its chain as I was cleaning my painting area in the basement.

This morning I was in the fugue state that I now call "twilight" between asleep and awake, and I started to visualize creatures, including dragon, wolf, elephant, a giraffe, and an anteater. I thought, "Wow giraffe and anteater; that's new and different; I haven't seen those guys before. And then I read a tribemate's posted class journey where he had giraffe and anteater guides.

I had another lucid dream. I was flying through galaxies at a high rate of speed, like being in a wind tunnel. I was lying flat, facing down and flying upward, away from Earth, but my hair was pushed out above my head, even though it should have been blown the other way. I realized I was dreaming and kept telling myself not to be afraid. I then flew back over the upper west side of Manhattan where we used to live and realized I was dreaming. Then I was lying on a sidewalk just outside of Riverside Park like I had just "come to" after the breath had been knocked out of me. It was now daylight. Two teenage boys were prodding me with their feet. I told them "I am dreaming, and you are just dream characters." Then they were talking; their mouths were moving, but no sound was coming out. I got up and started to walk up a flight of outdoor stairs. I was wearing a dress, and they kept pushing up against me. I kept telling them "I am not afraid; you are just dream characters. Do you know you are dream characters?"

March 24

We had a lovely session of pack cuddling this morning after meditation. I had a dog on either side of me, each with their head on a shoulder—Bella nestled between me and Rich and Chip on my right. A moment to treasure.

I had a good stride run today and a yoga class. I am making progress on balance. It is snowing now; it's actually pretty. I believe it is our last spring in the Midwest, so I vow to appreciate it.

I am going to paint this afternoon. It feels like so long since I have painted, and I miss it a lot. I have been trying to keep the house tidy for showings. I am going to the messy part of the basement and keep everything confined to that area and clean up after I am done. Tonight, I am cooking tofu in the air fryer.

Emma:

Mason just called; he stopped by to see Gussie and had her on the phone with him. She has been given some pain medication in the hospital. She told me she is hallucinating and seeing lots of bright colors and flying unicorns. She said she is happy, and she thanks everybody for their unconditional love and support. Then Mason coached her to say good night, and that was the end of the call.

March 25

Gus is being disruptive, and the nursing staff is getting frustrated. She wants to smoke and to go back to Vista Hope. They keep saying she will be discharged, but then one of her levels is not quite in the acceptable range, and they decide to keep her another day. Every time Psych comes to evaluate her competence, Gussie seems to gather some inner intelligence, and she comes across as completely with it. The evaluator always comes out and says, "She's fine."

Every time the nursing staff changes shifts, one of us has to call and repeat the same information.

I prepared a script and refer to it now when I call to check on each shift change. Our fear is Gussie will not be discharged correctly.

"Hi, I am Gussie's sister. I am calling to check on her. She is divorced; her children and all her siblings live out of state, so she has no family there. We have been increasingly concerned about her mental and physical decline. She had a DUI in Illinois a few weeks ago. She had a DWI in Missouri a few days later and spent the night in jail, where she tried to harm herself by throwing herself against the floor.

Gussie is in rehab at Vista Hope. Recently, while in the ER, she became impatient and checked herself out against medical advice, called a taxi, and purchased thousands of dollars of merchandise for flood victims. She was convinced to come back to the hospital. When she gets discharged, she is going back to Vista Hope. Please make sure that she gets discharged the correct way and let us know if you plan to discharge her today, so we can make sure Vista Hope is aware.

And today, happily, she was discharged back to Vista Hope, and she is there now and safe. So, I can put the script to the side for the moment.

March 26

I am learning to cook tofu, which is not as straightforward as it sounds. The trick in making it tasty seems to be to marinate it; I used Bragg's amino acids and nutritional yeast. After burning a batch, I realize it cooks best on a lower heat. Marinade and a 350-degree oven for thirty minutes works well; the air fryer is also a great tool.

I took books and flowered plants to the senior center here, and then we walked the dogs; it was nice to get fresh air, though it was very blustery.

Gus is following the twelve steps, which is great. But Donna is concerned about her medical stability, and she does not think they can treat Gus there for the whole length of rehab. There is a skilled nursing facility a block away called Lakeside. If Gus can transfer there, she could come every day for the AA lessons and stay in the program. The director of Lakeside agrees. Gus needs paracentesis regularly now, and she continues to decline in cognitive ability. She has periods where she seems very much out of it as well as times when she is completely lucid. Every time they do a psych evaluation, Gus comes across as totally in control.

March 27

Gussie is back in the hospital. Joe and Emma are with her. Gussie is jaundiced and only has a two- to three-minute attention span. Her MELD score is now 27. Her care team says she has a 30 percent mortality rate within ninety days (a 30 percent chance of dying in the next ninety days).

They got the DPOA signed and notarized, with Joe as primary and me as secondary. Gussie had no problem agreeing to sign it.

They had the palliative care team do an evaluation. One of the doctors said something to Gussie like, "So, you know you are dying, right?" and Joe and Emma said it took a couple of hours to get her to stop sobbing.

Gus has been demanding—sending Joe to buy her a new phone, asking for very specific food orders, and commanding the nursing staff to wait on her. Gus called Olive Garden and sent Joe to pick it up. He didn't know what she ordered and got out his wallet to pay. The tab was $400 with bags and bags of food for pick-up. She often goes AWOL, and they find her outside smoking.

Joe and Emma met with the psychiatric staff and went through Gus's whole history and explained about the concerning behavior during her shopping spree and that Gus is bragging about how wealthy she is and other delusions like believing she has a service dog named Scout.

I reminded Joe and Emma how each time there is a shift change at the hospital, Gus's story has to be repeated. So, they met with another shift of nurses and covered all the information again and made sure that the DPOA is now in place and that the note to call Joe or me is prominent in her chart.

Joe and Emma met privately with a family practitioner and explained that Gussie is so intelligent that she can easily fool the doctors and psychiatrists regarding her abilities.

The doctor explained Gussie is drinking too much fluid; the amount of liquid she consumes makes her sodium level low. They have put her on liquid restriction, which she ignores. She walks around the hospital and finds water, juice, and coffee.

Joe and Emma then met with Gussie, along with the doctor. The doctor said earlier this week her ammonia level was 22, and now it is 45. He scolded Gus for leaving the hospital, drinking too much fluid, and told her if she does it again, they will have to post somebody in her room.

March 28

I am in Missouri again. After all the care to make sure to update the hospital every shift change, Gus was mistakenly discharged. She set a trash can on fire outside the hospital and was arrested; she is in jail. When we realized she had been discharged, Teresa, Bethany, Joe, Emma, and I frantically started calling the police, Vista Hope, friends, and taxi companies, and finally found out she had been arrested.

The hospital had transferred her to a different floor so Gus could have access to palliative care. The staff on the new floor did not know the story we have been repeating to each new shift. Gus started to become difficult, demanding to go smoke, and when the team refused, she insisted she be released. Her levels were OK at that moment; psych came to evaluate her and decided she was not a danger to herself or others. So, they released her and somehow didn't see the DPOA or any notation to call Joe or me or to transfer her to Vista Hope.

Joe and Emma were driving home from their visit with her and were almost back to Iowa when it happened, so it was faster for me to go. I grabbed my pre-packed bag, Rich took me to the airport, and I made the flight just as they closed the door.

It turns out that burning a trash can is now classed as a felony in a new class of public burning crimes. Gus cannot be released without a hearing. The hearing will not be before tomorrow. Bail needs to be set. She cannot be released from jail tonight; she will have to spend the night.

We have to find a bail bondsman and an attorney that can handle this kind of felony. Releasing her from the hospital was a huge mistake. Vista Hope will now not take Gus back; she is too sick. She needs to go to Lakeside. Lakeside is happy to take her, but since she was not transferred properly from the hospital, she will have to pay out of pocket.

The sibs are furious at the hospital, frantic with worry about Gus, and highly frustrated about the red tape involved in figuring out the next step. My emotions once again seem muted. I am annoyed and concerned but feel pretty steady and ready to take action as each next step reveals itself.

We divided up the most recent to-do list. I am calling the jail to let them know the severity of Gus's physical and mental condition and see if there is anything I can bring her tonight if she definitely can't be released.

Teresa is finding an attorney and updating Mason and the kids. Bethany is finding a bail bondsman. Joe is calling the hospital to find out if they will properly transfer her. Emma is going to triple confirm that Lakeside will take her and update her closest friends.

I got to Columbia and checked into the Holiday Inn. I called and talked to the jail, and they took down the information but would not release any information to me or give me any status update. No, I am not allowed bring her anything or visit until the hearing. No, they will definitely not release her before the hearing. I let them know that she tried to hurt herself when she was in jail a couple of weeks ago and that she is physically and mentally very ill. I asked them to please watch her.

I called Mason and asked him to see if he could find any of Gussie's checks at the house; yes. I will pick them up.

March 29

I woke up at 3:30 and could not go back to sleep, wondering how the day would play out and worrying about Gus in jail. I went to the twenty-four-hour gym for a run, showered and meditated, and called Rich and updated him. At 7 a.m., I had a conference call with Bethany, Teresa, and the bail bondsman. The hearing is set for first thing this morning. Once they find out the bail amount, we can get everything in motion. We have to pay 10 percent of the fine. So, if bail is $5,000, we will have to pay $500.

Teresa found an attorney. She is in court now, but I can meet with her paralegal. After the call, I went to meet with the patient services representative at the hospital and told her the whole story about the inappropriate discharge. She was sympathetic but of no help, even though I explained that we are not litigious, we just want Gus properly transferred from the hospital to Lakeside. Joe found out how to file a complaint, and he is writing it in case that will help.

I got Gus's checkbook from Mason and went to see the paralegal. She was compassionate and helpful. The attorney retainer is $1,000. The hearing had just taken place; bail is $4,500, and the charge is public burning. She knows the bail bondsman well, and we called him together; he is going to send someone to meet me at the jail. Veronica is her name. She also suggested, given Gus's erratic mental state, that we start pursuing guardianship.

I updated the sibs and drove to the jail, met Veronica, the bail-bond person, and we spent about twenty minutes doing paperwork. Veronica is a strong, confident tattooed twenty-something with her blonde hair in a ponytail. She knew exactly what to do and say at the jail. She said it would be up to an hour before Gus got processed out and so we sat outside and waited. I asked her about her life, how she got her job, and told her about Gus.

Veronica explained that the door to the jail sticks and when people are released, they try to push it open, and it seems like it's still locked. It can be very disconcerting for them, so when the buzzer sounds that indicates she is going to be released for me to tug on the door from my side to help her. It seems like I stood there for an hour, waiting for the buzzer to sound, and as I did, I prayed, *Help me take the right next steps for Gussie.*

Finally, the buzzer sounded, and I started tugging on the door, and I could hear Gussie sobbing as she thought she was still locked in. I yelled, "Gussie, *push!*" as I tugged. When the door finally popped open, she staggered into my arms, shaking and sobbing and was such a dead weight I sank with her to the ground. Veronica came over to help us; we were blocking the door. Gussie looked terrible. Her eyes were yellow and bloodshot. She had blood coming out of her nose and ears. The legs of her sweatpants were pulled up, and her knees and elbows were bleeding. She had bruises all over her legs and arms. There was no tie on her sweatpants and she was holding them up with one hand and had a bag in the other.

I have never heard anyone cry that hard in my life. She could barely draw breath. I held her and rubbed her back and tried to soothe her. Finally, when she started to calm down, Veronica helped us both off the ground, and we walked over and sat on a bench.

Gus started yelling at me, "Why didn't you bail me out?"

I said, "We did!"

"But why not last night?"

"Because burning a trash can is a felony, and they would not let us bail you out until you had the hearing and bail was set."

"Where's Joe?"

"He is not here."

"Yes, he is; I heard him, and he said, 'I'm coming to get you out.'"

"Sorry, Gus; it's just me."

Another round of hard sobbing. I went to the car and got her a bottle of water and tissues. Veronica got a call from campus police. We need to collect all of Gus's things she had when she was arrested; I said to give me the number, and I would take care of it.

I asked Gus if she was hungry, and she said she is dying for a Diet Coke and a cigarette. Déjà vu.

We walked to the car, and she said, "Take me to Vista Hope." I explained that they could not take her back; she is too sick, but I could take her to Lakeside, and she could continue her sobriety training and daily AA meetings there. Shockingly, she agreed immediately.

I took her to Quick Time and gave her some cash out of my wallet for Diet Cokes and cigarettes, and she said, "Jane, I am going to drink."

I said, "Gussie, please don't do this; you have made so much progress on sticking to AA principles."

She said, "Jane, I know I'm dying. I will go to Lakeside, but I have to have a drink."

I said, "I don't want to argue with you; will you look at me?" She turned and looked at me, and I took her shaky hands in mine, and we looked into each other's eyes. I said, "Gus, every day we are given a new chance to change our life. You have been doing so well; just make the choice that is right for you, and I love you no matter what."

I called Lakeside to say we were on our way and then went in and found her in the bathroom. She had a small bottle of vodka and was drinking it. I helped wash her face, arms, and legs as I swallowed down guilt and disappointment in myself to not have been able to stop her from this. Why couldn't I have found the right words?

Then she said she wanted to stop at Walmart, and I said no. She wanted to get a pedicure and go for a steak dinner with very specific side orders, and I said, "Let's get you all checked in, and then I will go get you takeout and bring it back."

We got to Lakeside and went in. It was a ranch-style place with several wings; a little run down but with a cheerful vibe. We went in the wrong door at first and set off the alarm. A lady with a bunch of plastic key rings on her arm came and said in a good-natured way, "Are you the one who is setting off my alarm?" and we liked her immediately. She got us to the check-in desk. As we walked the halls, I could see the residents in their wheelchairs perk up with interest at who the new person would be. I was happy to see that Gus was friendly with everyone.

We filled out all the paperwork, and they needed a check. I got Gussie's checkbook, wrote the check and had her sign it. The nurse walked us back to see her room; it looked spartan, like a nun's cell with a twin bed, a small dresser, a nightstand, a closet, a small private toilet and shower, and a TV. Gus asked her if someone came in to clean. Yes. Is there cable TV? Internet? Yes. I thought she might erupt in anger at the sparse accommodations, but she turned to me and said, "I *love* it!"

I had her sign a thousand-dollar check for the felony attorney. I left her to get settled in and drove down the block to Vista Hope to get her medication and belongings and got her carryout order.

When I came back in, she had showered. She had her Boone County Jail pajamas on and was walking the hallways, and the other residents were saying, "What were you in for?"

She proudly said, "Burning a trash can; it's a felony." She was going around shaking hands and introducing herself to everyone in the hallways: "Hi, I'm Augusta. I'm an alcoholic."

I drove back to campus police to get her things, including a cowboy hat, a guitar, and trash bags crammed with shoes and clothes. How had she managed to carry all this out of the hospital? I took the check to the attorney and updated Gus's contact information. I drove her guitar and things back to Lakeside.

I sat with Gus for a while after I came back. I had my laptop and asked her to try to help me complete her Social Security disability profile, but she could not focus. I filled out as much as I could. Then the business manager stopped in to say hi and said she would help Gus finish it. I thanked her profusely.

Gus dialed through some big mood swings as I sat with her; from "How can you guys still love me" to "I can't believe you didn't bail me out." She claimed they abused her in jail. I asked her about her shopping **spree**, and she erupted. "If you knew you were dying, and you could spend your money to help someone, wouldn't you do it?"

I asked her about setting fire to the garbage can, and she said they released her from the hospital, and she got angry.

Not wanting to agitate her further, I asked what she wanted to talk about, and she started talking about her sobriety lessons. She told me proudly that she had not had a drink in six weeks and that she had a chip. I looked at her thinking, "Does she *really* not remember she drank a few hours ago?"

She said she wanted to meditate together, so we sat on her bed together, and I led us in a simple meditation.

Then she said she was tired and wanted me to leave. We said, "Love you, see you, bye," and I texted the sibs and called Dad to give them an update when I got to the hotel.

After I meditated, I spent a few minutes in gratitude. I am glad I could be there and play a role for her. I appreciate being able to get to the feeling of equanimity. Yes, I feel emotion, but I also feel pretty under control, pretty resilient. I keep asking for help to take the right next step. I can't fully see what is ahead, but I think hidden forces are with us.

I am grateful for Mason. No one questions the divorce, but he clearly has great compassion and love for Gussie still. I am grateful for all the many people who have helped us as we have stumbled our way through the dramas of the past month.

March 30

I packed up, checked out, and went back to Lakeside. As I walked in, I wondered if this would be my last chance to see Gus in this life. She wanted to go to Vista Hope to sobriety class, and I facilitated a conversation between the two centers to make sure she can go but only under supervision.

Gus was distracted, argumentative, and kind of mean this morning. I just tried to absorb it without getting annoyed, and I think me being calm irritated her, but then her mood switched, and she was almost sweet at the end. She wanted to meditate together again. Then she gave me a bunch of papers she had written about how mad she was at all of us and why she hated us. Then she started raving about every grievance she ever had with each of us, moving from Teresa to Bethany to me, and to Joe. I listened and tried to be patient and let her get it all out. Then she calmed down and said how much she loved us all and how amazed she is that we have stuck by her. And she took the papers back and ripped them up. She asked me to never drink alcohol again, started to preach to me from the AA book, and said she had been sober for two months, and had a chip. I didn't even go there.

As I hugged her good-bye, I made her look at me. I had tears in my eyes, and I wanted to make sure we really saw each other. She got impatient and dismissed me with "Love you, see you, bye."

I gave the staff some cash to keep at the desk for her in case she had some kind of crazy craving and triple checked that they would supervise her when she goes out to smoke and that they will not let her off property except to go to Vista Hope. I let them know we were pursuing guardianship. They know to call Joe or me with any issues.

Gus now has a phone, so we will see how that goes; I am sure she will be texting like mad.

Then I drove to St. Louis, turned in the car, and made my flight. I got home about 4 o'clock, in time to take the hounds for a walk around the pond, meditate, and have dinner with Rich and Raleigh.

Joe:
Guys, I checked on Gus. She loves Lakeside! She said has started a gardening club and sent them out to buy some flowers to plant. She seemed happy when I talked to her. She now has her computer and phone, and she is texting and emailing a lot. I have access to her account, so I can see what she is sending

Teresa:
I checked on Gus too. Her moods were all over the place. I suggested maybe she might want to limit her texts and emails

just to family. She hated this idea. In addition to the gardening club, she has now also started an AA group. She told me she had been sober for six months now, and she had a new chip. She has also started an art club, and she is painting.

March 31

Gussie is now sending notes to people outside the family, so we are getting questions from folks who have not witnessed her steep mental decline, and we are bringing them up to speed. She can now have visitors, and we get reports from people who have stopped by to see her. Her visitors have questions about her being abused in jail, suing the hospital for releasing her, and bragging that she is going to take the family on a luxury trip. So now, we are helping friends and relatives go through the heartbreak of seeing Gussie in the last phase of her life.

Raleigh's flight home was delayed; he has been here the past few days. I made him hot whole grain cereal with berries and a smoothie, and then he went and lay down. Chip and Bella love him and hung out in his room. Our house was full today: Chef Joe, the refrigerator repairman, Christina, and house cleaners. It felt like the doorbell kept ringing. The lawn guys came to mow and trim when we were out playing with the dogs. Rich deals with this better than I do. I don't want to put anyone out of a job, but when we move and downsize, I want to simplify and be able to maintain the house mostly by ourselves.

Raleigh flew home this afternoon. It was nice having just our pack together tonight.

Chapter Ten
April

I have a feeling in April of breaking through to a new level of awareness.
I continue to have vivid dreams connected to the shamanic apprenticeship. The teacher certification portion of the Chopra Center meditation class begins. My "Blue Light" painting hangs in the Museum of
Art for a fundraiser. Gus's physical and mental condition worsen, and
she enters hospice care. I feel supported and guided as I play my role
as one of Gussie's caregivers. At the end of the month, I attend the
Seduction of Spirit retreat and feel a profound sense of healing.

April 1

The Teacher Certification portion of the class at the Chopra Center
starts today. I took the dogs out before meditation; it was a chilly,
starry morning. We got back in bed, and Rich and I had a little cuddle;
then we all did Deepak and Oprah's new meditation series on success.
Rich got us coffee. When we took the dogs out for their morning play
session, the sun was coming up, and the birds were singing their sweet
welcome-to-spring songs.

Rich is judging scholarships for Rotary all morning: the Service
Above Self awards. The kids do things like mentor kindergartners and

organize blood drives. He is in one of the inner-city schools. Good for them and good for him; I love seeing positivity.

I ran outside, did yoga, and painted. Rich and I had lunch together: vegetable soup and leftovers.

Then, we took the dogs for a *huge* walk letting Chip walk on grass for much of it so his pads would not hurt. It was a gorgeous day with lots of stops for sniffing and scratching. Rich and I had a sweet Monday night meeting. I checked on Gus, and she is holding her own.

April 2

Gus went for a paracentesis and got admitted to the hospital again. She is giving the nursing staff hell. She keeps sneaking down to smoke and has been calling and ordering food to be delivered to the hospital. They caught her in the lobby trying to leave after she called a taxi.

Today was Joe's turn to check on her, and as the drama continued, he sent updates. Gus went to the hospital gift shop and bought hundreds of dollars of merchandise: figurines, sports merchandise, cards, lotion, clothing, and so forth. She also had a box of liquor delivered to the hospital and flowers delivered to the Ronald McDonald house. The nursing staff has now put her in restraints, and they have taken her phone away. She is being monitored. She is absolutely furious.

Joe:
Just talked to her briefly on the nurse's phone. She is royally pissed, but I have not heard her this lucid for a long time. She said she wants to make decisions for herself; she said she "has it under control." Mostly she wants to stop "being a burden" to the rest of us, and she is extremely frustrated about her care. She was crying and ranting until they brought her dinner. The nurse, Natalie, said when we call, she gets more agitated.

April 4

The medical team at the hospital has placed Gussie on a ninety-six-hour hold, and she is extremely angry, screaming and raging. She is in restraints, and they can't get her medically stabilized. They asked one of us to come, and I am on my way.

They told us she is exhibiting signs of mania. I looked up the technical definition from the American Psychiatric Association, and the diagnosis makes sense; a manic episode may include inflated self-esteem or grandiosity, flights of fancy, distractibility, and activities with a high likelihood of painful consequences (e.g., extravagant shopping).

I got there too late for visiting hours and checked in with the nurse; Gus is asleep. I told her I would be there first thing tomorrow.

April 5

I meditated, worked out, and was at the hospital by 7:30 when visiting hours began. I went to Gus's room and had to hold it together when I saw her. Her skin and eyes were yellow with jaundice. She was in a red gown. Her bruised arms and legs were in restraints. There was a person watching her. It was pitiful. But I summoned up every reserve I had and said a cheery "Good morning, Gus!"

She glared at me and said "Me no talk you," which is what she said as a toddler. I laughed, and she chuckled and then started to cry.

I sat next to her and held her hand and let her get it out. She cried and said she is furious that she can't have her credit cards.

Then she accused me of treating her like she is five years old. She was articulate, cogent, and powerfully angry. I was kind of impressed actually. When I tried to explain that we were trying to help her, she said "No! I won't hear any more about all the crazy shit I did! No one believes I wasn't drinking, but I wasn't!" She confused the Walmart incident with the shopping spree in the hospital gift shop and the liquor store order, but I knew what she meant.

Then she said, "Look at me; I'm locked up like a criminal; is this what you want for me?" I sat next to her on the bed and scratched her back and tried to speak in my most soothing voice, and it seemed to calm her for the moment.

We met with six members of her medical team (Joe was there by phone). At the moment, she is stable medically, but the team has concerns about her psychological state. She is displaying manic behavior and cycling in and out of different mood states quickly. She is now deemed incapable of making decisions for herself. They will start some new medications to try to address the psychological issues. To do that and keep her safe, they recommend moving her to the psychiatric ward, which is attached to the hospital. There, she would not be in restraints, but it is a locked ward. Her medical team feels that she could be harmful to herself, and they say that keeping her there for now is the best decision for her.

She can have visitors there in a public supervised area. The visit protocol is to sign in, wait for an escort, get scanned by a security device, and lock up your belongings. We asked if she could smoke there; they said no.

We explained Gus's wishes; a private room with a bathroom and not to be under surveillance. They said it's not possible.

They talked about their efforts to not have her in restraints and how she fooled them multiple times and escaped. They explained, if they put her in the locked psych ward today, this will take her out of restraints. The length of stay will depend on how she responds to treatment. They are hopeful they can get her manic episodes under control, and she can go back to Lakeside soon. They will start with a ninety-six-hour hold that could extend to a twenty-one-day court-ordered hold. A social worker will be assigned.

They want Joe to come in two days to get the legal work done with them. They asked if we had a guardianship in place in addition to the DPOA; we don't, but we are ready to start the process.

Joe and I asked if there were any other options they could think of, but no, moving forward with the locked ward is the only viable option for now. I went back to Gus's room, dreading talking to her about this.

The doctor on duty, Dr. Green, said she would go with me and pave the way.

We walked in, and Gus started joking with the doctor; I could tell she likes her. Gus said, "Can you get me out of these restraints?" and Dr. Green said, "Yes, we were just having a meeting about that. She asked Gus if she would like to transfer to the locked ward.

And then Gus said, "I will do that for you, if you will let me have a smoke, a Diet Coke, and a paracentesis." Dr. Green agreed, and they went back and forth negotiating a few things, including wearing real clothes instead of the red gown.

Then, Gus had the staff bring all the things she bought at the gift shop: bags and bags of figurines, cards, statues with uplifting sayings. I asked the nurse if I could return them, and she said it was a special sale as part of a fundraiser and so, no. But Gus will not be allowed to keep these items in the psychiatric center.

I called her friend Jim to see if he would meet me and take the bags to his house until Gus gets back to Lakeside, and he said yes. They brought Gus's dinner. I sat with her while she ate, and she was calm.

I told her about my classes, the upcoming Seduction of Spirit retreat, and studying for the Chopra Center certification to be a meditation teacher. She wanted to meditate together, and we did.

She talked about dying and asked me what I believe. I told her I think our energy cycles back into source energy like when a wave becomes part of the ocean again and that it isn't painful or hard; I think it will be joyful and blissful. She asked if I would miss her when she dies, and I hesitated, wanting to say, "You're not going to die!" But I looked at her and said yes; I will miss her so much but hope and expect on some level we will still feel connected. She held her hand palm up, and I put mine on hers, and we just sat like that a while and cried.

Gussie asked, "Do you think I will be punished for the terrible things I have done?' I was tempted to say that she has already been living in a hell of her own making, but I didn't.

I told Gus I don't believe in a judgmental God and that one of my teachers says it is a tremendous act of courage to choose to incarnate into a human life, that *we* choose our life challenges for the purpose of spiritual growth. There is a larger story to each life, and I believe Gus is a very courageous soul. I told her that I see the divinity in her. She is loved. I see the beauty in her, the bravery, the grace, the joy, and the goodness.

I remembered reading an article about autonomous sensory meridian response (ASMR), where some feel a peaceful euphoria by hearing a soothing soft voice. And I scratched and rubbed her back and in my most soothing meditation teacher voice started very softly saying phrases, like "just breathe easily, relax, and feel peaceful. You are good, you are light, you are brave, and you are loved."

When they came to move her, I told her I would see her in the other wing. Even though she had eaten dinner, she gave me an order for specific food she wanted me to bring. I asked if it was allowed, and it was.

I borrowed a cart to take her bags of knick-knacks to the lobby, met her friend Jim, and we loaded them in his car. I gave him the update, and he said he would come back with me to visit her; what a good soul he is. I went to shop for her food and came back with bags of groceries.

We went through the whole protocol; I turned in the food to the attendant to be screened and taken up separately. The guard met us, and we put phones and my handbag in a locker. The guard used a wand metal detector on each of us, and then we went in groups in the elevator up to the visitor's lounge. We waited, and Gus came in. She was so furious she was shaking. She started screaming at me and said, "How could you do this to me, Jane?

I was speechless for a moment; she must have forgotten she agreed or she didn't understand what she agreed to, and she said, "This is the psych ward; they *die* in here. I would never do this to you; I demand that you get me released immediately!"

The guard was standing near and speaking quietly into some kind of walkie-talkie. I tried to speak soothingly and get her to sit down and said, "Look, Jim is here," and she said, "Good, I have a witness who is on my side." I said "Gus, we are all on your side."

She sat. She shook her finger at me and said, "What if the situation were reversed and you were put in the psych ward against your wishes; what would you do?" I thought about it for a few minutes. I looked at her, grabbed her hands and said, "I would pretend I was Mahatma Gandhi or Nelson Mandela, and I would love my captors and treat them peacefully and meditate until someone came to let me out." And she said, "Fuck you, Jane. I am going to kill myself in here, and then it will be on you." And she told the guard she wanted to leave.

I stood up with her and said, "Gus, don't let us part this way," and I tried to hug her, and we both started crying. As she was leaving, I called out, "I love you, Gussie."

Jim handed me a handkerchief as I sat trying to process all that had just happened. As we waited for the next supervised trip down the elevator with the guard, he reassured me that her being here is necessary; and told me the delusions he and his wife Glenna had observed in their recent visits with Gus.

As we talked, the room attendant came over to us. Her name badge said Keisha, and she asked me, "Was that Mrs. Saxe?" And I said yes and introduced myself and told her that Gussie is my sister. She said that Gussie taught her son in school; she was his favorite teacher. Gus encouraged and paid attention to him, and he had found a pathway through music that made a big difference in his development. I thanked her so much for telling me and asked her to please watch out for Gus. She said she would.

I went shopping and got Gus a few pairs of underwear, some oranges and apples and sour candy she was craving, an adult coloring book and some crayons, and I took them back to the attendant. I called the nurse's desk to check on Gus.

The nurse said soon after I left, Gussie complained about abdominal pain. They took her down to the ER to have it checked out, and she called a taxi from the group phone and tried to leave. So, she is now considered an "elopement risk," and her phone and visitation privileges are restricted for a few days. I asked if I could talk to her, but the nurse said she was now sleeping. I asked if I could visit in the morning, and she said, please, no. They want to start her on her new medication and see if that makes her less agitated. She can have visitors again when she is calmer, probably in two days. So, I wrote Gus a letter that I will leave with the attendant and booked a flight home.

I updated the sibs and told them I am feeling very low, wondering how I could have handled things better. I have an image that we are all Bobo dolls, getting punched down and having to spring right back up again. Interestingly, I was recently writing how calm and resilient I am. Maybe not so much.

April 6

Home. Today I caught up on my shamanic apprenticeship and my Chopra Center teacher certification program. I found a book Paul loaned me and wrote him a letter.

Dear Paul,

You have been on my mind so much lately.

I am decluttering the house, giving and throwing things away, and keeping only what is really precious. (Sometimes I feel like my possessions own me and not the other way around.) The Goodwill store here has a donation drive-through, and I have been making a trip or two a day. I'm starting to get to know all the staff members there. The decluttering feels very good.

Here is an idea while I am on my detachment from possessions kick; what if we agree not to send each other birthday and Christmas gifts going forward? (I reserve the right to send you art if you want any, though.) I feel good letting go of "stuff." Tell me if you are OK with this and let me know what is going on in your life, please.

I digitized all of our photos. I actually threw away the boxes and boxes of real photos. It took some time to gin up the courage to do that. Old letters from high school boyfriends went, too. I can't believe I kept them for forty years.

Now I am down to the hard part that takes a while—getting things back to their rightful owners and making sure that really special things get handled the right way and giving away paintings.

The house is showing, so we have to live in it "staged" with everything off the counters. I hope it sells soon. I am ready to move to the mountains.

Among my most favorite treasures are all the letters and cards you have sent me and the books you gave me. All of those are saved and going with us.

I have been reflecting on our friendship as I go deeper in my spiritual practice. Friendships like ours are rare, and I am so grateful for you in my life. It's not a coincidence that we "re-met," and we have so many similar interests.

Enclosed is your copy of *Tell No Man* I borrowed. Thank you for letting me keep it for so many years. I love this book.

You know that Gussie is very sick and near the end of her life. She is suffering; it is hard to watch. We both went through this in the late eighties in New York with so many friends who died. But somehow when it is your little sister, it's very poignant. So, it is not the easiest moment in life, but much of my days are filled with tremendous joy as well.

Thanks for being such a great friend! Love,
Jane

April 7

I logged onto my teacher certification class on the Chopra website. Because of all my prior reading, I am not behind. I am very excited to learn more about Ayurveda and go deeper into Vedanta, which starts soon.

I realize the AIDS benefit where my donated painting will be hanging in the Columbus Museum of Art is tonight! I threw on a little black dress, and we went.

It was a perfect seventy-five-degree early spring evening, and it felt good to get out and do something fun. There was a big, fashionable crowd at the Columbus Museum of Art. Art for Life is sponsored by Equitas Health and is known particularly for HIV/AIDS treatment. The gay community in Columbus is very vibrant and abundant, and they were out in dapper style. At the outside entrance were drag queens welcoming everyone and looking gorgeous. How do they get their lipstick to gleam like that?

As we walked up the stairs to the gorgeous new wing where the silent auction was taking place, I felt a sense of "I can't believe this is happening," and "I feel like a fraud that one of my pieces is included in this great event with all the real artists," along with the dreaded, "What if nobody bids on it?"

And I had a momentary crisis of knowing that almost no one would "get" the painting—a blue light being? Come on; what are the chances someone will recognize that it is a piece of spiritual art?

But when we walked through, there were people looking at my painting; pointing to it, and commenting on it. I was hoping they weren't saying, "Oh God, here's another painting my five-year-old could have done." Rich heard a lady say it looked phallic. A couple of well-dressed dudes said, "Oh ... I like this." I think Rich was more excited than I was. He spent a lot of time in front of the painting, and he got the roving photographer to come by and get us both in a shot with the painting. Rich looks very handsome and fashionable in a blue cotton sport coat and black shirt.

There was a very professional looking sign next to the painting that said:

Blue Light
Jane Ramsey
Liquid Acrylic on Canvas 48 x 52
Minimum bid $1,500

The bidding was done by mobile device. I kept sneaking a look to see if anyone had bid yet, and Rich was telling me, "Stop looking at your phone." I just wanted it to get above the minimum bid of $1,500, all the while thinking, "Who would pay that much?" As we were walked into the room for the live auction, I saw the first bid come through, felt so relieved, and just started to relax and have fun. Every few minutes a new, higher bid would pop up.

The live auction for the very expensive pieces started at 6:30. (My piece was not included in the live auction.) Before the auction, there was a special presentation about Danny. His wife, Bea, was there to say a few words. We talked to her for a few minutes; she is doing well and was happy for all the publicity his piece was getting for a great cause. His piece had been on the cover of the catalog for the show, and I felt so grateful and honored to have a painting hanging in the same place as his art.

I saw many people who knew me from work and from community things, and they said, "I saw the piece by Jane Ramsey, but I didn't think it could be you!" So, I felt validated that I had somehow transitioned from corporate geek to artist, and I had several people come up to me and say they loved the piece.

Rich leaned over to me during the live auction and said, "Ace, these are your people. You have found your audience!"

The live auction was conducted by a professional auctioneer from New York Christie's, who was also a member of the gay community who really knew how to get the crowd going. The bidding went sky high for the live auction pieces. I was feeling very gratified, remembering all of my friends and colleagues who died of AIDS in New York in the eighties. They were serving Red Bull and whiskey, so there was plenty of adrenaline in the room.

I looked at my phone and saw the high bidder at $2,650 was Bethany! I quickly texted her and said, "You rock, but stop bidding. I will be humiliated if someone in my family buys it! I will paint you one for free!"

And then I watched in hope for the next bid, and there was one! It went for $2,750. Danny's piece sold for $31,000!

I think I can now put "artist" on my business card. So, the vision I saw at Jean Houston's salon came to be; one of my pieces was hanging in a public gallery space.

April 8

Trying not to be too messy in our "staged for showing" house, I am painting a new light being painting for Bethany and documenting it via video; everything from cutting the canvas to mixing the paint.

Feeling more like a legitimate artist, I let all my friends know that I am giving away art for any charitable cause and posted photos of the paintings I have hanging in the garage and basement. I got some immediate interest and set times for folks to come by.

Today an estate auction guy came to tell us how an auction would work if we decide to sell our furniture and other belongings. Basically, they will come and photograph everything we want to sell, including art, and then advertise it online, as well as having movers come on the final day to take it out to people who have purchased the items. They take 33 percent of the proceeds. We are inclined to sell nearly everything. In a downsized home, we will need different dimensions of furniture anyway, and a move to the West Coast can be expensive. I feel remarkably detached from our "stuff," and it is freeing to think we will have fewer possessions.

We dropped the price, and now our house is trending #1 again on Zillow, but no showings are scheduled this week. At this point, every space has been organized, so we would not be embarrassed for anyone to open any door or drawer. The messy part of the basement still has paint drips on the floor, but every time I paint, I leave it tidy.

I was reading about how to ask the universe any question. You have to make sure you are grounded and clear, and you are supposed to find out it if is OK to ask. If you get a yes to all of those, you can ask a carefully worded question.

So, I asked if we would be happy in the Palm Springs area. I got a big yes. And then I asked if we would be happy in the Indian Wells community we liked, and I got a big yes. I asked if we should continue to look in more places, and I got a no. I may have made it all up, but even if I did, it seems my own gut feeling is clear.

April 8

Gus keeps getting transported back and forth between the psych ward and the hospital. They are in the same large building but in two different wings, and just like two different divisions in a corporate enterprise—they have different cultures and leaders and don't always communicate well. We now understand that she really needs to be in a psychiatric hospital, and we researched moving her, but it's complicated by her legal situation, and her unique medical needs.

Meanwhile Bethany put in hours of effort to get a white binder back from the van that was impounded in Illinois; it is a notebook that Gussie insists she needs, claiming it has every important thing she values in life. Thus, Bethany has had to call, cajole, write letters, send a FedEx envelope, and so on. Finally, she got the binder and FedExed it to Gus at the hospital. Joe and Emma were there when the package came. Gus leafed through it and said, "Oh, this doesn't have what I thought was in there," and she tossed it aside.

Joe:
Apparently Gussie went around to everyone in the psych ward, including the staff, and asked for donations to her church. If they didn't contribute, Gussie told them they were going to go to hell.

Today we had a family Zoom call to talk about next steps for Gussie. She is so miserable. They are severely limiting her water intake. We wonder if it is time to stop trying to make her well, which we think is not possible anymore, and move to making her comfortable. Emma and Joe captured our thoughts beautifully in a note.

Dr. Kelly,
We met when your team provided a palliative care consult for our sister, Augusta Saxe.

Since that time, Augusta has been back and forth between the hospital and the psych ward for treatment. She is currently on a twenty-one-day hold. Psych has now requested a palliative care consult, and her family strongly supports this as soon as possible.

We need your expertise to determine our options for Augusta's care. She was hospitalized with critically low sodium levels for several days, and she fights the liquid restrictions necessary to stabilize those levels.

We are no longer confident that Augusta's health (both mental and physical) will improve. It is not our wish to see her suffering in a hospital if there is no realistic expectation of lasting improvement.

- Currently she can't drink more than one liter of liquid per day.
- She can't shower or use the bathroom on her own because she will drink water.
- She has a commode by the bed—and uses baby wipes to clean herself.

- She can't have access to her phone because she calls delivery services or 911.
- She often can't have visitors because she gets too agitated.

While we aren't arguing the thinking behind any of these steps, we are wondering, to what end? We need help determining if she is at end of life, and request your assistance in making this determination. If she is at end of life, we would prefer she be in hospice and be allowed to die with dignity. She is miserable, and we are, too.

Also, she has two college-aged children attending school out of state, four siblings in four different states, and elderly parents (in failing health), living ninety miles away. If it is time to say goodbye, we want to be able to get people to her in time.

Thank you for any help you are able to provide.

Joe

April 11

I didn't sleep well, thinking about Gussie and sending her love. I appreciate the momentum of the routine of our day, which puts me in motion and gives me so many boosts of positivity. I am feeling pretty balanced despite the sadness.

I had a dream that I kept floating to the ceiling, and I had to keep asking Rich to lasso me to bring me back to earth. On our walk this morning, I felt I was floating above the sidewalk. Maybe I am meditating, journeying, and twirling too much.

Joe and I had a conference with Gus's medical team. We then set another family Zoom call with the sibs, Dad and Marie, Mason, Mark, and Mia.

We updated everyone on what was covered, proposed the sad next steps, and asked if anyone had a different point of view about the direction we planned to take. We went to each person individually and asked their thoughts and opinions. Everyone was in alignment. I captured it all in a note and sent it to the broader audience including Marie's kids and Gus's closest friends and all her caregivers at the different facilities:

Dear Ones:

Thanks to family, friends, and caregivers for the ongoing prayers and love being sent to Gussie. She is still in the psychiatric care facility, but we hope that she will be moved to a less restrictive and more comforting environment soon. Her sodium level continues at a critical level, and as a result, she has been restricted on the amount of water she can drink. This has been very tough on her.

We asked that the palliative care team at the hospital come in for a consultation and then had a phone conference with a big team of doctors, nurses, the social worker, the palliative care team, the medical director, and the chief administrator for the hospital. They let us know that Gussie now meets the criteria for hospice care. It was a very caring discussion, focused on trying to find best thing for her. They don't see a path for her to return to health. She is near the end of life. How near? It is hard to say.

We all got in alignment: if we can't get her healthy, then let's get her comfortable. It seems extreme to keep restricting water and doing things that make her miserable. We talked about the importance of her having dignity and being able to eat what she wants, to be surrounded by music, books, and people she loves. We want her to be comfortable.

At the end of the call, Dr. Kelly said that never in his experience has he seen someone with Gussie's diagnosis that still had their family and friends lovingly supporting them. He said most people in her situation die alone in the ICU with no one there. He said that our support system for her was remarkable for someone in her situation.

He talked a lot about the relief of suffering and the importance of dying with dignity and love. We want to express our gratitude to all of you. It has been incredibly challenging for her and everyone who loves her. I am very proud to have been a fellow caregiver of Gussie with all of you.

The next stage will be "comfort care" for Gussie where they treat symptoms, but she can eat and drink whatever she wants. She will first move from the psychiatric facility to a regular floor in the hospital. A permanent catheter will be inserted that will drain fluid from her belly.

There are some legal hurdles that must be overcome before she can move to the next step after that. The felony charge must be dropped, and emergency guardianship needs to be in place before she can be released to a skilled nursing facility. Joe has agreed to be the emergency guardian. With no local hospice facility, a skilled nursing center with hospice support is the best solution, so she will go back to Lakeside, which has been her goal.

Teresa and I are going tomorrow to talk to Gussie to make sure she wants to take this next step of hospice. Mark has been home from college this week and has visited her every day along with Mason. Mia is coming home to visit her. Joe and Emma and Dad and Marie will go this weekend, and Bethany plans to go next week.

The three- to five-day plan is to get her out of the psychiatric care facility to the hospital, with a seven-day plan to get her to back to Lakeside, and then hospice can support the team there.

Gussie wants visitors and cards. It is likely she will soon have her phone back, so you may hear from her directly. If you visit or hear from Gussie, keep in mind she may be in a confused state as a result of her sodium and ammonia levels.

Thanks for the ongoing support; I know we will all be praying for the opportunity to get Gus to a more comfortable place this coming week.

With love, Jane

When I landed in Kansas City, Teresa was at my gate. We stood, hugged, and rocked with each other for a few minutes. I am grateful we are going to do this together. We got the rental car and headed for Columbia. We called Dad and Marie on the way.

We checked into the hotel and called the psychiatric facility and asked to talk to Gussie. We told her we were there for a visit. She got excited and asked for all kinds of specific things: a very tart orange, a very crisp and juicy apple, steamed dumplings, some Chinese food with duck sauce, and a steak. We said we would do what we could before visiting hours began. We ran those errands, and Teresa and I talked about how we would broach the subject with Gussie about hospice. We rehearsed several ways to get into the conversation and then finally just sat together in the parking lot, holding hands, and each of us asking for guidance to get to the highest and best outcome. We got out of the car and walked toward the building, and I said, "We can do this!" and she said, "Right! Yes, we can!" and we kept trying to stay confident that this would go okay. And it did.

Teresa had not been through the protocol of the psych ward, and she has not seen Gussie in a couple of months, so I prepared her. We went in, signed in, got approved to visit, and waited for the guard and visiting hours. We turned in the food and stored our belongings and went through the process. Teresa was horrified; it felt like visiting someone in prison.

We finally got up to Gus's floor and asked to see her. We were in the large visitor's room with other patients and their families. We could hear Gus coming down the hallway: "Hello, Teresa and Jane!" She was so excited to see us, and we were thrilled to see her. Teresa was trying hard to hold in her shock at seeing Gus's jaundice and swelling, so I kept Gus talking while Teresa collected herself.

It was clear that Gus had rallied the support of a whole crew of staff, who were now her "posse." Keisha was there, and Gus was teasing her. An aide brought her a frozen popsicle. Gus's food we brought was delivered, and she ate it with great relish. She asked for water, and it was still being restricted. She complained about this, and it gave us our starting point. We told her that she had some choices and options to think about. She could stay and continue to have the liquid restriction, or she is now eligible for hospice, which means she could go back to Lakeside and have what she wanted in terms of liquids. She could smoke. She would have comfort care. But there is a chance that if she has as much liquid as she wants, she could slip into a coma and die.

She didn't respond at first. She had a paper bag and started pulling out papers and showing us pages she had colored. We admired everything she showed us. She pulled out more papers and showed us newspapers where she had circled items she wanted for her next apartment. She read us some stories she had written. In the midst of other conversations, she said that she is ready for hospice. Then other visitors, Jim and Glenna and the pastor from her church, came to see her. She told them that she is going to hospice. And before we knew it, visiting hours were over. She gave us a complicated food order and a list of **other** things she wanted, and we said we would see her tomorrow.

We called Dr. Kelly's office and asked if we could have a private visit with Gussie tomorrow, and he said he would arrange it.

Teresa and I had dinner at our hotel, and she went through the same process that Joe and Emma and I had done: to assimilate this current version of Gussie with the bright, vibrant, intelligent woman she remembered. She shed some tears, and we both had a couple of glasses of wine. I told her it makes me feel very conscious now when I have wine. It used to be automatic: come home, have a glass of wine.

And I still enjoy it, but it is very top of mind that I am drinking something that, for another member of our family, is a lethal weapon.

We talked for hours long into the night: memories of Gus as a little girl and young adult, speculating whether her mental illness contributed to her alcoholism, and wondering about the larger story of her life and whether there was some higher purpose to this very difficult incarnation. What lessons are we supposed to learn from being her siblings? We expressed our concern about Joe since the two of them are so close and our strong desire that Mia and Mark will be able to heal. We appreciated Mason and his ongoing love for her. We marveled at how all of us as sibs worked so well as a team during all of her many dramas, and we talked about what she would want at her funeral.

April 13

Teresa and I meditated and went to the hotel gym together and got coffee. I had to call in for a board meeting at the art college, and she went down to get some more coffee to give me some privacy.

Then Joe and I had a conference call with the guardianship attorneys. They explained that taking someone's freedoms away—their constitutional rights to drive, to vote, to choose where they live, and so forth—has to be approved by a judge, and affidavits are needed to prove that the person is not capable of making decisions like these for themselves. We explained that we were in a fluid situation and that Gussie was a lot closer to the end of her life than we presumed ten days ago when we hired them.

But, they helped us understand that since she may be very close to the end, we don't want some stranger deciding on end-of-life issues.

To Gussie's Support System:
Teresa and Jane reporting in. We spent time with Gussie yesterday. She is now calmer, clearer, and more aware. The new meds are helping. There was little sign of anger or mania. Mostly she was sweet, funny, and appreciative.

Last night and today in another private meeting, we confirmed that she understands her diagnosis, and she wants to move forward with guardianship and hospice. She understands that when she is allowed to have as much water as she wants, her health could deteriorate further, and she could slip into a coma.

She says is ready and willing to stay in a secure facility, and she is grateful Joe will be her legal guardian. Physically, she is in very poor health. Her belly and legs are hugely swollen. She has difficulty sitting. Her skin is itchy, and she is uncomfortable. She already needs another paracentesis and told us she now has fifty extra pounds of water weight.

She has won over the staff. The supervisor of the visiting room is a lady whose son was Gussie's student. She told us they were all rooting for Gussie to move to comfort as soon as possible, and she broke down crying when she talked about the contrast between Gussie as a dynamic teacher and Gussie today. We met Jeri, her social worker. Kate, the pastor, was there. Gussie is making art, which occupies her mind and keeps her calm.

Things are in motion for the felony charge to be dismissed, given her diagnosis. We still need the guardianship to be approved so she can be transferred. It has been a team effort. It feels frustrating to wait for her to be moved to a more comfortable place, so we appreciate continued prayers for things to move swiftly. She wants visitors and cards.

We will keep you posted as we learn more.

Love, Teresa and Jane

I am so grateful to be here with Teresa. Either she or I could have done it alone, but it was so much better with both of us. We went shopping for the obscure items Gus requested, and Teresa and I both got a salad, so we could have lunch with her.

We weren't constrained by time, and Gussie was excited to meet with us in the private room, though there was a staff member in the room as is required. Our conversations flowed with Gussie's thoughts and moods, and we drifted in and out of the same threads multiple times, letting her lead.

We talked about happy memories: all of Gus's visits in New York, the Broadway shows we went to, singing in the aisles at *Mama Mia*, and the shock we felt when we went to *Naked Boys Singing!* (and they really were naked)! We reminisced about our sweet Canyon Ranch memories. She and Teresa talked about her many visits to Santa Fe. We talked about Mia and Mark, their wonderful gifts and talents, and her dreams for them. She showed us her art.

We talked about death, and she asked several times if Teresa and I were really not afraid of death. We said we don't fear it. I said that she will be the first of all of us to know the answers to the big mysteries, and if she finds out it really is a recreational universe and we are supposed to just have fun, to please find a way to come back and tell me. This made her laugh.

Teresa told her what she thinks it will be like: a continuous feeling of joy, bliss, wholeness, and peace. I said I thought there would also be some element of continuing education and that maybe after each incarnation, we advance to a new stage of development. She said to watch for her in all the new babies that come, in case she comes back to our family. And we sat like that for a while, just talking, crying and laughing, holding hands, and rubbing her back.

Gus told us she had burned off a shit load of karma while meditating in this facility and compared herself to Nelson Mandela and Mahatma Gandhi. This made me happy; she actually found some peace here, and maybe the stupid thing I said to her did some good.

She wanted us to do a ritual with her, and so we asked the person sitting in the room with us to give us a few minutes of privacy while we prayed together.

Teresa and I flowed into it. We stood up and faced each other, and I said, "Let's raise our hands up," and we held our palms facing outward. "May peace, ease, comfort, gratitude, and joy flow through us."

Teresa said, "May we request help and loving energy from all those relatives and friends who have gone before us, including Mom, Gramp, Gramma, Ma, Grandpa Joe, Gay, Retta, Sis, Carol, Clara, Dolly, Rosie, and all others who love our family."

I said, "And we request the presence and support of our higher guidance. We want to express gratitude for our lives together, for the opportunity to be sisters, and for this chance to be together now in this moment. May we use discernment in decision-making with and for Gus in the next critical steps in her life. May she have the highest and best outcome and feel the great love we have for her."

Teresa said, "We request a healing white light to join us. Let's repeat together; please bring your light, love, and peace to Gussie."

When we sat back down, Gus said she was having a hard time sitting in the chair and needed to go rest. We were getting ready to say goodbye, and she started crying hard. We said, "We aren't saying our last good bye; we will still come tonight," and she gave us a detailed food order to bring and said, "Love you, see you, bye."

Teresa and I went out to the car and cried for a while. We went to buy her lotion, sweatpants, and undies. And then we went to procure all the strange and elaborate things Gus wanted for tonight: moo shoo pork with extra duck sauce, a potato pancake and a filet mignon from a restaurant downtown, and a sour Granny Smith apple.

We went back for visiting hours, knowing this would be our last chance to see Gussie in this life. I said to Teresa, "We can do this." And as we waited for the guard to take us up, some of her friends came— Pastor Kate and some friends from her church.

Gus was excited about her food and tasted it all. She read us a story and showed her artwork to everyone. Then she stood up and announced she was tired, and she was going to bed. We kissed and hugged her and tried to hold back the tears. With a final "Love you, see you, bye," she disappeared down the hallway.

April 14

To Team Gussie from Teresa and Jane:

Gussie has now been transferred back to Lakeside. A catheter is in place so that fluids can now be continually drained from her belly.

Hospice services started with her transfer to Lakeside; and they met her at the nursing home and started to make her more comfortable.

Teresa and I had good visits with her over the past couple of days. Though she was uncomfortable physically, she was funny, loving, and peaceful, more like her typical personality. We are grateful for the time with her. Mia and Mason are with her now.

She will have her phone and computer, and you may hear from her directly. If you call, visit, or get a note, just know that she still has periodic moments of confusion and fantasy with the extra fluid in her body.

She welcomes cards, notes, and visits. Thank you on behalf of the entire family for the ongoing prayers, support and love for Gussie.

Love, Jane

Jane:

I just talked to Gussie. She sounds good. The social worker is with her. She is giving away all the tchotchkes she bought in the hospital gift shop, and that is making her very happy.

April 16

I worked out after meditation. I spent a bit of time on the apprenticeship, but most of the day was focused on Gussie. My Seduction of

Spirit retreat starts tomorrow. I am packed but will make a last-minute decision about going depending on where things stand.

We have all agreed that we will have Gussie's funeral and memorial services a month or so after she passes.

Jane:

Just talked to Gussie. She was pretty out of it but made jokes. She hates the drainage, of course; she said it felt like she was constantly peeing down her leg. The nurse told me that there is so much edema, the drain cannot keep up with it. She said the morphine relieves her pain, but she doesn't like feeling so "out of it," now that she has gotten used to feeling sober. She said she loved giving away the trinkets she had bought for everyone.

She got a visit from three close friends yesterday. She said, "Blessings abound; I am the gratitude girl." As we were hanging up, the nurse was scratching her back.

Three hours later:

Teresa:

I just got a call from hospice. Gussie's condition has worsened, and they think she may die today.

Joe:

We are here with Dad and Marie. Gus is unresponsive but alive.

Bethany:

How is Dad?

Emma:

He and Marie are doing amazingly well. You don't get to be ninety years old without lots of resilience.

We told her she is surrounded by people who love her. We sang songs and told her it is OK to go.

April 17

I woke up about 2:30, and it felt to me that Gus was transitioning. I sat up and just held space for her and sent her so much love. Then I meditated and fell back asleep. When I woke up a couple of hours later, I had the text; she passed at 2:37 this morning. Mason was with her.

I worked out, and Rich and Bella drove me to the airport. My flight left at six a.m. I pull out the agenda for Seduction of Spirit. I have not focused on it at all. I hope I packed the right clothes.

I flew through Dallas to San Diego, and my flights were perfect. I got to La Costa about five thirty. My room is in the center of everything near the marketplace and gym—perfect. I meditated on the flight and was hungry, so I went to dinner, sat outside, and took in the view. It seems unreal that Gussie died today. The meditation retreat is going to be the perfect place to grieve and process it all.

April 18

I woke up early as I always do when I travel west. The gym does not open until five. I sat in the marketplace and drank decaf coffee and answered email until the gym opened. I had a long treadmill workout and then lifted weights, did some yoga and Pilates, and twirled. I showered and washed my hair. I put yoga clothes on, not exactly sure what to wear. I walked down the hill to the conference center to check in and get my packet. There will be a big crowd here; my guess is about four hundred people. My lanyard was a different color from most others; it was yellow, and it said, "On the teacher's path." Cool.

The doors opened at 8:30, and registration was quick, easy, and very organized. I saw on the schedule that Jon Kabat Zinn and Rupert Spira will both be here—very exciting. Talking to the other participants, it's clear that many come back to this event multiple times. There are vendors in the conference center lobby, selling beautiful spiritual art, jewelry, and books. I feel grateful to be here.

Those on the teacher's path are invited to sit down front on the floor. So, I did for the morning session. Amanda Rignalda welcomed us; she is lovely, a gifted teacher. I remember her from the Synchro-Destiny course. She talked through the week's agenda and introduced Roger Gabriel. He is our main teacher for the Primordial Sound Meditation certification course and someone whose articles and lectures I follow. I feel honored to see him in person.

Roger told us his background. Born in Liverpool, he has a lovely, engaging accent and a fun sense of humor. He first learned meditation in the United Kingdom in the early 1970s because, he said, he thought it might be a way to meet girls. It instantly became his passion, and he soon trained to be a meditation teacher under Maharishi Mahesh Yogi. After moving to the US, Roger began studying Ayurveda, the ancient Indian system of healthcare. In 1985, while helping to establish centers for Ayurveda and meditation, he met and became friends with Deepak Chopra.

Since then, Roger has assisted Deepak with numerous training programs, seminars, and workshops; taught thousands of people on all continents to meditate; and assisted in training hundreds of people to become teachers of meditation, Ayurveda, and yoga.

Roger told a story that had everyone erupting in laughter. He showed an old sepia-toned photo on the conference screen of a British Raj with an Indian servant who was fanning him with a palm frond. He pointed to the Raj and said, "That was me in a former life." He pointed to the servant and said, "That was Deepak," and now, my karma is to serve him who served me—or something like that. It was very cute.

Roger said he has been blessed to meet and study with great teachers in India and the West, and he has traveled extensively in India. He incorporates much of what he has learned in his practices and teaching. In 2006, Roger received his spiritual name Raghavanand from Shree Satuwa Baba Maharaji of Varanasi, India.

Roger led us through the first meditation of the week and asked us to settle in and be comfortable and close our eyes. Then he asked the four soul questions that I use to meditate twice a day. Who am I? What do I want? What is my purpose? What am I grateful for?

I sat enjoying the mediation with the hundreds of other people, and after some time had passed—maybe fifteen minutes—I noticed that I had a growing sensation of heat coming from my core, like extreme hot flashes that kept building. I thought it would pass, but it intensified. I was sweating profusely. I lost my mantra and had to open my eyes and take off my sweater. My hair was wet with perspiration. I was soaked through my yoga pants, and my bra was dripping. I didn't want to be disruptive, and I looked around to see if anyone had noticed, but they were all sitting there peacefully with their eyes closed. I took off my socks, fanned myself, and it seemed to get a bit better. I used my balled-up sweater to mop the sweat from my face and arms. I found a hair tie in my bag and put my hair up. And then I went back to my mantra and tried to just settle into it despite the dampness. The meditation seemed long—maybe forty minutes. When we ended, I had a sense of peacefulness like usual, but I was soaked. Happily, we took a break, and I went back to my room and took another shower, redried my hair, and changed my clothes. I put on layers so that I could peel the tops off if this happened again, and I put a pair of flat sandals on. I had a pair of cotton harem pants in my bag, and I put those on; they felt better than yoga pants. I stuck a small towel in my bag and hurried back to the session. All the seats were taken at the front of the room, so I sat in a chair in the general audience.

Roger was just introducing Deepak. Even though I was now sitting in the back and hundreds of people were there, it felt like an intimate experience. After seeing Deepak at the Sages and Scientists symposium and in so many different classes, including Synchro-Destiny, I got the feeling that this is his favorite audience. He seemed very candid and open. He and Roger were so easy with each other; it was obvious how much they like working together. They joked around, and the atmosphere was light.

Deepak started talking about unveiling reality. It was a long lecture, and I captured some notes.

He said, "In meditation, we begin by asking 'who am I?'" He is a Shakespeare lover and talked about Hamlet. The play is really about figuring out what is real and what is an illusion. There are questions of appearance versus reality throughout. Is the ghost of Hamlet's father real? Is he telling the truth about his murder? In everyday life, we do all kinds of things to uphold our self-image. But what is reality, and what is our true self?

Anything we can give a name to is a human experience. Humans have a particular type of consciousness—modes of knowing that are different than those of other species. Everyday reality is filtered through our own experience: religious beliefs, myths, science, and our own personal stories are influences. We can't know if there is a reality independent of the mind.

Within our conditioned mind is the prison of karma. He quoted Rumi, "Why do you stay in prison when the door is wide open?"

Our conditioned mind makes experience seem continuous, but in reality, our experiences are evanescent. He said, "Life is like a lucid dream."

"Now" is our connection to the timeless—the true continuity of life. You are the imperishable self.

Deepak talked about how excited he is that Jon Kabat Zinn and Rupert Spira are with us.

His personal yoga teacher is here, Sarah Finger. He talked about the seven spiritual laws of yoga and some of the principles of Ayurveda. He told us that he would be personally teaching us some sacred knowledge from the *Yoga Sutras of Patanjali* that he asked us not to share outside of the conference, so I am leaving them out of my journal. And then he opened it up to questions.

He was respectful and thoughtful with each question. Some were basic, and some were deeply thought provoking. Many people shared their personal experience as they came up to the microphone to ask their question. He was patient with each one.

We broke after Q&A, and lunch was set up as a buffet outside. It was a gorgeous, sunny day, and it was wonderful to sit outside. The food was delicious, marked either as vegan or vegetarian. It was all Ayurvedic. The tables were set in groups of twelve, so I joined a talkative, international group.

Everyone at the table seemed to know a lot about Ayurveda. Most had been to Seduction of Spirit before, and several had been on silent retreats the Chopra Center offered. It was interesting to meet all of these many people who are on a serious spiritual path. They said I would learn a lot about Ayurveda just by being here and experiencing the food.

In Ayurveda, there are six tastes or rasas: sweet, sour, salty, bitter, pungent, and astringent. Ayurveda recommends including each of the tastes in every meal. If you include the six tastes, your meal is more satisfying to the senses.

There were lentils and rice but also many kinds of warm vegetable salads with amazing dressings, many kinds of cooked vegetables, and also some cooked apples.

Lunch was not rushed, and there was time to go back to my room and call Rich before the afternoon session began.

In the afternoon session, we heard more from Deepak about the nature of reality. I took detailed notes. He alluded to some of the things that had been explored at Sages and Scientists and in the Synchro-Destiny course, talking about the origin of reality being outside our ability to explain it. Even mathematics can't be proven to exist outside our mental awareness of numbers. Nothing can be shown to exist outside our awareness.

Instead of asking how the world "out there" emerged from zero, we could start with the only thing we know with certainty and go from there. We know we experience reality.

Reality is experience itself. Every mind experiences sensations, images, feelings, and thoughts. Our mental activity creates our own personal reality. Reality can be explained as a state of awareness.

Creating personal reality is each person's joyful challenge. We can each elevate our inner world of awareness. We can all foster the evolution of consciousness. We can all reject the notion of separation and replace that with the idea of unity. This is how we can shift our reality.

Once we accept the idea that everything is an excitation in consciousness, the everyday world gets reduced to a dreamscape. You exist at the center of the dreamscape; you are that consciousness.

Ludwig Wittgenstein said, "We are asleep. Our life is a dream. But we wake up sometimes, just enough to know that we are dreaming."

After a good break, we came back to the afternoon meditation session that Roger led. I put my hair up in a ponytail and took off a layer, in case the heat response happened again. Once again, about fifteen minutes into the meditation, I experienced waves of heat coursing through my body from my core. I started sweating from head to toe and stopped meditating long enough to use the towel to wipe my arms, face, and neck. I looked around the room at everyone with their eyes closed and breathed deeply. I took a drink of water, and then when I felt a bit cooler, went back into the meditation. Again, the meditation seemed about forty or forty-five minutes long.

Then Deepak came back and started instructing us on some of the sacred teachings of the yoga sutras, which I kept out of my journal. Deepak will build on this each day. And then Roger instructed us how to transition from using the mantra to incorporating the sutra at the end of meditation.

After a brief break, we had the option of several yoga sessions including chair yoga. I chose the session with Sarah Finger. Each day she will dedicate the yoga practice to a spiritual law.

Today, Monday, was the law of giving and receiving. Sarah wove the law into the whole yoga practice, saying things like, "I practice breathing awareness in every pose" and "I acknowledge the gifts that life offers me" and "I allow, rather than force, my body into each posture." The mantra was *Om Vardhanam Namah*; I nourish the universe and the universe nourishes me. It was one of the most powerful yoga sessions I had ever experienced; I could sense the spiritual joy in Sarah and loved how accessible the session was. It was challenging but doable. The focus was on the devotion and the breathing as much as the posture itself, and Sarah gave modifications for every pose.

After yoga was an Ayurvedic dinner. Part of the teaching of Ayurveda is that lunch is the biggest meal of the day, so dinner was plenty but not enormous. And I felt very physically and emotionally tired and ready for bed and slept well.

April 19

I woke early and had tea before going to the gym when it opened at five. I did a quick interval workout and took a shower to make it in time for sunrise meditation at six-fifteen with Roger. Again, I dressed in harem pants with layers on the top; a tank top, a short sleeve shirt, and long sleeve shirt. Staff from the Chopra Center was stationed along the path with lanterns so that everyone could find their way in the dark. I took a shawl in case it was chilly, and a small towel in case the heat response happened again.

Roger was seated in the front, and there were rows of white chairs out on the lawn near the golf course at La Costa. Roger reminded us that noise is no obstacle in meditation, and when the lawn mowers started up as meditation began, we could see he was right.

I experienced tremendous internal heat again during the meditation, but the morning air was cool, and as I pulled the shawl off my shoulders and took off my outer layer, it was tolerable. At the end of meditation, Roger set the four intentions, and everyone repeated them silently:

- Joyful, energetic body
- Loving, compassionate heart

- Reflective, alert mind
- Lightness of being

Just as I opened my eyes, the sun peeped over the horizon; it was one of those phenomenal, memorable moments that felt like synchronicity.

We walked from meditation to yoga. Sarah Finger taught again today. It would be amazing to have such a gifted teacher on a regular basis. Sarah seems to radiate light. The law for Tuesday is the law of karma. The mantra was *Om Kriyam Namah*: "My actions are aligned with cosmic law." Sarah reminded us throughout the practice, "I am fully present with each body movement. I consider the consequences of my choices." She focused on awareness, being conscious of the choices we make. "Are my actions serving my spiritual growth? How do they impact those around me?"

Breakfast was on our own, so I went to the restaurant at La Costa, got an egg white omelet, and caught up on email. I got to the conference center early enough to sit down front on the floor and chose a place on the end so that if the heat response happened again and I needed to leave, it wouldn't be too disruptive.

Roger facilitated meditation again this morning. He reminded everyone that if they have significant sensations or emotions that it was just stress being released. He said that because we are meditating so deeply, so long, and so frequently this week that there may be a significant amount of stress being released. In regular life, this could be uncomfortable, but here at the retreat where no one has to drive or make big decisions and all the details like meals and the agenda are taken care of, it is the perfect place to experience deep meditation and release a lot of stress. I realized that I had been hanging onto stress related to Gussie, maybe for years. Though I am regular in my daily practice at home, this deep meditation is helping release stored emotion and the heat response is just that.

And, it happened again in the morning meditation: waves of heat roiling through from the internal part of my body. Again, I took time to come out of meditation for a few minutes, stripped off the outer layers, put my hair up, and used the towel to wipe down the sweat. As I did, I noticed several people throughout the auditorium sobbing quietly or gently moving to work on their own sensation in their body; they were experiencing different kinds of stress release. But no one cared; everyone was on their own journey. We meditated for about forty-five minutes, and then Roger led us in the special sutra we learned from Deepak yesterday and taught us how to link that to our regular meditation practice.

After the break, Jon Kabat Zinn came to speak to the group. I was excited to be sitting up front. He wore a pink shirt, and even though he is in his seventies, he looks and moves like someone much younger. He and Deepak clearly know each other well. Deepak introduced Jon and spent some time asking him questions like, how did you get started in meditation? Jon grew up in a family where his dad was a highly capable scientist and his mother was a painter. His father and mother saw with different eyes; they each had their own reality. In some sense, this expanded his interest in what reality really was; he had the perspective to see from both sides. Jon and Deepak traded stories about people who had influenced them, such as Phillip Kapleau, Huston Smith, Jiddu Krishnamurti, and David Bohm. They both have a love of poetry and quoted some of their favorites. They talked about consciousness and Buddhism.

Jon said that after he heard Phillip Kapleau speak, he started meditating and never stopped. The talk blew his mind. He said, "This is what I have been looking for my whole life."

He studied yoga and the Upanishads. Over time he began to train more in the bliss traditions and go on different retreats. He said the love affair was: how could I make a job for myself where I could be meditating all the time and share this pure potentiality with others?

In 1979, he began to bring meditation and yoga to mainstream medicine and bring relief to patients. Mindfulness-based stress reduction (MBSR) is now available in more than seven hundred clinics around the world. He said there are limits to what drugs, surgery, and psychological treatments can do. Challenging people to do something for themselves that nobody else can do for them helps mobilize deep interior resources. They discover in that process, that it can transform their relationship to suffering and pain, emotional or physical, or to mental processes.

He invited everyone to "drop in" every day. He does mindful yoga, and then he drops into sitting; he drops into the body and rests in awareness, wakefulness, and heartfulness. He suggests we drop in and rest also in daily life and to remember: "We are here right now; this is it." He says it's about being awake. Focus on the actuality of things as they really are. Capture your moments and pay attention; this is how we cultivate mindfulness; it's about being awake. The best we can do is to be the best version of ourselves.

He gave some advice to the group: beware the sage on the stage. Dive as deeply as you care to about the *teachings* versus the teachers. After a break, Roger led the group in another meditation. Again, I experienced the intense heat response.

The teacher's lunch was today, so I went to a specific room in the conference center and met with the Chopra Center staff and about forty others who were on the teacher's path. It was good to make new connections and hear how the staff will support our teaching efforts going forward. They talked about expectations for teacher's training, went through the timeline, and answered questions.

The afternoon session began with a recap of some research studies in the Seduction of Spirit retreat over time. The benefits of meditation begin almost immediately; the biological benefits at the cellular level are dramatic. In meditation, which is an inward journey, the mind-body system experiences deep rest as it transitions into a state of restful awareness. Rest is how the body heals itself. When we journey inward, we have expanded awareness and begin to release stress. In meditation:

- heart rate decreases
- blood pressure normalizes

- we breathe more deeply
- stress hormones reduce
- immunity is strengthened
- anxiety decreases
- our bodies produce more of the telomerase enzyme and anti-aging hormones
- inflammation decreases

Meditation gives us access to inner silence. When our mind and body experience less stress, we are better able to express the creativity and enthusiasm for life that derives from our soul.

Humans tend to look outside ourselves for happiness, fulfillment, and approval. Through meditation, we turn our attention within to rediscover the self, which is the source of all creativity, peace, and joy.

We practice meditation to restore the memory of wholeness, reconnect with the perfection that is already inside us, and then bring it back out into our daily lives. It's just remembering what we already know and then integrating it into our lives.

Next, Roger talked about the Software of the Soul. This was a refresher of what was taught in Primordial Sound Meditation. I took careful notes, realizing that I will soon be *teaching* this content.

The software of the soul is the conditioning of our past actions.

Quantum physics shows that a oneness exists between all creatures; we are all part of one unified whole: you, me, every tree, every plant, and every animal. Spirit is that field that connects everyone at the deepest level of existence.

The choices each of us makes differentiate one person from another. Memories and desires are created from our activity, which leads to more actions.

So, in the field of infinite possibilities, we each make our own choices, and this gives us individuality. My life is unique; your life is unique; we are only limited by our choices.

When we perform an action, (which is called *karma* in Sanskrit), it leads us to a memory of that action, (*sanskara*), and subsequent desires (*vasanas*). And the cycle continues on and on with desires leading to the next action.

I thought of an example I can use when I teach: "Imagine you go to the gym and you work out; that was the action and you enjoyed it and it made you feel good; now you have a memory of feeling good after the workout. That leads to a desire of wanting that same good feeling and that might lead to another action of going back to the gym again."

Memories and desires emerge from thinking. When we slip out of thought into the field of infinite possibilities, we step out of the prison of our memories and desires.

We transcend thought and slip into unbounded awareness when we meditate. Meditation allows us to move beyond limitations we create for ourselves and begin to reach our greater potential and move toward our higher and better self. As we meditate regularly, we expand that doorway a little more, and it is a cumulative effect.

Using a mantra helps to temporarily interrupt the activity of the mind and break the cycle of one thought that leads to the next thought and the next.

There is a Sanskrit term for this called *atma darshan*, which basically means glimpsing the domain of unbounded awareness. The mantra allows you to more easily glimpse that silent space between thoughts.

Next, Roger talked about the layers of life and showed a model developed by the sage Adi Shankara on the screens in the ballroom.

He said there is no distinct boundary between our personal and extended bodies. I got excited when I understood this; it is what I was trying to convey in my painting "City Girls." We are inextricably linked with our environment; it's part of us and we are part of it. I listened closely, knowing I would be teaching this to my students.

At a deeper level, we have what we call the subtle or psychological body where we have our mind, our thoughts, our ideas, and our emotions. A little deeper than that, we have the intellect, where we have ideas and concepts. More refined still, we have the ego. The ego is our self-image; it's not really who we are. It's who we think we are.

At the bottom of the model, we find our personal soul and the collective and universal domains.

Our soul is the individual aspect. According to Shankara, we arrive on the planet with a specific purpose and a set of talents. Given the right environment, the seeds sprout, and we are capable of expressing our gifts in the world. The second sheath of the causal body is the collective domain. This realm invites you to consider archetypes that you resonate with, like recognizing the gods and goddesses inside each of us.

I realize that the collective domain is what Jean Houston referred to in the salon during the archetype lesson, what Carolyn Myss referenced in her archetype exercise, what Deepak was alluding to in Synchro-Destiny, and what I connect with in journeys.

After I started using my own mantra I was able to more easily access this dimension of myself; that was the first time I felt the essence of my higher self.

Spirit links everything in creation. Meditation helps take us to these more refined layers. We pass through all these layers in the model until we reach the deepest level of silence. All these layers are part of the same wholeness; everything is joined and connected. Meditation brings that essence of oneness back into our lives.

Roger summarized: people are complex and multidimensional beings with many rich layers. We live life simultaneously on many levels, and when we have freer access to these different layers, we become more balanced and integrated.

So how are the soul and the spirit related? From the shore, the ocean appears to be infinite; it looks like it goes on forever. Think of the ocean as the universal spirit. But when we look at the ocean, we also see waves; each wave has its own individuality—the wave is like our individual soul that is an individual expression of the unbounded ocean. We can't separate the waves from the ocean just as we can't separate our individual soul from the spirit; it's part of it. I realize I used this same ocean and wave analogy in talking to Gussie.

After the break, Deepak came and taught the next of the sacred sutras. Then Roger led the group meditation, which led into the sutra practice. Again, I experienced extreme body heat and the sweating response. Then I again went to Sarah Finger's unforgettable yoga class.

And then Ayurvedic dinner. I realized I had not felt hungry this week at all; maybe there really is something to eating this way. Amanda reminded the group that tomorrow would be in silence. There was to be no talking until the afternoon session.

As I drifted off to sleep, I thought about the day and especially Jon Kabat Zinn's comment of "beware the sage on the stage." And I thought that he is right. Any teacher or metaphysical practitioner on this earth plane, no matter how enlightened, is still human, and humans inherently have blind spots, eccentricities, foibles and our own belief systems. I think back to corporate life when young executives would become disillusioned when one of their leaders did some less-than-perfect thing and how often I had to explain: yes, they are human. They make mistakes just like you and I do.

April 20

I did my now-familiar routine of short intense workout, shower, sunrise meditation, yoga, and breakfast. I loved doing everything in silence this morning. There was something so peaceful about not talking and communicating only with small gestures, head nods, and looking into people's eyes. The only words I spoke in the morning were at the restaurant when I ordered breakfast.

In the morning session, I again experienced the powerful heat response, yet now I almost welcomed it. I felt my body was purging deeply held toxins from all of those years of fear, anger, despair, guilt, and worry about Gussie. I wish all of my family could experience this freeing of stress. Even though I presumed I was mentally accepting the situation, my body must have hung onto deep-seated emotions.

Sitting in longer and more frequent meditations are getting at the deeper levels of what I was holding onto.

The law of the day for Wednesday is the Law of Least Effort, and Sarah wove it in beautifully into today's practice. "I accept my body as it is. I take responsibility for maintaining balance while strengthening my body. I practice flexibility in my thoughts and actions."

Deepak's lecture this morning was "How to Know God." I was excited because I recently read his book with this title. I took detailed notes. Deepak said he believes that the experience of God is available to everyone.

God is defined as infinite intelligence and therefore infinite creativity. When we create something new in our lives, we tap into the infinite mind. The miracles that are described in every spiritual tradition are manifestations of the creativity that we have access to when we tap into "the mind of God."

Einstein once said, "I want to know how God thinks; everything else is a detail."

Deepak said, "Creativity is a quantum leap in our consciousness. When we understand how miraculous healing occurs and why desires sometimes get fulfilled without any conscious effort on our part, then we have the ability to cocreate (with God) anything in our lives."

He explained that as we become familiar with higher states of consciousness, our nervous system changes so that we perceive things that we usually wouldn't in our normal waking state of consciousness. We begin to understand what Mohammed may have experienced when the angel Gabriel visited him, what Moses may have heard when he confronted God, or how Jesus may have performed the thirty-five miracles described in the New Testament. He said that there is a spark of divinity present in every being. When we pay attention to this spark and nurture it, it can become a brilliant flame that can transform our lives and those around us.

Hearing this makes me shiver. So maybe the "knowledge" and insights I have been gleaning are being allowed by my nervous system as I explore alternate states of consciousness. Maybe, as rudimentary as my explorations are, I am learning to glimpse some kind of a "visionary response."

At the silent lunch, I sampled the delicious Ayurvedic food and was mindful of each bite: a flavorful vegetable stew, spicy lentils with rice, a warm salad with bright vegetables, and some grilled tofu.

A feeling of gratitude washes over me; somehow being here and hearing everything is a kind of validation. There *is* more to life than what we perceive with our five senses. I can't wait to hear more.

After lunch, still in silence, I browsed the incredible art on sale. The artist displayed huge mandalas, like the ones I have been painting, but on large canvases; 36 x 36; 48 x 48. I inspected them trying to determine the technique. Surely, they are not hand-drawn because they are symmetrically perfect. Another mystery to solve but how inspiring!

In the afternoon session, Deepak talked about higher states of consciousness. I have now heard this lecture several times, but each time I hear it, I retain and understand more. Soon *I* will be teaching this content, and I wonder how to convey it in a way people understand it.

For me, just the confirmation that there *are* higher levels of consciousness is a tremendous feeling of—almost relief. Again, the realization solidifies inside me that there *is* more to life than what we experience when we are awake and asleep.

Deepak starts and reminds us that we are not our thoughts, we are not our mind, and we are not our body. It's our attention that localizes our nonlocal experiences.

When we slip into the gap, we meet the experiencer, which is the soul. The potential for all experiences is in the soul. We only know we've been somewhere nonlocal when we come out of it.

There are seven states of consciousness, and everyone can experience them on their spiritual journey. Each state of consciousness has its own biology. Each of them is only real when we are in it.

He talked about the three states of consciousness we are all very familiar with that we experience every day: waking, dreaming, and deep sleep. The average person is only aware of these three states of consciousness in their entire lifetime.

The brain functions are measurably different in each of these states. Brain biology and brain waves show precise and different characteristics between sleep, dream, and waking states of consciousness.

Deep Sleep (Sushupti Chaitanya)

This is a state that we slip into when we first fall asleep and we are sleeping very deeply with very little awareness. In this state, there is no thought. It's like we go back to our nonlocal ground state. There is no awareness of "me." In deep sleep, we consolidate memories, our body renews itself, and our immune system is strengthened.

Dreaming (Swapn Chaitanya)

Dreaming is a state where we release the emotional stress of the day. In dreams, there is more flexibility of space-time than in the waking state. Dreaming is the creation of an internal world, and it seems real at the time. Dreaming is more the dimension of our subtle body; it's not as clear as the waking state. In dreams, there is a subject/object split, so it's possible to identify the "I" or "me" and the "other." Dreams seem very real when you are in them. When we wake up from the dream, the dream loses its reality; it seems like a fabrication.

Waking (Jagrat Chaitanya)

This is where most people live their lives: an everyday, ordinary existence in a local state of consciousness in which the world appears to our senses as solid, structured, and bound by geographical space and time with linear time and logic.

The great yogis tell us that one day we will all wake up and realize that this relatively dull waking state, where we perceive ourselves as separate from everyone and everything is actually not real at all; it's more like a dream.

In this state, we experience ourselves and others as separate; we see a clear division between "me" and "other." Our experiences are stronger and seem more convincing than in the dream state and appear more real.

Just like the dream was real when you were in it, the waking state is real when you are in it. In enlightenment, you begin to realize that you can "wake up" from the waking state and go beyond this point. In this waking state, we are guided by habits, cultural coding, and personal conditioning. Our reality is structured by gender, physical characteristics, name, profession, family, and other affiliations.

We have been experiencing the first three states of consciousness, sleeping, dreaming, and waking, every day of our lives.

Transcendental (Turiya Chaitanya)

In this state, which we call Transcendental Consciousness, or *Atma Darshan*, we become aware of being and are conscious of being conscious; we are in the field of all possibilities, synchronicity, creativity, correlation, and unpredictability. We glimpse the soul in this state. Our intentions become very powerful, and we have a profound experience of connection, love, compassion, joy, goodness, and peace. At this level, we begin to lose the subject/object split and realize that I and the other are both contained within me. We experience more intuition, more insight, more detachment, and synchronicity. Intention becomes more powerful, and we have less anxiety and fear.

Every time we meditate and slip into the gap, we experience this fourth state of consciousness.

The first three levels of consciousness are localized; they exist in space and time. *Atma Darshan*, however, is nonlocal; it exists beyond space and time. This is why you are only aware of it after you come out of it. To experience anything, it has to exist in space and time.

Deepak and Roger talked about the importance of integration—having the experience of slipping into the gap and then integrating it back into daily life. Meditation is just a tool we use to enrich our lives, and we go from the deep rest of meditation to activity.

As we access our authentic self, we experience less emotional drama in our lives. Our relationships become more loving and compassionate, and we find a deeper, more caring relationship with the environment. With the experience of the silent witness, our biology also reflects greater balance.

Cosmic (Turiyatita Chaitanya)

Cosmic consciousness is the state in which soul consciousness gets stabilized, and the witnessing awareness is present all the time in waking, dreaming, and sleeping states. This state of consciousness is sometimes described in wisdom traditions as being both local and nonlocal simultaneously.

The silent witness self is unbounded, but the body and the conditioned mind are localized; "being in the world and not of the world" describes this flavor of cosmic consciousness.

In this state, even during deep sleep, our witnessing awareness is fully awake. We have the realization that we are not the mind-body physiology, which is in the field of change, but rather an eternal spirit that transcends space and time. The most remarkable aspect of this state of consciousness is the knowledge of our nature as timeless and eternal. We lose our fear of death.

In cosmic consciousness, we are in a state of grace, being taken care of by our innermost being. We are slowly detaching from the roles that we play, yet we still play and enjoy them. The mind is now fully awake, and we recognize the divinity within ourselves.

In this state, we tap into the place of our own mythology, and we can more clearly see where our personal story joins a more universal story as we tap into the archetypal realm. We can see our life in broader context and see the larger story of our life. We begin to see deeper meaning behind our experiences.

Divine (Bhagavad Chaitanya)

As we continue to meditate, divine consciousness unfolds. We can truly feel the presence of spirit in everyone and everything. The heart fully awakens, and the ego dissolves in love. Deepak talked about the story of Buddha's Lesson of the Flower. He held a flower, and his disciple Ananda was looking at the flower. He smiled at the Buddha, and Buddha smiled back and then left; that was the end of the lesson. All the other disciples went up to Ananda and said, "We saw a flower; what did you see?" Ananda said, "I saw the flower but I also saw sunshine and earth and water and rainbows and stars and galaxies and the infinite void. I saw the whole universe stopping along the way, pretending to be a flower." So, we begin to see the universe in all things and start to see everything at a more refined level. Some may see light around people or objects; some may become much more intuitive, even clairvoyant or clairaudient.

We recognize the divinity in everyone and everything. So, every object in the world can be seen with the deep sense of understanding and compassion. We start to be in touch with pure love. The ego stops challenging us. In this state the whole universe is like a speck of dust; God is not difficult to find but impossible to avoid.

Wherever we go we feel the presence of the divine. At this stage, we have an even greater conviction of immortality and the enduring presence of divine love. Divine consciousness also brings a deeper experience of liberation where we see the world as an extension of the beauty and love of our consciousness.

Unity (Brahmananda Chaitanya)

Unity consciousness is the state of being one with everything. We still maintain our own localized individuality, our individual expression of the totality, but realize that, at the level of spirit, there is no separation. There is no you or me, just oneness—the same witness. There is only one witness, and that is you. You are the witnessing awareness, and that is called enlightenment; infinite consciousness.

This state of enlightenment is sometimes compared to the drop of water that is experiencing itself as the ocean, knowing that it was the ocean the whole time. You and God are now one because there is no you left anymore. You are not the drop in the ocean; you are the ocean in the drop.

Sometimes when people try to conceptualize this, they may be afraid that in losing their old identity they will lose their existence, memories, and individual perspective. But enlightened beings don't see it that way. They understand that personal identity was an illusion to begin with.

They realize that nothing real or valuable is ever lost on the path to enlightenment. They are experiencing their original identity but are only now recognizing it in its completeness and its full glory.

Deepak and Roger said that just by going back and forth between local and nonlocal awareness during meditation, we begin to explore all the layers of our existence. These higher states of consciousness unfold naturally and spontaneously over time.

The Sanskrit expression for this realization is *aham brahmasmi*—I am the universe.

Amanda then came to the stage and said that we were free to move out of the silent part of the day. We took a break, and then came back for Deepak's lesson on the next set of sutras and then meditation.

Once again, I had the sensation of powerful waves of heat coursing through my body, with the sweat response, and I remembered some of the key messages about the law of the day: least effort. Just accept it as it is. Surrender; don't resist. Find the hidden meaning or gift in every situation. And so, I took a break from meditating, toweled off, and let myself imagine that this heat was burning up the toxins and stresses in my body, which will allow me to move forward with more grace. And then I went back to the meditation.

Amanda announced that tonight there will be a special lecture on Jyotish, which is Vedic astrology.

Yoga was great again with Sarah, and dinner was the perfect amount of food. I decided to go to the lecture.

The speaker was Brent BecVar. He explained how he got into the field. He had studied Western astrology and then moved into Jyotish. He was a Vedic teacher for the Chopra Center. Deepak invited Brent on a trip to Allahabad, India during which he had a life-changing direct encounter with Swami Vasudevananda Maharaj. It was after that encounter that Deepak asked Brent to develop the Vedic Counseling Program for the Chopra Center. Jyotish or Vedic astrology is an integral part of Vedanta; it is the science of light, or science of consciousness,a sacred subject.

He explained some differences between Jyotish and Western astrology. The Vedic chart is square versus the round Western chart. Vedic astrology gives a better view of a person's karmic tendencies and when such tendencies are likely to manifest.

He said that the times of life events are shown through a detailed system of planetary time cycles, called *dashas*. There is no corresponding method in Western astrology. Western astrologers who make a study of the subject often find themselves converting to Vedic astrology because of its greater scope, depth, and accuracy for predicting the future.

The basic difference between the two systems is that the Vedic zodiac is Sidereal and the Western is Tropical.

Brent showed some actual charts, including Deepak's Jyotish chart and explained how the chart will provide information about relationships, children, career, and even someone's dharma, or purpose.

My eyes were closing because of the long day but I decided to make an appointment for a Jyotish reading as part of my spiritual journey.

April 21

I went through my morning routine as usual. Today's law of the day was the law of intention and desire. "I am clear on my intentions for each pose. I surrender to the process. I practice present moment awareness with each posture."

Once again, I had the waves of heat pulsing through my body during the morning meditation and sutra practice, but it seemed less distracting and less violent.

Then Amanda talked more about the law of the day and how our intentions and desires are supported by cosmic intelligence. She described a process of listing desires, releasing the desires, and practicing present-moment awareness. To practice, think of something you want to create in your life. Hold the intention effortlessly in your awareness during the day. Allow the universe to organize things for you. See if and how it manifests while remaining open to other possibilities.

Then we went through an exercise and listed our desires; what do I really want? Amanda said, this gets simpler over time; we get clear as we focus on our heart; where intention goes, energy flows. We listed our desires in categories: physical body, material desires, emotional desires, purpose/dharma desires, spiritual desires, relationship desires, lifestyle.

I wrote my list for each category, and when I got to lifestyle, I got even clearer about my desire to move west and be able to see mountains out my window every day. I began to visualize my painting studio and a private, quiet space for studying and teaching. How cool if this desire would actually manifest.

In Deepak's lecture this morning, he did a deeper dive on the Eight Limbs of Yoga and then linked it to the laws of the day that Sarah has been weaving into our daily practice.

Deepak described how yoga has moved from relative obscurity to being offered in thousands of locations in just a couple of decades. Although yoga is commonly considered a fitness trend, it's actually the core of the Vedic science that developed more than five thousand years ago.

The essence of yoga is the union or integration of all the layers of life—physical, emotional, and spiritual. It is a practice for going beyond the ego's identification with the mind and body and directly experiencing our true spiritual self. Rooted in this connection to spirit, Deepak said, we are able to solve the challenges that arise in life with greater ease and grace.

The yoga sutras describe the eight branches or "limbs" of yoga, providing a clear roadmap for the evolution of consciousness from ordinary states of awareness such as waking, dreaming, and sleeping—to the higher states of consciousness.

Beyond looking at yoga as just a way to exercise the body, the deeper meaning and gift of yoga is the path it offers us into the timeless, spaceless world of spirit. Yoga teaches us both to let go and to have exquisite awareness in every moment. In this expanded state of consciousness, we experience freedom from suffering. We remember our essential spiritual nature, and life becomes more joyful, meaningful, and carefree.

The afternoon session featured Rupert Spira.

He came to the stage wearing a cardigan sweater; I resonated with his calm voice and gentle presence. He sat down and spoke slowly and clearly about being aware of being aware.

He said it is impossible to experience the appearance of awareness. We have no experience of a beginning to awareness; no experience of its birth. We have no experience that we, awareness, are born. Likewise, in order to claim legitimately that awareness dies, something would have to be present to experience its disappearance. Have we ever experienced the disappearance of awareness? If we think the answer is *yes*, then what is it that is present and aware to experience the apparent disappearance of awareness? Whatever that is must be aware and present. It must be awareness.

He also said love, peace, and happiness are inherent in the knowing of our own being. In fact, they are the knowing of being. They are simply other names for our self.

Then he led us in an exercise saying, "I am aware that I am aware." I somehow lost time during the meditation and had to gently come back into my body.

After the break, Deepak taught the next layer of sacred sutras, and then we did the afternoon meditation. I experienced the heat sensations, but they were more muted than in the morning, and I was able to make it through the hour easily.

In the evening session of yoga, Sarah again focused on the law of the day.

At dinner, I realized that I felt loopy, and someone said, "Well, if you attended every session, you had nearly four hours of meditation today; maybe that's why." At the dinner, I discovered that many of the participants didn't attend all the sessions; they looked at the schedule and picked and chose which session to attend. This shocked me; I had never considered skipping a session for a spa treatment or just to take a break. No one else at my table had been to the sunrise meditation session. I didn't judge them but was surprised; every session seems so precious to me, and I don't want to miss anything.

April 22

I did my morning routine of workout, sunrise meditation yoga, and breakfast. The law of the day was the law of detachment. Sarah wove it into our practice: "I relinquish my attachment to the outcome of the pose. I cultivate an attitude of curiosity and wonder. I release into the full potential of each posture."

I got warm in the group meditation, but the impact was even less than yesterday; I must have moved through much of the stress. The hour seemed to go by quickly.

In the general session this morning, Deepak focused on the idea that "You are the universe" and the notion that "universe" is a human word. I felt riveted; this is the topic he and Menas Kefatos were talking about at the Sages and Scientist symposium that I found so engaging.

He said that the universe that you and I experience is in human consciousness. Unless we know the nature of our consciousness, we will not understand how we participate in creating both a personal and a collective reality. The universe is in the experience. It's not just out there; it's also "in here."

Then he talked about Einstein, quantum physics, the use of imagination to solve problems and gravity, how atoms behave, and supernovas.

And then he told the story of Einstein meeting the great poet and philosopher Tagore and the connection the two men felt. Tagore said "this world is a human world ... the world apart from us does not exist. It is a relative world, depending for its reality upon our consciousness."

Then Deepak did his sutra teaching for the day and took questions. I had two questions prepared and stood in line for a microphone until it was my turn.

I asked Deepak, "I once read that when a person meditates, they burn karma; do you believe this is true?" and he said "Definitely," and he talked about ourselves after conditioning; when we are born, we are like a fresh snowy white cloth. Then conditioning happens from our parents, bosses, and all of our life experiences, and thus, our cloth becomes dingy and dirty. Every time we meditate, it is like dipping the cloth in a stream of clear water. Each time, some of that conditioning washes away, and the cloth become cleaner every time you dip it in the stream.

I thanked him and asked my second question, "I once heard someone muse: "What if we live in a recreational universe? Can you tell me where this idea generated?"

Deepak said, "Yes, this is the concept of Lila or Leela. There is a question in Hinduism about whether Brahman had some purpose in creating the world. The concept is that the world is merely a spontaneous creation of Brahman. It is a Lila, or sport, of Brahman. It is created out of Bliss, by Bliss, and for Bliss."

Then Deepak said goodbye to everyone; he had to fly out that afternoon.

Amanda announced a special guest yoga instructor would teach after lunch. And she said the afternoon session would be a surprise.

The special yoga instructor was an adorable six-year-old; the youngest yoga instructor in the United States. He had a sweet nature, a big afro, and a great story. He learned yoga with his mom when she was going for cancer treatments. He did an awesome job.

I went back to pack before the afternoon session.

In the afternoon session, we went back into silence and formed two large human circles, one inside the other. Soul-filling music was playing. We moved from person to person, holding palms out to one another and gazing soul to soul into one another's eyes.

Then they turned up the music, and we had a big dance party in the ballroom that was now empty of tables and chairs; it was fun and a great energy release.

We did the afternoon meditation outside, and then everyone broke to get ready for the party. At the party, there was a talent show, dinner, and dancing.

April 23

The law of the day was the law of dharma, and Sarah also covered Sunday's law, which is the law of pure potentiality.

During the practice, she reminded us, "I am awake to the gaps between breaths and movements. I honor my talents. I cultivate an attitude of service." She said that dharma evolves throughout our lives. Our ultimate dharma is to be self-realized—to learn our lessons and to be on the path of awareness.

After breakfast, I checked out and took my bag to the conference center.

We did an extra-long morning meditation, and then Roger and Amanda wrapped up the week. On the flight home, I typed up all my notes from the session.

As I fly, I think about how good I felt eating Ayurvedic food this week and consider whether it is time to draw a clearer line in the sand on what I do and do not eat.

I think about some of the discussion this week: mammals are close to humans; they give birth to live offspring. They nurse their young from their breasts. They have a neo-cortex. They have emotions. I am ready to take at least one step and say I don't eat mammals.

I tried to feel my way into the notion of "I don't eat pork or beef, but I eat fish and chicken. It's not making the full leap to being vegetarian, but it moves me along the path in a natural way. At least it would be a conscious, thoughtful choice. If you were to consider it from the standpoint of minimizing harm to sentient beings, a nonmammalian diet is only partial. But it is a step. Then chicken and fish can be decided later. I don't know how Rich will feel about it. I know some Buddhists are omnivores, but I suspect there is a thoughtful choice in there somewhere along the way, like making sure the food comes from the most humane source.

I try to decide if I can now fully answer the question of who I connect to in meditation and if it is the same essence I journey to. Are my guides external beings, or are my guides and dream messages really just created by my higher self, my own internal guidance system? If that's true, messages like "prepare for death" are just my own intuition or my own internal higher intelligence system at work. This seems to resonate; I think I am just finally tapping into my own higher intelligence.

I have heard many different names for the nonphysical: guides and angels; entelechy and archetypes. I now believe strongly we are all extensions of source energy; we are all vibrational beings, and we must somehow connect back to a bigger vibration that we were part of before we were born in this life and that we will be absorbed into again. So, when I connect to my higher self in meditation, see my light beings, feel Bhodi, journey to Hawk, or invoke Leonardo in front of a canvas, are those all connections to the same energy? I believe they are part of something I am also part of. But, are there higher and lower vibrations within the energy? I have to keep this on my open question list.

Rich and the pups picked me up at the airport. How good it is to be home.

April 24

We meditated and got coffee. Rich played golf; I painted. We drove around to see everything greening up and beginning to bloom. The dogwoods and cherry blossoms are coming. Lots of daffodils are starting to peek out.

I recapped the whole week for Rich when I got home last night. He agrees, suggesting let's try it on eating no beef or pork and see how it feels. Raleigh is here with us for a few days; beef and pork are staples in his diet, so we will need to prepare options at mealtime.

I went to the basement, retrieved Bethany's painting, and looked at it from all angles to consider my next step. I recorded a video segment laying out choices and sent it to Bethany. She says she likes the feeling of being with me when I am painting and loves seeing how it unfolds. I feel this one is emerging on its own, and I am just facilitating, providing the paint and the arms and hands.

We got carryout so we could order fish, and we got Raleigh a pork chop, which he loved. After dinner, I went to the basement and painted another layer on Bethany's painting. It is emerging as a gold light being surrounded by teal and magenta. Chakras are partly visible. As I have painted, I have also embedded subtle sacred symbols and numbers along with prayers and intentions for Bethany's health and prosperity. The painting might be done. I will let it dry and take another look then.

I have been thinking about Deepak's response to my question and did some research about releasing karma through meditation. I found an article by Roger Gabriel on the subject.

Through meditation, our consciousness expands, helping us to reduce the impact of contracted karma. The practice also gives us the awareness to avoid creating new karma and dissolve stored karma.

Karma is locked away in our memories and desires, both of which are in the mind.

The karma being processed during this incarnation is in the conscious mind, while the remaining, stored karma is lying dormant in what we refer to as the unconscious mind. Meditation takes us beyond the mind to the realm of infinite possibilities. We transcend thought, memories, and desires.

The journey back and forth from local to nonlocal "washes" the karma on all levels. This is exciting news for those of us on a spiritual path. We all have the potential to be enlightened in this lifetime. The contracted karma will be released one way or another during our life:

By making conscious choices, we can avoid adding karma to the bag.

Through the process of meditation, we can transcend any karma left in the bag.

April 25

The shamanic apprenticeship this week focused on death walks (times of loss and transition; cycles of death and rebirth). The advice is to pay attention to your body; it's telling you what you need to know. Learn what makes you fluid, agile, and resilient. Can you lose your agenda and pick up Spirit's agenda? Learn the lesson: I'm not being picked on; I am being refined. I wonder if witnessing Gussie's pain was a death walk.

I took Bethany's painting and hung it in my big easel upstairs in the studio so I could see it in the light. I like it quite a bit. I did another video and sent it to her to see what she thought. I also gave her another option of a different painting in case she liked that one better. She said she loves the yellow light being. I declared it done. I rolled it up and sent it in a tube. She will frame it there.

We drove around with Raleigh to see spring budding and then had a simple supper with corn relish, green beans, orzo, and some salmon.

April 26

It was so fun painting Bethany's painting; I want to make more art that is for a specific person with sacred intentions embedded. It is fun to ponder how to do this.

My days seem remarkably free now, and I find myself missing Gussie. We are planning her services for next month when the kids are out of school

Raleigh left today. More friends and neighbors stopped by to get paintings I am giving away. I take a picture of each one that is leaving, and it makes me happy to think of them in a new home. I let "City Girls" go. I will paint the girls again when we move. Maybe they will be mountain girls.

Roasted vegetables. Two chilly, windy walks. I painted in the messy part of the basement and then tidied it up for a showing. It will be nice to sell the house and get settled so I can keep my painting area messy all the time.

Rich played golf. I took some books and magazines to the senior center during the house showing, and the dogs came with me. I like it when the showings are close together because the house stays pretty clean; it's just a matter of inspecting for dog hair and then doing the light, candle, and music routine.

Chapter Eleven
May

In May, I savor the sweet routine of our days: meditation, exercise, fresh air, painting, class time, healthy food, and working with Rich on our partnership. Gussie's funeral and celebration of life services are held, and we celebrate dad's ninetieth birthday. The main phase of the shamanic apprenticeship is winding down, and I prepare for final testing and certification from the Chopra Center.

May 5

Pink cherry blossoms and white dogwood are blooming; everything is lush. Rich calls these clear days where you can almost taste the sunshine "chamber of commerce" days. It's hard to believe the rainforest-like beauty in contrast to the stark, brown desolate landscape of two months ago.

We spent much of the week outside: biking, planting herbs, and watering new sod. I planted flowers on Beau's grave. It's a strange comfort to know that while his ashes will stay here in Ohio, memories of Beau will go wherever the pack goes—and I can almost feel it in the air; we will be going soon.

We are still making small philanthropic donations in our Ohio community, thinking, "Until we are not here, we are here." We often now talk about the law of giving and receiving and consciously realize that even very small gifts, like a smile or opening a door or anything good that can be done for someone, helps cultivate the feeling of circulating love; in giving, we receive. We helped pay for a trip to Cedar Point and got a nice note back.

Dear Rich and Jane,
I want to express my gratitude for all that you have done to
help our kids climb the mountain to college. I shared the
Cedar Point trip with our eighth-graders this morning and our
joy was amazing to see!
Much love and respect, Alex

However, after my time with Jean Houston, and through work in the apprenticeship, I feel my philanthropic interests becoming more global, and Rich is right there with me. I have chosen Mercy Corp as the group I am supporting through regular intentions and attention. As I have followed them, I have become increasingly moved by their stories, particularly as they have helped in the aftermath of natural disasters, famine, and refugee crises.

Charitable institutions and humanitarian groups, like people, are never perfect. But there is a lot I like about Mercy Corps. They are secular and nonpolitical. In crisis, they believe in the power of human potential, and they help communities grow stronger, believing that local people are the best agents of their own change. They partner to address root causes of conflict, help farmers be more productive, empower girls and women, and much more. We are now supporting them philanthropically.

May 10

Gussie's funeral and celebration of life memorial service have come and gone. Mia, Mark, and Mason planned the celebration of life event attended by hundreds of Gussie's former students. Moving tributes and stories, incredible music, poetry and love abounded. Teresa delivered the eulogy at both services. I was proud that the whole family agreed to be transparent about Gussie's alcoholism and mental illness.

Teresa started off by thanking everyone who came and by talking about Gussie's life from toddler to adult. She spoke about Gussie's close love and friendship with Joe, her love of music, her time as music teacher, and her award-winning honors choir and children's chorus. Teresa described Gussie's natural generosity and beautiful spirit, but further explained:

In addition to all that was so beautiful about Augusta, there was a dark place in her too. She was an alcoholic. For years, she tried to get well. We felt helpless watching her sink further and further into her alcoholism. We all had feelings of anger, confusion, fear and sadness. For so long there was hope, too, that things might change.

We know that alcoholism is a disease. She fought that demon on a daily basis for the last decade, and many days she defeated it; those were sweet victories for her and for her family. But the days when the demon was stronger were terrible days, and she could not win no matter how hard she tried. She stopped teaching a few years ago when her health was too bad to continue. The last few years were very difficult for her, for Mason, and for the children. She tried several jobs that didn't work out. She fought many battles but could not stay sober for very long."

Her family experienced heartbreak, financial burden, tears, anxiety, frustration, fear, anger, and so many other things. We wanted to help her find her way back to that beautiful woman who wanted everyone to love music. In the end, our lesson was to not give up on the ones we love, that tough love didn't help her, and that caring and compassion at the end was the best choice.

The past few months were torture for her, her children, and her family. We all learned. Hidden within her addiction was mental instability. We know that people do not choose addiction; there is a trigger caused by a need to stop the pain of the depression and anxiety and the demon that plagued her. It is hard to say these things, but to not mention her struggles is to let her die without the acknowledgment of the strength she often glimpsed and tried so hard to maintain.

In spite of all Gussie's difficulties, and as hard as her life was, she found ways to make it beautiful. Her music, and especially her choirs, were an amazing gift. Her love of others and her compassion and generosity made other people's lives better. And her greatest achievement, along with her husband Mason, is the two beautiful young adults they created together. Mark and Mia are exceptional, gifted, amazing young people. Despite the fact that they faced huge challenges growing up, Mia and Mark are talented, strong, confident, and ready to make their mark on the world.

And then Teresa paraphrased a speech by Physicist Aaron Freeman to NPR in 2005 where he talks about the physics of death. He says:

Remember first law of thermodynamics—that no energy gets created in the universe and none is destroyed. All the energy, every vibration, every BTU of heat, every wave of every particle that was our beloved Gussie remains in this world.

All the photons that ever bounced off her face, all the particles whose paths were interrupted by her smile, by the touch of her hair, hundreds of trillions of particles, have raced off like children, their ways forever changed by her. And these photons were gathered in the particle detectors that are the eyes of those who love her. And those photons create within us constellations of electromagnetically charged neurons whose energy will go on forever, and ever, and ever …

And if you don't have faith … if you don't believe that she is still here simply on faith, it's fine. You can measure. Scientists have measured precisely the conservation of energy and found it accurate, verifiable, and consistent across space and time. The science is sound, and we can all be comforted to know her energy is still around. According to the law of the conservation of energy, not a bit of Gussie is gone. She's still here; she's just organized a little differently.

Goodbye, dear Gussie. Your humor, compassion, generosity, and lovingkindness will continue to inspire us forever.

May 20

For our dad's ninetieth birthday party, he wanted just a simple celebration; his request was that everyone go to Mass with him. And we did, before an afternoon reception with punch and cake, in a hall decorated with family photos. Over a hundred people came to honor him.

I got some private time with him to read him a letter I had written:

Dear Dad,
I am very grateful for the spiritual inspiration you have given me. Your life-long devotion is one of the reasons I've spent time and energy seeking greater understanding of different belief systems and how people who have really thought about it answered the big existential questions: why are we really here and what is it all about?

I have deep reverence for people of faith, born from watching your mother, you, and your brothers and sisters practice your faith daily in thought, word, and deed. I can see that you have lived your life in a state of grace.

I believe that the face of God looks different to different people but that we all can get to the same place, entering the same beautiful room from different doors.

I'm grateful for the belief in a soul, in immortality, and in the idea that there is something bigger than each of us, that we will be together again after this life.

One of my teachers believes that before we are born, we choose our families. We choose our parents and kids and siblings, and we have a say in the challenges and lessons we will experience in life. I think this is a pretty cool thing to ponder. I'd choose you all over again. Happy ninetieth birthday!

Love forever,

Jane

May 21

I have enjoyed every aspect of my teacher certification at the Chopra Center. It is rigorous but a beautiful process, and I relished going deeper in my understanding of Ayurveda and Vedanta. Reading the Upanishads, the Rig Veda, the Bhagavad Gita, and so many of Deepak Chopra's books in advance was wonderful grounding, and it kept me from becoming overwhelmed taking the shamanic apprenticeship at the same time as the Chopra Center course.

When I am certified, I will be able to give my students their own Sanskrit mantra; I see this as a great honor. I will be critiqued while teaching all the segments of class, and I will be evaluated on my content knowledge and teaching presence. There is also an extensive written exam.

Another requirement is to memorize and be able to chant the Shanti Mantra, a chant full of ancient meaning that honors all the many teachers that have gone before.

Although it is not required to graduate, I have also registered to attend a week-long Ayurvedic experience at the Chopra Center called Perfect Health. I think this will give me deeper understanding and make me a better teacher.

May 25

The shamanic apprenticeship continues to deepen, and the lessons become more complex. I think of each new journey as a chance to keep strengthening my spiritual muscles and experiencing connection with nonphysical energy. Often, my rational mind rebels. I continue to remind myself that it is OK, even if some or all elements of the journey are an exercise in pretending. Imagination is a gift that children have in abundance, but most adults keep it firmly hidden away. Even if I am only exercising imagination, that is still a part of my higher intelligence.

Finally, after months of learning we were finally given permission to "do" things in the shamanic realm. My fellow apprentices and I started by doing things for ourselves. I made myself an extrovert for the first time in my life and experienced a week of an easy, outgoing, chatty nature, which was quite freeing. At the end of the week, I undid it and reverted to my typical personality.

My tribe has plowed our way through months of tough feedback from our teachers. We shared our journeys and learned from each other's mistakes as the teachers critiqued and explained alternative choices of direction.

In learning to journey for clients, we began with Tribe Mates, and the teachers provided detailed critical review of our work. We were asked to go back again and again and correct small mistakes in technique. Though I do not expect to journey for clients in the future, I still enjoyed this level of rigor and scrutiny and began to gain confidence that I was making connections to source energy.

We spent weeks studying Norse runes. I did extra research on binding runes and created some I felt were powerful and beautiful. I wove them into my art, feeling their power and ancient history.

The apprentices, under close supervision, created personal rituals for altar, space, and clearing methods, use of runes, our own set of intentions for working with others, creating a medicine bag, and developing ceremonies to the four elements (fire, water, earth, and air energies).

In addition, with the support of my teachers, I also studied Egyptian mythology, posting my journeys, so my teachers could monitor my progress and insights.

May 29

My designated sabbatical year of deep spiritual study is coming to an end. Someday I want to do sacred travel to Machu Picchu, Lake Titicaca, the Nazca Plains; to the Holy Land, to an ashram in India, and most of all to Egypt—Cairo, the Giza Plateau, Elephantine Island, Philae, Edfu, and the Luxor Temple to deeply study Egyptian mysteries.

For now, instead of going physically to Egypt, I have gone there in my studies and journeys. I read *Shamanic Mysteries of Egypt* again and again, following the recommended meditations and journeys for what the authors call "the first and second great round." These are iterations of ancient rituals to reclaim divinity while maintaining humanity and are written by Nicki Scully and Linda Star Wolf.

The Egyptian *neteru* resonate strongly with me and make me feel connected to a high vibration. They seem to be forms of source or archetypal energy that are particularly enlivening for my imagination: Anubis, the opener of the way; Khnum, the master craftsman; and Sekhmet who plants seeds of sacred purpose. Thoth inspires illumination, and Ma'at, makes it clear that the true purpose of all life is to know one's self; the more we seek to find divinity outside of ourselves, the more we are allowed to see that is has always been there within. Khepera is a guide to help me be a co-creator of my own reality, my own universe. Hathor, medicine woman guide, tastes from her cauldron to see if the flavors of my life are coming together. Sothis, the Bodhisattva star goddess, encourages me to share what I have learned, to help others on the path to ascend to higher levels of consciousness, and Ptah, the deity of craftsmen and builders, inspires a desire for a world rich in beauty where no one is hungry and there is abundance for all.

Chapter Twelve
June

In June, I begin to feel as though I am moving into more conscious orchestration of my life and enjoy the feeling of living life on multiple levels. I still feel I have one foot planted in the real, material world of everyday life, but I feel more constantly aware that I am much more than my mind, my body, and my thoughts. I attend the Perfect Health retreat at the Chopra Center to learn about Ayurveda.

June 1

Perfect Health is the Chopra Center Ayurvedic Lifestyle Program. Ayurveda is a 5,000-year-old healing system from India that offers a guide for a life of happiness, vitality, love, and purpose and is derived from the Sanskrit words *ayus*, meaning life, and *veda*, meaning wisdom. Ayurveda teaches that humans are fields of intelligence in dynamic exchange with the energy and information in our environment. Health is a state of vibrant balance in which all the layers of life are integrated.

As instructed, I began to prep for Perfect Health the week before I went, eating the recommended vegetarian diet and taking Gugullu and Triphala herbs.

Class began at 7:30 on Monday morning in the Dharma Room at the Chopra Center. There were twenty-nine people in class—four men and twenty-five women. We were greeted by Dr. Sheila Patel and Michelle White.

Dr. Patel was one of my teachers for Primordial Sound Meditation, and I was excited to see her in person. We went on a tour of the center and saw the private meditation room that had two special reclining, zero-gravity, grounded relaxation chairs—special chairs from the "earthing" company that provides products to ground you to the earth for a rejuvenating effect.

We saw the Chopra Center treatment rooms, the medical offices, the larger community meditation and yoga rooms, and the La Costa spa where many of the treatments would take place.

Dr. Patel explained that disease is a physical imbalance and/or emotional turbulence. Ayurveda aligns us with our natural cycles; it is based on timeless principles from the laws of nature.

This program is a detoxification, rejuvenation, and a purification to get rid of *ama*—toxins that interfere with the natural state of health.

The program addresses mind, body, and spirit. At our seats, each of us had a box containing "Purify" product—the first part of the cleanse protocol. This was a container of gluten-free fiber, some special supplements, a bottle of special oil, and a specially designed mixing container with a blue lid that contained a wire spiral to help mix water with the fiber. We all took the first dose together; everyone shaking the mixture and waiting for someone to take the first swig of the fiber solution, supplements, and oil. It didn't taste bad, but we were all wondering if we were going to need to make a fast break for the restrooms.

They also gave us a tongue scraper and some "swish" liquid to use for oil pulling.

My beloved meditation teacher, Roger Gabriel, delivered the next lecture. He reviewed the five elements: space (*akasha*), air (*vatu*), fire (*tejas*), water (*jala*), and earth (*prithivi*). The three Ayurvedic Doshas are derived from the five elements. These Doshas are responsible for every function of our mind and body. The three Doshas are known as *vata, pitta,* and *kapha.*

Each of the participants had completed a detailed mind/body questionnaire prior to arriving, so everyone knew their Doshas. My primary Dosha is a blend of Pitta/Kapha in my body, and my mind is Tri-Doshic: a blend of all three.

This was a detailed lecture with information about the qualities of each Dosha, significant attributes, physical characteristics, temperament, how things look when the person is in and out of balance, and stress responses. Physically, Vatas are typically thin and light; when out of balance, they are anxious and worried and have delicate digestion. Pittas usually have a medium build and when out of balance can be irritable, harsh, and judgmental. Kaphas tend to be heavier set with an amazing ability to get good sleep. When out of balance, they can be clingy and too attached.

He went on to explain that unhealthy lifestyle choices can cause imbalance in the Doshas. The lecture was followed by lunch (lentils and rice) and the first spa treatment, called the Odyssey.

My spa treatment that day was in the La Costa spa. I put on my robe and sat outside under a perfect seventy-degree day amid colorful plantings and serene spa music. The Chopra-trained therapist, Sonia, explained the treatment before I started and said she would "hold silence" during the treatment so I could relax and enjoy it but said to speak up if I needed anything.

She chose the spicy/sweet aroma appropriate for my Dosha. The Odyssey began with *garshana,* dry skin brushing using silk gloves to stimulate the skin and lymphatic system. Next, she covered me in a warm herbal oil for the *abhyanga* (oil massage) with special friction strokes designed to move the oil deep into tissues to loosen stored toxicity. *Vishesh* followed—slow, penetrating strokes to enhance relaxation and the elimination of more toxins. The treatment ended with *marma* therapy, a light touch in several points on my face, feet, and other points to awaken inner energy. Like a door or pathway, activating a marma point opens the inner pharmacy of the body. Touching a marma point changes the body's biochemistry and can unfold radical, alchemical change in one's makeup. Stimulation of these inner pharmacy pathways signals the body to produce exactly what it needs, including hormones and neurochemicals that heal the body, mind, and consciousness. This deep dimension of marma therapy has the potential to unfold spiritual healing. After a few minutes, I could not tell where Sonia was touching. Was she on my face or the soles of my feet? All of the above? Sonia left the room for fifteen minutes at the end so I could meditate with my mantra while on the table. I felt blissed out and lost time, because I was asleep or maybe because I was in the gap.

Covered from head to toe in fragrant oil, I then headed to the steam room to let the healing continue. I rinsed with cold water as advised but left the oil in my hair. I was happy they had advised to pack comfortable clothes that could withstand oil; my harem pants and an old cotton top were perfect.

As I made my way back to class, other classmates wandered in, many still in their robes, also covered in oil and seeming slightly dazed. We spent the afternoon in meditation and doing yoga; took another dose of the fiber, oil, and special supplement protocol; and had a light dinner (lentils and rice).

The cleanse was gentle and productive with no aggressive bloating. We had homework: a journal exercise to identify emotional or physical toxicity.

Am I holding on to self-negating labels about myself? What choices am I making that are keeping me from being healthy and balanced? What heath challenges am I dealing with that I would like to see resolved?

June 2

Tuesday morning. I didn't sleep well; I had a headache, hot flashes, and woke up at 3:30 and couldn't go back to sleep, so I meditated awhile and then went to the gym when it opened at five o'clock.

The cleanse protocol continued with the fiber, oil, and supplements. After the gym, I came back and had a cool bath before 6:45 yoga and then group meditation before breakfast. I felt hungry, and my head ached. Breakfast was oatmeal with cooked fruit. Most classmates felt pretty OK—a little bloated and some had headaches.

The morning lecture was about Ayurvedic philosophy about bringing the body into balance, using food as medicine. The teacher was an integrative nutrition consultant. Next to Prana or breath, eating is our most vital bodily function. Prana is the same as chi; it can increase cell to cell communication. We store emotions in the energy body; two-thirds of disease is psychospiritual. To create and maintain a healthy physiology, our food must be nourishing, our digestive power strong, and our elimination efficient.

Our digestive power, which is known in Ayurveda as *agni*, is comparable to our inner fire. When our digestive power is strong, we can extract the most nutrition from our diet. When our digestive power is weak, a residue of undigested substances is left behind in our body. This toxic reside is known as *ama*. Ama can lead to many health problems including constipation, fatigue, bad breath, and low energy. With my lifelong raging appetite, I wondered—*do I have much ama?*

The idea is to minimize ama and maximize *ojas*, a biological substance that is the end product of digestion. It is the foundation of our immunity and longevity. How do we tell if our ojas is balanced? We feel rested, energized, contented, and peaceful. Our skin glows, our mind is clear, our body gives off a nice smell and feels light, our digestion is strong, and our tongue is pink and clear. We rarely get sick.

Ayurveda teaches that heat and oil can help remove ama. From the treatment yesterday and those to come over the next days, it is clear that the use of oil is fundamental in Ayurveda. Ginger tea and other warming herbs help with vasodilation. Their joke was that we "dilate," so we don't die early. They mentioned the importance of steam and sauna—not overdoing it—-just enough to break a sweat because sweat is detoxifying.

We learned guidelines for healthy appetite and digestive efficiency, including not eating unless you are hungry, eating only to the point of satiety, and avoiding other activities while eating.

Ayurveda prefers food that is warm and cooked versus cold and raw because it is more nourishing and grounding. A whole food plant-based diet is healthiest. Spices help us secrete enzymes. Lunch should be the biggest meal of the day. We learned about the six tastes to include in each meal for greater satiety and maximum nutrition: sweet, sour, salty, pungent, bitter, and astringent. Some foods have multiple tastes: berries are sweet, sour, and astringent. Black beans are sweet and astringent. Asparagus is sweet, bitter, and astringent.

We should eat not only for our body but also for our mind. We learned about foods to balance and pacify Doshas as well as foods to avoid; for example, Pittas should eat cool foods and liquids and favor sweet, bitter, and astringent foods. Grapes, melon, cherries, apples, and oranges are better for Pitta than grapefruit and sour berries.

For each Dosha, there are specific spice blends that assist with digestion, and these were on each table and labeled as Vata, Pitta, and Kapha.

Armed with this new wisdom, I was hungry and ready for lunch, which was rice and lentils. But there was also a very delicious, warm cauliflower soup. Today we had a silent lunch. We were to appreciate, bless our food, and enjoy each of the tastes. At lunch today, we were each given a ginger elixir shot with advice not to chug it, just sip it.

Before today's spa therapy session, I took a walk and sat outside in the shade and enjoyed the gorgeous, sunny day while doing my journaling exercise, writing down the physical and emotional sensations I am experiencing. The instruction was to observe without interpretation any areas of constriction or discomfort, such as headache, hot flashes, poor sleep, or achy neck and back.

Today's spa session was at the La Costa spa, and my therapist, Gina, came to greet me. I let her know about the headache, hot flashes, and achy feelings. She apologized that I was going to really feel hot for part of the treatment, which she called S-A-N, for Shiro-Abhyanga-Nasya.

She said my symptoms were normal; it is the release of stored toxins. I said, "No worries; I'm all in for the whole experience."

She directed me to sit in a chair at a side table, which had a steam machine under a tented piece of fabric. The steam was directed at my face, and I inhaled the minty menthol aromas with the steam. I began to sweat profusely, and Gina let me open a side vent in the steam tent, encouraging me to hang in there and keep opening up my sinus passages. After I emerged from the steam tent, Gina placed warm towels on my face and did a head massage. She said that the massage would help open up the *srotas* in my head, neck, and shoulders. She explained that *srotas* are channels throughout the visible body as well as at the "invisible" or subtle level of the cells, molecules, atoms, and subatomic strata. It is through these channels that nutrients and other substances are transported in and out of our physiologies. It is also through these channels that information and intelligence spontaneously flow. When the flow of appropriate nutrients and energies through these channels is unimpeded, there is health; when there is excess, deficiency, or blockage in these channels, disease can take root.

As I continued to sweat, I kept telling myself I was letting toxins go, which helped. Then, Gina led me across the room to a sink, which had a blue ceramic neti pot next to it. Gina said that the blue pot was mine to keep, and she mixed warm saline solution and added it to the pot. She directed me to lay my forearm in front of the sink, to insert the neti pot spout into my nostril *before* tilting my head sideways, so my face was horizontal. I followed Gina's direction to open and breathe through my mouth while she gently poured. After a few seconds, the water began to stream out of the lower nostril. I used half of the solution in the first nostril and saved the remainder for the second. Gina handed me some tissues. In between nostrils, I stood up and gently blew my nose to clear it. After the flush, she said adding oil (*Nasya*) to my nose afterward was a very important part of the process to lubricate and protect the sinuses. She handed me Q-tips with herbalized oil to put in my sinus passages but said that in the daily practice, my pinky would work just fine. Then I went to the massage table and got more massage for my head, neck, and shoulders. My nose ran the entire time. So much for not having much ama.

The late afternoon lecture was the spa director. She was caring, hilarious, and irreverent, and I loved her. She explained all the treatments we had already gotten and would receive and answered questions. She explained that the therapists are all highly trained in Ayurveda and that each treatment is tweaked for our personal Doshas and any issues we are currently experiencing. The therapists discuss each attendee and what their needs are and make sure they work as a team to address any health concerns. They are all trained to see everyone as divine and to have reverence for all. I thought, "So, when you become cranky, irritable, gassy, and are covered with sweat and mucous, they keep telling themselves you are enlightened beings." Some of the treatments to come sound a little scary—especially Netra Basi, which will take place on Friday.

The lecture was followed by group meditation and yoga. I took the evening dose of the fiber, oil, and special supplement protocol and had a light dinner (lentils and rice). I was trying to be strong, but I really wanted different food tonight. I kept having a little fantasy about a piece of grilled salmon, a salad, asparagus, and a glass of wine.

June 3

Wednesday morning. I was so clogged in my nasal passages that I couldn't even get my new neti pot to clear them. I was blowing my nose all night and hardly slept. And this morning, shockingly, I was constipated, which seems impossible given all the fiber I have been taking. Yes, I concluded that I have a lot of ama to get rid of.

I feel gross; bloated and quite cranky. Since I couldn't sleep, I took my morning fiber to see if that would get things going—it didn't—so I got dressed and went to the gym. After a lackluster workout, I came back, had a bath, and went to yoga. I found out in talking to my classmates that I am not the only one who is constipated and stuffy. Micole taught yoga and led us in meditation; she is one of my favorites.

After meditation, we had breakfast: oatmeal and cooked fruit with some ghee. Ginger tea. Still no relief after breakfast. Michelle came in and asked who needed a laxative. Me! And several others in the class. One of my classmates, Louie, had the same miserable nose stuffiness I did; and he is also Pitta Dosha. Interesting.

The morning lecture was one of the medical staff talking about emotional freedom. Like each of the other lecturers, she told her personal story and how she ended up at the Chopra Center. Each story we heard was inspirational about some type of health wake-up call and a subsequent return to balance.

She talked about the universal desire to be happy and how, ultimately, we learn that our happiness comes from connection to our higher self. Beyond physiological needs, humans need attention, affection, appreciation, and acceptance in order to feel complete. When our needs are not met, we feel distress, pain, and sadness, and if these feelings are repressed or retained, it can lead to depression anxiety, guilt, or hostility.

She talked about the need to metabolize and clear the residue of emotional pain. We actually store unprocessed feelings within the psychological layer of our being. Impressions of loss, disappointments, traumas, and betrayals are seeds in our subtle body waiting to germinate. When we recognize our emotional triggers, we can begin to identify and clear the residue of unprocessed emotional pain. Transformation begins with awareness.

Some signs of emotional toxicity are fatigue, irritability, lack of enthusiasm, depression, emotional reactivity, and cynicism. Healing our emotions requires acknowledging the sensations as we feel them in our body and listening to the messages they convey.

She referenced work by Marshall Rosenberg to develop skills of conscious, nonviolent communication in order to diagnose what is happening within us and move to clearing it.

She talked about the tremendous health benefits of meditation including changes in gene expression and chromosomal improvement.

I had my medical consultation in the late morning with one of the mind/body doctors. She studied my tongue, took my pulse, and said my pulse was very Pitta, but my tongue was a Kapha tongue in its shape and the coating. She reviewed the detailed health questionnaires I had completed before coming the program. She gave me many recommendations to address hot flashes, night sweats, insomnia, thyroid health, and even nasal congestion. Some of the suggestions surprised me but made sense, like getting a humidifier for the bedroom. She said it is fine for me to eat the raw fruits and vegetables I have been craving, though it is not recommended for most Doshas. She said to think of wine as only an occasional treat for special occasions.

Lunch was soup, ghee, rice, and lentils. I felt bloated and yet quite hungry.

The spa treatment this afternoon was srota clearing: a therapeutic massage that used different techniques to completely relax the body and clear channels of circulation. The therapist used herbal oil to encourage the movement of toxins. I had to stop several times to blow my nose. I had meditation time at the end and then went to the steam room when, finally, my nose started to clear.

The afternoon lecture was incredibly interesting: a hypnotherapy session with Maureen Pisani. She had a delightful accent (she is from Malta) and a great story about how she came to the Chopra Center. She had everyone laughing as she told jokes and drew maps of the brain and talked about the roles of the different hemispheres, the pituitary gland, the hippocampus, and the amygdala. She talked about stress and brought up examples like getting your divorce papers and sitting on an examination table in a paper gown, waiting to receive test results.

She talked about the conscious versus the subconscious mind. The conscious mind is the part that is aware of what is happening while we are in a normal waking state, about 12 percent of our capacity. It is aware of those things that we sense when awake, such as sounds, touch, sight, taste, and so forth. The conscious mind distinguishes between good and bad, and healthy and unhealthy—basically, it is the part that rationalizes. The unconscious mind is in charge of 88 percent of our capacity. It keeps us sitting up, regulates body temperature, and gives meaning to the symbols that we read. Basically, she said the unconscious mind runs the show.

Our daily lives are heavily influenced by our subconscious minds. Will power alone is often not enough to change habits and patterns. Suggestions to the subconscious mind can become integrated into our sense of self and begin to change behavior. In a hypnotic state, we can be more open to suggestion. Hypnotherapy can be used to treat many conditions including phobias, sleep disorders, depression, stress, PTSD, grief, and loss.

She asked the group what issues we wanted to improve in their lives; we said, "Better sleep, better health, more joy and happiness, and inner peace." She then took us through about a twenty-minute relaxation technique, bringing in the visualization of colors and using the sound of her voice to go deeply into the activation of the unconscious mind. She talked about the fulfillment of the desires the group had mentioned. She had some private sessions times available, so I made an appointment.

This was followed by group meditation and yoga. I took the evening dose of the fiber, oil, and special supplement protocol and had a light dinner: carrot and ginger soup, lentils, and rice. I worked to rise above crankiness and to appreciate the food and the view.

The journaling tonight was to imagine releasing completely all the physical and emotional issues I had listed in the past few days, to journal about how it would feel emotionally and physically to eliminate each issue, and to lie down and perform an abdominal self-massage, moving my hands clockwise as I bring attention and awareness to each issue I want to release.

I released constipation, crankiness, stuffy nose, headache, neck ache, hot flashes and poor sleep and imagined feeling light, cool, happy, and well-rested.

June 4

Happily, I am no longer constipated, and my headache and stuffy nose are gone. I feel thinner and my mood is back to happy normal. I slept better and had a good workout in the gym before yoga and meditation.

I was very hungry for breakfast.

Today's morning lecture was about our inner pharmacy, using Shankara's model of the Layers of Life and the point that life is an interplay between the environment, mind, body, and soul. Our sense organs—ears, skin, tongue and nose—are the gateway through which we experience the world. Our body tissues are created from the foods we eat; the composition of our minds is created from our sensory impressions. Sounds, touch, sights, tastes, and smells can all be used to balance, nourish, and heal.

Sound and vibration are powerful in healing. Sound can be used to create harmony and coherence within our body, mind, emotions, and spirit. Sounds that heal are called primordial sounds—vibrations of nature, which are subtler than words or language. Wind, rain, and singing birds are examples of primordial sounds. Our personal mantras that are used in silent meditation serve as a vehicle to quiet the mind and expand awareness.

It is also possible to chant or tone certain sounds to awaken different energy centers of the body. We learned the classical sounds for toning chakras and took a deep breath and together sounded each tone while placing attention on the area of the body for each chakra as follows:

First chakra	Base of the spine	*Lam*
Second chakra	Below belly button	*Vam*
Third chakra	Solar plexus	*Ram*
Fourth chakra	Heart	*Yam*
Fifth chakra	Throat	*Ham*
Sixth chakra	Brow	*Sham*
Seventh chakra	Crown of head	*Aum*

Sound and vibration enlivens and soothes.

Next she discussed the importance of touch. In the daily treatments with therapeutic massage, a pharmacy of healing chemicals is released from our skin. In addition to feeling good, regular massage and loving touch nourish and detoxify the body's tissues, calm the mind, stimulate skin to release the self-healing chemicals, improve circulation, increase alertness, and facilitate detoxification and improved immune function.

Daily self-massage with oil is recommended—self *abhyanga* (abee-yan-ga).

The oil to use is specific to your Dosha; Vatas respond best to heavy oils like sesame or almond. Pittas do well with cooling oils like coconut or olive. Kaphas respond best to lighter oils like safflower or a warmer oil like mustard. Dry skin brushing with silk gloves are also beneficial for balancing Kapha.

She recommended keeping an old towel handy to stand on in the bathroom; to heat the oil by placing it in a plastic squeeze bottle and warming it under tap water. She demonstrated starting at the feet and moving up toward the heart to properly drain the lymphatic system, using long strokes on the arms and legs, circular strokes on the joints, and back-and-forth strokes on the chest and lower abs. Don't forget toes and ears. Shower or bathe after the massage.

Staying on the subject of touch, she recommended multiple hugs a day—at least five.

Moving on to healing through sight, she talked about the importance of focusing on healthy images from nature. Gazing at a beautiful sunset can help our bodies generate soothing, pleasurable hormones. Watching a violent movie can cause us to release stress hormones. Choosing nourishing visual input is as important as choosing nourishing food.

Visual patterns like those found in nature and sacred geometry can also have a powerful effect to soothe the mind. These primordial shapes can generate increased coherence in our brains.

Mandalas and the Sri Yantra symbolize the creative forces of the universe.

Healing through taste was the next topic—the importance of the six tastes and the importance of eating multi-colored food. Aromas can trigger healing power through smell. Our sense of smell connects us directly with emotions and memories. Through neuroassociative conditioning, we can link a healing response to the experience of a particular smell. If you inhale a certain essence that you particularly like when you are feeling relaxed, your body will start to associate pleasurable feelings with the use of the aroma, and soon just the smell will evoke a heightened state of well-being.

Pittas tend to like sandalwood, mint, rose, jasmine, ylang-ylang, and lavender. This completely resonates with me. She also said that along with the importance of laughter, a good belly laugh enhances immune function for twenty-four hours.

Lunch was vegetable soup, ghee, rice, and lentils with steamed vegetables including heirloom cauliflower that was purple and green.

The spa treatment today was *shirodhara* where they used a tremendous amount of fragrant oil in a light massage over the scalp, face, and body, and then a soothing stream of warm oil is poured over the forehead to calm the nervous system, integrate mind and body, and activate the third eye. This was a blissful treatment that ended with private meditation time, and I felt spaced out and disoriented when it was over. The advice was to keep the oil on for as long as possible. I was happy I had cotton harem pants and an old cotton shirt to wear. Most classmates just stayed in their robes. They gave everyone a cloth hat to wear to cover our very oily heads for the afternoon.

The afternoon included a very interesting lecture by Michael Mastro on the subject of Vastu Shastra, a 10,000-year-old Indian science that was the precursor to feng shui involving the science of harmony and prosperous living by eliminating negative and enhancing positive energies around us. It keeps the energy moving in the home to keep us from disease. The speaker designs homes and offices so that they are in harmony with nature. He has done many significant projects in Silicon Valley and regularly appears on TV. He talked about the importance of clearing clutter because clutter creates stress in the home. It is best to face north or east for optimum health and productivity.

He also talked about having beautiful altars in the home in order to manifest your intentions and to lay the altar out as follows:

NE	Water element
SE	Fire element (candle)
SW	Earth element (plant and/or crystal or a bowl of rice)
NW	Air (incense or a bell)
Center	Intentions

I had time to steam and shower before group meditation and yoga. I had to shampoo my hair multiple times to get all the oil out.

I took the evening dose of the fiber, oil, and special supplement protocol and ordered soup, a baked potato, and a vegetable salad for dinner as a break from lentils and rice.

The journaling exercise tonight was about bringing in intentions that I would like to see manifested in my life. Now that I have eliminated and released some things I no longer want in my life, there is room to bring in things that are nourishing into the empty space. I listed the things I want to see in my life: health, gratitude, abundance, daily joy, finding my dharma, graceful aging, and love and passion with Rich. I was directed to lie down and do the abdominal self-massage while picturing these nourishing things entering through my breath to every cell in my body.

June 5

Friday. I slept well last night and woke up very hungry. I feel a little thinner today, but there is no scale in the room, so I will have to wait until I get home to know if I have lost any weight.

The daily routine was very familiar now: fiber and oil protocol, yoga, meditation, and breakfast.

I met with Michelle, who gave me a huge packet of specific information from the doctor and other therapists, including a detailed explanation of the Pitta/Kapha Dosha, including the effects of balance (lustrous complexion, perfect digestion, strong appetite, balanced intellect, contentment, strength, vitality) as well as the best forms of exercise and recommendations for staying in balance, including the best beans, rice, vegetables, and fruits; meal suggestions, supplement suggestions, the daily routine, an article about journaling, an antiinflammatory diet, chakra chart, and so forth.

Today was the spa treatment we were all wondering about called Netra Basti: a specialized eye bath designed to calm and cool the eyes. Ghee is used because of its soothing and cooling properties. Ghee helps to draw heat out of the eyes, which are a seat of Pitta. An Ayurvedic foot massage encourages the energy in the body to flow unimpeded, thus allowing the body's own healing potential to be stimulated. The treatment ends with Marma point therapy to enliven the ability of the body to know how to heal itself.

My treatment was in the Chopra Center today in one of the beautiful spa suites with its own bathroom. Sean was my therapist. I started face down, and he began with oil on my head and body. When I turned over, he used oil on the front of my body and face and then made a sort of dam around my eyes with dough. He put some sterilizing drops in each eye and asked me to close my eyes. He then put warm ghee on top of my eyelids, and I could feel some of it seep out under the dough dam into my ears. It smelled great; I kept fantasizing about popcorn. Then he asked me to open my eyes, and I did eye exercises looking left, right, up, down, and making circles with my eyes as he directed. He left the ghee on as he did the foot massage and marma point therapy. He used a soft cloth to wipe off the ghee that was still on my face. He gave me meditation time before I got off the table. My eyes felt very moist and soothed.

I steamed and showered before lunch, which was rice, lentils, and mulligatawny soup.

The afternoon lecture was about daily routines. The doctor who spoke is a functional medicine expert. She said that sometimes it takes a crisis to discover our true self and our higher purpose.

She talked about the importance of taking time to detoxify the whole body and all of our organs; doing this regularly can bring us in balance, using the beautiful ancient healing practices of Ayurveda.

She reminded us of the wonderful practice of following the recommended daily routine, which allows our bodies to align with the day because our hormones rise and fall with the movement of the sun. She went into more detail about the tongue cleaning, neti pot, and oil pulling and explained that a healthy microbiome protects us against germs, breaks down food to release energy, and produces vitamins. An unhealthy microbiome is the precursor to every chronic disease, and this starts with the gut and the mouth. Oil attracts heavy metals and toxins, so oil-pulling and tongue cleaning can reduce the toxins in the first part of the digestion process so that our gut stays healthier. Recommended routine:

Morning

Wake without an alarm by 6 a.m. Brush teeth and clean tongue. Use the neti pot. Do oil pulling. Yoga. Meditation. Strength and cardiovascular workouts. Bless your breakfast. Bless and thank your body. Oil massage. Bathe. Perform morning work/activity.

Afternoon

Eat the biggest meal of the day. Bless your food. Sit quietly for a few minutes after eating. Take a short walk to aid digestion. Perform afternoon work/activity. Meditate around sunset.

Evening

Bless your food. Eat a light dinner. Sit quietly for a few minutes after eating. Take a short walk to aid digestion.

Bedtime

Minimize intense work after dinner. Be in bed with the lights off by 10:30.

She talked about the benefits of a regular occasional simple fast and/or cleanse, perhaps with the change of seasons. Some people do this monthly or even weekly.

She also talked about the importance of recapitulation where just before you sleep, you take a few minutes, tap into the witness, and review the day without judgment, just thinking about all the moments of the day and releasing any emotion about what happened.

She also talked about the importance of "grounding"—taking off our shoes and walking outside barefoot, which helps to reduce cortisol levels in the body.

She also said that if we do nothing else, keep meditating twice a day; it is the most effective way to continue positive momentum and can lead to all the other positive changes in a timeframe that feels right for our bodies.

Then we took a group photo and walked over to the gym for a fun dance class called Groove before yoga and meditation.

The journal exercise for today was to imagine that all the toxicity in my body had been eliminated and that I am moving forward in balance and perfect health. I was directed to say how I am feeling physically and emotionally: lighter, grateful, happy, healthy, and energized.

Review the list of things you want to continue or bring into your life:

- Continue to "eat the rainbow."
- Continue focus on more of a plant-based diet.
- More legumes.
- Continue meditating.
- More yoga.
- Follow the daily routine.
- Bless my food.

June 6

Today is the final day. I slept well and went to the gym before yoga and meditation. Breakfast was fun, catching up with classmates before everyone departed.

Today I had a private hypnotherapy session with Maureen in the morning and a Jyotish call in the afternoon.

I felt a real connection with Maureen. I had made a huge list of everything I wanted to focus on, reviewed it with her, and together we decided to focus the session on improved sleep and unlocking creativity.

I named some colors I wanted associated with each, and she put me in a relaxed state and recorded the hypnotherapy session. She immediately sent me the twenty-minute recording; I am to listen to it as I fall asleep for the next twenty-one days. I'm optimistic that I will start to see improvement.

The final spa treatment today was Ghandarva. It was at the Chopra Center in one of the deluxe treatment rooms. Ghandarva is based on the theory of vibrational medicine. Everything in the universe resonates at an optimal frequency. The chakras, bones, and organs in the body all resonate at different frequencies. The body is in a healthy state when each cell resonates in harmony with the whole being. When there is a blockage, the frequency of the body part in question is altered. The vibrational disharmony in the body allows illness to settle in. Sound and hands-on energy work can help break up, release, and even dissolve the blockages that exist in our body. Ghandarva therapy also affects brain wave activity, allowing for meditative states.

Sean was the therapist again. I had an oil massage to a recording of "singing bowls" of different resonances. After each section of massage, he also went to play an actual singing bowl that was in the room that corresponded to each area that was being treated and was in alignment with the recording. At the end, he left the room for fifteen minutes so I could meditate to the vibrations. It was lovely, and I felt very awake and energized at the end.

Then I was off to say goodbye to classmates and have a final lunch and steam and shower.

The last journal assignment for the week was to sum up the week and imagine what your days will be like when you incorporate some of these new tools into your life:

It was an unforgettable week. I feel inspired to continue to blossom into a full-spectrum life that includes many of the healthy elements I have been exposed to this week.

I see myself as vibrant and healthy, continuing twice daily meditation and daily yoga. I see myself consciously and gratefully consuming freshly prepared, multicolored, mostly plant-based meals. I intend to pause and bless my food before the first bite and take time to appreciate its source and the fact that what I consume transforms into my very tissues.

I visualize spending time in nature on a daily basis and appreciating the shapes and sounds of the outdoors.

I will continue my daily routine and will now begin to include neti pot, Abhyanga, and oil pulling while being conscious of nourishing myself to bring about feelings of contentment and peacefulness— signs that *ojas* is present and flowing.

Before I left the Chopra Center, I had a Jyotish call with Brent Bec-Var, who I first saw at the Seduction of Spirit retreat.

Much of the reading centered around Rich and our marriage. He explained that I am a double Taurus because I was born close to sunrise.

Rich's rising sign is also Taurus. Taurus is ruled or represented by the planet Venus. Taurus people are sensual and appreciate fine things like food and wine, fine art, textiles, and good design. They like harmony in nature and have a rich sensual connection. But they may have issues with control and want to hold on tightly to things they love.

The real work for Taurus in life is to learn to love in all the ways possible and yet to allow for the cycles of life to have their own freedom; that is part of the balancing act.

The fact that Rich and I both have Venus in the rising sign is extremely good; he said we see each other through the eyes of love. This resonates with me.

I also have a double strong Saturn, which can keep me constrained and impact confidence but can also signify gifts of like self-discipline and hard work. I have Saturn on the seventh house of partnership and marriage.

We each have Venus in earth signs, so we have an easy ability to support each other's desire natures. We can easily be in harmony, be friendly, and want each other to succeed.

We both have the moon in complimentary elements, and both have the moon under the influence of Mars and Saturn. He explained, it's like we both have our foot on the gas and the brakes at the same time, which is a remarkable combination of push/pull tension in the mind; Brent is amazed at the parallels in our charts. There may be empathy for one another because of the similarities.

The best antidote to this combination is to put the gearshift in neutral every day through meditation. So, meditation is very good for us, and meditating together is awesome. He was delighted to hear that we meditate together daily; this will continue to bring wholeness, presence of mind, peace, and integration of body, mind, and spirit.

I have Saturn in the seventh house of partnership; that is highly valued in India. This indicates a commitment to marriage, but it may require some conscious intention to spark things up, pay attention to the other, and imagine what enjoyment would be like for my partner. What would nourishment be like for my partner? Meditation is the most intimate thing we can do together.

He tells me that we both have a beautiful heart with Jupiter in our fourth house, and that also gives good real estate karma.

Brent says that we have a great partnership, but there would have been risks if we had married young. I laugh and tell him we *did* marry young and about our divorce and remarriage. He notes again the remarkable similarities in the charts and says that even though there was a break, the karma indicates that the break was not final and that we have a much stronger commitment now.

Both of us have gone through a transit of Saturn over our moons. I am just now finishing it, and Rich is at the end of it. It is called Sadi Sati. I am now embarking on a whole new seventeen-year period of Mercury.

In the couple of minutes remaining, I asked him about my purpose or dharma. He can see in my chart that I have felt compelled to go on the spiritual journey. There isn't just one dharma or purpose in life; it is a state of mind that asks, How can I help? How can I serve? How do I align to play my part?

He sees roles in partnership, business, communication, and art. I will have to make another appointment to learn more.

June 19

I met Abigail for a quick trip to Chicago for a belated birthday celebration. We met at Midway Airport; our flights got in within twenty minutes of one another. We shared a happy hug and then took a cab to the Ritz Carlton. Our room was ready; it was large with an excellent view. We left our bags and went out into the blustery day for lunch.

Walking down Michigan Avenue the winds were high, temperature was low, and we were cold. We had a great long lunch at Valero, complete with Prosecco. We shared a kale and Brussels sprout salad with chickpeas. Abigail got the pasta, and I got the salmon. It was a fortifying lunch before we headed off to the windy architectural tour on the First Lady Cruise Line.

The boat was packed with tourists. Our docent was extremely knowledgeable about every architectural style from art deco (the LaSalle Wacker Building) to historic (the Tribune) to modern (the Willis Tower—formerly Sears tower).

I found two old running headbands and a pair of gloves in my handbag; we pulled on the hats and each wore a glove with both hands tucked in. We walked back to the Ritz, bumping in and out of stores along the way to warm up. We went to Nico Osteria for dinner.

We wanted a table overseeing the kitchen, so had a drink at the bar while we waited. Our topics spilled over from lunch: Abigail's kids and work; my classes, apprenticeship, teacher certification, and spiritual adventures. Abigail asked thought-provoking questions.

"Do you still believe in God after all your spiritual endeavors?"

I replied, "Yes; more than ever, but my concept of God is evolving. The Vedas say that seeking God is like a thirsty fish looking for water; what we seek is all around us. Our minds focus on duality; me as a separate being from God and everyone else. They say God is reached by transcending and realizing that we are all one."

Abigail thought about this and asked, "How do you transcend?"

I said, "In meditation for sure; but also, in anything creative where you have expanded possibilities and have that strong feeling of being connected. When I paint, it's like a meditation."

She asked, "How do you think about God now?"

I said, "That's still one of the big mysteries. As a kid, I thought of God as an old man on a throne in heaven. In Catholic school, I got confused; was God loving or all-powerful or a harsh judge or all of the above? I never bought into the notion that there was one segment of mankind as the exclusive group who would get to heaven. I still wonder if the best explanation is some kind of universal force of balance or cosmic law. So, I'm not sure how to think about God now, but along the path, I notice things falling away and I feel loved."

Abigail asked, "What have you noticed falling away?"

I thought about how to phrase it and said, "The need to hang on to me and mine; the fear of death; the need for status. Now I feel a connection to everything around me; I feel *safe*; like I'm living in a state of grace. I feel more able to cope with the chaos in life. I feel—connection."

Abigail pressed further: "What or who do you feel connected to?"

I said, "I guess my current version of God. It's hard to describe, but it feels…completely pure. Maybe pure awareness, pure intelligence, pure creativity, infinite potential, oneness. And in my mind, I now think of that as Source or Spirit. I know this force is genderless, but I like to think of it as feminine. Right now, when I pray, in my mind I call Her the Holy Spirit."

Abigail laughed. "Wow, Holy Spirit almost sounds like you have come full circle."

I laughed, too. "Yeah, they talked about the Holy Ghost in Catechism. I don't think they thought of Her as feminine though."

Abigail continued with her questions, and I felt so much love for her, appreciating that she was trying to deeply understand.

"Is meditation the path you have chosen to connect with God?"

I said, "Yes, meditation, painting and other kinds of devotion. I like all types of meditation, but using my own mantra has been especially powerful for me; it is part of Raja yoga. I think meditation is the path I have been seeking all my life."

Abigail asked questions about the apprenticeship. "Will you call yourself a shaman?"

I replied, "No, the apprenticeship has been incredibly valuable. It has taught me to use my imagination and tap into the subconscious part of myself, to truly believe that it is possible to connect to nonphysical source energy. It taught me comfort with the irrational way beyond my five senses. But my call is not to journey for clients. I think the apprenticeship served to teach me that there are many interpretations of the nonphysical: guides, angels, and spirit animals, and they all can be valid. And, it led to the pathway of studying mythology and other ancient belief systems."

Abigail asked, "So, what's next?"

I brimmed with excitement as the words spilled out, "I am passionate to teach meditation. When I started meditating with my own mantra, I felt I got to a whole new level of experience, and now I can't wait to help students on their path. My secret dream is to somehow combine art and meditation. I think creative expression and meditation can help people become more balanced, to be more grateful, vital, energetic, peaceful, and joyful; to develop greater abundance and loving relationships in their life; to help them find their purpose and use their gifts and talents to live a more full-spectrum life.

And the best way to be a good teacher is to practice what I teach; to keep going deeper into meditation, continue to learn, continue to focus on health, keep painting, and figure out a way to combine creativity and meditation.

When we got to our table overlooking the kitchen, we could see other foodies surrounding us that were taking dinner very seriously. Abigail talked to the salad prep chef in the kitchen to decide what to order. We shared some grilled asparagus. I got the arctic char and Abigail got orchietto pasta. It's so fun to watch a good kitchen team at work; they were calm and efficient, and they seemed to love their jobs.

We had a lovely, chilly walk back to the Ritz. There were two enormous slices of chocolate cake with candles in the room. Over cake, Abigail asked me to name the most profound things I came to believe or understand this year. I laughed and said I had been working on that very list on the flight. As Abigail made some phone calls, I got my laptop:

- We are not separate from God; there is divinity in each of us; we all emanate from the same source and are all essentially one. We are just fields of energy; I am, you are, they are; every rock, tree, plant, and person is part of that field.
- The people we meet and feel a connection with are not random. We are all part of the same source of energy, and there are key people in our lives who carry out certain roles to help us learn the lessons we are intended to experience. Many believe that the obstacles that we face are chosen before birth, that we choose our family, our bodies, our personalities and the people who dance in and out of our lives. We choose

these people who have agreed to help us learn the particular lessons we need in order to grow spiritually.

- We all have access to higher guidance; we reach out all the time. It even happens in our sleep; our guidance is always there. Everyone can learn to be more intuitive and to begin to trust hunches and instincts. You may not become clairvoyant, but you can become a better leader, partner, parent, or human by tuning into your higher guidance.

- There is a larger story to our lives, a divine design. Sometimes the story feels like a romantic comedy, sometimes a tragedy. Falling in love, the end of a career, the death of someone we love —it all makes more sense when viewed from the altitude of a larger story. When we are born, we step onto the stage of the play of our life, which will inevitably contain love, adventure, pain, joy, and heroism. When unplanned and unexpected events take place, some interpret this as chance, some as karmic destiny, and others believe the universe is intervening. I have come to believe that it is all part of a greater story and that subtle or hidden forces play a role.

- Yet, even when unexpected things happen, we are free to choose our response. We hold the remote control to the movie; we can change the channel. Our intentions and choices create our reality. We are always free to respond at the highest level. We can all use more of our potential and live more of a full-spectrum life through the choices we make. We can choose to keep growing, to continue to expand our horizons; we can choose a more dynamic life with less struggle and more fulfillment.

- Whatever spiritual path you are on can help you advance toward enlightenment (we are all headed to the same room though we can choose our path of entry). Everyone is on his or her own journey, studying a curriculum that makes sense to them. Including a spiritual tool like meditation into life can open the door to the higher self, and I think it can only deepen your faith in whatever belief system you have.

- Pain is inevitable, but suffering is optional. Suffering comes from a focus on me and mine: attachment to my body, my mind, my possessions, my reputation, and my relationships. It is possible to detach and see that we are not our body, our thoughts, our mind, or our ego. We are not our pain; we are something larger. Each moment gives us an opportunity to step beyond illusion into freedom. Examining beliefs, abandoning them, and returning attention to the present can help alleviate suffering, as is living in the awareness that nothing in the universe is personal.

- Our body and mind are what localize the nonlocal; if they are in good working order, our instrument will receive clearer signals. Exercise, rest, heathy diet, creative expression, and meditation help us be at our best. Unforeseen things will always happen in life; being able to respond from our healthiest, most balanced place is the best way to cope so that we can respond at the highest level.

- Our body is just a suit we inhabit in this lifetime. We are having an *embodied* experience. There are experiences in embodied life we cannot get in any other way; experiences we cannot have without encasement. For a soul to experience embodied life, to grow, to unfold, and to become, it not only needs to wear a body suit, it needs to deeply embrace and be embraced by the physical, creating a full and healthy relationship with our body. Our body is intelligent and unique. Meditation helps us be even more tuned in to our body and to trust the signals it sends.

I read the list to Abigail, and she said she wants to be my first meditation student. Before we drifted off to sleep, Abigail asked me one more question:

"How do you reconcile what you now believe with others' belief systems?"

I said, "I have deep respect for others' beliefs. I still say to myself and sincerely to them, "You may be right." I think we won't completely know until this life is over. And I'm OK with the mystery."

June 20

The next morning, we went to the gym, meditated together, and took a walk down to Millennium Park for our annual visit to "Cloud Gate" by Anish Kapoor. The massive and elegant sculpture is shaped like a bean and reflects the Chicago skyline. It is balanced on its ends, so you can walk underneath it. Eighty percent of its surface reflects the sky.

We talked about what easy travel companions we are, with similar interests and body clocks; we are both foodies and appreciative of just taking the day for what it brings without being overscheduled or fussy.

Chapter Thirteen
July

A year has passed since I began my journey. I am filled with gratitude as I reflect on my process, the things I learned and my insights. Now, in living daily life I often feel that life has taken on added facets. I still experience normal daily life in a three-dimensional world but now also sense more. I think of it as a sense of nested realities: "I am an atom, a molecule, a cell, an organism, a body, a soul, divine." Some of my teachers talk about walking in multiple worlds; I now understand what this means.

July 4

This is the one-year anniversary of me keeping a journal, a year of the most profound learning in my life. I found a quote by Mark Twain, which captures how I feel about my journey.

> Some things you can't find out; but you will never know you
> can't by guessing and supposing; no, you have to be patient
> and go on experimenting until you find out that you can't find
> out. And it is delightful to have it that way; it makes the world
> so interesting. If there wasn't anything to find out, it would be

dull. Even trying to find out and not finding out is just as interesting as trying to find out and finding out, and I don't know but more so. (Mark Twain, *Eve's Diary*)

I'm glad I had the chance to discover things on my own instead of just adopting someone else's interpretation. I tried different ideas on for size to see what resonated with me, suspended disbelief and judgment, and said to myself, "Let me just experience this with an open mind; they might be right about that."

In my circuitous path of stumbling from one thing to the next, I got direct experience, and the vision quest felt uniquely mine. I felt like an explorer. I realize that I could have taken a more direct route, a shorter path in a faster vehicle.

Now, in hindsight, I realize that my desire for answers is pretty universal to those who are seekers, and there is nothing remarkable in all that I experienced.

There are tons of books, videos, articles, and shows that cover every topic I explored. I'm grateful I didn't know them when I started because, for me, the journey of self-realization was half the fun. My exploration meandered from one thing to the next. What if I had seen Afterlife TV a year ago? I might have had earlier insights, but in a strange way, I appreciate them more because the insights, having been sought, seemed to unfold for me as I needed to receive them. I have been able to experience things, ponder them and draw conclusions for myself.

But I'm glad to know about other sources now because what I discovered is being reinforced, and I am still learning. Many days now in the gym, if I am not watching something about art, I tune into something captured on Chopra.com, Sounds True, YouTube, PBS, Ted Talks, Hay House, a talk by Eckhart Tolle, a podcast by Teri Uktena, or some other inspirational program, whether it's Oprah on Super Soul Sunday, Wayne Dyer in his movie *Shift*, Esther Hicks channeling Abraham, Afterlife TV, or Bill Moyers (in his 1980s PBS show featuring interviews with Joseph Campbell, *The Power of Myth*, or his later show *Faith and Reason*).

I am now making a new list of questions to research.

The work of scientists who explore and try to prove mystical concepts through scientific methods is very appealing to me. I continue to read books by Amit Goswami, a quantum physicist, who wrote many great books, including *God Is Not Dead: What Quantum Physics Tells Us about Our Origins, How We Should Live*, and *Physics of the Soul*.

I have to read his work very slowly; the ideas are rich and layered. He proves the existence of God, souls, and reincarnation, using quantum physics concepts. He says that people of genius are a proof of reincarnation.

Goswami says we have a learning agenda for our life, a dharma, so that when we fulfill the learning agenda we bring to the current life, life becomes full of bliss, and if we find bliss in our lives, we must be following our dharma.

I recently read *Real Magic* by Dean Radin. The subtitle is *Ancient Wisdom, Modern Science, and a Guide to the Secret Power of the Universe*.

Even though I am just an ordinary person instead of being a scholar or scientist, I find these works to be accessible if I go slowly and think carefully about each concept.

July 5

I'm back where my journey started: at Canyon Ranch with my family. There is a palpable void; we all feel the pain of Gussie's absence, yet it is healing to be together in a place she loved.

We are hanging in there. Joe is slimmer now than in high school. Emma is managing through her hip pain with a positive attitude and neuromuscular therapy. Teresa is the upbeat encourager, though she keenly misses Gus. Sasha, grieving herself, somehow helps us all keep it light. Mia is with us this year. I think it helps her to be with us and it helps us to be with her. She calls Teresa, Bethany and I "the aunts," and we love it. With her dancer's grace and flexibility, she did the splits in aerial yoga today. Bethany, the self-proclaimed "leaker" can't seem to stop crying for long, but she also gathers enough composure to tell some jokes, stories, and memories that make us laugh.

Each time one of us walks by the gong sculpture, we ring it, and it reverberates through the property; we hear it wherever we are. It reminds us that Gus is with us still.

We did a ceremony for Gussie as she wished, in the midst of a rare Tucson rainstorm. We remembered the Gussie that we want foremost in our memories. I said,

> We have grieved her death and mourned the loss of her, and now our love for her will continue on in a new form. Our love is a vibration: a transformation of energy from one state to another.
>
> We are not stuck in loss or separation. Our love flows, and we realize our oneness with all things. Gussie's life and how it touched each of us is part of our truth. As we become closer to living our truth, we also begin to live our greatness, using more of our capacity and potential.
>
> Let that capacity be like a powerful rising flame that purifies us, now as we stand here together in this place Gus loved, and let us heal as she would want us to. Let's move beyond pain. Let's recognize the divinity within us and know that she is divine also.
>
> In our truth, we recognize all that Gussie dealt with in her life. But today, let's remember the things we most loved about her and also make a commitment to her to embrace health, wholeness, happiness, gratitude, and peace, and let the memory of her in this place be a catalyst for our continuing evolution through this life together.

Then each of us spoke, saying something we most loved about Gussie and something that we will make a commitment to going forward—something that she inspired in us.

And in the midst of many tears, each of us told a happy or proud memory of our dear little sister, made a commitment to our own progress, and released her ashes into the wind.

July 6

I review from my red notebook what I set out to do. I accomplished much of what I envisioned: to be active and healthy with daily nourishment of mind, body, and spirit; learning; laughter; love; daily pleasure; connection to family, friends, and community; great sleep; exercise; fresh air; vibrant fruits and vegetables; intimacy; travel; painting; meditating; and helping others find laughter, fulfillment, and gratitude.

My red notebook is now completely full. After it filled, I started typing my daily journal. The daily practice of recapitulation has been therapeutic. I flip through the filled notebook and reflect on the events of the year.

I recall my fears in the beginning: How will we change? Will I be happy? What do I believe in? I recall not knowing where to start, beginning to express myself spiritually in art, stumbling to answer the existential questions, and yearning to find a way to get closer to God. How I struggled to let go of ego. I smile as I remember delving into the laws of the universe that opened the door for me. All the books I read. Decluttering and detachment.

I reminisce about going deeper into meditation, worry about Gussie, our dad, and Raleigh, and beginning to see myself as an artist. Getting my personal mantra and sensing nonphysical source energy for the first time. The entry of Chip into our lives, the Soul Beliefs class, and learning about nonlocal awareness.

I leaf through pages and look back fondly on my struggle to answer the question about destiny versus free will, and I remember the notion that we plan our lives and how shocking that idea was to me.

Studying Vedanta starting with the Upanishads will always be linked in my mind to the Europe and bike trip. I reflect on staying at the villa in Umbria and memorizing the Gayatri Mantra. Going to Barcelona and reading the Bhagavad Gita for the first time. Studying Buddhism. Painting "City Girls." Gus's health decline. Studying numerology. Going to the salon at Jean Houston's home and Jean's prediction about painting being part of my dharma. Meeting Robin. Learning about archetypes and karmic lessons. Thanksgiving in Napa. Animating paintings. Reading the Yoga Sutras of Patanjali. Having the astrocartography session. Deciding to put the house on the market and move to the mountains. Finding a new medium with liquid acrylics. Taking the Synchro-destiny class. Creating the Light Being paintings. Exploring past lives and learning about dharma. Using brain catalyst technology. Working on our marriage. Learning the Mahavakyas, more about karma and higher states of consciousness. The Science of Happiness class. Spending six weeks in California and falling in love with it. Attending the Sages and Scientists symposium. The teacher certification for Primordial Sound Meditation. Deciding to eat a more plant-based diet. My painting in the AIDS fundraiser. The Perfect Health retreat. Beginning and ending the year at Canyon Ranch.

I think with gratitude about the insights and lessons from these amazing experiences. I start a new page in the notebook. How have I changed during this pivotal year?

To be able to find the quiet days so enjoyable is a great, happy surprise. I don't miss corporate life.

I have become more reasonable in my workouts. I'm taking it easier with the goal to stay strong, resilient, and injury free and still be at a healthy weight. I think this is possible.

Daily fresh air has been such a gift. I can't wait for our next chapter where we will be able to be out in nature even more.

Rich and I are very good. Our marriage has gotten stronger. We joke that we are grateful to not only love, but still like each other after nearly forty years. We have both evolved so much. We are still having our weekly marriage check-in. It's usually fast now. "What could I be doing to be a better partner to you?" "Nothing, Jane. Now that we use GPS instead of relying on your map-reading skills, life is basically perfect."

My studies have been tremendous. From Science of Happiness to the shamanic apprenticeship to Primordial Sound Meditation teacher training, I have loved learning and experiencing. I see learning being a big continuing endeavor.

Keeping this journal has been instructive. Every wisdom tradition says that the answers are within us. And meditation asks you to go deep to try to answer the question "Who am I?" Themes and insights are easier to see when you peer inside.

If I had to choose one thing that was most impactful for me in the last year, I would have to say meditation. It seems that every class, every new course of study, every insight keeps coming back to the idea that making spiritual progress is an inside job; it is necessary to go within, and meditation is the best vehicle for me.

I take a look at the philosophical questions I wrote down at the beginning of the year. It would be arrogant to say, "I know the answer." But the fog is starting to lift; I know what I now believe:

What is the meaning of existence—the purpose of life?

Many of my teachers agree that the purpose of an individual life is the same as the cosmic purpose, which is to manifest the possible. And yet, I also now believe it is about finding your own path to happiness. The size of the stage for the production of life is not what matters. One person can have a huge impact and find joy just by interacting with family, friends, or seeming strangers.

My teachers have taught that we are here:

1. To know ourselves at the soul level
2. To discover our purpose in this life
3. To learn the lessons we are meant to learn as we discover who we are

Meditation has helped me discover more about who I am and allowed me to get clearer on how to create life as I want it to be—to find my own path to happiness. The idea of creating more capacity in our own human potential continues to inspire me. I want people to be able to bring more of who they are to the world and use their gifts and talents to make a difference and find fulfillment.

I keep hearing that we are entering a time of world-wide awakening. This idea excites me, and when I see the negative rhetoric, divisive behavior, nationalistic "me and mine" behavior, and the fear, I wonder if the extreme drama playing out could finally be the catalyst that is needed to force people into a new dimension of thinking that will pave the way for a more collaborative, cooperative, positive, synergistic era to come.

People are looking for meaning. As members of humanity, we are all connected; we are all part of one thing.

Deepak Chopra has a vision that inspires me: he wants to get a billion people meditating. He says this is enough critical mass to change the vibration level. As a teacher, I want to play my part. I read that those who are currently on earth decided to come during this time, which could be a great widespread awakening; it might help souls get on with their unfinished business.

I believe that cultivating creative expression is also a form of self-actualization; I am excited about the next chapter in my desire to combine meditation and art.

How did we get here?

I am drawn to the idea that we agreed to come—that we chose our life in some way.

Do we really have souls?

I believe the answer is yes. Amit Goswami has even "proven" it with quantum physics.

What is my greater purpose; do I have a "soul mission"?

I now believe that we have multiple purposes in life and it is beneficial for each individual to do the work to answer this question. At the beginning of the year, I guessed the next chapter for me had something to do with inspiring people to live a conscious, full, abundant life and to broaden perspective to see all in God and God in all.

Now my scope is even clearer: I will help people see the larger picture of their lives, to inspire them to live their best life in healthy balance, and to nourish creative abilities. I will joyfully be a lifelong seeker who embodies the notion that we are all one. I will encourage people to recognize, cherish, and use their unique gifts, pursue their dreams, and create their own reality.

How should I live my life?

Ethically, with as much love and compassion as possible and live a life full of learning and discovery. Treat everyone as an equal; see the divinity in everyone.

What happens when we die?

When we die, our energy transforms but remains a part of source energy. Like an individual wave, it spikes up for a moment and then curves back on itself and once again becomes inseparable from the ocean.

What is God's or Spirit's true nature? What role does she, he, or it play in our life?

This is one of the mysteries I will lovingly continue to explore. I think often of the blind men and the elephant. Each person grasping their part of the elephant believes they have an answer. Each of our answers are probably only a tiny fraction of what will be known.

I believe that there is divinity in each of us and that we are supported and loved.

What do different wisdom traditions believe?

In my studies, the best source I came across to address this question was a book written in 1958 by Huston Smith: *The Religions of Man*. I have read the book so many times, it has fallen apart, and I keep it together with rubber bands. Smith discusses the spiritual meaning that Hinduism, Buddhism, Confucianism, Taoism, Islam, Judaism, and Christianity hold. Smith repeats throughout the book the theme of having a wide enough perspective to appreciate different views.

He mentions Socrates, who said on his deathbed, "I am not an Athenian or a Greek, but a citizen of the world." He borrows Nietzsche's image of the Cosmic Dancer who lightly turns and leaps from one position to another to reach out with interest and curiosity to see what has interested others, to enlarge our understanding and awareness, and to see the world through the eyes of another. He quotes Arnold Toynbee throughout. Toynbee was once asked who the greatest benefactors of mankind are, and he answered, "Confucius and Lao Tse, the Buddha, the Prophets of Israel and Judah, Zoroaster, Jesus, Mohammed, and Socrates."

The major wisdom traditions all contain some version of a core belief in the Golden Rule. Yet sectarianism and exclusion are prevalent.

I believe that there are many paths to enlightenment and that any belief system is a doorway to the same room. I am particularly drawn to the explanation of this in the Bhagavad Gita:

Whosoever comes to Me, through whatsoever form,
I reach him; all men are struggling through paths
which in the end lead to Me. (Gita)

Which traditions believe in reincarnation?

Reincarnation is a central tenet of all major Indian religions: Jainism, Hinduism, Buddhism, and Sikhism. The idea of reincarnation is found in many ancient cultures: A belief in rebirth/metempsychosis was held by Greek historic figures, such as Pythagoras, Socrates, and Plato. It is also a common belief of various ancient and modern religions such as Spiritism, Theosophy, and Eckankar, and as an esoteric belief in many streams of Orthodox Judaism. It is found as well in many tribal societies around the world, in places such as Australia, East Asia, Siberia, and South America.

Although the majority of denominations within Christianity and Islam do not believe that individuals reincarnate, particular groups within these religions do refer to reincarnation.

In December 1945 works containing tenets of the early Christian religion were found in Upper Egypt, a location where many Christians fled during the Roman invasion of Jerusalem. Undisturbed since their concealment almost two thousand years ago, these writings contained the doctrine of reincarnation that was taught among early Jews and Christians.

Have any of these ideas ever been scientifically proven?

Amit Goswami has used quantum physics to show the compatibility of science and spirituality, and Bruce Lipton uses biology in a similar way. "Scientifically proven" may be a stretch, and faith will always play a role. But they both show scientific evidence to validate spiritual beliefs. In *Real Magic,* Dean Radin outlines forty years of controlled experiments that demonstrate that thoughts are things, that we can sense other's intentions and emotions from a distance, that intuition is powerful, and that we can tap into the power of intention. David Bohm used quantum physics to show the totality of existence as an unbroken whole. Investigative journalist Lynne McTaggart shows that the human mind and body are not separate from their environment and that consciousness shapes our world in *The Field*.

Which wisdom traditions believe in the laws of the universe? Who set them down originally?

They seem to underpin all wisdom traditions. They are attributed to Egyptian philosopher Hermes Trismegistus.

Which is true: do we have free will, or is there a divine plan for us?

I now believe that both notions are valid. My current belief is that there *is* a general plan that is decided before we incarnate, and yet there *is* free will to make choices and decisions along our paths.

These are my placeholder answers after a year of seeking. Some seem rudimentary, as though I have only just begun to understand.

I am sure as I look back at them after more years of experience, these answers may seem like just a starting point. Yet, at least I have clarity about what concepts make sense to me. I am so grateful for this year of discovery and continue to have a tremendous desire to study, learn, experience, and understand.

As I look back on the year, I am amazed by and grateful for what I have had the opportunity to do.

As I look forward, I want to continue to savor each day, my family, and friends, and enjoy life to the fullest. I want to keep teaching meditation, making art and deepening my spiritual path. I can't wait to develop what I believe is my next purpose by combining meditation and creative expression.

As I reflect, I now understand that the harder we strive to make sense of things, the more clearly we begin to see ourselves. The more we seek to find divinity outside of ourselves, the more we are allowed to see that it has always been there within.

As we were flying home from Canyon Ranch, we received an offer on our house. The next week, I graduated from the first portion of the shamanic apprenticeship and the teacher certification at the Chopra Center. And so the next adventure began as we moved west.

Epilogue

Six months later

It is just before sunrise. Rich and I are seated on an outdoor chaise lounge facing a mountain range, meditating. We are in California at last. We have settled into our new home; it has wide, sweeping views of the mountains, palm trees, green grass, and bougainvillea. It is the perfect size—just big enough but completely manageable on our own without much outside help.

It all happened effortlessly as often happens when the right path begins to unfold. Our home sold in Ohio. We bought a new house that had just been finished in the community we wanted. If we had built the home, we would have chosen virtually the same cabinets, counter tops, and fixtures. The move was simple; we sold or gave away most of the contents of the Ohio home and bought new, simple furniture.

Rich's office is perfect with gorgeous views of the San Jacinto Mountains. I have a separate casita for my office, painting studio, and meditation teaching space with wonderful natural light, blissful solitude, and a view of the Santa Rosa Mountains.

I finished my website and have a small but growing practice as a meditation teacher. I teach my classes online to students all over the world. I am creating a curriculum to combine meditation and art. My cherished routine continues in the new location: meditation, exercise, learning, painting, gratitude, daily joy, and lots of love.

Letter to the reader

This book is my story. The events and insights all took place. The names of my teachers and books are all real. However, names of some friends, family, and places have been changed. The timing and sequence of events have been altered to help with the flow of the narrative and place it within the time frame of a year. For example, the salon with Jean Houston actually took place in August; the Sages and Scientists symposium was in September. "Gussie's" illness and decline took place over a longer span of time. In some cases, events have been merged: for example, combining feedback from two metaphysical readings into one, synthesizing multiple conversations into one dialogue or two trips to the same place in one.

I embarked on a vision quest to seek answers to the mysteries of life. My family, friends, and some of my students knew about the journal I kept and asked me to outline the steps I took. This book was born as a result. If you have finished this book, there is a good chance that the idea of going deeper in your spiritual practice resonates with you.

At the end of my year of deep discovery, I found that everything I needed to know had been there and available inside myself all along. The best advice I can give you to access your own inner wisdom is to begin or strengthen a daily meditation or other contemplative practice. Techniques abound. Find one that resonates and stick with it. Following any of the Oprah and Deepak 21-day guided meditation series is a wonderful way to begin.

I have now been meditating for more than twenty years. I have experience with many kinds of meditation, and I love them all. They include guided meditation, mindfulness, movement meditation, lovingkindness meditation, body scans and relaxation, Kirtan, breathing techniques, and using brain catalyst technology. Personally, I have found mantra meditation to be the most powerful and effective for me because it gives me a focus that allows me to move beyond thought to the silence within.

Meditation has had a tremendous positive impact on my life. I feel more grateful, vital, energetic, and peaceful, and I see abundance and happiness growing in my life. Meditation has also had a great impact on my relationships.

If you would like to learn more about the type of meditation I teach, please feel free to go to my website to try some of the complimentary meditations and pranayama on the site, or sign up for a class at jramseyvisionquest.com

In addition to going deeper spiritually, I sought balance in body and mind during this pivotal year. To develop my mind, I took classes and read books that supported my journey. Many of these are listed in the bibliography. To be healthier in my body, I continued a commitment to daily cardiovascular exercise, including walking, regular high-intensity intervals, weight lifting, getting fresh air, eating the rainbow in vibrant fruits and vegetables, doing yoga and Pilates, and getting sufficient sleep. I also explored Ayurveda and brought new practices into my daily routine from this ancient tradition. Links are referenced in the following bibliography.

Namaste,

Jane Ramsey

Bibliography

Abrams, Nancy Ellen. *A God That Could Be Real: Spirituality, Science, and the Future of Our Planet*. Boston: Beacon Press, 2016.

All Online Music Production Courses—Berklee Online. Accessed January 09, 2019. https://online.berklee.edu/faculty/david-mash.

"Atheism." Wikipedia. January 03, 2019. Accessed January 09, 2019. https://en.wikipedia.org/wiki/Atheism.

Awaken. Accessed January 09, 2019. http://www.awaken.com/2018/05/deepak-chopra-explains-the-deeper-meaning-of-yoga/.

"Barnaby Marsh." Institute for Advanced Study. Accessed January 09, 2019. https://www.ias.edu/scholars/barnaby-marsh.

"Bernardo Kastrup." Google+. Accessed January 09, 2019. https://plus.google.com/+bernardokastrup.

Brussat, Frederic, and Mary Ann. Brussat. *Spiritual Literacy: Reading the Sacred in Everyday Life*. New York: Simon & Schuster, 1998.

"Buddhism and Modern Psychology." Coursera. Accessed January 09, 2019. https://www.coursera.org/learn/science-of-meditation.

Byrne, Ronda. *The Secret*. Place of Publication Not Identified: Simon & Schuster, 2009.

Campbell, Joseph. *The Hero with a Thousand Faces*. Novato, CA: New World Library, 2008.

"The Chopra Center." The Chopra Center. Accessed January 09, 2019. https://chopra.com/.

Chopra, Deepak, and Minas C. Kafatos. *You Are the Universe: Discovering Your Cosmic Self and Why It Matters*. London: Rider, 2018.

Chopra, Deepak, and Rudolph E. Tanzi. *Super Brain*. Bath: Paragon, 2013.

Chopra, Deepak. *Buddha: A Story of Enlightenment*. New York: HarperOne, 2008.

Chopra, Deepak. *How to Know God*. London: Ebury Digital, 2008.

Chopra, Deepak. *Perfect Health*. New York: Simon & Schuster, 1995.

Chopra, Deepak. *Quantum Healing*. Place of Publication Not Identified: Bantam Books, 2015.

Chopra, Deepak, and Simon, David. *The Seven Spiritual Laws of Yoga: A Practical Guide to Healing Body, Mind and Spirit*. Hoboken, New Jersey. John Wiley and Sons, 2004.

Chopra, Deepak. *Super Genes: Unlock the Astonishing Power of Your DNA for Optimum Health and Well-being*. Place of Publication Not Identified: Harmony Crown, 2017.

Coelho, Paulo. *The Alchemist*. HarperCollins Publishers.

"Dacher Keltner." Wikipedia. August 08, 2018. Accessed January 09, 2019. https://en.wikipedia.org/wiki/Dacher_Keltner.

DailyOM—http://www.dailyom.com/.

Dawkins, Richard. *Unweaving the Rainbow: Science, Delusion, and the Appetite for Wonder*. London: Folio Society, 2009.

Dennett, Daniel C. *Darwin's Dangerous Idea*. Simon & Schuster, 1996.

"Dr. Dan Siegel—Home." Dr. Dan Siegel—Books—The Developing Mind. Accessed January 09, 2019. https://www.drdansiegel.com/.

Easwaran, Eknath. *Bhagavad Gita*. Place of Publication Not Identified: Nilgiri PR, 2019.

Easwaran, Eknath. *Upanishads*. Place of Publication Not Identified: Nilgiri PR, 2019.

"Eliot Deutsch." Wikipedia. November 20, 2018. Accessed January 09, 2019. https://en.wikipedia.org/wiki/Eliot_Deutsch.

"Emiliana R. Simon-Thomas | Profile." Greater Good. Accessed January 09, 2019. https://greatergood.berkeley.edu/profile/emiliana_simon_thomas.

"Esther Hicks." Wikipedia. January 08, 2019. Accessed January 09, 2019. https://en.wikipedia.org/wiki/Esther_Hicks.

Frankl, Viktor E., John Boyne, and William J. Winslade. *Man's Search for Meaning*. Boston: Beacon Press, 2017.

Gabriel, Roger www.rogergabriel@chopra. com

Gefter, Amanda. *Trespassing on Einstein's Lawn: A Father, a Daughter, the Meaning of Nothing, and the Beginning of Everything*. New York, NY: Bantam Books, 2014.

Gethin, Rupert. *Foundations of Buddhism*. Oxford: Oxford University Press, 2014.

Goswami, Amit. *God Is Not Dead: What Quantum Physics Tells Us about Our Origins and How We Would Live*. Charlottesville, VA: Hampton Roads, 2012.

Goswami, Amit. *Physics of the Soul: The Quantum Book of Living, Dying, Reincarnation, and Immortality*. Charlottesville, VA: Hampton Roads Publishing Company, 2013.

Harris, Sam. *The End of Faith: Religion, Terror and the Future of Reason*. London: Simon & Schuster, 2006.

Harris, Sam. *Letter to A Christian Nation*. London: Transworld Digital, 2011.

"Hay House." https://www.facebook.com/hayhouse/.

Hay House. "The Shift by Dr. Wayne W. Dyer." YouTube. June 29, 2009. Accessed January 09, 2019. https://www.youtube.com/watch?v=wEM0SF04Rw4.

Hindu Wisdom - Nature Worship. Accessed January 09, 2019. http://www.hinduwisdom.info/quotes1_20.htm.

Hitchens, Christopher. *God Is Not Great: The Case against Religion*. London: Atlantic Books, 2007.

"Home." Eckhart Tolle—Official Site - Spiritual Teachings and Tools for Personal Growth and Happiness. April 23, 2019. Accessed January 09, 2019. https://www.eckharttolle.com/.

"Home." Mpho Tutu Van Furth. Accessed January 09, 2019. http://www.mphotutuvanfurth.com/.

Houston, Jean. *A Mythic Life: Learning to Live Our Own Greater Story*. London: HarperSanFrancisco, 1996.

Houston, Jean. *The Search for the Beloved: Journeys in Mythology and Sacred Psychology*. New York: J. P. Tarcher/Putnam, 1997.

Houston, Jean. *The Wizard of Us: Transformational Lessons from Oz*. New York: Atria Paperback, 2016.

"Interview with a Vedic Scholar: Dr. David Frawley." Ayurveda | Everyday Ayurveda. August 23, 2016. Accessed January 09, 2019. http://everydayayurveda.org/interview-with-a-pandit-dr-david-frawley/.

"James Mault, MD." The Chopra Center. September 06, 2016. Accessed January 09, 2019. https://chopra.com/bios/james-mault-md.

Jamison, Stephanie W. *The Rigveda*. Oxford: Oxford Univ. Press, 2014.

"Jitish Kallat." Wikipedia. November 22, 2018. Accessed January 09, 2019. https://en.wikipedia.org/wiki/Jitish_Kallat.

"Joel Primack." Wikipedia. February 02, 2018. Accessed January 09, 2019. https://en.wikipedia.org/wiki/Joel_Primack.

"Jon Kabat-Zinn." Wikipedia. October 19, 2018. Accessed January 09, 2019. https://en.wikipedia.org/wiki/Jon_Kabat-Zinn.

"Joseph Campbell and The Power of Myth | Shows." BillMoyers.com. May 23, 1988. Accessed January 09, 2019. https://billmoyers.com/series/joseph-campbell-and-the-power-of-myth-1988/.

Kaplan, Aryeh. *Sefer Yetzirah = The Book of Creation: In Theory and Practice*. Boston, MA: S. Weiser, 1997.

Lipton, Bruce H. *The Biology of Belief: Unleashing the Power of Consciousness, Matter & Miracles*. Carlsbad, CA: Hay House, 2016.

Marcinak, Barbara. *Bringers of the Dawn*. Rochester, VT.: Bear & Company, 1992.

McTaggart, Lynne. *The Intention Experiment: Using Your Thoughts to Change Your Life and the World*. New York: Atria Paperback, 2013.

"Menas Kafatos." Wikipedia. December 21, 2018. Accessed January 09, 2019. https://en.wikipedia.org/wiki/Menas_Kafatos.

"Mitleid, Corbie" Accessed April 03, 2019. https://corbiemitleid.com/"

"Moira Burke." Wikipedia. September 17, 2018. Accessed January 09, 2019. https://en.wikipedia.org/wiki/Moira_Burke.

Myss, Carolyn. *Sacred Contracts: Awakening Your Divine Potential. New York*. Harmony Books, 2002, 2003

Natarajan, Priyamvada. *Mapping the Heavens: The Radical Scientific Ideas That Reveal the Cosmos*. Place of Publication Not Identified: YALE University Press, 2017.

Oprah.com. Accessed January 09, 2019. http://www.oprah.com/app/super-soul-sunday.html.

"Our Team." Kiss the Ground. June 28, 2018. Accessed January 09, 2019. https://kisstheground.com/about/our-team/.

Patañjali, and Alistair Shearer. *The Yoga Sutras of Patañjali*. London: Rider, 2002.

Faith and Reason. PBS. Accessed January 09, 2019. http://www.pbs.org/moyers/faithandreason/.

"Furst, Dan" Accessed April 03, 2019. https://danfurst.com/astrocartography-readings/

"Poonacha Machaiah." The Chopra Center. September 07, 2016. Accessed January 09, 2019. https://chopra.com/bios/poonacha-machaiah.

"Preview: The Four Horsemen of New Atheism Reunited." New Statesman. Accessed January 09, 2019. https://www.newstatesman.com/blogs/the-staggers/2011/12/richard-dawkins-issue-hitchens.

Radin, Dean I. *Real Magic*. New York: Harmony, 2018.

"R/Buddhism-Venerable Thich Nhat Hanh Beautifully Explains the Concept of Dependent-Origination Using a Table as an Example." Reddit.

Accessed January 09, 2019. https://www.reddit.com/r/Buddhism/comments/2hoemg/venerable_thich_nhat_hanh_beautifully_explains/.

Rice, Robin https://www.robinrice.com/.

Richert, Scott P. "What Is the Catholic 'Guardian Angel Prayer'?" Thoughtco. Accessed January 09, 2019. https://www.thoughtco.com/the-guardian-angel-prayer-542646.

"Rick Stollmeyer." The Chopra Center. August 27, 2016. Accessed January 09, 2019. https://chopra.com/bios/rick-stollmeyer.

Russell, Cameron. "Cameron Russell." Ted. Accessed January 09, 2019. https://www.ted.com/speakers/cameron_russell.

Salman. "Sages & Scientists Symposium 2016 with Deepak Chopra | ARHT Media Inc. | Leaders in Holographic Telepresence." ARHT Media Inc. September 09, 2016. Accessed January 09, 2019. http://www.arhtmedia.com/sages-scientists-symposium-2016-with-deepak-chopra/.

Śańkara, Prabhavananda, and Christopher Isherwood. *Shankara's Crest-jewel of Discrimination (Viveka-Chudamani)*. Hollywood, CA: Vedanta Press, 1978.

"SAS16." The Chopra Foundation. Accessed January 09, 2019. https://www.choprafoundation.org/events-initiatives/sages-scientists/sas16/.

"Satya Hinduja." SoundCloud. Accessed January 09, 2019. https://soundcloud.com/satyahinduja.

Savary, Louis M. *The New Spiritual Exercises: In the Spirit of Pierre Teilhard De Chardin*. New York: Paulist Press, 2010.

Schwartz, Robert. *Your Soul's Plan: Discovering the Real Meaning of the Life You Planned Before You Were Born*. North Atlantic Books, 2009.

Schwartz, Robert. *Your Soul's Gift: The Healing Power of the Life You Planned Before You Were Born*. Whispering Winds Press, 2012. https://www.yoursoulsplan.com/rob.schwartz@yoursoulsplan.com

"The Science of Happiness." Greater Good Science Center. Accessed January 09, 2019. https://ggsc.berkeley.edu/what_we_do/event/the_science_of_happiness.

Scully, Nicki, Linda Star Wolf, and Kris Waldherr. *Shamanic Mysteries of Egypt: Awakening the Healing Power of the Heart*. Rochester, VT: Bear &, 2007.

Seale, Alan. *Soul Mission, Life Vision: Recognize Your True Gifts and Make Your Mark in the World*. Red Wheel, 2003.

"Shamini Jain." Michael Criqui | UCSD Profiles. Accessed January 09, 2019. https://profiles.ucsd.edu/shamini.jain.

Shin Dharma Net. Accessed January 09, 2019. http://bschawaii.org/shindharmanet/studies/coarising/.

Michael Franti & Spearhead. https://michaelfranti.com/.

Simon Leung. "Simon Leung." YouTube. Accessed January 09, 2019. https://www.youtube.com/user/simonleung.

Smith, Huston. *The Religions of Man*. New York: Harper & Row, 1958.

"Sonja Lyubomirsky." Wikipedia. December 26, 2018. Accessed January 09, 2019. https://en.wikipedia.org/wiki/Sonja_Lyubomirsky.

"Soul Beliefs: Causes and Consequences—Unit 1: Historical Foundations." Coursera. Accessed January 09, 2019. https://www.coursera.org/learn/soulbeliefs.

"Sounds True." Wikipedia. April 02, 2018. Accessed January 09, 2019. https://en.wikipedia.org/wiki/Sounds_True.

"Sridhar Solur." The Chopra Center. August 27, 2016. Accessed January 09, 2019. https://chopra.com/bios/sridhar-solur.

"Stuart Hameroff." Wikipedia. July 21, 2018. Accessed January 09, 2019. https://en.wikipedia.org/wiki/Stuart_Hameroff.

"Subhash Kak." Wikipedia. January 08, 2019. Accessed January 09, 2019. https://en.wikipedia.org/wiki/Subhash_Kak.

"Support Regenerative Agriculture." Kiss the Ground. October 17, 2018. Accessed January 09, 2019. https://kisstheground.com/.

Theise, Neil D. "Neil D. Theise, MD." Neil D. Theise, MD. Accessed January 09, 2019. http://neiltheise.com/.

Tolle, Eckhart, and Russell E. DiCarlo. *The Power of Now: A Guide to Spiritual Enlightenment*. London: Yellow Kite, 2016.

Toynbee, Arnold J. Top 25 Quotes (of 53)." A-Z Quotes. Accessed January 09, 2019. https://www.azquotes.com/author/14748-Arnold_J_Toynbee.

Uktena, Teri https://www.akashicreading.com/

Rutgers University "Soul Beliefs: Causes and Consequences with Daniel Ogilvie and Leonard Hamilton." YouTube. June 09, 2011. https://www.youtube.com/watch?v=3pWgWzFzwyk.

"Unweaving the Rainbow Quotes by Richard Dawkins." Goodreads. Accessed January 09, 2019. https://www.goodreads.com/work/quotes/3323916-unweaving-the-rainbow-science-delusion-and-the-appetite-for-wonder.

"Up Close & Personal with Upasna Kamineni"—Times of India. The Times of India. January 15, 2017. Accessed January 09, 2019. https://timesofindia.indiatimes.com/entertainment/telugu/movies/news/upasna-kamineni-interview/articleshow/53208976.cms.

U.S. News & World Report. Accessed January 09, 2019. https://health.usnews.com/doctors/paddy-barrett-1052596.

Walsch, Neale Donald., and Frank Riccio. *The Little Soul and the Sun: A Children's Parable Adapted from Conversations with God*. Charlottesville, VA: Hampton Roads Pub., 1998.

Weiss, Brian L. *Many Lives, Many Masters: The True Story of a Prominent Psychiatrist, His Young Patient, and the Past-life Therapy That Changed Both Their Lives*. Simon & Schuster, 2012.

"What Are the 8 Limbs of Yoga?" The Chopra Center. April 19, 2017. Accessed January 09, 2019. https://chopra.com/articles/what-are-the-8-limbs-of-yoga.

"What Is a Chakra?" The Chopra Center. October 03, 2018. Accessed January 09, 2019. https://chopra.com/articles/what-is-a-chakra.

"What the Buddha Taught." Wikipedia. July 04, 2017. Accessed January 09, 2019. https://en.wikipedia.org/wiki/What_the_Buddha_Taught.

"William Mobley." Michael Criqui | UCSD Profiles. Accessed January 09, 2019. https://profiles.ucsd.edu/william.mobley.